The Best Short Stories 2023

The O. Henry Prize Winners

Guest Editor:
Lauren Groff

Series Editor:
Jenny Minton Quigley

Anchor Books
A Division of Penguin Random House LLC
New York

The Best Short Stories 2023

To Laura and Elliott
—Lauren Groff

Contents

Foreword

Lauren Groff is the guest editor for this year's collection of O. Henry Prize–winning stories, but perhaps it would be more accurate to describe her as the presiding curator, producer, and wizard of the anthology. A supremely talented short story writer herself, Groff brought her prodigious literary gifts to bear as both reader and judge; after observing the dedication, seriousness of purpose, and sheer energy she devoted to assembling and editing this collection, a fitting subtitle for 2023 could have been *Trying to Keep Up with Lauren Groff.*

While her own stories mesmerize, populated with characters that Lorrie Moore has called "bewitched eccentrics," Groff's love of the short story transcends the ways in which she herself chooses to use the form. She seeks stories that take risks and surprise, and her wide and inclusive search for the best examples of those took her around the globe this year. This collection includes two brilliant stories published abroad in English—a first for the O. Henry: "The Blackhills," first published in *The Stinging Fly* in Ireland, and "The Mother," which first appeared in *Disruption: New Short Fiction from Africa,* Short Story Day Africa. Their respective authors, Eamon McGuinness and Jacob M'hango, are making their American debuts in this book. Groff also selected three stories in translation, two from Spanish and one from Danish, and chose works by writers of many different origins: Nigerian, Venezuelan, Danish, Spanish, Fujian, Irish, English, Munsee Lenape, Mexican, and North American. Furthermore, in a move that is probably unprecedented in the O. Henry Prize's history, Groff selected twenty stories from twenty different magazines and literary websites, including two brand-new journals, *Astra* and *The Drift*. Each magazine has its own beat, and by carefully determining the order in which the stories appear, Groff orchestrated a coherent and thrilling reading experience.

O. Henry's friends established the O. Henry Prize in 1919 to honor him with a memorial that, in their words, would "strengthen the art of the short story and stimulate younger authors." The talented group of 2023 O. Henry Prize winners is a clear demonstration of the ongoing vigor of the short story form, and we hope that their craft, imagination, humor, and insight will inspire readers, writers, teachers, and students everywhere. O. Henry was an anti-snob, and in that spirit his eponymous prize is not meant to foster a club of literary insiders, but to provide an exciting and accessible sampling of many of the absolute best contemporary writers. Every year we include at the back of the book an updated listing of journals with their contact information, which we hope writers both aspiring and established will find useful.

In 1909, the year before he died, O. Henry conducted an "autobiographical interview" for *The New York Times*. It appeared under the title "'O. HENRY' ON HIMSELF, LIFE, AND OTHER THINGS; For the First Time the Author of 'The Four Million' Tells a Bit of the 'Story of My Life.'" To a question he asks himself, O. Henry answers, "Yes, I get dry spells. Sometimes I can't turn out a thing for three months. When one of those spells comes on, I quit trying to work and go out and see something of life. You can't write a story that's got any life in it by sitting at a writing table and thinking. You've got to get out into the streets, into the crowds, talk with people, and feel the rush and throb of real life—that's the stimulant for a story writer." In the "Writers on Their Work" section at the back of this book, the prize winners share with us some of the real-world inspirations that sparked their creativity.

I find that O. Henry's prescription is also true in reverse. Many of us can't fully appreciate life, can't truly take in "the rush and throb" of humanity, at a game, on the sidewalk, in a store, or at a party. When we get home and can sit and think about what we observed, then, absorbed in solitude, the words of a gifted writer can put us more deeply in touch with everything that our own experiences have awakened in us. So we venture out, as we should, to our work or on our adventures—and, oh, as the pandemic recedes, how we appreciate more than ever being able to immerse ourselves in the busy and stimulating world. But then we can return to our home, to our room, to this precious gift of stories, to listen to life at our own volume and speed.

—Jenny Minton Quigley

Introduction

If heaven exists, it must exist in the form of a clean and quiet house, a comfortable chair near a snoring dog, a glass of cold wine, and a lapful of short stories. I love the short story form with a wild-eyed passion, the fervor of a street-corner evangelist who dresses up in robes to shout at pedestrians about angels and harlots and the seven-headed beast of the end of days. But short stories are, to me, closer to the dawn of days; they are quick, breathtaking windows into other humans' souls, which is where the infinite resides, in my personal credo. The story form is infinitely malleable, gorgeously economical, and endlessly surprising; it is long enough to lose oneself in, short enough to deliver a satisfying gut punch. I say this to contextualize why, when O. Henry Prize series editor Jenny Minton Quigley asked me to be this year's guest judge, I must have terrified her by responding in enthusiastic all-caps within thirty seconds of her invitation.

It has been a delight to revel in short stories the past several months, to read hundreds upon hundreds, written by people from all over the world, with so many exquisite voices and so many idiosyncratic understandings of what a short story is and what the form can be stretched to do. I could have selected five times as many great stories and made five equally marvelous books; alas, I could only choose twenty stories for this year's anthology, the book you are holding in your hands.

But, oh, what brilliant stories these are. I know it is the custom for the writers of such introductions to shout out each contribution by name with a compliment, perhaps a way of justifying for a large audience choices that are so deeply individual and subjective. I wonder, however, if this practice risks minimizing or simplifying the appeal of deeply complex stories like those that are found in this anthology, each of which is excellent in multiple, and sometimes even contradictory, ways. Instead, I'll say that each of these stories had to pass a few rigorous tests, the first and most important of which was that they had to show some sort of thrill or risk in terms of language or structure or plot or enigma; something in the story had to deliver a sharp blue jolt of electricity to my nervous system.

The second test was that each of the stories had to subvert my expectations, and some succeeded to the point where they made it past my deepest, most ingrained antipathies. For example, halfway through the year, I asked Jenny to please stop sending me any more first-person stories because, while there were so many perfectly competent ones coming to me, I began to resent being anchored again and again to individual consciousnesses; I began to feel at the center of a sucking collective whirlpool of anxious solipsism. It's true that ours is a largely secular time, and some of us are urged to self-help, self-care, self-seek; far too many others among us subscribe to a sort of cranky and (to me) unbearably myopic libertarianism. All of this, mixed together, leads to a culture of somewhat hypertrophied individualism, a large-scale cult of the singular self. Perhaps because of this, the godlike third person, peering down at the story's characters from its distant hover, like an enormous all-seeing hawk, can feel uncomfortable to contemporary writers. Jenny did mostly stop sending me first-person stories, but some eventually broke through to the final anthology because the writer was doing something new, or the story throbbed with vitality, or made me see the familiar world as warped or strange. In addition, I used to have a screaming aversion to stories in the second person, but—welp!—not anymore, because of a single brilliant example in this anthology that smashed the aforementioned dislike to smithereens. An excellent story can, indeed, break open irrational hatreds. This is one of the great gifts of narrative. This is also why so many of us need to fling our phones into a bog and start reading literature again.

The final test for each story was that I had to remember it weeks and months after I first read it. This was harder than it sounds; halfway through reading for this anthology, I contracted COVID-19, and I was in such a state of brain fog for so long afterward that I genuinely feared I'd never be able to write a sentence again. Brain fog also made reading far harder; every time I sat or lay down to read, I'd fall asleep within an instant. So I began to read while marching around the house, driving my dog and children bonkers, and after some time, I grew to love this form of moving meditation. I knew a story was good if I started stepping to its rhythms. I kept finding smart stories to throw into the enthusiastic *maybe!* pile. This stack grew until it was taller than my dog, which is saying something, as she's a leggy labradoodle whose snout rests comfortably on my hip when I am standing still.

With this final test, there was a sort of natural winnowing that happened; some stories I found excellent on first reading, but then I couldn't remember them. It may have been my brain fog, or it may have been because our aesthetic sense is fickle and often dependent on things outside our consideration when we encounter art; perhaps we had insomnia the night before, or the coffee from our favorite café was cold and bitter, or someone was nasty to us on the internet and it threw off our taste for the piece at hand. Which is to say that the stories in the towering *maybe!* pile were likely deserving of being in this collection, but also that art finds us at the time that we need it, or when we can be open to it, at moments when we are vibrating at the frequency that the art is putting into the world. The self is unstable and shifts so radically through our days and years that it's unrealistic to presume we'd respond the same way to any piece of art every time we encounter it.

Mostly, in the end, I was building the collection slowly, story by story, balancing one story against another, trying to get a feel for the whole collection. While I do love the individual short story with a proselytizing fervor, if it's possible I love the well-thought-through collection of short stories even more. The best collections have an invisible architecture to them, in which the first story asks a question or makes an argument, and this initial question or argument is then fractured and complicated by the next story, and so on, story by story, until the glorious grand finale that, upon ending, sends a sort of prismatic light shooting back into daily life. I was trained early in this kind of aesthetic construction; it was probably my first serious artistic love. I was a child of the eighties, an adolescent in the early nineties, and I owned first a beige Fisher-Price tape recorder, then a giant black boom box, and out of these I made mixtapes assembled with extreme thought and care, the covers decorated with magazine collages and Wite-Out and nail polish, my most legible block handwriting listing the songs on the insides. This was before music could be found with a few strokes of a keyboard; to claim a song heard on the radio, we had to sit for hours with our finger on the record button, just hoping that when the song we longed for would finally play we'd recognize it by its opening bar. To assemble a mixtape, we put careful thought into the pace of the songs, the speed, the key they were in, the kind of beat they bore, the quality of the singers' voices, the genre of the music, the way that the energy moved from song to song, the emotional place where all the songs, together, ended up. Mostly we thought about the person we were making the mixtape for: what we knew they already liked, what we thought they might like, what we wanted them to feel when listening to this beautiful thing, this gift of art, that we'd made for them.

This anthology was assembled for you, dear reader, to give you a sense of the enormous range and capacity of the contemporary short story, to make you laugh, to bewilder and delight and scare you, to show you the thriving ecosystem of the short story as it existed in the world this strange third pandemic year, and to give you a glimpse of the extraordinary diversity of voice and journal and nationality and subject matter that the short story, most vibrant of narrative forms, encompasses. You will certainly like some of these stories more than others; some will be set at your current vibration levels; it seems likely to me that others that you may not appreciate just now will find you where you will be at some point in the future. If our adolescent mixtapes were a shy declaration of affection, please accept this year's O. Henry anthology for what it is: a loud declaration of love.

—Lauren Groff

The Best Short Stories 2023

Ling Ma

Office Hours

H OW SHE USED TO SMOKE in his office, back when the University allowed that in campus buildings. He didn't smoke, but allowed her to as she sat on the sofa across from his desk. Or rather, he didn't object, and even set out a little dessert plate as an ashtray. Maybe because it gave them both a pretense for talking longer, for the extra duration of a cigarette, then two, then three. So that by the time she graduated, she was a chain-smoker.

She had taken several of his courses, mostly on cinema. She read the assigned Gombrich texts, studied the Muybridge prints, wrote a paper on close-ups of Falconetti's face. After class, she would drop by his office hours to continue their class discussion. "Let's hear it" was the first thing he'd say when she arrived. During her junior year, they would talk for an hour every week.

Over time, their conversations began to drag, usually when he started pontificating about how he'd never intended to be a career academic, and devolved into complaints about the institution. Though flattered that he confided in her, she grew a little bored. He had the dream job of watching movies and writing about them.

He was both an involved mentor who frequently solicited her

opinions and a raging, pacing animal, sour about where he had ended up in life.

Once, she had offhandedly mentioned that she was tired and couldn't wait to sleep. "So go home then," he snapped. Taken aback, she explained that she didn't have enough time to go home before her next class. "You can take a nap," he said, and offered to leave his office so she could sleep on the sofa.

"Where would you go?" she asked.

"I'll go to Holy Grounds," he said, referring to the basement coffee shop in Godspeed Hall. He shuffled some papers on his desk. "I'll take these papers to grade with me."

Except when she lay down, he didn't leave. Maybe she'd already known he wouldn't. He remained behind his desk, and the sound of pages turning, the quick swipes of the pen as he scrawled devastating comments on students' papers, served as the white noise that lulled her to sleep. She thought of his pen scrawling over her body, his sharp razor-point tip marking her with corrective feedback in corrosive industrial ink.

When she awoke, he already had his coat on. "Okay?" he asked as she sat up.

"Okay," she said, a little embarrassed. "Was I asleep for long?"

"No, not at all," he said. "But office hours end in two minutes."

Whereas she had wanted to be the object of his gaze a little longer. She liked being warmed by his interest without ever yielding to it. The naps began to occur, if not frequently, then enough to set a precedent. The rust-colored sofa was mushy but comfortable. He never seemed to mind, and after a while, she no longer felt self-conscious about languishing in the amnion of his office. When she woke up, he would say, "Okay?" and she would reply, "Okay," and leave.

It was a drafty office. She seemed to hear wind whistling from the walls. Leaving Godspeed Hall, she would bury her face in the collar of her coat, redolent of a tangy pine, not of him exactly, but of his office, as she walked across campus on those winter afternoons, the sky already dark.

There was no sofa in her apartment, no bed. She slept on an inflatable mattress, reinforced nightly with a bike pump. Her parents had remortgaged their house to afford her private-college tuition, and she didn't ask for more. With her wages shelving books at the library, she subsisted on spaghetti and apples. These were supplemented by appetizer spreads laid out at receptions following English Department events. After lectures on the decline of the novel, the failures of empire, she pilfered smoked salmon, soft cheeses, even the decorative garnishes—star fruit slices, caviar ruffles.

On weekends, there was usually a party. Her classmates, freed from their wealthy families, cosplayed as struggling intellectuals. With ham-handed irony, they put out cellophane-wrapped Twinkies, Ding Dongs, MoonPies on faux-silver trays, snacks they wouldn't eat themselves. Their privilege was always betrayed by some outlandish gesture, like a mariachi band, in full regalia, hired to play in the living room. If the potent coke, the immaculate sound system, didn't tip you off. The careless way they walked through snow in suede Nikes.

The last time she remembered seeing the Professor was after leaving one such party, a few weeks before graduation. She had been standing on a street corner late at night, waiting for a ride. It had begun to rain lightly. He had been walking his dog. Like most older faculty, he lived near campus.

"I like your dog, Professor," she had called out. It was an excessive, girthful dog, a slobbering Bernese mix.

"Oh, good," he said, as he neared. "My dog is your dog."

"Oh, good. I was about to clone it. What's its name?"

"Nemo."

"Hi, Nemo! Nemo, did you know that your name means 'no one'? I'm sorry!" The dog withstood her overzealous petting with sober dignity.

The Professor also waited until she was done. "Do you have a strategy for getting home?"

"Yes." She didn't mention that she had been waiting for "the drunk van," a campus weekend service that deposited inebriated students at home.

He studied her, then pointed across the street, at Godspeed Hall. "That's my office."

"I know." Though actually she hadn't known. Her surroundings suddenly reoriented themselves around her: she had been standing on the wrong corner for pickup. "It's a nice office."

"Thank you. If you'd like to dry off, you're welcome to it." He added, clarifying, "I could give you the keys. I won't be in until Monday."

"I'm fine." She smiled to show him so.

"I see." He hesitated. "You're graduating in two weeks. What's next after this?"

"I don't have anything lined up." On the other side of graduation was her actual life, the slow narrowing of possibilities that would catch her and freeze her in a vocation, a relationship, a life. She intended to avoid that slow calcification for as long as possible—if only by refraining from making any crucial choices. In other words, she was moving back home. She added, "I want your job one day." Maybe she was saying it just to see his response.

He smiled. "You can have it. This is my last year."

"You're retiring?" The surprise of this news sobered her a little.

"I've probably overstayed. Once you're tenured, you never leave." Nemo tugged on his leash, but the Professor made no indication to move. "Meanwhile, the gap between you and your students widens. You get older, while they stay the same age, year after year. Like vampires."

"Well, sounds pretty nice to me, at least the tenure part." She didn't know what to say. He was not happy. He was just a person. "I've really enjoyed your classes, Professor." She wanted to add more. How watching long films in the campus screening room, as they did in his class, made the Midwestern winters bearable; how she appreciated his clear, straightforward lecture style; and how, unlike other faculty, he never wielded his knowledge as a weapon against his students. She lacked the finesse in the moment to convey this.

He was still speaking, had been for a while, trying to give last words, advice. "The sanest way forward—you have to learn how to split yourself up, like an earthworm."

She didn't know what he was talking about. Instead, she followed his gaze to Godspeed Hall, then looked back and forth between them. It made her dizzy. "Whoa," she said aloud, to herself.

"I think Nemo is getting restless. I should be on my way." He nodded at her. "Get home safe. And if I don't see you before graduation, stay out of trouble."

Stay out of trouble. There it was. She didn't like how he code-switched at his whim, wavering between treating her like a peer and like just another student. As if he had never encouraged those hour-long discussions in his office, or called her a kindred spirit. Maybe he was demonstrating that he could dictate the terms of their association however he chose.

She watched as the Professor walked across the street with Nemo. They ambled across the quad, then entered Godspeed Hall, where, through the stairwell windows, she saw him enter the third floor, where his office was located. The clock tower indicated that it was nearing three in the morning.

She did not know him that well, she reminded herself. She had just been his student, a vampire. Whatever he was doing, it was really none of her business.

Her default position was that of a dog fighting out of a corner. For much of her adult life, she had assumed this defensive crouch, tensed to prove herself against all odds at all times. She did not have the assurance, like many of her peers, that if one thing didn't work out, there would always be something else. Maybe this desperation was how she had managed to end up on the tenure track, doggedly persisting through a complicated gauntlet of grad school and postdocs and fellowships until she finally found herself gainfully employed as an assistant professor at her college alma mater, where the fights were imperceptible because everyone had too much to lose, and there was no corner.

The Film and Media Studies faculty holiday party was held in a circular brick tower that typically served as the department conference room. She sipped rosé next to the window, a heavy wool coat over her other arm as if she were ready to leave. Surveying the event space, she did the usual reconnaissance: There was the one who bludgeoned her with compliments, vague in content, exclamatory in delivery. There was the one who always cut her off midsentence. There was the one who leaned in too closely and asked, in a hushed, solemn voice, "So how are you doing?," as if only they could be the facilitator of her feelings. This dance of feigned, unearned intimacies, playing on endlessly at every meeting.

But anyway. She was showing her face. She was engaging. And Carolyn was half-heartedly fêting her.

"Hey, before I forget. To your book," Carolyn said, raising her glass and clinking it against hers. "Will you sign my copy?"

"Absolutely," Marie replied, though no copy materialized.

"You must be so busy after book release. I'm sure you're being heaped with accolades."

"I'm just glad it's done." Her book, on cinema of "the face," had been released by a university press at the beginning of the semester.

Carolyn leaned in meaningfully. "How are you feeling about that?"

Marie wasn't entirely sure what the question was. "Well, it always takes longer than you think." She cleared her throat. "Do you have any interesting plans for holiday break?"

"We're taking the kids to the Adirondacks. We all need the detox, you know?" Carolyn waved her jittery hands, glistening with rings. "It's crazy how busy things get during the semester. I'm serving on, like, ten committees." She looked at Marie curiously.

"Ladies." Sean approached, placing his hands on both their backs. He was her least favorite. "I presume you're teaching next semester."

"Yes." Carolyn and Marie nodded in unison.

"I presume these courses have titles." Sean looked at Marie. He didn't ask her questions so much as issue statements that she could either confirm or refute.

"Well, one course is called 'The Disappearing Woman,'" Marie said. "We start with the genre of women's films, then we look at contemporary heroines. You know, *Vertigo, L'Avventura* . . ."

He sipped his wine, glanced around the room. "Oh, that's fun," he said, after waving at the program chair across the room. She couldn't tell if he was pretending, this nonchalance. "So I assume the woman always disappears by the end."

"I guess the course title should come with a spoiler alert." She too sipped her drink.

"You know, I've found in my experience that students respond best to genre surveys rather than courses built around a theme."

"Depends on the syllabus, I'm sure," she said benignly. He hadn't been teaching at the University much longer than she had, maybe a year or two. She turned to Carolyn. "What are you teaching this spring, Carolyn?"

"Oh, just an introductory survey of silent film." Carolyn shifted warily. "I have to run. I promised the sitter I wouldn't be late tonight."

"Anyway," Sean resumed, ignoring Carolyn's retreat. "I would take a look at some of the course listings from years past to give you the right idea of what works best."

"I have, but thanks." Marie looked around the room, scanning it for reasons to excuse herself. Colleagues encircled one another, then broke apart periodically to form new groups.

She spotted the Professor, speaking to someone across the

room. She startled. It wasn't his appearance that was surprising—though he looked, for lack of more elegant descriptors, frail and decrepit. She hadn't seen him in maybe fifteen years, not since college. She'd thought he had moved away after retirement.

On cue, he looked up and caught her gaze.

The Professor wanted to see his old office, which now happened to be her office. And so they walked across the dimly lit quads in the snow. He walked with a cane, and hid his winces with every step. He was speaking to her as if they were picking up midconversation, across the span of more than a decade. He said, "I'm very ill. The treatments aren't working."

"Is it serious?" she asked, knowing well that at his age, all illnesses were serious.

"It's terminal," he said matter-of-factly. "I don't have long, though there are differing opinions about how long."

"I'm sorry." Her pat response sounded so trivial. They made their way to Godspeed Hall in silence.

When she opened the door to her office and switched on the fluorescent lights, he looked around at the now-bare walls and new, plywood furnishings, the empty bookcases, the little mini-fridge plugged into the corner outlet. She wanted to apologize for not having properly made the space her own.

He turned to her. "You don't use this office?"

She thought of how she used to nap on his rust-colored sofa, now gone. "It's mostly just for meeting with students." She preferred to do her scholarly work at home. "Anyway, would you like some tea?" When he didn't respond, she said, "Is there any drink that you would like?"

"I would like you to keep an open mind." He was studying the closet behind the desk. Then he opened the door, revealing an old armoire, the only piece of furniture that remained from his time. She watched as he struggled to move it.

"Here, let me help you," she said. But he had already slid it to the edge of the closet. From the drag marks in the floorboards, it had probably been moved this way many times.

"There," he said, satisfied. "Now turn on the light, please." When she pulled the drawstring, the bare bulb dangling from the ceiling clicked on. The light revealed a hole in the wall, something that she had never noticed before. It was large enough that a person could easily enter it.

"Is this extra storage space?" She knew it was not.

"No, but you'll see." He stepped through the hole until he was almost fully submerged inside the wall. She didn't move. Sensing her hesitation, he turned around. "Okay?"

"Okay." As if in a dream, she followed him. On the other side is where the story begins.

The passageway led outside. She looked around, allowing her eyes to adjust to the darkness. To their left, a cloister of coniferous trees, swaying in the breeze. It had stopped snowing. Or, actually, there was no snow on the ground at all. It was not even cold. The air felt soft and supple. It was almost warm, a summer's night.

She said, "I have never been to this part of campus before." And then waited for him to correct her. They were not on campus, or even near it.

"I used to come out here when I had your office." He was still looking around.

There was a full moon in the sky, the only source of light. It illuminated what looked like a country road, a two-lane stretch that receded into the distance.

She wanted to take off her coat, but to do so would have been to accept the plausibility of her surroundings. "Where are we, Professor?"

He pointed to a pine tree some yards away. "Do you see that cup over there? On the ground?" She squinted. There was a white paper cup at its base. "It's a cup of coffee. Can you take a look?"

She walked over to the tree and picked it up. It was a Solo cup, filled with what appeared to be fresh coffee, lightened with cream. "It's a cup of coffee," she echoed.

"Is it still warm?"

"Yes." She brought it to him, but he didn't bother to examine it.

"What if I told you I left it there years ago, on my last day before retirement?"

"But it's still warm." Heat emanated from the cup.

"Yes, that's my point." He paused. "What I can tell you is that I have visited this place hundreds of times, at all hours, across all seasons. It is always night here. The weather is always the same, warm and temperate."

She studied the coffee cup in her hand. The paper sleeve was imprinted with the logo of Holy Grounds, which had closed years ago.

She looked around again, studied the space. "Where does that road go?" she asked, gesturing to the two-lane freeway.

"I don't know. I've never seen a single car go down it." He was looking at the sky, the full moon. "It's always the same," he reiterated.

She set the cup down in the grass. It had been burning her hand. "Why did you show this to me?" she asked. When he didn't answer, she repeated the question.

It was only after the Professor had passed, during holiday break, that she entered the passageway again. The University memorial service, scheduled shortly after New Year's, was held in the same circular tower room as the faculty holiday party.

She had not expected the body to be on view, half the casket opened to expose his face, pale and frowning. Looking at this presentation, she felt that she didn't understand anything.

Something he had once said in a lecture: "It is in the most surreal situations that a person feels the most present, the closest to reality." What film had he been speaking of? She wished she could ask him now.

Sean approached, clearing his throat. "So I hear you're presenting at HFF."

"I think I'm subbing for someone else who wasn't available," she obliged. She moved away from the coffin, not wanting to hold the conversation so close to the body. Sean followed.

"Huh, so you replaced someone." He took a sip of wine.

"That's my impression. But I don't know." She was downplaying it. The Humanities Futures Forum—or "huff," as everyone called HFF—was an annual weekend fundraising event, attended by major donors to the University. Though everyone bemoaned it as a dog and pony show, that didn't prevent the scorekeeping over who was asked to present.

He was looking at her, not saying anything.

After a pause, she asked, "What about you? Are you presenting at HFF?"

He ignored her question. "I presume you have ideas about what you're presenting."

What if she just didn't respond? "I'm not sure yet. Maybe something on cinematic fantasy or dream spaces. Like *The Wizard of Oz*, or maybe *Stalker*."

"Fantasy space." He nodded slowly. "Well, you could devote the entire session to all the Tarkovsky films alone."

"It's just a twenty-minute presentation." She held her smile. "But I'll keep that in mind."

"But, c'mon, Tarkovsky. There are so many films that would fit that theme. It would be easy to create a presentation just around that." He looked at her closely, waiting for her to acquiesce. "Wouldn't it?"

Marie smiled benignly. "I should go and pay my respects."

In her time at the University, she had begun to dislike Sean intensely, but as a point of pride she couldn't quite commit to her dislike. He seemed unworthy of any intensity of feeling, he who made his students call him Doctor.

But today, at the beginning of the new year, at the memorial for her former professor, the prospect of seeing someone like Sean regularly, of forever dodging him at receptions and cocktail parties, of treading lightly while serving on the same committees, of presenting at faculty meetings, just seemed intolerable, fucking impossible.

During holiday break, she had been thinking of leaving the University. Then she thought of leaving academia altogether. When she brainstormed about what else she would do, where else she would go, her mind drew a blank.

Across the room, attendees clustered around the Professor's widow, elegant in her charcoal dress, and their surviving grown children, who had flown in from East Coast cities. "He wanted to go on his own terms," the widow said. "He decided when he wanted to stop the treatment. So I'm glad he was able to wield some control over the process, at least."

"And what about you? How are you doing?" Carolyn cooed to the bereaved woman. "I am so sorry. You must be so exhausted. Now, please tell me there's someone taking care of you." Her voice was subsumed by the cicada chorus of others' condolences, their voices metallic and mercenary.

Marie placed her glass on a table and left.

It was still bright outside, at least for a January afternoon. She walked across the quads, and retreated to her office, where tears did not come. In the silence of not crying, she heard the wind whistling from the closet. Of course she moved the armoire. Of course she stared at the opening. Hostile to new knowledge, she had not been into the passageway since he had first shown it to her.

Now she entered again, for the first time by herself.

When she emerged on the other side, it was night, just as it had been before. The towering pine trees rustled in greeting, unloosening a familiar pine scent. The inky sky above hosted a scattering of stars, the full moon.

She moved through the clearing uneasily, aware of the exit at all times.

Spotting something on the ground, she saw it was the paper cup of coffee, where she had placed it last. It was still warm. Hot, even. She took a sip, scalding her tongue. Then she downed the rest of the cup.

On Wednesdays, she taught "The Disappearing Woman." The class consisted of a screening followed by a discussion. That week, in the February thaw of spring semester, they watched *Ghost World*, released in 2001, a year many of her students had been born. In the end, Enid, the teenage protagonist, gets on a mysterious bus and seems to leave town. The credits rolled.

Marie flipped on the fluorescent lights in the screening room, and looked around at the fifteen students. "So, what did you think?" She liked to begin with general questions, allowing the students to choose the topics, before she zoomed in on specific subjects.

After a moment, Zach spoke. "I didn't get the ending. I mean, I like that it's kind of open-ended, but it feels like a cop-out. Enid just gets on this special bus and goes where?"

She tried to reset the question, to anchor them in the source material. "Well, the ending seems to serve as a refutation of some kind, with Enid opting out of the town on this mysterious bus. One way to approach this is to ask: What is *Ghost World* trying to refute? Are there specific scenes that suggest an answer?"

When Marie started out as a teacher, she had directed all her efforts toward appearing unafraid. But training yourself not to appear afraid was not the same as training yourself not to *feel* afraid, the difference between pretending and being. She had taught long enough that as soon as she slipped into the classroom, she became another person entirely.

"There's a lot of anxiety around this idea of authenticity," Abby offered. "Like, the fake-fifties diner that plays Top 40 music. Or the art teacher who has these narrow parameters for what qualifies as art. Enid and Rebecca are always hyperaware of what's inauthentic."

"Yeah, but wherever Enid ends up, she's only going to see

inauthenticity and hypocrisy. There is no place she's going where she's not going to see that," said Grey. "What kind of place could the bus take her that would meet her standards? That place doesn't exist."

Sarah added, "Enid gets to disappear, but most of us can't do that. Most of us are like Rebecca: we're critical of the world but we still have to live in it."

Abby interjected: "But that's the fantasy, right? That there is an escape, there is a way out of . . ." She trailed off, then restarted. "The movie doesn't show you the answers. The ending simply opts out. It's an aversion."

After class, Marie returned to her office and, through the closet, entered the passageway. She referred to the outside area as "the chamber." Initially, it had served as a discreet area to smoke, a habit she had picked up again after the Professor's memorial. It was often after class that she did this, or before a long faculty meeting, or in the middle of a lecture by a visiting scholar. She would lock her office door, remove the armoire, and go through the wall. She lingered in the clearing near the entryway, blowing her smoke into the cool night air, surrounded by those swaying trees. The pleasure of this place was its extreme, surreal privacy.

Over time, her visits had become more exploratory.

In the chamber, there was the road and there were the woods. She skirmished in the woods occasionally, but didn't venture far. There was the sound of water, a brook, maybe, but she never went in that direction. The Professor had said he didn't know how large the forest was. He had gotten lost there once, and had emerged days later, at a loss to explain his disappearance to his wife, who had filed a missing person report. He had warned Marie not to get lost.

Using a key chain flashlight to guide her, Marie walked along the silent road, which hosted no vehicles, no cars. She would never get lost if she stuck close to it; it would always lead her back to the entryway. There were flowers that grew in the ditches, thistle and yarrow and hyssop, some sagebrush and chamomile. She went for a mile this way in the moonlight, collecting flowers in her hands. She didn't know how far the road unfurled, but she had never reached its end. The deeper she went inside the chamber, the more apprehension she felt. She would only walk for as far as she could walk back.

The road reminded her of her lost year. After graduation, she had moved back home, to the same house her parents had remortgaged to pay for her college. For almost a year, she had lived like a dilettante, sleeping in too late too often and watching movies during the day. In the evenings, while her parents worked the dinner rush at their restaurant, she would often find herself walking alone along a freeway near the house.

The freeway cut through a landscape of strip malls that all seemed to converge at one giant intersection, a collusion of Target, Starbucks, Orangetheory Fitness, the Home Depot with the notorious parking lot that had served as the scene of a shooting. She would go into these stores and buy products of little import—a box of health bars she would never eat, a tube of mascara—but that gave her an excuse to walk around. It was a time when the future could have been anything, been anywhere. It was so open that it could actually crush her. That was what she felt on those nights after graduation, especially along the stretches of freeway where the streetlights gave out.

She had offered to work at the restaurant her parents owned, but they wouldn't let her. They hadn't sent her to the University just so she could assume their livelihood, just so she could return. She had been named after Maria from *The Sound of Music*, the first film her parents had watched in America, swept up in the exploits of the nun who leaves the convent to become a governess. "Climb every mountain," the mother superior sings, urging Maria to leave, to see the world.

That whole sequence, the Professor informed her once, had been censored in Germany, deemed too obscene. "A nun advising a young woman to leave the convent and explore the world, the subtext being to sow her wild oats—well, it was more outrageous than any graphic scenes," he had said.

When she thought about the Professor now, she could understand, in a way she had not before, his unhappiness in his position. She remembered, most of all, his complaints—the pressures of teaching, how little time he had to work on his next book, the bureaucratic gridlocks of the admin, the chair's shortsighted decisions, the misanthropy of certain colleagues. She could also see how, in the midst of his unhappiness, he had created the terms of their relationship. How he had encouraged her to attend his office hours, had curtailed meetings with other students to speak with her, had engaged her in emails that had nothing to do with class, and of course those naps he'd allowed her to take. Even the act of disclosing his dissatisfactions . . . All those little actions had had the effect of making her feel like the exception.

It was to his credit, maybe, that nothing had ever transpired between them. Maybe he had wanted her to initiate it, absolving him of liability. But she never did. She was content with the faint affect of romance, rather than its realization. By senior year, the Professor had become a little colder, more dismissive and impatient. However subtle, these changes in his demeanor were noticeable enough that she stopped going to office hours. In the absence of his attention, she was ashamed of her reliance on it. She was naïve, a clear windowpane.

And now here she was.

At a certain point, she stopped walking along the road and pivoted to return. She dropped her bouquet of collected flowers. She had been creating a mourning bouquet. But in what way was she supposed to mourn? What right did she have?

And, anyway, she had brought flowers from the chamber into her office before, arranged them in a beautiful vase, and they had decayed instantaneously in front of her, as if in a time-lapse video. What remained were moldy, phosphorous, blackened stems, water that smelled like rotting teeth. What came from that world was not meant to live in this one.

The Humanities Futures Forum began on a Saturday morning, and would last throughout the weekend. The donors filed in, wearing polo shirts and sports jackets. The lecture room was designed like a conch shell, spiraling downhill toward the speaker, who stood at its carpeted bottom, looking upward at the audience.

As everyone took their seats, the lights dimmed.

The projector turned on, and she began to speak into the microphone, welcoming them to the presentation. "Cinema, as they say, is the space of fantasy. Today, I'd like to show you clips from two films, forty years apart: *The Wizard of Oz* and *Stalker.*"

The presentation screen lowered from the ceiling. A black-and-white clip from *The Wizard of Oz* played. Dorothy wakes up in her uprooted house, which has been blown away by a tornado, and the door opens onto the Land of Oz in full color. This was followed by a clip from *Stalker,* showing a group of men riding a train into the Zone. The switch again from the sepia-toned film into the full-color foliage of a new realm.

She had to remember to hold the microphone closer to her mouth. She started her sentence, then stopped and repeated it. "In each film, we journey through an alternate reality, a fantasy space, a second site—if you will—that is not of our world."

In the darkened room, she looked at the impassive faces of the audience, the wealthiest alums who were now major donors to the University. A few jotted down notes in their new University-issued notebooks and pens. HFF was technically a showcase of the University's programs, but it was mostly just classroom cosplay for them. The campus served as an elaborate set that allowed the donors to pretend they were still college students.

She continued, "Whether this alternate site is called Oz or the Zone, they share one similarity. The travelers within it move toward a central apparatus, a place where their wishes are said to be granted. For Dorothy and her friends, they are seeking out the Emerald City, where the wizard resides. In *Stalker*, the travelers move toward the Room, a fabled space that will grant each passenger his subconscious wish."

Again, the screen played clips from each film. The projection showed an image of the Emerald City, followed by an image outside of the Room.

Periodically, the donors moved to the back of the room and helped themselves at the refreshments table, which was piled with finger sandwiches, cheese and crackers, fruits and canapés, buckets of champagne, an iced tea station.

She was a donor to the University too. Every season she received a routine phone call from the fundraising office, soliciting alums. She gave them her credit card number, allowed them to charge her fifty dollars. Of course, these donors must have already paid off their student loans.

She continued with her little presentation. "I can't help but observe that in each film, the protagonist never has an elaborate wish. The Stalker has guided others through the Zone many times, but has never entered the Room. And after a hard-won journey to find the wizard, Dorothy's only wish is for a return to normalcy, a return home. Fervent, elaborate wishing, as suggested by the actions of our virtuous main characters, can only be folly."

When she was finished, she answered questions as the refreshments table was replenished by the hired catering company. Then the next group of donors came in, seated themselves. And she went through the presentation again, then held another question-and-answer session. Then the same thing. When she was done with that, another group came in. She repeated the process.

After the final presentation of the day, Marie understood what she had to do. She crossed the quads in the direction of Godspeed.

Inside her office, she opened the closet, pushed aside the armoire, and, like many times before, disappeared into the chamber.

This time, she bypassed the road and went into the woods. It was hard to see at first, the full moon's light obscured by the foliage, by tangled tree branches. She brought out the mini flashlight on her key chain.

It wasn't as if she knew where she was going. But she followed the sound of water, which led her to a stream, glinting in the dark. Further passage into the forest was blocked by the water, which emitted a tinkling sound. Or, no, that sound wasn't water. There was something moving low to the ground, on the other side of the stream.

She stood up warily and backed up. The creature was bounding toward the bank. Reflexively, she aimed her flashlight toward it. "Oh," she said. It was a dog, thirstily lapping at the water's edge. A Bernese, collared, with jangling tags. It belonged to someone.

The dog's reflection on the water's surface was soon joined by the reflection of its owner.

She looked up. The figure was standing at a distance. It didn't shift when she shone her flashlight at it, and the beam was too weak to reveal a face. He was wearing his mackintosh and loafers, his standard dress on campus.

She glanced back at the water's surface. She was able to see a face only in the watery reflection. Was this him or a facsimile? A chimera?

She spoke, her voice tremulous and uncertain. "Professor?" she said. There was no answer. Slowly he turned and moved away, the dog by his side. She stepped closer to the stream, raised her voice this time. "Nemo?"

This time, the dog stopped and turned to look at her. It barked before catching up with its owner. Across the stream, the two figures disappeared into the woods.

.   .   .

It was the recurring sound of something hitting the wall, a hard clacking, that made Sean step out of his office and investigate. He had been working in Godspeed that Saturday, trying to finish an essay. The building was typically quiet on the weekends, and he'd been counting on that quiet to focus.

The door to Marie's office, just down the hall, had been left open, but she wasn't in. He stood in the doorway, glancing at her desk—which was strewn with personal items sloppily spilling out of her leather tote—before quickly stepping inside. Hesitation implied wrongdoing.

It was freezing, was the first thing he noticed. She had left the window open. The sound had been the flapping of those blinds in the wind, smacking against the frame. He closed the window. Godspeed was an old building, with a tricky heating system. Any temperature drop in one room would lower the temperature of the entire building, thus kicking the heating into overdrive and rendering all other offices even hotter. Of course, she probably hadn't considered this when she'd opened the window for that gratuitous blast of cold air. It was typical of how she moved through the world—carelessly, with shortsighted selfishness. If he brought it up to her, she would apologize only to humor him.

She must have been in the middle of something, then hurried away, leaving her belongings strewn out. On her desk, there was a phone, some extension cords, skin-care products, a burnished leather day planner. Anyone could come in and rifle through them.

He would hear her steps in the hallway if she were approaching.

This is what he was thinking when he was interrupted by the closet door opening. He glanced up just in time to see her stepping through it. "Ah, I didn't realize you were in here," he said, hiding his surprise. Then, sternly, he added, "You left the window open."

"Oh, I wasn't aware. I'm sorry." She smiled, then gestured to her open day planner in his hands. "Find anything interesting in there?"

"It fell on the floor. I was just putting it back," he lied.

"Okay," she said brightly. Whether or not she believed him, she didn't seem invested in finding out.

"You weren't here," he added unnecessarily. "Sorry, the window—"

"It's fine. Anyway, I'm off to the HFF reception." She paused, then asked, "Would you like to come with?"

"Oh, uh—I have a few things to do in the office." It might have been the first time she had ever invited him to anything.

"Are you sure? I hear there's an open bar. Donor events are always the most flush." She smiled conspiratorially.

"I know," he said stiffly.

She was gathering her things back into her tote. "Are you done with that, or . . . ?"

He looked down at her planner in his hands. "Oh, I wasn't—"

"It happens." There was no trace of suspicion in her voice.

Sean looked at her. Something was off, her lack of suspicion or irritation. He cleared his throat. Resetting the equilibrium, he said, "You should really keep the window of your office closed in the winter. It forces the heating system in the building to over-compensate, overheating everyone's offices."

She nodded. "That's right. I keep forgetting. I'll make sure to keep it shut next time." As if to herself, she said, "I should write a reminder on a Post-it."

"See that you do." He slipped out into the hallway, back to his office, where he closed the door and sat down at his desk.

He pivoted back to his laptop, the cursor blinking at him. None of the words he had just written made sense. He was very quiet for a moment as he heard her footsteps descending the staircase. From his window, he saw her leave out the front of Godspeed, her coat flapping behind her.

He got up and moved down the hall to her office again, trying the knob. As he'd anticipated, she had not set the door to self-lock. Someone like her always left a trail of oversights.

He looked around again. She had materialized out of seemingly nowhere.

He opened the closet, which felt drafty and smelled like the outdoors. Like her office, it was mostly bare, save for a piece of furniture, some kind of antique dresser. It took a moment before his eyes adjusted, and he recoiled at a blotch of black mold growing across the wall. His first instinct was to blame Marie for not having called building maintenance earlier to eradicate it. A breeze filled the closet. It took another moment before he realized it was not mold.

At first he approached the opening cautiously, ducking his head inside. He couldn't see anything. Then, unable to stop himself, he rushed through the passageway.

It did not lead to a storage space, as he had thought. He was outside. It was a clearing. He could see the silhouette of a figure standing there smoking, the back toward him. Even though he could not see the face, he knew immediately. That was her hair, the same wool coat. Was that really her, though? Who had he just seen leaving the building? He felt tricked. He hastened his steps toward her, intending to take her by surprise. "But I just saw you leave!" It was a cry both triumphant and confused. He had found her out, caught her in something—he didn't know what.

His exclamation made the figure startle. She turned around and looked at him, the cigarette falling from her mouth. It snuffed out when it hit the ground.

Catherine Lacey

Man Mountain

I CANNOT SAY I FULLY UNDERSTOOD where it came from, but I think we all understood, in a way, where it came from. Not physically where it came from—I mean, no one could really explain that—but the mountain's sudden appearance was at least understandable from a metaphoric, philosophical, and/or emotional perspective, which is to say it made sense astrologically even if it did not make sense logically.

Logic and reason (remember reason?) had long ago fallen out of fashion. The calm among us—and there were still a few calm among us—kept saying there was no need to worry, that history was cyclical and we had simply entered a recurrent era of abject chaos. This was the "Goodnight Mush" part of the century, time for the chrysalis to turn soupy. This was the year a mountain spontaneously materialized in rural Kansas, one kilometer high, composed entirely of semiconscious adult men.

When I heard about the Man Mountain I was, of course, at the gym. Those of us who were not comforted by the historical view of the contemporary moment—a nagging sense of being prewar—had taken matters into our own hands in the only way we could—that is, symbolically—and begun training for the figurative and literal wars that were both imminent and present. Most of the women I knew (though I only really knew or seemed to know the people who also spent most of their waking hours at the gym) kept strict training schedules in Muay Thai, jujitsu, boxing, or semi-acrobatic styles of weight lifting. In an era of perpetual crisis, we soothed ourselves by caring inordinately about how tall a box we could jump onto, or how much we could deadlift, or how many times we could flip a truck tire. In idle moments, we imagined perfecting the form of our pull-ups, our push-ups, our jabs and jump squats, and we pitied the women who still did yoga, except the ones who did that torturous heated variety with their tongues sticking out, contorted and menacing and psychospiritually weaponized. They were all right—mostly—though we felt they had not yet realized that inner peace was a patricapitalist fantasy and the only reasonable thing a woman could do now was amass an antiestrogenic cluster of meat around her controversial guts and train for battle.

"Our Bodies, Our Machines," we said. There was no time for softness. There was no time for time. Sometimes, between sets, we would look at each other and just say what year it was—could you believe it? And no one could believe it—then we would return with new hostility to our routines, laboring until we were sweating blood, spitting blood, until blood soaked our hair and slicked our limbs, until blood issued from our every pore and pit.

So when news broke about the Man Mountain I just thought, Uh, what? Then, like so many unbelievable things, it became completely believable, and all there was left to do was to climb it.

Not to blow my own horn (but also not to apologize for blowing my own horn, because what else are you supposed to do with your own horn) but I probably ranked in the top tier of nominally amateur American athletes most prepared to conquer the Man Mountain. I don't know how you could have polled for that, but I feel confident that it was, and still is, true. I'd spent a lot of time at my local climbing gym, then a few other climbing gyms, then I went rogue and started climbing straight up buildings, trees, gates, traffic lights, anything. Maybe I didn't have time to eat solid food anymore and maybe I wasn't being an effective employee and perhaps I didn't have an actual human-on-human relationship in my day-to-day, but none of that mattered anymore because I was no longer exactly human, but something closer to a spider—spindly and silent and menacing, frightening nice people as I hoisted myself onto their balconies.

So I drove straight to Kansas and, uh, *whoa*. The pictures and the videos and the three-dimensional animated renderings of the Man Mountain did not really convey the thingness of this thing. It was a real stumper. It was, I don't know, a feat? But whose feat? A feat of what? Several television trucks were there, but none of the reporters could look away for long enough to read their teleprompters. Policemen and National Guards and SWAT teams idled in dark hordes, but there seemed to be no agreement about how to proceed—which way to point the guns, whether it was a crime scene or not, whether the Man Mountain needed protection from the people or whether it was the other way around. Some UFO enthusiasts had gathered, smug and reverent, and there were several varieties of cult members and leaders, many forms of clergy, druids, leftover Y2Kers, a few seemingly unaffiliated drum circles, and so on. Each of them claimed the mountain as confirmation of whatever they needed confirmed; it had been prophesied, and now was a time for great rejoicing and repentance and sudden death. They looked up at the large Kansas sky, gleeful and reassured.

I stood away from the crowd. An expectant solitude washed over me as I contemplated the possibly sinister and as yet unknown force(s) that could have created the Man Mountain, and my understanding of the basic foundation of reality shifted beneath my feet. It was reassuring, at least, that something literal and serious had occurred in this time of chronic indifference and rumor. The Man Mountain was not contingent or theoretical. It was not a think piece. It was here and large and undeniable. The few who attempted to take photographs of the Man Mountain all failed, as the feeling of being in its presence resisted digitization. It was the only event for many years that lacked an obvious political narrative or conspiracy or apocrypha.

The base was exceptionally easy to scale, almost as if it had been designed this way. Holds were plentiful and well spaced. I grabbed a foot, an elbow. Thighs and buttocks gave gently beneath my feet. Up close, none of the men seemed to be asleep, exactly, yet none were quite awake. Most of their eyes were shut or fluttering, and all of them held slight grins, as if they understood and accepted the strange enormity of their predicament. Every limb I held as I scaled seemed to teem with itself, forcefully occupying its place in the pile. There was no passivity here, no victimization. The Man Mountain was, I inferred, a wonder of sheer will.

About thirty feet up I came across Justin.

Justin? What are you doing here? Whoa! Justin!

His eyes shocked open like he was a corpse in a horror film, which would have startled me if I hadn't been engaged in military-grade stress training for several years. Justin began to move his mouth, the muscles as loose and uncontrolled as an infant's.

Hey.

Yeah, I said. *Hey.*

A broad man sandwiched sideways in the mountain created a ledge I rested on to talk to Justin.

It's been a while, I said.

Yeah, he said.

Are you all right? Do you want me to, uh, help get you out of here or . . . ?

Nah.

Cool. Okay. Well. Maybe I'll see you around?

Justin didn't reply so I kept on moving upward, but what did I even mean: *Maybe I'll see you around?* Around what? Around when? Recently my emails had started writing themselves—I would click to open a reply, then the computer would just take over and words appeared on the screen, words I recognized as unremarkably my own. Even our emails knew, for absolute certain, that no one had said anything unpredictable in many years.

And when, exactly, had I even met Justin? I couldn't remember if he was someone to whom I'd given my vague approval or whether he was someone I suspected capable of performing the acts of evil so casually enjoyed by those with disposable incomes and frictionless societal existences. I was pretty sure we'd met at a party hosted in a town house owned and renovated by a tech start-up. A large fiberglass horse took up much of one living room. It seemed several young men lived there, and several maids would appear and clean it when one of those young men summoned them through one of the apps that had been developed by the start-up they'd started. A grove's worth of potted fig trees filled the rooms, all of them well cared for, some of them fruiting. One room was arranged with sofas and armchairs that looked like the cartoonish inflatable furniture sold in late-nineties American malls, only this furniture did not deflate. These chairs, you had to live with them.

Justin had been playing a vintage pinball machine under a black crystal chandelier while explaining some complex opinion to another man, or maybe Justin was the one listening instead of speaking or maybe Justin and I observed these two men by the pinball machine or perhaps Justin was someone else entirely. It's difficult for me to remember, as this was a very long time ago, at least one presidential era into the past. In fact, Justin may not have been either of those men but instead the one who had either invited or escorted me to the tech town house, and if that is the case then I am even less sure about how I first came across Justin and now that I think of it I am less sure about his name being Justin, or—another likely case—half or more of the men in that town house were named Justin. At the time I thought an important part of being a human was appearing before other humans and demonstrating the facts of your humanity—your name, age, origin, collegiate affiliations, career, ambitions, social standing, and whether you slept in a bed with another person and if so what sort of genitalia that person had and if not what sort of genitalia you would accept on the body of a person with whom you might consider sharing a bed.

But then I joined a gym and realized that it is totally possible to commit to a life lived primarily within one's legal, corporeal limits, and of pushing one's living corpse to the outskirts of its abilities, of measuring out the finite weeks in leg, arm, back, or ab days, of monitoring the fluctuations of a body fat percentage, of scrupulously observing the material intake and output of one's body, of tracking the incremental progress of how well one is able to pick something up and put it down again. There was nothing, it sometimes seemed, that I couldn't lift and set down again, nothing I couldn't climb, nothing I couldn't put below me.

Anyway, I soon realized my ascent of the Man Mountain was going a little too easily—it just wasn't the challenge I'd been hoping for as I wasted all those hours driving to Kansas. In boredom, I stopped on a man situated horizontally in the pile much like the man I'd perched upon to talk to Justin, and in fact this man looked so much like that last man that it might have been the same man and turning to my right I found, again, Justin's face, his eyes just as wide as before.

Hey, Justin 2 said, but I could not bring myself to reply. Had I somehow climbed in a circle? I had, I thought, been climbing straight up. I looked down at the spectators and SWAT teams and television trucks below; everyone was still staring up or moving around haphazardly, pacing, confused, aimless. I leaned back against the chest of a man in a pale green polo shirt. *Hey,* Justin 2 said again, but I didn't have any ability or desire to speak to Justin 2 for the first or second time. Something was not right. Something, maybe, was very wrong.

A foot jutted out right next to my head—it wore a polished

leather shoe and a sock patterned with little red and blue birds flying to and from and with and against one another. The ankle of this foot seemed to be in good condition, probably had a decent bone density, healthy ligaments. I'd once seen someone drop a sixty-pound metal orb on his bare foot and as the orb rolled off, his foot seemed smaller than ever, but by the time the ambulance came the foot had swollen to the size of a small head. The guy on the other end of that foot was stuck in bed for months, losing all his life's gains, all his strength evaporating in his inaction. To get out of bed he needed permission from both his feet and one of them would simply no longer give it. His foot, it seemed, could not forgive him.

And what part of my body would someday not forgive me? I often succeeded in never thinking of such things by thinking instead of inputs and outputs, measures and reps, by focusing on progress and never on ends. But here on this heap of men, everything seemed closer than ever to ending, and all at once I was engulfed by a great arbitrary vortex that goes by the name of God.

All those heights I had climbed, all my strength, all my effort and torn muscle rebuilt and rebuilt, not even God could see it, and I knew that then, or I felt that I knew it, or maybe I just felt a breeze and knew it to be the cool and apathetic gaze of God. I was in a race against my own potential weakness and I was winning and I was losing.

Hey! Justin 2 said again.

No, I thought, that's quite enough. I simply cannot tolerate being so social anymore, not today, not in this crisis. There were just too many people in this Man Mountain, and I had not come here to make friends—I had come here to climb! Well! I wasn't going to waste my little time anymore. I started scaling down the Man Mountain, which is always awkward looking and never quite as easy as going up. I passed the initial Justin, who calmly watched my descent, but then I passed Justin again, and though

I quickened my pace, I passed yet another Justin or perhaps the same Justin and when I looked down to estimate how close the ground was, it seemed I hadn't moved any closer to the base of the mountain.

Then, as if this world had spontaneously begun to understand my trouble, a rope ladder dropped from a helicopter. I leaped to and ascended it, and how strange it was to realize that climbing something as unusual as a pile of men could be so boring while climbing something as unremarkable as a rope could be so thrilling. The wind whipped up by the helicopter blades rushed through my four actual and my four invisible limbs and for a few moments everything I'd ever done seemed worth the hassle. God could take me or leave me.

In the helicopter several reporters were huddled, and one of them had a large microphone she held to my mouth as she shouted questions over the helicopter's nearly deafening whir: What were the Men of the Man Mountain like and what were they doing there in a pile like that and what did I think it meant and did I think the federal government should intervene or should they leave it up to the state of Kansas and what would I like to tell the American People and did any of the Men in the Mountain say anything to me and did I say anything to them and did I suspect foul play or divinity and, yes, most important, did I think the Man Mountain was an Act of God?

I wanted to answer the reporter, but I didn't want to answer her questions. I shook my head, so she reshouted her questions, all of them the same, just louder, meaner. How could she have known that I, a human spider, can hear very precisely through both my ears and the extremely tiny and biologically complex hairs that cover my body and limbs? She couldn't have known. The truth is that spiders and humans know very little about one another, and human spiders know even less about themselves. I tried to answer her questions, but my ears were bleeding. I'm simply too sensitive. I just want to climb on everything, keep climbing on everything up and always up, to reach the top or die trying. I tried to speak; I may have spoken. Perhaps I should have kept quiet. Below us everyone kept struggling and failing to know how the world had come to this, and above us no one even bothered to ask the question.

Jonas Eika

Translated from the Danish by
Sherilyn Nicolette Hellberg

Me, Rory and Aurora

IT WAS ME, RORY AND AURORA, back then they lived in a flat
smack up against the tracks. Crawling back and forth between
their living room and bedroom was like taking the train, Rory had
punched a big angry hole in the wall one day while Aurora was at
church, like the tunnel on that train line. Well, one day Rory said
he didn't love Aurora anymore, and looked at me with eyes I think
I'd call turned around, I mean they were looking as much into his
own brain as at me, and seeking affirmation both places. I said
why and didn't feel like talking about it when she wasn't home,
and in a way I was their child, so how was I supposed to talk to
him about it anyway? My main interest, besides running away
with Aurora, and I would never get her to agree to that, was to
keep being their kid. She's always out and about, he said, she's not
interested in *our* life anymore. Kiss my ass, I said, and went to bed
with a rancid taste in my mouth because of what his *our* implied,
that something like a his-and-my life could exist without her.

Luckily she came home and threw her puffy jacket on the floor.
I could tell from the sound of fabric collapsing and the way she
sighed, a drawn-out, useless whistle like electric signals moving
through a burned-out computer. Where have you been? Rory

asked. At the church, Aurora said. What'd you make? Enough, she said, and dumped all the money on the table in the kitchen, where he was making leek soup. I could smell it by the sweet, oniony steam seeping toward me in bed. The room was nearly dark, bundles of warm light poked through the hole in the wall. Headlights slid over the ceiling, which was shaking from the trains. Does it really take all day to sell your shit to the faithful? Rory said. Does it take all day to steal vegetables for your soup? Aurora replied. Who's the one with a baby in their belly? I was lying halfway down the gap between the two mattresses, my shoulder blades against the wooden pallet, which I had found out walking one day and dragged back home—like how a cat brings in dead birds, Rory had said, and it was fair enough: I was quiet and cuddly and almost never in the way, I registered everything that happened in the flat. A little food was all I needed but I could easily go a day or two without. And every once in a while I'd come home, guilty and proud, with some sort of junk they hadn't asked for but had to accept: a wooden pallet, a board game, a lump of amber. Ceramic shoulder pads Rory would put on when he got drunk. There wasn't any shame in letting them take care of me, it was hot and sometimes turned us on, but it would have hurt if I couldn't return the favor.

Later—I must have been sleeping—they got into bed all stiff and stubborn with the silence they brought with them from the kitchen table. The air grew hard between their shoulders where I was curled up, and then Rory turned onto his side and snuggled up to Aurora, saying hey or babe or some other conciliatory thing. I wanted to join in as usual, to wedge myself between their laps and start on both of them while they kissed, but it was their fight and I guess their makeup too. I wriggled to the foot of the bed, crawled out and lay down under the pallet. Rory rolled onto his back again, his bony body closing the gap between the mattresses. He pulled his butt cheeks, which were above my chest, up and away from me as his shoulder blades pushed against the pallet, so his lower back became an arched bridge of skin. It smelled like sweat loosening the dirt he had accumulated during the day.

And then it was Aurora on her belly between the mattresses, pressed softly against the crisscrossed planks. I laid the palm of my hand against one of them and could vaguely feel the weight of her belly through it. Involuntarily, and with a sense of irritation that exceeded the tenderness, I felt for a second entirely equal with the creature on the other side of the wood and the belly skin and whatever else was shielding it from me. Dropped into this cramped flat, it would have to find its place in Rory and Aurora's life, between the furniture and piles of clothes, the way they'd been living for a while. Who knew why that baby had chosen to come here. Who knew whether the world you were in before you let yourself be sucked into conception was as barren and formless and freezing cold as mine had been the night I met Rory and Aurora at that bar eight months earlier. They were out drinking up the last of her severance check, celebrating her return from rehab, Rory was glowing. I had gone out hoping someone would buy me drinks and offer me cigarettes, and they did. They told me about their lives, that they had moved to London because Aurora got a job as a teacher at a local school, which she lost soon after when she lost their child in the sixth month and went to the dogs, and I loved sitting there hearing about it. I loved the lack that was so clearly part of their lives, since they were babbling about it to a stranger between giggles that made their martinis spill. It was paranoid and hot how they were getting closer on both sides. I followed them home because I was hungry. The sex and fun we had was so good that they let me stay, or maybe they were just sympathetic to my situation. Or maybe they were sympathetic *because* we had such a good time together, so in that sense I also invested some of my personality that night. I followed them because I was hungry. Next thing I was in love with Aurora.

Now I was climbing back into bed and falling asleep to her breath. Her hand on my shoulder shook me awake, did I want to come with her? Rory was still sleeping.

She preferred to work alone, probably knowing that we would never really do anything without her, so it felt special to be brought along. Sitting across from her on the train going backward, watching things disappear. A timid streaming orange light in the leaves and the rails and the rail workers' bodies, like they hadn't returned to themselves after sleep. Their hammering sounded daring and impossible so early in the morning, coming through the window with the cold air. And with the whirring of the train's frozen axles. Aurora said, Hold your breath!, and I blocked my throat as the darkness was pulled over us. The friction of the train on the rails sounded stifled and secret. In the light from the other side of the tunnel, she let her breath leak slowly out between her teeth, her hand slipping the pills into her coat pocket, and I coughed mine out with a gasp. A pair of coattails flapped out of the train compartment after the man who had been sitting next to her. *Vowels,* that's what we called those pills, because they softened you up and made you receptive, starting with a round feeling and a light in your mouth, your throat, your belly and so on, until your whole body was a glowing processor just waiting for data, which was probably why City Church was the perfect market; affiliated with the rehab center, it was full of addicts who had turned to God or were trying to. The vowels, like the service, lasted for about an hour and were usually a prelude to acid, a way to prepare for the actual trip, so Aurora could get a bag of one hundred for £50 and sell them on for £1 apiece. She would prop herself against the wall by the entrance, then push off with her shoulder and greet people as they arrived. She pulled them to her, calling them by name, and leaned into them with her voice. A kind of smoothing, a leveling of features into a dull plate of a face, marked the majority of these people, and from where I was standing it looked like Aurora was pulling them out of their sameness one by one and really seeing them. I thought about whether it felt that way for them too. Whether she could do that while selling them drugs.

What surprised me that day, and what I think Aurora brought me along to see, was how they remained seated when it was all over. From the moment I had taken the pill—in sync with a hundred other hands rising from pocket to mouth, a hundred throats stretching and swallowing when the prelude began—the service had seemed to be elapsing in parallel with my trip, expanding in time with the space being cleared out inside me. As if its composition were encoded into the chemical formula of the pill. Afterward, there was only the comedown. I was all tied up inside and couldn't feel a thing. And that felt like an awful weakness in light of the service and the way the prayers, the organ music and the priest's gesticulations had filled me up. Now it was quiet, the priest had left, and all around me people remained seated with the saddest faces or their eyes closed, afflicted by something they preferred to deal with in the dark. They sat slumped and shaggy, but seemed at the same time infused with a mystical will to be present in this *after,* a persistence that went far beyond what the pill could give them. But Aurora! She wouldn't budge either, didn't react to my elbow poking her side or my feet tapping the floor. Of course she sat through the service so people could see that she didn't split as soon as she had milked them, and when the dealer is tripping too you know the product is good. But why was she still sitting there—and with that belly too, shouldn't she eat something soon? Her abdomen was bulging in the light from the barred windows above, trying to get her attention, just like me. She stayed that way for hours. And the church actually wasn't even a church, but a bare room without ornamentation, just concrete walls and ten rows of folding chairs set up for the occasion.

Back home in the kitchen, Rory had a roast in the oven and two homeless men at the table who looked up at us friendly and embarrassed when we walked through the door. Dave and Sully, he said, introducing them with an outstretched palm, we got to talking up by the corner shop. Aurora hid her confusion, probably so that they wouldn't feel unwelcome, went over to greet them with me at her heels and turned to Rory, who had his head in the oven: Food's ready! Over dinner he tried to keep the conversation going, mostly talking about Aurora—only three weeks till she's due but she's still bloody working nine to five—while a tone of accusation crept into his voice. Yeah, things are a bit tight right now, Aurora said, looking at him, especially if we want to be able to afford a roast now and then. She ate very little. And now she's taking Casey with her too, Rory continued. Yeah, I said, I'm not doing much anyway, so I get to go to work with Mum! And I'm here all day thinking about them, Rory said. Well, you've got friends up at the park, Dave said, implying Sully and himself with an almost noble nod back and forth between them. I smiled, feeling really wretched, sad that they had to step right from the street into this family drama, probably the first home in which they'd set their wiry feet in a while. Rory had insisted they take their socks off and rest their feet on a stool under the table. They were sitting very awkwardly, unable to relax or give in to the reclined position their raised legs demanded. They reeked much worse than we did, everyone could smell them. When Rory offered for them to stay the night, something happened that went way beyond this covert marriage dispute and the discomfort of sitting in the middle of it. Dave, he was the one who did the talking for both of them, looked down and said, Thank you but we can't. But it's freezing cold outside, Rory continued, and the shelters, aren't they all closed now, until Dave said, We wish we could accept the offer. You're very nice people. But you see, it's not easy being comfortable in someone else's home—it can make us really sad, Sully added—we can't do it for your sake.

Later, after we had said goodbye and closed the door behind them, we stood in our respective corners of the kitchen, staring into the living room. It was so full of their honesty and our pent-up conflict that we had two possibilities: either cry or shout at each other, either fight or be sad by ourselves, so we went straight to the bedroom—Rory through the door with Aurora at his heels, me through the hole in the wall—and met in bed in an indecisive embrace. Sex between the three of us could never become that self-contained formation that shut out everything else, the snake biting its own tail, we were always trying to open and extend the pleasure, with hands and mouths, across the mattresses, through the room, up and out of the building. While the train screeched through every ten minutes. Water glasses rattled on the night-stand. The flat bulged red with heat against the night's blue-black. The air was riddled by traffic moving in all directions, up to the satellite and back again. Someone shouted, started running after someone else, *Hey, you!* Cars accelerated and hit the brakes at the foot of the bed. Aurora's belly was bulbous with visible veins, we navigated around it with caution. At one point I was on my knees with Rory inside me and Aurora lying diagonally in front of me. I was sucking on her nipples and could have sworn some milk came out, just a few drops. Just a second of that body-warm, sugary, a little oniony, a-little-too-soon liquid in my mouth, and right after, an impulse to suck away, to drink so much that it would fill me all the way up and push out Rory's cock, but there wasn't any more. It's not that I didn't appreciate his presence, but there was a longing inside me to be alone with Aurora and be pure milk. Sometimes when he fucked me I could feel so specific and demarcated, bound to the bed. The morning after our first night together he made scrambled eggs and said I should stay around. So strange sitting there together, eating breakfast in a T-shirt on a cold stool, like the two of us were going to be a couple, but then he said, I think Aurora would be happy if you were here when she came home. Rory had a way of being in the flat without her, always in the process of taking care of something or other, which I really liked about him. He would gently rearrange the furniture and clothes, wipe the crumbs off the table, make the bed and air the place out. Water the plants with a spray bottle and nuzzle the leaves between two fingers, count the cash and meticulously decide what kind of soup he would make today, and which ingredients he'd have to steal for it. He dragged everything out, as if to fake a household and make it last until Aurora got in—maybe that was part of why he wanted me to stay? Back then she would come home early, and we would have started flirting around noon, stirring up a mood she could wade right into and release. Later, if he hadn't already that morning, Rory would go do the stealing, and then me and Aurora would make out hungrily and wait to do more until he got back home. A lot of me loved her exclusively, wanted her now and all to myself, but 1) that would ruin their marriage; 2) then I might have to leave the flat, or at least not be under Rory's care anymore; 3) I cared a lot about Rory too; and 4) it was because of their marriage, with my place in the sweet spot between them, that I could even be close to Aurora in the first place. Without them I might lose her for good.

Now I was looking up and saw a guilty but also kind of outbound expression in her eyes. I looked over my shoulder and realized that they were responding to Rory's, which were looking at her the same way as when we had come home late that afternoon: an injured look that expressed the same feeling that I had had next to her in the City Church all day: she was on her way out. She was turning toward something that made her stay in her seat much longer than necessary, forget to eat and drink, and that made her care about everything but her sales, the baby and us waiting for her at home.

Six months later, I suddenly spot the reflection of the man in the dull gray trench coat in the glass I'm looking out of. In the opposite window, he's sitting with his hands in his lap, letting himself be rocked by the swaying of the train on the tracks. He's staring straight ahead at the empty seat across from him, apparently so familiar with the scenery on this route that he can just as well let it slide blurrily by. Who knows what it's like: being a dealer, spending your days on those efficient, silent transactions. Recognizable, at this point even familiar, buyers in the seat across from him, who he can't talk to or really look at, just a second of eye contact to confirm the imminent sale. Maybe it's not only a matter of discretion, maybe he actually prefers it that way, cutting straight to the bone of the transaction: in the dark of the tunnel handing over a ziplock bag with a right hand, taking the cash in a left, getting up and leaving the car before it gets light again. The train turns softly to the left, setting course for an arch of brown bricks that frames a darkness for me. Two deep breaths and I block my throat, haven't been able to breathe in tunnels ever since Aurora told me you couldn't. It's a game she used to play. Hidden by the dark and the mechanical rumbling, I get up and walk over and kneel on the seat behind the dealer. I dip my hands into each of his coat pockets, close them around whatever they're holding, pull them out and walk fast out of the car.

An hour later I'm knocking on Rory and Aurora's door. It hurts in my bones going over there, knowing that I have to see them again, but I really need the money. The sight alone of Rory's puzzled face in the cracked-open door almost makes me cry. He lets me in, and then I'm standing there looking around the kitchen, at the evergreen countertops with all of his lists on them, at the toaster and the kettle, in the yellow glow of the ceiling light. I can feel how my body is sucking everything in because it has forgotten and knows that now's the chance to get it back: the piles of clothes, the draft and the knots in the floor, the smell of Rory's soup, the jagged hole in the wall, Rory, his birdlike body in the kitchen, I swallow it all and hold it inside my wide-open belly. Then I take two steps forward and look into the bedroom to the right. Aurora is sitting on the edge of the bed, rocking a cradle on the floor. Something awkward about the way her arm is extended, she must have sat down like that as soon as she heard it was me. The baby is quiet and barely visible between the hat and blanket, snub nose and a tiny open mouth. What's up? Aurora says. What've you got? I take the bag of vowels out of my pocket and say, There's ninety-eight, I took two already. Where'd you get them? she asks. Don't worry about it, I say. You can have thirty pounds, she says. You know I know what they cost, I say. I want forty, minimum. You get thirty, she says, even more resolved . . . Listen, I don't want to know where you got those pills, but if our guy has lost one hundred, and then we buy half the usual amount the next day, how do you think that's going to look? No matter what, I'm gonna have to spread those ninety-eight out over a few weeks, or months . . . Fine, I say, thirty, that's fine.

I handed her the bag of pills. She handed me £30.

I still don't know how we ended up with that cruel transaction. Was it my indecisiveness, my inability to take a stand in the fight, that let the two of them close around each other? Was I just too passive, a kind of pet, was I becoming too dirty and unkempt? Or was it the baby, the arrival of the actual baby, that inevitably excluded me? That would be really ironic, because it was most likely conceived the night we first met. After Dave and Sully left, we lay in bed and counted back to that night, and I felt fertile for a second, or at least beneficial to my surroundings. Me and Rory were curled up on either side of Aurora, who was sitting halfway up in bed, each of us with a cheek and a hand on her belly. You've never been so pregnant, he said dreamily. Soon there'll be a baby here. He gestured panoramically across the room like it was a showroom for their life after the birth. I realized that the child, or at least the dream of a home that the child was supposed to fulfill, was Rory's most of all. He had never really been good at anything, but the flat was his to arrange, to potter around and display at the end of each day. A helpless living creature here would make him indispensable. The next morning I was awoken by the door slamming, jumped out of bed and caught up with Aurora halfway up the street. Hey, you're pulling my love out of bed way too early! I said, smiling, and grabbed her collar. I didn't think you wanted to come, she said. Her face was blank and exhausted in the headlights of the cars driving by. Sometimes she looked almost wounded by fatigue, it was really cute. I just don't understand what they're doing in that church, I said, why don't they get up at the end? I don't think I can explain that to you, Aurora said, it's a kind of meditation—But I want to be part of it, I said—on the hangover, she said, the state that comes after. Okay, come on then.

The City Church was in East London, Stratford I guess, in a remote industrial neighborhood twenty minutes walking from Leyton station, and the patients had already served their five hours when we got there a little before eleven. That was how they paid for their stay at the rehab center, Aurora told me, by working it off in the factories. The whole complex was owned by one of the private companies that the state had started using to contract its social services. People were sent here after being on welfare support for a long time, as a kind of combined detox and job training. Even from a purely therapeutic standpoint, the work played an important role, Aurora explained; getting sober was all about rediscovering your functionality, teaching yourself each day that you're good for something. In the work halls, screens listed the day's productivity stats, and once a month you had to sit in the observation room to watch the *big picture* and be reminded of each person's indispensability on the production line. But *I* always felt totally replaceable, Aurora said. The days I produced the most, it was like it was running right through me. What do they make? I asked. Turbines, computer chips, that kind of thing. A bell rang, or the sound of a bell was played from speakers on the roof of the church, and a few minutes later people left the factories lining the road, and walked down the sidewalk and across the gravel parking lot. There was something protracted and uncertain about their movements, on the way to yet another demanding job, one they weren't sure they could complete, but also something serene, a kind of faith, maybe, that it was worth doing anyway. On the way into the church, which was actually an empty factory, a box-shaped building with peeling walls and the trunks of demolished chimneys sticking out of the roof, they stopped by Aurora to exchange £1 for a vowel with a handshake or an embrace across her belly. She was pale and professional in the late-morning sun.

Inside, we sat on folding chairs, swallowed our pills and listened to the prelude. After a few minutes I felt the light of the vowel expanding my body, activating an alternative nervous system that was directly connected to everything around me. My skull and my rib cage enveloped the hall, the organ and the sermon quivered inside me. As the priest pronounced the blessing he melted into my spine with a fluid click, pushing my ribs from each other with his arms. Our addiction was a hallmark, the sign of a foundational weakness and impotence that we had to accept in order to let God accomplish inside us that which we couldn't do ourselves. And when we speak of God, we mean God as *you* perceive him. He said that several times.

There's nothing to say about the séance after the service. No altar, no ornaments in the empty, square room, could distract me from the unbearable feeling of paralysis or permanent sedation of my soul with which I was left after the trip. Even the light was useless, falling without shadows or nuances, it probably hadn't been changed since there was a factory here. After a few hours I started getting hungry, and what about Aurora, could she feel the baby complaining inside her? Was she ignoring it like she was able to ignore her own hunger? The air was greasy from the gas that had been burned in the room. Grease got stuck in my eyes and the roots of my nails, and I felt the creeping griminess I remembered from living on the street, before I moved in with Rory and Aurora, in an inhuman crowd of people and vehicles. It's a boundless space, not fit for living, you can't tidy or clean or decorate anything. You own nothing around you.

When the bell finally rang again, who knows when, we got up in a daze from our folding chairs and left the church in the opposite direction of everyone else. They squeezed past us, heading toward the back wall. On the threshold I turned around, grabbed Aurora's hand and watched them disappear through a double door made of dark green metal. They stepped out onto a muddy field, in the dusk that fell murkily into the church. What are they doing? I asked. The rehab center, Aurora said, it's on the other side of the field, and pulled my arm. I hesitated for a second, trying to make out a building, but saw only blue-gray fog framed by the doorway, and the patients sliding away, disappearing into it, one by one, in the middle of the field.

Several worn faces looked up at us as if we had interrupted them in the middle of a sentence or a prayer. At least ten homeless men and women were seated around the table, on the two bar stools in the kitchen, on the floor against the opposite wall and on the windowsill, with their bare feet resting on stools and piles of clothes, in a stench that made the flat swell. It was completely silent for maybe five seconds, until a bony woman with long, iron-gray hair burst out laughing from the window and said, They weren't expecting *that*, were they now! Just look at those two! Rory laughed too, goofily resting his hands on our necks. But they're totally speechless, the woman said, haven't they seen a homeless person before? And in their nice little living room too. Come on, give them a break, Ellen, said a slightly younger man at the kitchen table, let them get through the door, all right? And I'm not doing that, or what, Ellen said, not giving them a chance? No, you're not, the man said. I'm just teasing them a bit, she said, just joking around. I mean, they look like they're at the zoo! And that's no problem *at all*. That's just *fine*. We are a bunch of old seals, the two of us and the others, a flock of crows, free birds in a cage that's too big? No, we're not, there was a third who said, we're wild dogs, and then their eyes and voices kind of let go of us and turned to each other, so we could throw off our jackets and turn to Rory, who was awkwardly stirring his soup. His cheekbones shone boyishly in the steam. Up in front of the shelter, he said quietly, I stopped by on the way home from the shop. And they were all standing there freezing and their numbers weren't getting called, you know, it's completely packed tonight. There's a storm coming. So I said they should come over here to warm up and have a bite to eat . . . You know, honey, I want us to be able to take *care* of people here, just provide the bare necessities. That's why we have a home, right? Someday you'll be old too! Ellen shouted over everyone else. She had gotten up from the windowsill and was hanging in the middle of the room, her crinkled skin aglow like a paper lamp, like an ancient creature on speed. Ellen, Rory said, and went to meet her on the floor. Calmly, he placed his hands on her shoulders and looked her in the eye, as sure of himself as he was when he stole. Do you think they understand the insanity of being sixty years old? she shouted. I don't think they do, Rory said. They're not listening to me, she said, they all think they'll just die in their sleep whenever they're ready. But you know a thing or two, Rory said, that's for sure. Yeah, just look at me, Ellen said. Here I am, spent my whole life on the street, getting ready to die, and still I'm afraid! Still, I want my life. I can't take it anymore, not for another second. Don't think about that right now, Rory said, it's time to eat. I made pea soup. She thought about it for a second. Yeah, she said, sinking into herself, I'm so hungry.

The rest of the night he took care of everyone, ladling and clearing the table, moving things around and making soft encampments out of pillows and clothes, with a new spring in his step. And at the same time he was trying too hard, wriggling his hips, carrying four bowls of soup with demonstrative ease whenever Aurora was watching, as if to say, Look! You too could be this nimble and caring if you hadn't spent all day wearing yourself out in the pews. I leaned toward her, attempting to squeeze myself into the place he was trying to appeal to. I avoided making conversation with the homeless people. In the corner of my eye, they were a wall of voices, a grayish fog, and I felt ashamed. But I couldn't see anything in them but fatigue. That deep, undying fatigue that takes over a face and settles inside it. Too much bad weather and bad sleep, too much noise, abuse and traffic, that was all they expressed. That was what scared me about them, the way their features had yielded to a far-too-general and shared condition. It hadn't happened to me, not in the year and a half I was living on the street, which was part of why I was able to find a clean set of clothes, dress up, go to the bar and flirt my way home with Rory and Aurora. Now they were saying good night, and I hurried after them into the bedroom. We got into bed and listened to the storm and the snores of the homeless people. One of them had put their feet through the hole in the wall. I had the urge to chop them off at the ankles.

On the train the next day, both Aurora and the trees on the other side of the glass, which I loved, and in which the sun slowly rose, were dead to me. In the church, when the high started to fade, I recognized the down as the same condition of insufficiency: not being able to give the world back the meaning I knew it had, for me too. For hours I sat there, feeling that absence, and it hurt in my bones like they were crumbling.

Aurora shouted hi and walked straight to the bedroom in long leaping strides to avoid stepping on anyone. They were everywhere and more since yesterday, strewn across the floor, talking and tea-drinking, slumped over like the participants in a shabby symposium. I was on the toilet, my butt cheeks freezing, when her voice cut hostile through the wall, quickly followed by Rory's. Without being finished I pulled up my pants, ran across the living room and stopped at the door to the bedroom. Do you have any sense, Aurora was shouting, do you have any idea what it's like? If you're so fucking pregnant, Rory said, why don't you come home and relax when you're done working? Why are you staying out so late? But you've got a room full of people! she said. Yeah! I said, and took a long step into the room, maybe you should be taking a little more care of *them*. I nodded in the direction of Aurora's belly. This all started long before I started helping those people, Rory said, and don't you try to teach me anything! You're the one out with her all day, what the fuck are you thinking? I'm taking care of her, I said, and looked at Aurora. As she stood there on the bed, emaciated and bulging like a chicken carcass picked clean, with one hand under her belly and the other raised at Rory, I realized that I had completely forgotten about her in the church the last few days. I felt the kind of sadness that collapses in your belly when you realize the person you love and live with is lonely. In the hallway, some of the homeless people were pulling on their boots. Rory ran over and blocked the door with outstretched arms. But you're already here! he said. We don't want to intrude, they said. It's just a little squabble, he said, lowering his voice, the kind of thing that happens when you live together. My wife . . . it really doesn't have anything to do with you. Stay, won't you? He came back in, got up close to Aurora and hissed into her ear: Come back home to me when you've done your thing. The violent potential in his voice reminded me of that night when the pot of soup was steaming away in her absence. All of a sudden, he got up and hurled it at the wall and made the hole through which the homeless people's awkward silence was now audible. There was soup everywhere. Then you get rid of all these people, Aurora said. If you don't come home late again, he said.

That night, I was awoken by the sound of scratching. It lasted for five seconds at a time, accompanied by a sharp and dry vibration in my spine, like someone was running a barber's knife slowly down it. I lay there, getting scared, heard someone breathing between the scratching, counted to three and rolled fast onto my stomach. Between two of the pallet planks I could make out the bottom of a face, a small, tight mouth without lips, which opened and said sorry. What the hell are you doing! I said. You can't sleep there, you really can't. But it's just me, she said—Ellen, I said—I like it here, it's better than the living room. Her breath was sweet and dry. We debated a bit. She sounded harmless and frail in the dark, and I couldn't be tough. Okay, I said, and turned onto my back, but can you at least stop scratching? I'll try, she said, and started up again a while later. And then I couldn't help but imagine that we were buried together like a married couple, Ellen below, tirelessly scratching the lid of her coffin. It's like that for some people, I think it is, maybe for most; they have to lie in the ground and practice dying because they didn't manage to get ready while they were alive. Their whole existence reduced to a dry breath in ash, a leg stretching, the sound of nails on wet wood.

The next day I couldn't even enjoy the service. The high, the way the vowel turned me into one big glowing nervous system, felt mostly like an opportunity or a demand I couldn't live up to. The hunger and numbness that would follow shone dull and desertlike through the euphoria, and drove it away. I had the thought that this feeling would never stop, and couldn't shake it off. It made my intestines contract, and then I felt a jab, like from a little piece of cold iron, deep in my belly. Some of me passed through the hole in a quick and piercing movement, as if it were being snatched up by a bird of prey, into some foggy, directionless landscape, but it didn't make me less sad.

I still don't understand, I said when we were sitting on the train headed back home. Aurora turned her face from the glass and looked at me. She was actually ugly, or at least each individual feature was unattractive—snub nose, narrow pursed lips, dull eyes set deep in her face—but she was beautiful. I don't understand why you take those pills . . . why you hang around after. Oh, Casey, she said, exhausted, you've been there too. How would you explain it? Terrible, I said, I just feel weak. Me too, said Aurora . . . but that feeling, it's like it's right for me. I think it's what I am. Are you scared? I asked. Of what? The baby, I said. Why, it's coming either way. But you can still be scared. Ahead, the dark semicircle of the Thames tunnel approached behind her. It rose and gradually filled more and more of the gray sky, and as we entered it she said, I'm just tired, Case. I'm so tired of waking up every morning at the crack of dawn with this light in my body. I wake up with such a dumb, totally physical *appetite for the day* when I should stay in bed. And with a baby in my belly when I don't feel like it . . . like it should be there. There shouldn't be anything there. It makes me so hateful.

The train raced through the tunnel, both jangling over the

tracks and drifting away, the darkness expanding the space. The exit signs swished by, gave way to Aurora's face. I reached a hand across the table and placed it on her wet hands. But I'm not scared, she said. I couldn't come up with anything else to say besides that I was there for her and would play with the baby and give it milk at night when she didn't have the energy, and then I could see it: me and the kids, there were two of them now, wrapped in our blankets in front of the television before Rory and Aurora got up. Rory had built a loft in the living room.

The flat was aired out and the makeshift beds cleared away, but it was full of people whom he must have picked up as soon as he realized we weren't coming back early after all. There was something pointless and impotent about his protest now that he had said it out loud. Like stirring a pot full of water. We woke up around midnight to a fresh wet mattress. Aurora pushed us away, panting through her contractions alone. The light from the cars slid bluish across her forehead and hair. Two of the homeless people came in to ask whether she was okay. I hurried to push them back into the living room, where the others were sitting up in their beds, not knowing what to do with themselves. I started tucking them in, pulling the blankets up to their chins, placing a hand on their foreheads, but stopped when Aurora came out of the room, and ran to grab her hospital bag instead. In the middle of the room, she hesitated and said to Rory that she refused to give birth until they were all out of the flat. He turned to them, clapped three times and asked them to leave. Get them out of here! Aurora screamed. They hastily threw on all of their layers, laced up their boots and walked past her with their eyes on the ground. Let's get going, Rory said. Her too, Aurora said . . . Casey too, she repeated without looking up, but sent an exhausted nod in my direction. Get her out! Rory turned toward me, and he was about to get it past his lips when I handed him the bag and left, on legs that felt ancient and foreign, through the door, down the stairs and out onto the street.

I took the train to Stratford and walked straight through the empty church. In front of me, still framed by the wide-open iron door, the field and the overcast night sky slid into a big pile of mud. It thawed and received me to the ankles. There wasn't a single light or star, only the cold, wet wind I imagined was coming from the sea to the east. What was there for me in the east? I walked back and forth, all around, in and out of the mud that was warmer and sweeter than the air. My eyes adjusted to the darkness, but then came the fog. I lay down on my stomach and fell asleep. At some point, I was awakened by some sticky sounds, and out of the damp, white fog there came two, then ten, then twenty and then a whole crowd, muddy and tired like me. I slid in between them and walked alongside them. When we reached the industrial quarter by the City Church, I followed them into a random hall and stamped computer chips for hours. After the service, I followed them back across the field, found a bed that was free in a room for five and was inaugurated into group therapy: taking turns, you talked for fifteen minutes about whatever you were feeling, while the others listened without judgment and helped you get to the Hurt, the places where the pain lay hidden. Reaching them would cause bodily reactions: sweats, shakes, farts, tears, yawns and laughter. I slept and ate and showered, serving my five hours at a new factory each day. Everywhere the buzzing of machines, and the fixed direction of the production line that I started to follow from hall to hall. In the factories closest to the church, work was easy and manual. We welded computer chips, cast rotor blades and fans, put together plastic and electronic parts, carrying out a few motions in a process that resulted in a processor, turbine, or motherboard. Farther out they were assembled into respirators, and in an adjacent hall, into servers that were transported to a building about the size of two football pitches and full of server racks in dead-straight rows. A set of keys and a laptop were pushed toward me through a crack in the wall, and for the next five hours, I followed the others: strolled up and down the rows, connected the computer to the servers that lit up red and followed the troubleshooting instructions on the screen until they stopped. Meanwhile, I saw glimmers of what was stored on them: data about individual patients, their productivity stats, medical files, records, transcripts of group therapy. Much of it was quantified, entered into charts I couldn't interpret. That I could move freely between the halls also meant I didn't have to work, I knew that. But I wanted to see where the respirators ended, and the hours of repetition made my grief foggy and mechanical, my feeling of not meaning anything to anyone. I missed Aurora all the time. One morning, in the parking lot in front of the church, someone recognized me and asked where she was. She needed to take care of some things, I said, as people flocked around me. She told me to tell you guys to go on without her. The last part just slipped out, but they looked like they understood. And without the vowels, one of them said. We need to continue authenticating our addiction. Some days, when crossing the field, a bird of prey would emerge from the clouds, and we would lean our heads back, watching it dive with its long, stiff neck and its claws. At the rehab center, we had the afternoons off and could relax in the rec room, where the lighting was low and ambient. It made you want to sit on the rug or in one of the furnished corners and chat with the other patients, or with the nurses moseying about at our disposal. There was always someone to talk to. And I discovered a pressing need to talk, a whole database of thoughts, feelings, fantasies and memories and quiverings in my nerves, that suddenly became accessible to me. Things felt true when I said them aloud. One day, with the help of a stolen ID, I entered the fenced enclosure farthest from the church, wearing a lab coat like the other employees I had seen coming out of there. The tall brick building was full to the rafters with a cool, rattling sound like wind in fallen leaves. Separated by stands bearing respirator equipment, hospital beds were arranged side by side in long rows, sixty or eighty beds total, housing the Newly Dead: warm, breathing, urinating and pulsating corpses that blood was being drawn from and drugs were being tested on, until it was time to harvest their organs. I was careful not to bump into their bare feet, their fresh faces. I recognized some of them from the center: people who had committed suicide or overdosed, I had seen the nurses rushing to their rooms with the defibrillator.

Gabriel Smith

The Complete

IT WAS THE NO-SUMMER SUMMER. Nobody had to work so we ate and drank in the streets. We shared stories and videos of mob violence, food shortages, burning buildings, black men beaten or shot to death. The climate changed in faraway places. The Americans ended the endless war. A sleepwalking woman attempted her former commute and stepped in front of a high-speed train. At the Empty Olympics in Tokyo, athletes quit and we were so happy for them. A billion animals died in one Australian fire. The air was allegedly full of bad particles.

A Jew dies. He ascends to heaven. At the pearly gates, he is introduced to Saint Peter.

"We have one entry requirement for Jews," Saint Peter says. "To get in, you need to tell a joke that makes God laugh."

The Jew is confused.

"And if God doesn't laugh, you stay in purgatory until you can think of a joke that makes God laugh."

"Can I have some time to think about it?" the Jew says.

"Don't tell that one," Saint Peter says. "He's heard it before."

So the Jew sits on a cloud outside the gates and thinks for a while. When he's ready, he tells Saint Peter, and Saint Peter summons God to the gates to hear the Jew's joke.

"What have you got for me?" God says.

"Well—" the Jew says. Then he tells a long and involved joke about the Holocaust.

God doesn't laugh. He looks shocked.

"That wasn't funny," God says. "That's just awful. All those poor people."

"Well," the Jew says, to God, "I guess you had to be there."

So: here we are, on Earth, specifically London, right now. It is a Sunday morning and the no-summer summer of 2021 has slipped into fall. Everything is in short supply. We have all given up on shopping lists. I do not remember the last time we had any weather.

Last night, an Australian girl told me that time itself felt different to her.

"Like even how I move through reality," she said. "It used to feel staccato. Like moments. Now it feels like a wash."

It was four A.M. and we were on the fire escape of the warehouse she lives in, smoking.

"What do you mean?" I said. I was coming down off a Vyvanse. I couldn't think of anything else to say.

"Like I'm asleep in the backseat of a car. And every so often I wake up and see a road sign, and think, O, I must be here. Then I fall back asleep."

I hear about a staff member at Marylebone Underground Station who, after twenty-odd years on the job, goes insane and begins to use the intercom system to disseminate his apocalyptic agenda, reading passages of Dante, Blake, Milton in place of the usual messages about masks, delays, suspensions in service.

"I get it," a friend tells me, after the anecdote is related to us. "You go under the ground and sit in the dark for an unclear amount of time. You feel movement but don't actually see any for yourself. Then you ride an escalator into the light and you are somewhere else entirely. How could you watch people experience that all day without cracking?"

Personally, I often dream I am on an endless series of connecting trains, heading toward an unfixed destination.

"In Freud," another friend, who also rides trains while asleep, says, "the train is symbolic of death. The journey across the Styx, into the unknown, etc."

Another friend tells me the root of "confused" is "fused with," meaning putting two unconnected things together.

The rich leave the planet for fifteen minutes at a time.

We all become increasingly convinced by street preachers.

In Venice, Harry and I run into a girl he used to fuck. He feels awkward because he hasn't told her that he has a girlfriend now. Between her starters and mains she comes over to the table where we are drinking.

"We're going to this party later," she says, gesturing at her friends. "I'll text you."

"Sounds fun," I say. Harry kicks me under the table.

"What do you do?" she says, to me.

"I'm a writer," I say.

"What are you working on?"

"A Vietnam War novel," I say, which is what I say when I can't be bothered to explain.

"But gay," Harry says.

"Yeah. Like *Brokeback Mountain*," I say, "but in Vietnam."

"Sounds interesting," she says.

"A GI falls in love with a Vietcong," I say, "but they can never be together."

"Are you gay?" she says, the way Italians do.

"He is," Harry says.

She goes back to her meal. We get the bill and leave hastily.

On the way to another bar, Harry puts on a potentially Vietnamese accent and says, "I wish I knew how to quit you."

We are hysterical. We repeat it for the rest of the night.

As for me, I go on dates that go nowhere. A girl who was fired from the circus for sleeping on the job. A girl who had recently discovered that her doctor boyfriend of three years had lied about being a doctor, had two other secret girlfriends, had committed faux malpractice by taking her on a date to a morgue after-hours. A girl who grew up with a cemetery in her garden and buried dead frogs in it amongst the hundred-year-old human graves. A girl who had been a child Christian pop star. A girl who sends me pictures of herself naked, tied to a chair, her body covered in meticulous wounds inflicted by a Palestinian artist who mixes blood in with his oils. A girl who threatens me at length with an expensive Japanese knife. How could I bring a child into this world, they often say, then we fuck raw. The news says that nobody is having sex right now. I contract a disease and learn to play dumb.

Speaking of, I was about to kiss this one girl by the Thames, in the last locked-down winter, with snow falling. She knew I was going to kiss her. But we were playing the game: how long can we make the conversation last before that happens.

This fucked-up guy came up to us and asked for money.

"I hope I'm not interrupting something," he said, in a rude and sarcastic voice.

"You know," the girl said, handing him a crumpled £5 note, gesturing at the snow, "the Eskimo have over a hundred ways to say 'fuck off.'"

I found that very charming. I hope she's reading this.

Another thing she told me: on a long enough timeline, old flames are just cold ashes caught in wind, and every store is a pop-up.

I am fifteen. I haven't fucked, but Harry and Millie have. Millie's parents go away so she invites me and Harry and Jacquetta to spend the night. We shoplift alcohol, hop the train.

Millie meets me and Harry and Jacquetta at the station. Harry and I perform for the girls, tell the Pope Joke, making sure it takes as long as possible.

"That punch line wasn't worth it," the girls say.

But they laugh and laugh the whole time.

Here's the joke. The Pope is in America. He is doing a papal tour of the United States. He does a Vegas residency. When this finishes, the next stop is Los Angeles.

The Pope typically travels in the Popemobile, a high-security, bulletproof luxury car. But the Popemobile is back at the Vatican having work done. So instead, the Pope is being driven in a limousine, by a new, American driver.

On the morning the Pope is due to travel to Los Angeles, the driver goes up to the Pope's hotel room and knocks for him. The Pope opens the hotel room door. He is wearing the full papal getup—hat and all—as he has an engagement in Los Angeles that afternoon.

"Your Holiness," the driver says, "I am your driver, and your car is ready."

"Thank you," the Pope says. Then he pauses for a moment. He looks troubled but excited, as if there is something he wants to say. The driver notices.

"Is there anything I can help with?" the driver says.

"Actually," the Pope says, "there is."

"What is it?" the driver says.

"Before I was Pope—when I was a cardinal, and before that—I loved to drive. Driving was my great joy. Aside from God, it is my one true love. But now I am Pope, I am never allowed to drive. Instead I am driven everywhere in the Popemobile. It is very, very sad. Perhaps the great sadness of my life."

The driver agrees that it is sad, but reluctantly. He knows what is coming.

"So my one request to you," the Pope says, "is that you allow me to drive the limousine from here to Los Angeles."

"Your Holiness," the driver says, "I can't do that. I will lose my job."

"I beg of you," the Pope says, "honor my request. I will make it worth your while. Eternal life. Riches. Whatever you want can be yours."

The driver thinks for a moment.

"The Vatican is the richest organization in the world," the Pope says, "and nobody will ever find out."

"All right," the driver says, "but please, Your Holiness, do not violate any traffic rules. Don't run lights or stop signs. Drive sensibly. Do not speed."

The Pope grins a menacing grin.

"Of course," the Pope says.

The girls on the nowhere dates all listen to podcasts that say the future has been killed by seemingly abstract things.

The boys I am friends with all listen to podcasts by people who haven't yet heard the future is dead. On the boy podcasts the talk is of interplanetary colonization, the power of batteries. The hunting of rewilded animals.

I have attempted to listen to both, but don't have the attention span for either, though I appreciate having the ability to pause a person midsentence.

We have all lost our sense of smell, taste. The share prices of food delivery services have skyrocketed. I speculate on perfume, and plagiarize wherever possible.

I steal a novel idea from a Reddit comment. The novel is about a young man and his best friend. The young man is me. The best friend is Harry, my real best friend.

The novel opens with us having so much fun. We have been friends our whole childhood. We do not need anyone else. We are young and drunk and feel invincible.

We decide to drive Harry's car fast down country roads. Harry sees a deer and swerves to avoid it.

I wake up in the hospital. I am informed that Harry turned into an ash tree, died in the crash. I was lucky to survive.

I am crushed by grief. I recover from my injuries, though I retain a limp from where my femur was shattered.

Alone, I rebuild my life. I spend years moving between bleak jobs and bleaker houses in London. I miss my best friend so much.

One day I see a very beautiful girl sitting alone under a tree. The day is windy and I see her blond hair in the wind, the deep blue of her coat. I go introduce myself and see the deeper blue of her eyes.

We fall in love. She has lost someone, too. Slowly we learn to let go of our grief together.

We find okay jobs: not much, but enough. Years pass. Not everything is perfect. But we make it work.

We move to the countryside. She learns she is pregnant. We get married. I am so happy. We have a beautiful daughter. Then we have a beautiful son.

When Jacquetta and I were in love, we would often spoil social situations by telling the Pope Joke together. But eventually she laughed less and less, until she stopped telling it with me, and just became another person who found the Pope Joke annoying.

Here's the thing: you can't start telling new jokes just because people have gotten bored of your old ones!

I give up on a novel about a girl who changes universities because her father is dying, and she needs to be near him to care for him.

She falls in with a group of friends who are obsessed with a videotape of an episode of an old sitcom.

They are obsessed with the videotape because every time they watch it, it changes, as if by magic. The story always stays the same, but details are different: it is raining, or a character is wearing a deer costume, or affecting a bad French accent.

The friends have various theories about why this is—the most compelling being that the tape is a link to parallel universes, a new one produced every time the sitcom's showrunners made a creative decision.

The girl becomes obsessed with the tape, too, and falls in love with one of the boys, though he has a girlfriend. The girl and the boy meet in secret to fuck and watch the tape. But instead of the episode playing in full, the tape gets stuck in a loop, and the title credits just spiral over and over, punctuated by VHS snowstorm.

The boy feels guilty. He drives his girlfriend into the forest to come clean. They argue. He turns into an ash tree. He dies in the crash.

The girl is heartbroken. The girl falls out with the remaining friends, who blame her for the boy's death. The tape is lost, too.

The girl's father finally dies. She graduates alone.

Years later she meets with one of the friends, ostensibly to catch up, but really to speculate about where the tape might be. They agree, sadly, that it was likely incinerated in the crash.

. . .

When Millie and Jacquetta are out of the room, Harry and I steal vodka from Millie's parents and pour it into the stolen cider cans so the girls get drunk faster. Nobody has told us yet that you are not meant to do this.

By midnight there is a layer of frost on the garden trampoline.

I climb onto it and tell Jacquetta to as well. We jump and the frost shatters.

I push her so she falls over.

Then I let myself fall beside her.

The night is clear and behind the clouds our breathing makes, we can see stars. I pretend I don't know what they are called so she will name them for me. She is so thin and shivering. I prop myself up on my elbow and kiss her and wow wow wow wow wow.

We are middle-aged now, my wife and me. We move to a larger house in a deeper part of the countryside. In the garden is an ash tree. Outside, at night, having a rare and secret cigarette, I notice something strange about the ash tree: it seems to, occasionally, become two-dimensional.

But when I walk up to it, it's regular.

The ash tree bothers me. I continue my life, but begin to obsess over it. Sometimes the tree is flat—like a poorly rendered object in a video game—and sometimes it is fractal, somehow four-dimensional, growing constantly and visibly, and reaching out to me, and at the center of it there is some kind of strange blackness that's a deeper black than anything I have seen before.

Slowly my obsession with the ash tree takes over my life. I stop going to work. I lose my job. I ignore my beautiful wife and my beautiful daughter and my beautiful son. I sit in the garden all day, staring at the deep-black thing at the center of the tree.

My wife and children become increasingly concerned. I am committed to and then discharged from a mental hospital. Doctors try to break the spell. A hypnotist is hired. But I cannot help returning to the tree. I cannot keep away from the deep black thing at the center of it. I sit out there day and night. The black thing grows and grows, until it's almost all I can see.

And one day I fall into it. The black thing.

I'm in the black thing for a while.

Or, it feels like a while, but it also feels like no time at all.

I wake up in a hospital. I slip in and out of consciousness. When awake, I beg to see my wife, my children. When asleep, memories of my life come to me, discordant and scattered.

One day, in the hospital, I have the strength to look down at my body. It is the body of a young man. I panic. How old am I, I ask a nurse. What year is it.

Twenty thirteen, she says. You are nineteen years old.

I ask her about my wife, my children. You're not married, she says. You were in a car crash.

You've just woken up from a coma. You are very lucky to be alive.

It eventually becomes clear that my whole life—since the car crash in which Harry died—has been a dream. None of it was real.

My beautiful daughter, my beautiful son. My beautiful wife. None of them real.

I have nothing to live for anymore. I see the window from my hospital bed. It looks like it opens. So I decide to throw myself out of it.

In the no-summer, I get on heroin, then off again. In New York friends and friends of friends overdose, die. In London, while we are all meant to stay home, the police seize vast amounts of cocaine and the price skyrockets. Benzos become cheaper than ever. When we are told to leave our homes, cocaine gets cheap again. We share conspiracy theories. Fentanyl is China's revenge for the Opium Wars. Midcentury is out. We start decorating our homes and restaurants and bars in the Empire style. People say that it's the twenties again, that all the Americans are moving to Paris. But none of them ever seem to actually arrive.

So they go downstairs to where the limousine is waiting. The driver hands the Pope the keys, and the Pope, in his big Pope hat and dress, gets into the driver's seat. The driver gets into the back of the limousine, invisible behind the blacked-out windows.

As soon as the car reaches the highway, the Pope breaks his promise. He puts his foot to the floor. The limousine does 90, then 100, then 110. The driver grips the armrest in terror.

They pass a cop car. The cop sees the speeding limousine. He starts his engine and gives chase.

The cop catches up. He flicks the siren on and off. The Pope pulls over.

The cop gets out of his car. He walks over to the limousine, stationary now on the shoulder of the highway, and knocks on the window.

In the backseat, the limousine driver is terrified.

I used to believe that for my little stories to feel real to the reader, they had to be staccato: structured, fixed in time, a list of moments.

I remember reading an essay by someone saying that because of capitalism, or something, we cannot imagine fictions that exist past "a list of real moments, fixed in time." Like a shopping list.

Now I'm less sure.

I think, now, I want my stories to feel like being asleep in the back of a car, waking briefly, and thinking: O, I must be here. Then falling back asleep.

I couldn't tell you the last time I made a shopping list.

. . .

A man dies. He wakes, a waiting room. Saint Peter—extremely tired—tells the man to take a ticket and a seat. There are other dead people there. The dead seem bored and restless. Behind Saint Peter's desk, there is a staircase made of clouds and bathed in golden light, going up somewhere, and also a disgusting-looking escalator which leads down somewhere dark.

Eventually the dead man's number comes up on the screen so he goes up to the desk. God comes out to meet him. He is disheveled, unshaven. He has bags under his eyes. He smells of cigarettes.

"I am sorry for the wait," God says. "I am so burnt out. I'm really tired. I haven't had time to pay much attention. You were good down there, yeah?"

"I'm not sure it's for me to say," the man says, "but yes. I was a good Christian. I loved my neighbor. I was kind. I made some mistakes, of course, but I think that I left the world a better place than it was when I came into it."

God doesn't seem to be listening. He is looking around the waiting room. He rubs his palms against his temples and then wipes his bloodshot eyes.

"Yeah, cool," God says. "Listen, you didn't do any gay shit, did you?"

The man pauses. He isn't sure what to say.

"Well, I—"

"Yeah," God says, "down there, pal."

I see Jacquetta sometimes still, in Soho coincidences, on medium terms. In her face and the bend of her elbow are the dropout futures we spent years talking about. Probably in mine for her, too. But I don't ask, and it goes unsaid.

Most recently, when I saw her, she told me: the purpose of fiction is not to manifest the incomplete.

. . .

I ask another friend if time feels different to her. We are in the BFI bar on the South Bank. She is a writer too. But while I was making my staccato and structured stories, she was making stories that sat outside of time entirely. A series of beautiful images.

"There wasn't even a summer," she says. "Of course it feels different. I feel as if I've fallen out of place."

I ask her if she's changed what she's writing.

"Yeah," she says. "I just want to do things with plots now. I love competent stories. I've gone trad. As a reaction to time being different, maybe."

I tell her that's so funny. I feel the same but I am doing the opposite. We have swapped entirely.

In the fact-checked news, a cop dies, then does not die, from accidental fentanyl exposure. The Taliban hang, then do not hang, an American soldier from a suspended helicopter. Ghislaine Maxwell appears at a fast-food chain, until she doesn't. The North Koreans sometimes have missiles.

I speak to my friends in jokes, ironies, yeses when people ask reallys. I take to issuing my own corrections. People DM my Twitter saying: I don't know if you're joking, but . . .

I give up on a novel about a girl who involuntarily throws up everything she eats. In the sick, every time, is a beautiful vomit-slicked pearl. As if she's part oyster.

I give up on a novel about a girl who visits an old writer by the sea. He was in love with her dead mother, but it was unrequited. When the old man dies, he leaves the girl his slowly eroding house. It is full of half-finished stories.

I give up on a novel about the death of a charismatic publisher. A cohort of his students who have not seen each other in years attend his funeral, stay in his home after. Together they remember their teacher, remember how to write. The reader pieces together the students' stories into some greater, more meaningful narrative.

I give up on a novel about the town I grew up in, the lives of the people there. But with an algorithm as a narrator, rather than a human.

All of these have the same title: *The Complete*. So the cover says, *The Complete Gabriel Smith*. A little joke.

But, in hindsight, a funnier title would have been *The Incomplete*.

The Pope rolls down the limousine window when the cop knocks on it. The cop sees the Pope sitting there, in his Pope dress and big Pope hat, his Pope hands at ten and two.

The cop looks at the Pope. He almost says something. Then he doesn't. He just makes a hand gesture for the Pope to stay put. Then he walks back to his cop car, and sits back down, and gets on the radio to his superior officer.

"Chhhhk," the cop says. "I've just pulled over someone going one ten on the highway. Over."

"Chhhhk," the superior officer says. "So arrest them. Over."

"Chhhhk. I think it's someone famous. I'm not sure what to do. Over."

"Chhhhk. That's great. It'll be great publicity. Is it an athlete? A pop star? Over."

"Chhhhk. More famous than that. Over."

"Chhhhk. A politician? Who? Over."

"Chhhhk. No," says the cop. "Even more famous. Over."

"Chhhhk. More famous?" the superior says. "Just tell me. Over."

"Chhhhk. Well," says the cop, "I think I've just pulled God over. Over."

"Chhhhk. You've pulled over God? What? Over."

"Chhhhk. Yes, I think I've pulled God over. Over."

"Chhhhk. Have you gone mad? Why do you think you've pulled over God?" the superior officer says. "Over."

"Chhhhk. Well," the cop says, "his limousine is driven by the Pope."

That's the punch line!

Gordon Lish said that for writing to be interesting, each sentence has to wholly reject the preceding one. A neat trick.

"Of course," a writer friend says, "if you extrapolate that rule to the length of a short story or a novel, the shape you get is a spiral. Something constantly folding in on itself."

"That's how a joke is structured," a comedian friend says. "A premise, and then a surprise. Something that's the opposite of the premise, that doesn't fit with it at all. So much the opposite that it's the same thing. But new."

"The spiral is the shape of life," another friend tells me. "Moving forward in time, but constantly trapped by and falling backward into memory. Like *Sans Soleil*. Or *Vertigo*."

"The spiral is everywhere in the more mathematical arts," my grandmother says. "Music, painting. The Fibonacci sequence. The golden ratio. The fractal growth of plants and trees."

The current of memory is getting stronger. Boats against it, etc. But I don't know anyone who knows what it is that we're rowing toward.

On Greek Street, I watch a middle-aged man undress completely, then wrestle another middle-aged man, also naked, their dicks right-angle retracted in the cold.

Earlier in the night, in the smoking area of Trisha's, the middle-aged man tells Harry and me about his new, second wife.

"You think you'll never fall in love again," the man says. "That's bullshit."

"Right," Harry says.

Later in the night, waiting for a short-supply Uber, a drunk Egyptian man invites me and Harry to a brothel.

"You guys are best friends," he says, once we decline. "I can see it! Don't let that go."

"Chhhhk. Roger that," I say. "Over."

One can imagine, using Lish's rule, a story that's a mathematically perfect spiral. Forward in time, and backward in memory, perfectly synchronized. Whether imagining something means it exists is another question entirely. I like to think it does. I promised myself I would never write about writing. So self-indulgent. Lol!

I try to leave my hospital bed to throw myself out the window. But I am so weak I collapse.

The nurse asks what I was trying to do. I tell her about the dream. That I have lost my best friend in the car crash, and my wife, and my children. That I have lived a whole life and it has disappeared. And now I am alone. Everything I have ever loved.

Your best friend isn't dead, the nurse says.

He's in the next ward over. He's going to make it.

At first I do not believe her. I have lived decades without him. I have dealt with the grief.

But then, there he is, at my bedside, and we hold each other while I cry for all of it.

I rebuild my life. I move between bleak jobs and bleaker houses in London. I have my best friend back, but I am haunted by memories of my wife, my children. It is all I can do not to kill myself.

I do not want to have to live another whole lifetime without her.

Then, one day, walking alone in a park, I see a flash of blond hair from behind a tree, caught in the wind. The sleeve of a deep blue coat. Perhaps the deeper blue of her eyes.

That would be where the novel ends.

. . .

And so we wait it out. The endless nodding, the slip of it all. The cemetery frogs, the wet market of the soul. The evening applause and the midnight alley-oop. The live streams of the dead. A skyful of Saint Peters, eyes wet with tears.

At the height of it, after the no-family Christmas, but before the New Year, a friend called me from her parents' home, late at night.

"Christmas purgatory," she said, referring to the days between Christmas and 2021, the Year of Disappointment.

"I worry I've died. And I'm in actual purgatory," I said.

"Maybe," she said. She was falling asleep on the phone. I asked her if she felt the same.

"Can I have a little time to think about it?" she said.

"Go to sleep," I said, or maybe she said, I don't remember, "I'm sure it'll feel different in the morning."

Jamil Jan Kochai

The Haunting of Hajji Hotak

Y OU DON'T KNOW WHY, EXACTLY, you've been assigned to this particular family, in this particular home, in West Sacramento, California. It's not your job to wonder why. Nonetheless, after a few days, you begin to speculate that the suspect at the heart of your assignment is the father, code-named Hajji, even though you have no reason to believe that he has ever actually completed the hajj pilgrimage to Mecca. In fact, Hajji hardly leaves home at all. He spends hours at a time wandering around his house or his yard, searching for things to repair—rotted planks of wood, missing shingles, burned-out bulbs, broken mowers, shattered windows, unhinged doors—until his old injuries act up, and he is forced to lie down wherever he is working, and if he happens to be in the attic or the basement, or in some other secluded area of the house, away from his wife and his mother and his four children, sometimes he will allow himself to quietly mutter verses from the Quran, invocations to Allah, until his ache seems to ebb and he returns to work.

When Hajji has exhausted himself, he often retires to the living room, where he watches murder mysteries or foreign coverage of conflicts in Islamic countries. If his wife, code-named Habibi, is in the kitchen, and if she isn't already chatting with one of her many friends, most of whom you know Hajji despises, he will request a cup of tea and ask about his mother's health, which is never very good, but Hajji's wife doesn't tell him this, because his mother, code-named Bibi, is sitting just a few feet away, and though she doesn't acknowledge her son's presence, Bibi is always listening.

From early dawn, when she wakes to pray, until late at night, before she falls into a fitful sleep, Bibi nests in a corner of the living room, on the farthest edge of the second couch, and listens to the television at an incredibly low volume, listens to her son and his wife in the kitchen, to her grandchildren on their phones, to the Quran on an old radio that she smuggled out of Afghanistan forty years ago, to the flushing of the toilets in the house, to the wind in the trees that her son planted near her window, to the gentle burbling of her oxygen tank, and to the constant thrumming of the house, and she reports back all that she hears to her only living brother, in Afghanistan. Thanks to Bibi's keen ear for even the most minute details, her calls are thorough and uncompromising. She knows when her grandchildren are constipated. She knows when her son and his wife are secretly fighting. She knows who is peeing too loudly or cheating on exams or missing prayers. Through Bibi's many reports to her brother, you begin to gather snippets of Hajji's history: his former life as a mujahid in Afghanistan; his trek from Logar to Peshawar to Karachi to California; his wedding; the births of each of his children; the children's gradual loss of Pashto; their gradual increase in insolence; the trucking accident that destroyed the nerves in Hajji's neck and shoulder; the court cases that led to nothing; the betrayal he felt when his second-eldest son, code-named Karl, decided to become a Marxist while studying at Berkeley; his depression; his total disillusionment with the American justice system; his anger; his rage; his softly bubbling fury.

In another life, you think, Bibi might have been a spy.

Hajji's eldest son, Mo, gets home from his job at Zafar's butcher shop in the evening. He wears a blood-splattered smock, an Arabic *thobe,* and a heavy beard. Every night, Mo's mother scolds him for not having washed his smock, which smells like a massacre, and every night Hajji defends his son, who smells, he says, like a man. Mo begs his mother's forgiveness with a laugh and sits beside his father. In English, Mo asks Hajji about the current condition of the *ummah,* which translates roughly to "community," but which actually refers to a supranational collective of Islamic peoples.

"They hope to destroy our *ummah,*" you record Hajji saying, in English, before he gives a recap of all the bombings, massacres, war crimes, protests, shootings, kidnappings, and assassinations that have occurred in the past twenty-four hours. Mo listens quietly, only occasionally asking a question or muttering a vengeful prayer.

The rest of Hajji's children arrive as dinner begins.

Lily, the youngest, sneaks into the kitchen and asks her mother which dishes have been prepared without meat.

Lily has recently, and secretly, become a vegetarian. Two weeks earlier, she came home weeping to her mother after having witnessed the vehicular maiming of a duck that was crossing the street with a line of her ducklings. Lily had cradled the duck in her death throes, surrounded by her little ducklings—which, Lily swore, were crying out for their mother. Together, Habibi and Lily wept for the little orphaned ducklings. Later that day, Lily informed her mother that she could not bring herself to eat the chicken korma she had prepared, and Habibi decided not to scold her (a decision she would come to regret). At first, it was only chicken, but then Lily confessed to her mother that she could no longer stomach beef or lamb, the rest of the culinary trinity of Hajji's household. Habibi made an effort to explain to her daughter that vegetarianism was a slippery slope toward feminism, Marxism, Communism, atheism, hedonism, and, eventually, cannibalism. "Animals are animals," her mother explained, deftly, "and humans are humans, and when you begin mixing up the two you will find yourself kissing chickens and eating children."

Lily swore that it was a matter not of ethics but of physical repulsion, and that with time, *inshallah,* she would be able to eat all her favorite dishes again. Habibi relented, and for a few days the secret remained solely between mother and daughter, until Mary, Hajji's elder daughter, turned toward her sister one afternoon, in the room they had shared since Lily's infancy, and asked her how much weight she had lost.

"None," she said, too quickly, laughing. "I'm as chunky as ever."

But she *had* lost weight. Two pounds.

"Then why do you look so pale and self-righteous?" Mary asked, continuing her interrogation. Sharp, uncompromising, and with an excellent eye for weakness—a trait that, you assume, she inherited from her grandmother—Mary has many talents (deception, introspection, manipulation, a high pain threshold, and embroidering) that are wasted in Hajji's household, where the girls are allowed to go only to school or to the mosque and then must come straight home.

It's really a tragedy, you think. She could have been a fine spy.

In the end, Lily confessed her sin to Mary, who immediately mocked her. "Idiot," she said. "You're short enough as it is. How do you expect to get taller without protein?"

"I'll eat beans."

"Beans? How many beans? This room isn't ventilated enough for you to be eating beans all day."

"Please," Lily said. "Don't tell."

Mary laughed and promised to snitch as soon as she could, which was a lie, of course, because Mary wasn't the sort.

During dinner, Lily is always careful to serve herself a heaping portion of chicken or kebab or kofta, but while she eats her rice and fried vegetables, Mary, an avowed carnivore, nonchalantly clears away Lily's meat. Hajji, fortunately, never notices. He eats with perfect focus. In total silence. And with his fingers.

Habibi, on the other hand, hardly eats. She is all questions and stories. She wants to know about Mo's butchering, Mary's studying, Lily's friends, and even Marvin's gaming. In response, the children tease her, which, at times, upsets Hajji, but Habibi always takes it in stride. She is—in your professional estimation— the beating heart of the household. Not only does she take on most of the chores; she also actively organizes the entire social life of the family—dinners and parties and showers and gatherings and even the occasional communal prayer. Seemingly at war with the hundred silences that fill her small house, she is almost always on the brink of shouting in Pashto or Farsi or English or sometimes Urdu. She chats so much on the phone, outside in the yard, inside in the kitchen, with her gloomy husband, her spiteful mother-in-law, her eclectic children, and her many, many friends, that you end up spending half your time at the office skimming through hours and hours of Habibi's gossip, translated from your audio recordings by an officially sanctioned team of Afghan American interpreters, who are only ever provided with fragments of her statements, in the hope that they won't figure out whom, exactly, they are interpreting. Habibi's relentless chatter, however, is not completely useless. Every night, before bed, she calls her family in Afghanistan, some of whom still live in a small village in Logar Province, which, according to your research, is currently under the control of the Taliban.

The word comes up sometimes amid Habibi's barrage of Pashto and Farsi. Her "*baleh*"s and "*bachem*"s and "*cheeka*"s and "*keer*"s.

"Taliban," she will whisper into her phone, as if she knows you are listening.

Just the sound of it makes your heart race.

After dinner, Marvin and the girls rush off to their rooms while Mo, his parents, and Bibi drink tea in the living room. Inevitably, the conversation turns to Mo's prospects for marriage. Habibi has a niece in Kabul, a midwife and a beauty, who speaks English, Pashto, Farsi, and Urdu. "She is almost too good for you," Habibi says, laughing. Hajji has a niece in Logar, only sixteen, wholesome, holy. She has memorized half the Quran, and her father is a respected mullah in the village. What Mo's parents don't know is that Mo is already in love with a girl at Sac State. They are constantly messaging, conversing, and Snapchatting. Mo writes her secret love poems on his laptop. Horrendous verses that he is rightfully embarrassed by. Sometimes, when he thinks he's alone, he recites his poems quietly.

His love, you hope, will save him.

At night, Hajji and his wife are the first to go to bed. The next morning, they will wake up at dawn—Hajji because of his pain, and Habibi because of Hajji's pain. Both Marvin and Mo pretend to fall asleep, but when Mo thinks Marvin has passed out he sneaks downstairs with his laptop, and, as soon as he does, Marvin climbs out of his own bed, performs *wudhu,* and begins to make up all the prayers he missed throughout the day. Though Marvin has earned a 3.8 GPA in his first semester at UC Davis, though he works part-time and donates money to Afghanistan, his parents often scold him for not praying, not reading the Quran, and Marvin never utters a word in self-defense. And yet here he is, in the middle of the night, praying in secrecy, away from the approving eyes of his mother and father and brother and grandmother, reciting verse after verse from the Quran, in a voice so soft and melodic that it almost brings tears to your eyes.

Downstairs, Mo descends into forums. Swaddled in his father's woolen shawl—the very same shawl that Hajji used to wear in the days of his long-ago jihad—Mo watches clips of American bombs falling on Iraqi cities, Afghans bearing witness to ISAF executions, Muslim boys being burned alive in Gujarat. He watches these clips for hours, his head bobbing, his eyes bleary, until his beloved, mercifully, notices that he is online and commands him to go to sleep. Upstairs, Mary is reading Mo's messages. She has hacked into his Facebook account and watches his conversation play out in real time. She is a ghost on his profile, always careful to read only what he has already read and to leave everything else untouched. Such potential, you think, such a pity. Lily, in the bed next to Mary, is sketching pictures of ducks and ducklings and ponds and ducks crying into ponds and ponds expanding into oceans and ducks in flight and ducks walking and ducks dying, and she takes pictures of these charcoal portraits and posts them to a private Instagram account, which Mary can also, secretly, access. In the room adjacent to the girls, Hajji and his wife have a quiet argument about his wife's brothers. You recognize their names and suspect it has something to do with the fact that they were employed as interpreters for the U.S. military in Afghanistan. Hajji, you know, considers these men to be traitors. Eventually, Habibi turns away from her husband, mutters something under her breath, and cries herself softly to sleep. Hajji does nothing to comfort her. He sits up in bed, wheezing with pain or regret, and stares out the window at the dark street, where Mo is now shad-owboxing beneath a streetlight. Tucked away in her corner of the house, Bibi sits up at the same moment, in the same manner, and stares out her window at the same streetlight. She, too, watches Mo strike at invisible enemies.

When the family finally sleeps, you listen to them dream.

In the course of the next few weeks, you search for clues, signs, evidence of evil intentions. But to no avail. Life merely goes on.

Hajji repairs a window he broke while attempting to repaint his mother's room.

Cold floods the house.

Bibi moves into the boys' room, and the boys sleep in the liv-ing room. No longer able to sneak away from each other, they carry out long conversations before falling asleep. They discuss their family's finances, their suspicion that their father is hiding bills from them. They plan to confront him but never go through with it.

When they sleep, both of the boys snore, Marvin whistling and Mo sort of growling, and the girls, whose bedroom is closest to the living room, complain to each other all night. The timing of the boys' snoring is uncanny. There is a certain rhythm to it. When Mo murmurs, Marvin bursts, and when Marvin quiets, Mo roars. The girls refer to it as "the symphony." Eventually, though, the girls fall asleep and you become the sole listener.

Mo notices blood in his stool but doesn't go to a doctor.

Mary earns a 4.3 GPA for the semester, and Hajji buys dough-nuts for the whole family. They all sit in the living room, eating doughnuts and drinking tea, and Bibi jokes that now they won't have to sell Mary for a pair of goats. The whole family laughs as though in a scene in a sitcom.

While Habibi's husband is out buying supplies from a hardware store, she receives a call from her parents, in Kabul, and discovers that her mother is seriously ill. She tells no one and leaves to visit her brothers across town. Soon afterward, Hajji returns home to find her missing. He goes from room to room, calling her name. For the first time in weeks, Bibi speaks to her son, informing him that his mother-in-law is sick.

Tech workers from the Bay Area have moved into the neigh-borhood. Property taxes are rising. Bills stack up. Hajji needs help but won't tell his sons, because he doesn't want them to take on more work. He borrows money and credit. He buries the bills at night like corpses.

Habibi receives another call from her parents. There will be an operation. It's the heart, of all things. Habibi tells only Hajji, but Bibi, of course, finds out.

In a moment of weakness, Lily eats a Slim Jim that she shop-lifted from a gas station near her school. At home, she vomits the processed meat for several minutes. Though everyone assures Hajji that Lily will be fine, Hajji insists on taking her to the emergency room. "As long as we have Medi-Cal, why take the risk?" he argues. An hour later, Hajji and Lily return home from the hospital, and Hajji informs his wife that Lily has become a vegetarian. He asks her to keep it a secret. "For now," Hajji says, "she doesn't want anyone else to know." Habibi promises not to tell a soul.

One afternoon, while her father sleeps and her mother cooks, Mary shuffles through Hajji's mail and discovers past-due bills, three or four from the same creditor. She picks a few of the most urgent (electricity and internet) and rushes upstairs. On Poshmark.com, she sells her own lightly used sweaters and jeans and T-shirts, which she has embroidered with characters from popular animes—Sailor Moon and Totoro and Naruto—and, in the course of a week, pays her father's bills online.

Habibi tells Marvin about his grandmother's upcoming surgery. "Do you think she will forgive me for abandoning her in that city?" she asks him. Marvin pretends to pause his video game, even though he is playing online, in real time. He sets his controller aside and listens to his mother's fears without responding. He is killed over and over again.

The stack of bills lightens, but Hajji hardly notices.

When her husband is out, Habibi calls Karl in Berkeley. They chat about his stomach, his rent, his studies, his protests, and his prayers until Habibi begs him, once again, to renounce Communism and come home. Karl argues that his father, more than anyone else, should be sympathetic to his cause. Habibi begins to weep and Karl mutters an excuse and hangs up. You wonder which of your colleagues is surveilling Karl.

While Hajji watches Al Jazeera—video footage of a young Afghan farmer being executed by an Australian soldier plays on the screen—Mary curls up next to him and picks at the flakes of dried skin in his beard as she did when she was four years old. According to Habibi, this was her special ritual before sleep. Now Mary has a bottle of olive oil in hand, a tiny dollop of which she pours into her palm and runs through her father's beard. The execution is played again. After being mauled by a dog, the farmer, Dad Mohammad, lies on his back in the middle of a field. His knees are drawn up to his chest, and he is clutching red prayer beads. A soldier stands over him with a rifle. "You want me to drop this cunt?" he asks. There is the sound of a shot, and the footage cuts to black. When Mary is gone and the news segment is finished, Hajji sits alone in the living room with the TV turned off. He runs his fingers through the moistened strands of his beard and seems surprised by its softness.

On the night before Habibi's mother's surgery, one of Habibi's brothers visits for the first time in months. Mary is the only one who doesn't acknowledge him. In their shared room, Lily attempts to persuade her sister to forgive their uncle for his many insults, attacks, jokes, attacks disguised as jokes, and threats. But Mary refuses. "Mom will understand," Mary says, but you're not so sure. That night, Habibi and her brother sleep on a red *toshak* in the living room and quietly pray for their sick mother. In the morning, the news is good, and you cannot help sighing with relief.

Six months into your assignment, you begin to doubt your purpose. Hajji is falling apart. His doctor has advised him to undergo spinal surgery that may leave him paralyzed. In another era, in a different body, perhaps Hajji could have been dangerous. But here, now, debilitated by pain and trauma, the old man is no threat at all.

You should update your superiors. You should advise them to abort the operation. But you won't. Not now. Not when Mary is about to apply to colleges, not when Mo is planning to propose, not when Marvin is making new friends on campus, not when Habibi's parents are applying for a visa to the States, not when Hajji is deciding whether or not he will go through with the surgery, not when Bibi is losing touch with her brother, not when

Lily is on the brink of an artistic breakthrough. There's too much left to learn.

But then, on a cold summer night, when the rest of the family has driven down to an aunt's house in Fremont, Hajji heads up to the attic to fix a pipe. You watch him prepare his tools and climb his ladder and enter his soaking attic, and, in a fine mist of leaking water, Hajji fidgets with the pipe until he mutters "Shit" in Pashto. He crawls back through the water, but on his way down he slips off the highest rung of the ladder and falls onto the hard tile beneath him. Though the fall must have been only ten feet or so, Hajji has landed awkwardly and broken his leg. He lies on the floor, on his back, staring up at the attic from which he fell. You know for a fact that Hajji has broken this leg once before, during the Soviet occupation, when a Kalashnikov round pierced his fibula and forced him off the battlefield for six months, during the heaviest period of fighting in Logar, and that this injury probably saved his life, and that his living—while his brother died, while his sister died, while his cousins and friends and neighbors all died—has haunted him his whole life.

A minute passes. Two. You know that Hajji always forgets his cell phone in the kitchen and that the kitchen is approximately twenty yards away from the spot where he lies on the floor, unmoving, and that he will have no other choice but to drag himself there and call for help. And yet he doesn't move. You listen for his breath and hear him rasping. Water drips from the trapdoor to the attic, and Hajji lifts his hands and washes his face and his arms and his hair as if he were performing his ablutions. It's at this point that both you and Hajji notice the small puddle of blood forming under his head.

Hajji pleads to God, and you hear him, and you answer.

The ambulance arrives shortly afterward.

The next day, as soon as he returns home from the hospital, Hajji purchases a phone recorder on Amazon and, when it arrives, has Marvin hook it up to the landline. No one questions him.

No one argues. He listens to hours and hours of recordings in his bedroom, alone or with Habibi, and during awkward moments of silence, pauses in conversations, he stops and rewinds and listens again. "Do you hear it?" he whispers to Habibi in Pashto. "The breathing?"

She waits and listens again and nods her head.

You know this is impossible. You know there is no way for them to hear you, and yet, when you are listening to a conversation, and there is a pause, a silence, you find yourself holding your breath.

Hajji becomes relentless.

He searches for you on the phone, in the streets, in unmarked white vans, in the faces of policemen, detectives in street clothes, military personnel, and his own neighbors. He searches for you at the hospital, at the bank, on his computer, his sons' laptops, in webcams, phone cameras, and on the television. He searches for you in the curtains and in the drawers of the kitchen and in the trees in his backyard, in the electrical sockets, the locks of the door handles, and in the filaments of the lightbulbs. And, even as his family protests, Hajji searches for you in shattered glass, in broken tile, in the strips of his wallpaper, the splinters of his doors, his tattered flesh, his warped nerves, and in his own beating heart, where, through it all, the voice whispering that he is loved is yours.

Lisa Taddeo

Wisconsin

NINA DROVE FOR FOURTEEN HOURS, stopping only to pee and eat a hot dog at a roadhouse. All her life she thought the middle of the country had moose and blue trucks and men with tall hats. But it turned out to be limestone and crippled people with no jobs.

On the road she felt the desire to have sex clearer than ever. A virgin, Nina couldn't determine the locus of the need. But when she found herself behind a truck carrying sections of gas pipe, she became transfixed by the bright, aggressive cylinders.

She'd been fingered, of course, by Ryan S., who had sustained the same pimple since freshman year. In his basement, with the Schlitz sign and the colored Christmas lights and the mom on the phone upstairs. He had this terrified look on his face the whole time, like he was waiting for her to blast off into space.

—Okay, that's enough, said Nina, after two quiet minutes. She imagined a black-and-blue inside of her. A week later, by the time she felt untouched enough to masturbate again, it was the same day she got the news at school. Principal Field walked into her AP Spanish class. He had a green-hued face and looked like the Incredible Mr. Limpet.

—Nina, he'd said. Out in the hall he told her there'd been a car accident. A seafood truck. No turn signal. It was her mother who had no turn signal. It seemed important for the principal to inform Nina it was her mother's fault that she was dead.

She was eighteen in one month and would go to college in four. Her mother, a widow with no close friends, had guilted her into staying close to home, so Nina had enrolled at Rutgers. She'd share a dorm room with a girl named Elizabeth. On the phone, Elizabeth sounded like a nerd who'd never suffered, or eaten lobster.

Nina inherited $47,000 plus the house to sell or rent. She was a virgin queen. Proprietor of flat sheets and a garlic press. The idea that she could have gone to Tulane, Pepperdine, McGill. Nights she sat in her Volkswagen in the parking lot of 7-Eleven and watched kids her age, washed in the fluorescent light of eleven P.M., emerge with Slurpees and frozen Snickers.

Days she packed up the house. Aunts and cousins came to help. Some pilfered silver candlesticks and cigarette cases. One outright asked for the gold leopard ring with the emerald eyes and the tennis bracelet from Macy's that Nina helped her father pick out. Her father was dead, too. But his death suddenly seemed like a tornado in a far-off state. Now it was her mother's handwriting in the margins of cookbooks that sent Nina to puke in the bathroom.

She'd saved the nightstand for last because it had been her mother's private zone. There was no lock, and Nina didn't remember having been explicitly forbidden to open the drawers as a child, yet it was the most prohibited space. For all its intrigue, there might have been her mother's vagina inside—metabolized via death into a velvet change purse. Two days ago, she'd opened all the secret drawers and emptied them. Then she shut them because open drawers were the mark of entitled slovenliness. She sat on the Persian rug. It was cream and sapphire, like jewels in sandy countries. She pulled at its tufts. The carpet was her mother's prized possession. Nina could drop on it anything she wanted now. Pear nectar, nail polish. The death of one's parents tendered an unholy freedom. But suddenly the rug belonged to her, and it was worth a lot. So the freedom was short-lived. She petted the tufts down and read all the emails.

There weren't so many, but it took her a long time to absorb each one. It seemed likely they'd been in the nightstand like this even when her father was alive. The audacity was shocking. And yet none of it was effectively sinful; the emails predated her parents' marriage.

The man's name was Jon. Nina liked the name; the omission of the *h* was jaunty.

He started his notes out, *Hey hey.* He used ellipses with extra dots. At some point he'd gone to Peru, and when he told Nina's mother he was back in town, she could feel the brightness in her mother's reply, a schoolgirl exultation she'd never known.

> *Hey hey back in town. . . . .*
> *its been a struggle getting back into the swing of things.*
> *The trip was unbelievable, Peru is a beautiful country.*
> *Rob told me you guys got pretty drunk the other night at*
> *back bar.*
> *You have to be careful when Danny is pouring, he'll light*
> *you up if your not careful.*
>
> *Wisconsin, welcome back.*
> *Not sure what other night you're referring to, I haven't*
> *been to harry's in a while and the last time i met rob*
> *there, i didn't drink more than a few beers. But I did go to*
> *spring lounge a few nights ago, and I remembered about*
> *your hands.*

Poor Mother, thought Nina. Maxine had taught her how to read men. Partly, this was why Nina was a virgin. She could see through all the boys her age. Sleeping with one of them would feel as if she were letting all of them get away with something.

Maxine had been so methodical in her teaching that Nina had expected to find a playbook somewhere. Among the many inconceivable things about Maxine's death were the lessons she hadn't yet taught her daughter, the balance of the dark arts.

What Nina saw now was that her mother had not been born with her wisdom. She did not come out of the womb unflappable. The rest of the emails between Jon "Wisconsin" and Maxine told a dark, slippery tale. Jon was married. He and his wife and their young son lived on the Upper West Side. Maxine had been writing a story about the men on Wall Street, back in what she called her former life, as a reporter for a small paper. The affair lasted a few months. From what Nina could tell, there were less than seven meet-ups during that time. Her mother had done most of the soliciting. Cloaked as they were in bravado—*Going to Yankees game, have fun at work sucker!* and *Just back from Barcelona, feeling slippery*—her mother's words were so obviously steeped in desperation. A thin and lonely woman eating quinoa in a studio.

The thing that did not predate her parents' marriage was the newspaper clipping of the married man's dead son. A four-year-old who'd drowned in a Wisconsin ice-fishing accident. The paper was yellowed and soft. It had been handled a lot. The accompanying photo was a picture of the boy on a shining dock in red swim trunks. He had a ruddy and beautiful face. Nina thought of her mother running her hand across the clipping, crying about a child she had never met.

After thirty minutes on the internet, Nina knew the man's address and 70 percent of his trajectory. Jon Dunham lived in a house on the banks of the Bois Brule, in Winneboujou. He was fifty-three. In a recent but pixelated picture, he was holding a trout the size of a corgi. He had a big, manly nose, blue eyes, and wavy hair. He was objectively even more handsome than Nina's father, who had been hit on by many of Nina's friends' mothers.

Jon Dunham and his wife had split up shortly after the death of their child. She kept the apartment in Manhattan, and he withdrew to their summer cabin in Wisconsin. He competed in fishing competitions but otherwise lived the quiet, retired life of a suffering rich guy.

If his boy, Charlie, had lived, he would have been five years older than Nina. He would have been the kind of handsome that was in short supply. Not like the baby pricks her age who worked at Hollister and had boring, rippled chests. Nina had many feelings about the dead kid and the man who was clearly Maxine's longtime obsession. But mostly she looked upon her parents' meet-cute in a new light. The story had been spun like a downtown fairy tale, true love dusted with cigarette ash. One windy but warm spring evening, Maxine walked into McSorley's alone, the points of her heels a quarter inch deep in sawdust and peanut shells. *Easy pickings,* Nina's father, Richard, had said. *Every guy knows that when a girl goes to a bar by herself in high heels.* They talked for hours, but some psycho hairdresser also tried to take Maxine home. *He kept buying tequila shots and fruitily kissing your mother's hand.*

At midnight Richard picked up Maxine's gray felt book bag and waited by the door. *It had all of her Post-it notes inside,* he said, *so I knew she'd come with me.* The McSorley's story. It was all dartboards and sweetness and dark ales with creamy heads. An evil villain to boot.

That night, which they celebrated thereafter as their anniversary because of the love-at-first-sightness, coincided with the last email from Jon Wisconsin, which said something to the effect of, *All we had is dead, as I am dead; marry another.*

A couple of months later Maxine and Richard tied the knot in an ugly church on the Gowanus. Maxine wore red, nobody important came, and they were pregnant with Nina by the chalky end of the summer.

. . .

The clouds of Wisconsin were fat dragons. There were silos and rainbows. As Nina neared the river, the farms gave way to white-tail deer and log cabins.

She'd called ahead. He had a house line. His voice was slow and twangy. She told him whose daughter she was. Said she'd be passing through the state on her way to college. He acted like her mother was a normal old friend. Probably, like everyone, he liked a nice mystery. For her part, Nina did not tell him that Maxine was dead. Many times, over raw dough or garlic skipping in oil, her mother said to her, You will never be hurt by a man. I am making sure.

During one of these kitchen confidentials, a few days after her first period, Nina asked,—But what if I want to be hurt? She had just seen something on HBO, where someone sexy said, Love hurts.

—What? Maxine said. No. This is about self-awareness. This gift I'm giving you, what I teach you every day, self-awareness, and awareness of everything around you, you won't be able to eat a lunch with someone without knowing they don't want to tip the waiter as much as you do.

—What if I never fall in love?

—You'll be lucky. But it's impossible. No, you'll want to fall in love. There's no life without it.

—You were irresistible to Dad.

—Yeah, her mother said, like that. Maxine's eyes were warmish but always looking out of windows.

It was early morning when Nina reached the town line of Winneboujou. Driving through the night made her feel like a warrior. Now she napped for a few hours in the backseat, leaving open the glove compartment where Maxine had spilled her Shalimar around Easter.

Jon's house was off a dirt road rimmed with pine and white birch. Ten degrees cooler between the trees. The branches and the dark road looked wet. Nina wore a white tank top and jeans and the leather sandals her mother had worn two weeks ago. Her hair felt dirty but looked good. A mile away, she had applied mascara and poppy lip treatment. She played "Carey," by Joni Mitchell, for the seventeenth time.

His driveway was circular and the house was no summer cabin. It was modern and imposing, many windows and dark fantastic wood. She wished she had a dog because she would have turned to it now and said, What in the fuck am I doing?

She parked her little car next to his forest-green Suburban. Her mother had always waited on stoops for her. They fought and she never gave her enough cash for a night out, but Maxine waited on stoops, dyed blond hair shivering in the breeze.

Here now was her mother's former lover, waiting the same way, next to piles of neatly cut wood. He wore a fishing vest. His cargo pants were taut against his thighs. She didn't try to stop herself from noticing that. She got out of the car and found her feet had fallen asleep.

—You must be Nina, he said.

—I am.

She liked the way he looked at her, not fatherly at all.

—Driving to Stanford, how proud your momma must be. Nina had nothing in the car, not even a toothbrush.

—Yes, she said. She walked toward him. They didn't shake hands or embrace. She stood on the ground and he stood on the steps above her.

—I have to say, it was surprising to get your phone call. I haven't seen any of my old friends in years, my New York friends. I barely go back. They barely come here.

—Too bad for them, it's beautiful, Nina said. And it was. So much river-cooled shade and glands of sunlight slipping through the branches.

—Don't tell anyone, he said. He indicated the doorway, which she walked through on her tingling, small feet.

There was one of those horizontal fireplaces sandwiched

between burnt wood. The walls were wide cedar planks and the whole house smelled and looked like an oversize sauna. The kitchen was austere, steel and gloss.

—I have some Blue Moons on the porch, he said. Or lemonade iced tea.

—Blue Moon is great.

The porch overlooked the bank of the river. Two Adirondack chairs. Two silky Weimaraners that barely acknowledged her.

—Porgy and Bess, he said, pointing at the dogs. They're both ladies. Indifferent as cats. He opened a beer off the lip of a firepit and handed it to her.

—Wow, she said, the river is gorgeous. I heard this was a great river for fishing.

—Do you fish?

—No, but I'd love to learn someday.

—How much time do you have? he said. Birds chirped high up in the trees. The air smelled fresh and she felt only the missing, suddenly—the trips to Harmon Discount Cosmetics and Blinds To Go—without the irrevocability, the grass over gravestones.

They were in waders and out on the river by two. He said the afternoon was terrible for trout traffic, but it was all they had. The water was bright cold and Nina loved it. She ran her fingers through the film-colored current.

—The thing you learn right away about fish is they exist without you, Jon said. He was casting a line. He'd shown her how to slit a hook through the pulsing body of a pink worm.

—Memorial Day, he continued, whatever day you get off from work, doesn't mean jack shit to these flat fucks.

She followed him as they walked hip-deep through the water. He asked her why she chose Stanford, and she thought of her boring roommate and her boring state college in shitty New Jersey.

—Because it's the best, she said.

He smiled and nodded. He had a scrape of stubble across his cheeks and chin. It was stippled with gray. He pointed west.

—You see, he said, right here is where the fur traders came through, they'd take Lake St. Croix down the St. Croix River into the Mississippi. But the Brule is fishing first. These waters have been fished by Eisenhower, Grant, and Hoover. Calvin Coolidge ran the country from the banks of this river in 1927.

—Do you prefer to fly-fish, or . . . this? Nina asked, looking at her ecstatic worm.

—I use a net, I use a line. I use whatever the fish want, whatever I think the fish want.

Maxine had always acted like nothing a man would say, nothing darling, could be applied to her. Jon had both their beers in the pockets of his vest, and he'd pass Nina's over at exactly the times she wanted it.

—I close my eyes, he said, closing his eyes, early on a cold fall morning. I've got a piece of bread buttered, some black coffee in a thermos, or I ate cornflakes at the house, but usually you get up, you don't wait around, you don't sit at your table, you get right out to the river. Before I go in, I close my eyes and I visualize those brown beauties coming to me. But that's where it gets tricky. That kind of thinking right there. That's where you can get all wrapped up in the wrong stuff. See, the fish. You have to count on them. Your whole day counts on the fish being there. The fish don't know that. They don't care either way. People who think it's inhumane, you got your vegetarians and whatnot. Those cats get it wrong. I don't think the fish mind being caught. But they also don't mind not being caught. You see? It's the indifference that can kill you. But that's not the fish's fault.

—Oh, she said. Yes.

She'd forgotten how magical springtime could be. The way the sun chose certain leaves to burn. The skin on her arms was warm.

Death was a part of life. The natural order. But she, Nina, was alive, and who knew for how long?

Jon placed the rod in her hands and guided her arms back with his. His chest was very close to her back.

There was a tug on the line. It felt like a whale. She yelped and he laughed.

—You've got the touch, baby! Woo hoo!

Then they were reeling something in together. Every time the line slackened, she thought it was gone, but then the tug would come again. There was a brilliant little anxiety to it. When the fish got close, Jon took control of the rod; her arms were still laced with his. Suddenly there it was in his hands, slipping and smooth.

—Hoo ha! This right here is prime certified, Grade A Bois Brule steelhead. Hopefully you can stay for a light, early supper. We'll roast her up respectable with some oil and lemon. Kid, you've just caught your own dinner.

Nina smiled. She was not upset that this made her feel good. This was a fatherly thing, but she welcomed it all the same. For a second, for the briefest of seconds, she thought: Well, maybe it can be this. Instead.

—Hey, Nina said, did my mother ever talk to you about me?

—I have to tell you, he said, the reason I was so surprised to hear from you, Nina. I haven't spoken to your mother in nearly twenty years. She emailed me, a few years back. But otherwise, no. We've both been busy and I've been out here in no-man's-land. I would love to ask you how she is. I'd love to know how she's doing.

—My mother died, actually.

She had said this a number of times. To Verizon account specialists. To bank tellers. In the supermarket once, after Gloria, the checkout lady who loved them both, asked, Where's your mother at, kid?

—When? Jon said.

—The funeral was three weeks ago.

—Jesus.

He embraced her. The river squelched between their bodies. She told him about the emails, all printed out.

—Oh, he said. She told him about the clipping of his late son. She told him she'd come here because she figured he must have been important. She let that statement hang, like now she was thinking he was not that important after all.

He asked if she would like to shower off the river. Inside, he showed her to a steam stall with slate floors. It smelled like a spa, unused and eucalyptic. He gave her two large towels and said he'd wait downstairs.

She put her dirty clothes back on after. Minus her underwear, which she threw out in his wastebasket. The rough crotch of her jeans gouged around between her thighs.

She walked past the long fire. On a side table there was a picture of him holding his newborn son. Beside it, a wedding picture of him and his wife. She was glorious, blond and calm looking. He wore seersucker.

She found him in the kitchen, filleting the fish she'd caught. He'd changed into dark sweatpants and a hooded sweatshirt.

—Oh, did you shower, too? she asked. She held herself like she was in a German film.

The month after Richard died, they'd gotten into the bluest of fights. Nina said to Maxine, *I wish it were you instead of him.* They had the difficult relationship of mothers and daughters. Two cats, sharing jewelry and milk. But they understood one another. They never tired of talking to each other. Maxine had said, *I wish it were me, too.*

There was a bottle of Sancerre open. He was sipping from a short glass. The fish on the cutting board looked elegant and clean.

They sat down to eat at the glacial Corian table in the kitchen. It was informal but classy. Everything about him. The fish smelled deeply of herbs. Its silver skin glistened with oil.

—You caught a beauty. Beginner's luck, some of my fishing buddies would say. But they're bitter old farts. I say you have talent.

—I'd like you to tell me about my mother, said Nina.

The dogs were sitting side by side, looking out the sliding glass doors at the deck and the full moon.

He looked at her shoulders instead of her eyes. They were round and smooth. It was the shoulders on a woman that died first. Nobody knew this. She was more beautiful than her mother had been. Those plump lips.

—What do you want to know? he said, pressing his hands in prayer.

—How you met, and then. The rest.

—All right, he said, sipping his wine. All right, all right. Wish I'd cracked something stronger. Well, we met in a bar. She was doing a story. She was twenty-six or so. I was about a decade older. She interviewed me for her story. I gave her some good quotes about the collapse of Wall Street.

—Harry's bar?

—Yes. Have you been? No? It's this old Wall Street joint. Underground. Kind of place you have no idea it's been raining until you step outside.

—Then what?

—She emailed me a few days later, asking could we meet again. I said, Sure. Of course.

—This was spring?

—It was late spring, like now. The day was bright and cool, like the inside of a church.

He paused to savor his words.

—I'd told her we had to meet someplace way above Wall, like it was espionage. I got to Spring Lounge before her. How about that place? It's this great spot. Maybe now it's overrun with kids, with tourists. But then it was still hip.

—What did she wear? How did she look?

—She walked in wearing pigtails and a leather halter top. She looked very good. Pretty.

—Hot?

He was a man who didn't mind certain discomforts. He nodded.

—What were your thoughts? When you saw her.

—What was I thinking? I don't know. What any guy thinks.

—And your wife—

—Was at home.

—Did you feel guilty?

—Not at that time. We drank a pitcher of beer. I complimented her on some things I'd read. I have always been a gentleman, and I sensed she was unused to that. We got buzzed enough to move on to Tom & Jerry's. My other favorite spot. I smoked a one-hitter on the way. I kicked up my accent.

—How did you know she liked accents?

One of the dogs barked, and the other followed. He told them to quiet down. He turned back to her.

—All women like accents, he said, winking. At the next place, he continued, we drank G&Ts and our knees touched. It was erotic, but it was also like a first date. I told her something to that effect.

—She knew you were married?

—She knew I was married, we both felt it at every moment of the evening. Of course you wonder if it would have been as good, had I been single. That sounds wrong, but. The illicit is really something remarkable, you know. My wife that night, I'd told her I'd be getting a few drinks with the boys, I told her to go ahead and order a pizza.

—Did you love your wife?

—Very much, he said. I still love my wife.

—What did you feel for my mom, in relation to how you felt about your wife?

He laughed and folded his arms. She was just a girl, he could see that now.

—I have a friend from around here. He's just remarried, to a Peruvian girl. They've known each other four months. There's a picture of him he sent to all of us, he's standing there with the new Peruvian wife, holding her fat seven-year-old boy in some Peruvian water park. He says things like, Happy birthday, Wife! He's so jolly. I don't think she knows a lick of English. In a year his face will be puffy with vodka and salted nuts, all over again.

—Life is a cycle, is what you're saying.

—I felt excited about your mom. He paused, remembering the evening in question. It was, now that he'd called it up, one of the more pleasant evenings of his life. The sky was purple. The air was warm. He'd felt like a man in the truest sense of the word.

—Did anything happen that night?

—My wife was blowing up my phone. Women can feel things, across avenues of taxicabs. I'm sure I don't need to tell you. The same way some men can feel about fish, where they'll be, like, diviners. I'm not one of those, but my granddad was. And his dad before him. It ended with my father. My pop went into finance, and then I went into it worse. So we left. Outside in the street I hailed her a taxi, I opened the door for her.

He paused again, remembering the moment.

—I said to your mother, Can I kiss you on the mouth?

A tangible shudder ran through Nina's body. She hadn't touched her fish. They were almost through with the bottle of wine.

—How was it?

—It was short. It wasn't too much. But. Yeah, it was nice.

—And this went on for a few months?

Alone in his brain, he remembered those months. How another, younger woman could make you feel like a god. He thought, in particular, of the night he'd walked Maxine home from Harry's. He'd thrown her up against a brick wall as she swung her bare legs around his waist. They walked, drunk on that feeling, down Broadway, stumbling across the road, kissing and holding hands. A car honked, slowed. The driver gave them the finger and they laughed. He carried her inside and the bottles in her little bar stand shook. He threw her on the bed and he remembered seeing the digital clock as he knelt between her legs.

—Yes, he said, there were a few evenings but not too many. I had a new son. And that night I had to go.

—That was the beginning, Nina said. You had the power from the start. Is that right? You knew.

He looked at her, this young woman, who had a whole life to live.

—Listen, he said, taking Nina's hand in his, I did see a look in her eyes, but, kid, you have to understand. I'm like the fish. I promised her nothing.

His bed was larger than a king. It was white and gray and very soft and maid-clean and the corners were maid-tight. It was all windows, his bedroom, and Nina could see the river through the thin trees, and the tangerine flames in the firepit that were still rising and spitting.

Like the billions of girls before her, she thought, So that's sex. It was good. She'd felt, during the best part of it, about two minutes in, that a light had popped on inside her. He was an excellent kisser. He had a nice, strong body for an older man. She hadn't come, but hadn't expected to. She'd faked it, handsomely. Arched her back and said *fuck yes* over and over until he came, too. She let him come inside of her; she'd been on birth control for months. He'd asked her well ahead so as not to ruin his good time. And she was full of all the things she shouldn't know yet. On account of her mother. The nest of hair around his balls was gray, and she could tell that he was pained by that.

He lay beside her, his arms folded behind his head. He'd been lying that way, on docks and on boats in the sun, since he was a kid. Now, having spent his desire on this girl, he had more space to access the memory of her mother. He remembered the day just before he called it off for good. He'd stopped by her place after work. She said she was making martinis. Maxine opened the door wearing a tight wool Henley, which stopped at her hips, and then only a pair of silk panties and high-heeled shoes. What? she'd said. Did you want to come in?

And the truth was he almost didn't. He thought, My wife would never do something like this. That one little thought mopped up so much of the guilt. It effectively wiped the past few months. Made him feel like he and his wife were on one level, and this young woman was merely a dirty massage that he would be able, in time, to metabolize into a minor transgression. In the end it hadn't even been difficult, to send her off. It hadn't hurt him at all.

Beside him he felt the girl grow cold, or bored. He hadn't been with too many young women lately, and he didn't realize how they were like the music they listened to—impressively effervescent but almost inhumanely forgettable.

—I'm no expert, he said, but I think that was pretty fucking great.

With his index and middle fingers, he skimmed her naked side.

—This could be very dangerous for me, for a lonely guy like me. Have you read any Simone de Beauvoir?

—No, Nina said, not taking her eyes off the plum night outside his window.

—"There are few crimes which exact a worse punishment than this generous fault: to put oneself entirely in another's hands and thus be at his mercy." In this case, *her* mercy.

Nina said nothing. First she felt the light that had turned on in her now go off, a small and quiet darkness, like a child's nightlight on a timer. Then she started thinking about her mother taking her to Nice Stuff, the absolute worst store in New Jersey, with shoulder-padded dresses and fitting rooms with stained curtains. Nina would sit and play on the floor, picking straight pins out of the carpet, which was a homely shade of blue that to this day could make her depressed on the spot. Her mother didn't shop for occasions, and she didn't even shop to buy. She just rifled through discount racks, pulling the price tag away from the material, looking at each one like it had disappointed her. There were multiple moments that Maxine was not fully present and Nina had felt it, even though she had never, until now, understood.

Whereas before sex lovers are united, in the shivery moments after, they are in different countries thinking in different languages. Jon Dunham's brain went to the dun place, the layer of river beneath the silt at the bottom. Often this happened when he had too free of a time; his son, his beloved Charlie, would come to him in rainbow fragments, a cruel kaleidoscope across his mind's eye. In particular, he was seeing the child eating corn on the cob, on the picnic table at the Lake House Club. The yellow-white threads between his little teeth, the butter spackled joyously across his lips and cheeks. The sun behind his head, lighting him like an angel. Your kid could eat corn on the cob just once in the hot sun and you would feel that memory forever. As though there had been more than just four summers.

—So that's sex, said Nina at last.

—Hmm?

—Oh, she said. I was a virgin.

She felt him start.

—It's okay, she said, I wanted to get it over with.

—Jesus.

—No, really, this was the perfect circumstance.

She heard him exhale all his breath. She waited, the way her mother had instructed her to wait, to keep a man suspended so that he might never regain his footing.

—It's funny, she said, I thought because of the timeline. I got nervous for a second, that there was a reason my mom had a whatever, a shotgun wedding, right after you dumped her.

—What are you saying, he said. What was this girl saying. Sometimes he felt so desiccated, so empty, like he was an ancestor already. He wore fur-trimmed anoraks in faded pictures. There was nothing left but bones and fishing hats. But then he'd remember he had no offspring. He would never be an ancestor.

He would die in this house. The maid would come and steal his scotch before reporting his body.

He'd tried, recently, to primordialize the death of his only son, like, yes, a woman I once knew birthed an animal and that animal perished. But it hadn't worked. The boy had been too real, too beautiful, a little man in the world, a wearer of Packers caps, a person holding up his four fingers in the months ahead of his fourth birthday. Jon Dunham was scraped. Once he'd been a selfish man, yes. Once he'd had all the reason in the world.

Nina watched the trees waving in the night sky. The river moved like a melting snake. The name Bois Brule, Jon Dunham had told her in the water, came from the Anishinaabe words Wiisaakode-ziibi, *"a river through a half-burnt woods,"* which was translated into French and incorporated into English. Bois Brule was also the brand name of the burnt wood planks throughout his two-million-dollar house. The house Nina had grown up in was aluminum sided and ordinary. It was close to the houses on either side of it. Her father had been an accountant, a different way to work with money. Nina thought how funny it was that some people went into careers that made a lot of it, and others did not. There was a feeling of owing her mother something. Not her mother, even, but her mother's life.

—What *am* I saying? she replied. The man she'd just *fucked*—oh my God, she'd finally done it—was shaking in the bed, but she did not turn to see his face. If she had, she might have felt terrible, and hurried to make it all better. She could have shown him the picture in her wallet of her father, with whom she shared a hooked nose. Told him that there was no question. But she didn't know this man's pain. She had only hers, and her mother's. The pain of women, who carry pain in buckets from a dipping rod across their shoulders. The pain of discount shopping, and waiting for homely phones to ding.

In the end, anyway, it wasn't Nina's fault. She was like the fish. She had promised him nothing.

Rachel B. Glaser

Ira & the Whale

IT IS DARK IN THE WHALE AND HOT. The air is difficult to breathe. Ira is coated in gunk, sweating in his black Speedo. The whale's heartbeat booms and echoes like a giant drum. It's intimidating. It sounds tribal, ritualistic, as Ira wades through the animal's stomach in shock, up to his knees in liquid goop.

He hears water gurgling and rushing. Mournful moos that go unanswered. Eventually his eyes grow accustomed to the dark. In murky gray scale he can make out the swaying surface of the goop, spotted with mounds of algae, dying shrimp, stray squid tentacles, and the occasional fish head. Surely, somewhere, there is a throat that presumably leads to the mouth, but Ira can't find it.

It must be a *magical* whale or the biggest whale of all time because its stomach seems infinite. Ira wanders for hours, passing sights he'd remember if he saw them again, but nothing repeats. He sees one of those intricate camp chairs floating in the muck. A Mercedes hubcap adorned with the gnarled skeletons of . . . Ira doesn't fucking know. He's just a graphic designer trying to get laid on Fire Island. In summers past he's visited with friends, but this time he's alone.

Liquid rains down on Ira and he closes his eyes and mouth. His body is bruised but still intact. He longs for his cigarettes—which are under his sun hat on his towel on the beach, near a hairy man in a tube top—but what he really needs is water. He wonders how long he can live without it. He dips his finger in the goop and touches his tongue. It's so bitter it burns.

The initial panic has dissipated and bleak reality is setting in. He'll never make it back to his Airbnb, which looked exactly like the pictures, only half the size. He sees his headstone—his name in a cold, boring font chosen by his parents. He's forty-four. His life has been average. It was his childhood dream to live in New York City and become an actor. He moved there for college but gave up on acting after one class. He still lives there, though he doesn't love it the way he thought he would. He shuffles between work and home, squandering his paycheck at a gourmet supermarket— the others depress him.

Ira has been single for much of his life. His hookups disappear back into the Grindr pool, rarely to resurface. He only likes a certain kind of man. They must be as tall or taller than him. He doesn't know why. And he doesn't like guys who are effeminate. Or overly masculine. They must know what's going on politically. No one religious, but he also doesn't want the lecture-y atheists or 24/7 activists. He wants someone he can make dinner with side by side while Schumann plays from his Sonos speakers.

Something catches his eye. Fabric from a . . . beach umbrella (?) has been stretched around a piece of coral, reminding him of that artist, the French guy who loved nothing more than to wrap things. Ira wonders for an insane moment if he is seeing art . . . but then remembers he is trapped in a whale and will die alone. He feels dizzy. A half-digested octopus floats by. This is, hands down, the grossest place he's ever been. It smells like rotting fish and vomit, with hints of mildew and Band-Aid.

He wonders how many notifications are accumulating on his phone. Flirtatious responses to the rare selfie he posted on Instagram last night. He imagines the picture—blown up and pixelated—greeting visitors at the funeral parlor across the street from his parents' house. As a child, he was mesmerized by the goings-on out his window, how wood boxes carrying corpses were delivered and received at a side door marked FLOWERS.

If he can't crawl out, maybe he can cut himself out. He passed a few sharp objects earlier—broken coral, giant crab claw—but now that he's looking, he can't find anything except an oar and some fish bones too small to do damage. His thirst is an unending tragedy. He feels like a child lost in an evil kingdom. Dizziness sends him stumbling.

Ira wakes up floating in the muck with a taste in his mouth like rotten strawberries. A bare-chested man is violently shaking him. Another man! It's a miracle! Ira is elated. "Hi," he says, his mind racing. What are the odds of two men being swallowed by the same whale?

It's difficult to see in the low light but the man looks to be in his thirties. He's wearing goggles. His bathing suit is in shreds. He's built, but not excessively so. Wet strands of dark hair stick to his forehead. Ira steps closer and stares at the man's face. He's . . . handsome. Ira wants to touch him. Hug him or rub his shoulder. Run his hands through the man's thick hair.

"You're alive," the man says coldly. He isn't tall but it doesn't matter. The air feels humid with desire. Ira imagines them fucking in the whale. Sex inside a body! That's crazy. The whale's heart thumps. Everything tilts and Ira grabs on to the man to catch his balance. The whale is on the move. When things level out, Ira waits a moment before letting go.

"I'm Ira."

"Austin."

Austin seems checked out as they compare stories. Austin saw the whale and swam toward it. Ira had been looking at a turtle, or maybe a rock *shaped like* a turtle, when he was covered by a massive shadow, then had the surreal sensation of tumbling down what felt like stairs. Austin seems like he's lost hope, but maybe Ira can restore it. Escaping the whale feels possible. "We can just break out, like in a prison movie."

Austin holds up a jagged piece of wood. "There's a hole I've been working on since I got here, but the skin's really thick." He stares at Ira like he's sizing him up. "Wanna work on it?"

"I thought you'd never ask," Ira says. He wades through seaweed, struggling to keep up with Austin. He fixes his eyes on Austin's muscular back. Austin doesn't seem gay, but still, Ira has to ask if he's here for Pride. Austin scoffs.

"You're looking for Jake."

"Who?"

"There's one other guy, but he's probably dead by now."

A third man! This can't be. Ira wonders if he's hallucinated Austin. That would be so Ira, to hallucinate a straight guy. "There's another guy in here?" he asks.

"He was gay. He made sculptures. You'd have gotten along."

"How do you know? You just met me." Ira needs water. His eyes burn. He notices sores on Austin's skin, then spots some on himself. It's probably from stomach acid. If he doesn't die of dehydration he will dissolve, slowly, painfully. Bile jumps up Ira's throat and he swallows it back down. He breathes shallow breaths.

It feels momentous to reach a wall, but the hole looks pitiful. It's more like a dent. It's hard to see. Austin jabs the hole with the piece of wood a few times, then hands it to Ira. Ira jabs it for a bit. The wall feels elastic.

"Use your whole body," Austin says. Ira leans into it. He gives it all he's got.

"No, like this," Austin says, taking the wood from Ira's hands and stabbing the hole with new vigor.

Ira thinks of all the straight men who have corrected him in gym class, at pool halls, at Home Depot. Smirking IT guys at work, disgruntled AAA men changing his flat tire. Ira's crush evaporates. Even if they work nonstop on the hole, Ira doubts they'll break through. And even if they did, they'd have to somehow puncture the whale's outer wall, which will be even thicker. They need a laser. A high-tech laser.

Austin answers Ira's questions as if they're an inconvenience. As if this asshole's got someplace to be. Ira loathes the straight people clogging up Fire Island during Pride. Didn't they get the memo? Did they just come to gawk? "Where's the other guy? The gay guy," Ira says.

"Probably decomposing somewhere."

Ira picks up some kind of bone and stabs the hole with it. He and Austin fall into a rhythm, alternating jabs, but it isn't clear if they are making progress. Ira's hungry. Only an idiot would starve in a stomach, his father scolds in his head. Ira makes a face—he hates seafood. He feels like he's about to pass out again. His eyes are on fire. "Can I borrow your goggles?" he finally asks. "Just for an hour?"

Austin shakes his head no.

"I need water," Ira whines. Austin ignores him. Ira drops his bone. "I'm taking a break."

"No time for breaks," Austin says. Ira hates being bossed around. It took him a decade to find a boss he could tolerate. "You're gonna die in here," Austin says. "Do you wanna die?" Ira says nothing. "Well, I can't die in here. I won't. I'm fucking engaged." Austin jabs the hole. Bits of whale flesh float away in a bloody clump. Screw him and his hole, Ira thinks, wading away.

"You're weak!" Austin shouts after him.

"You're trash!" Ira screams back. He can hear Austin cursing at him and it gives him a strange satisfaction. I'll just take a short walk, he decides. Hours pass. It dawns on him in short painful moments that the wall was a good place to be. He should have kept wading along it. The wall led to somewhere, and in his haste, he's wandered back into infinity.

Fuck it. He'll just die. What does it matter? He's already lived the best years of his life. Getting old is depressing. He wades with his eyes closed but they still burn. When he opens them, everything looks dreary and endless. His mind flickers off and on. His body will never be found. His friends and family will assume he drowned, which is embarrassing because he's actually a decent swimmer.

Ira passes out and is shocked to wake up still in the whale, delirious from the heat. He thrashes around in a burst of energy that only lasts five minutes. His skin has the awful texture he saw on Austin. He thinks of his parents sorting through his apartment, finding the bottle of lube in the back of his sock drawer. To live is humiliating but to die is worse.

He thinks about his first real crush—his socially awkward junior high Latin teacher. In high school, he kissed a boy at a Gay-Straight Alliance dance, but then nothing else happened for years. Ira remembers his first boyfriend, George, whom he lived with the summer between sophomore and junior year at NYU. George was super tall, kinda fat, slightly stupid. They watched action movies, ate pizza, had sex—that was their routine. They always got pizza from the same place. The mushrooms were from a can, the peppers small green squares. They relished the homoerotic moments in the movies—a man hanging from a cliff, grabbing another man's strong hand.

It seemed like their relationship could have gone on forever, but it didn't—it ended the following semester. It seemed like it would be the first of many relationships, but it wasn't. Ira usually lost interest after a few dates. After the first fights. Whenever he became serious about a guy, he started noticing their little tics. Everyone proved to be intolerable up close. But all the men he's ever been with now seem wondrous and unique. People who will never live again.

Ira has gotten used to the whale's heartbeat and can go long periods without noticing it, but he sometimes becomes fixated on it, waiting for it, listening to it, terrified of it. He craves water, air, sky. He hears a distant droning melody. He's going crazy, his mother tells his father. He was always crazy, his father says. A jellyfish swims by, grazing his leg. Ira leaps away, tripping face-first into the sludge. A putrid taste fills his mouth. The warm liquid oozes into his ears. He lies at the bottom of the stomach in misery. He'll just die and get it over with. He tries to will himself to stay under, but he rises back up. He tries twice more and stays under longer but surfaces again, sputtering and dripping with goop. He'll just have to die the slow way—waiting for it to overtake him. It could be days.

He sits down, up to his shoulders in muck. He feels pressure to have deep, sincere, leaving-this-world thoughts, but decides that's just homework and fuck homework. He tries to think of the best sex he's ever had. He recalls various encounters but can't wring any pleasure from them anymore. When he thinks of his friends, he feels anxious. He's been meaning to call them back.

Ira zones out. He sees his fourth-grade classroom. The Burger King logo. A photo of Guns N' Roses he masturbated to as a teen-ager. His lungs ache. There isn't enough air in the air. Probably he's hallucinating the droning melody, but he finds himself wading toward it. The goop is thigh-level. He limps past the remains of a seal. His legs seize up with cramps. He sees movement ahead and keeps wading. His eyes burn but he must see this. A blur, possibly a figure. It has to be. He wants it to be. Are those its legs? It has a head. Yes, it's a figure, and he can tell by the way it moves that it's not Austin. It's a man trudging through dark wads of seaweed carrying what looks like a basket.

Ira's heart races as he wades toward the man, who moves in rhythm to whatever he's singing. He's thin and pale. His flaccid penis bounces with each step. His pubes are bushy. There is some-thing familiar about him. He is either the flamboyant man who single-handedly got the dancing going at Sip·n·Twirl the other night, or just the same kind of man, who is rare in life but in abundance on Fire Island. Men like this have always captivated

Ira but he's sometimes felt jealous of their freedom. Watching the man, it seems obvious that his joy is irreverent and radical, that someone who can create fun from thin air is a magician.

The man sees Ira and stops in his tracks. "Oh my god," says the man, swinging his basket. "Who are you?"

"I'm Ira."

The man shakes his hand. "I'm Jake." His voice is high and spirited but not annoyingly so. It's amazing to see another face. Jake has small features, a prominent forehead, and short, thinning hair. His skin is more decomposed than Austin's, which makes it hard to tell his age, but he looks older.

"Are your eyes burning?" Ira asks, squinting at Jake.

"Yes. Can barely see a thing."

"Austin said you were probably dead. I was working with him on that hole."

"That *stupid* hole! I spent hours on it," says Jake. "It's never gonna give. The skin is too thick! I told him so many times. But he didn't like my idea."

"What's your idea?"

"To get pooped out the butt."

"What about the throat?" Ira asks. "Can't we climb it?"

"Maybe. If we can find it. I've been looking for days, but this place goes on forever. I'm just trying to eat as well as I can and entertain myself when possible." He pulls something out of his basket.

"Sushi?" He drops little bundles of seaweed into Ira's hand and Ira stuffs one into his mouth. It tastes terrible, but he makes a show of enjoying it. Jake looks proud.

"We need to find the throat or something sharp," Ira says. "Which way?"

Jake shrugs, then chooses a direction. As they wade side by side, Jake plucks shrimp from the surface and eats them. His voice is lilting, musical. His stories take unexpected turns. His line of questioning is natural and thorough, and Ira talks about himself for longer than he intends. Their taste in books is pretty different, but they like a lot of the same movies. Ira has never kissed a woman, but Jake once had sex with one. It's thrilling to have a real conversation. A couple of times, Ira catches himself forgetting where they are.

Jake is convinced they're in a blue whale, but Ira is sure that blue whales are extinct. Occasionally they pass one of Jake's sculptures. All are in disarray except for a spiral of shells pressed into a dolphin carcass, which Ira compliments. Jake seems pleased. He asks Ira questions about design and Ira tells him about the font he made this past year, called Ethics—with narrow *o*'s and robust *r*'s—and how his coworkers never responded when he emailed it to them. Jake asks Ira what his favorite logo is and Ira says it's still the Nike swoosh. Jake's is the NBC peacock.

"That's so gay," Ira teases.

"It really is."

"What does a peacock have to do with TV?"

"A peacock *displays,* baby."

Ira is too light-headed to keep talking but happy to listen, so he asks Jake to tell him "everything." Jake says he grew up in Virginia in a big house with a big family. He studied drama in college and acted in a few plays, then entered a career in customer service, first in department stores, then in hotels, where he grew restless. He became a flight attendant on boring short-haul routes, eventually working his way up to be the head steward in first class. For many years he traveled all over the world, until his drug habits, which he'd always had, grew in scope and intensity, becoming a madness that disassembled his life, costing him his job, his husband, and his West Village apartment. His sister pretty much kidnapped him and drove him to a treatment center where he suffered and played board games. Now he lives alone deep in Queens, head of customer service at Target.

Beams of light flutter over them. Ira shivers in excitement. His eyes dart frantically from one beam to another. "Did you see that?" Jake asks, grabbing Ira's arm. The light comes in thin waves, illuminating, for the first time, the ceiling, which is bluish black and dripping. Jake goes wild, screaming and dancing. They must be in the throat! Ira rejoices. He'll live differently this time! He'll go places and he won't spend so much time on his phone.

They must be in the throat, but Ira can't see it. As far as he looks there is only the ceiling. Maybe the mouth is still hopelessly far away, and the light is just traveling as light often does. A beam passes over Jake and for a fleeting moment, Ira sees his face in remarkable detail. It looks full of humor and intelligence, though prematurely ancient.

"We have seen the light!" Jake shouts with what's left of his voice.

"But where's the throat? The walls?" Ira demands, desperately throwing out his arms.

"We must be really close," Jake says. The light suddenly vanishes. Ira's stomach feels like lead. "Come back," Jake pleads. They wade around in the dark, waiting. "It's going to come back," he insists a few minutes later. "Any second now. I just know it's going to come back." But it doesn't. Neither speaks for a long time.

Jake concocts a plan to make the whale cough them up, but none of the ingredients are available to them. They begin bargaining with God or whoever might be watching. If they escape the whale, they promise to spend the rest of their lives volunteering at charities. "Or at least a good portion," Jake adds.

"At least fifteen hours a week."

"Really? Fifteen?" asks Jake.

"Too little?"

"Fifteen is a lot," Jake says.

They are disintegrating. Jake looks half-dead, but Ira keeps telling him he looks great. Ira is forlorn. His legs ache with each step. His skin burns. Eventually he gives up praying for light and just focuses on Jake's voice. It's a beautiful voice, though it has been weakened by hours of talking and is now a whisper.

They find a floating island of seaweed and plastic. Jake crawls onto it and lies down. It bobbles but supports him. Ira crawls up too. Plastic bags, plastic cups, huge spools of knotted nylon ropes, a calcified surfboard, jagged pieces of kayaks. The seaweed stinks like rotten eggs. Ira lies next to Jake and drifts off. He sees a night sky or large expanse of water. He dreams they are discovered by the flashlights of scuba divers. Ira wakes up and sees Jake's eyes are closed. He jostles him but Jake is unresponsive. His friend! He'll never get to talk to his friend again. He'll just have to lie here, next to Jake's dead body, until he dies too.

Liquid rains down. "I hate when it does this," Jake says, lips barely moving, like a ventriloquist. Ira bursts out laughing. "What?" Jake asks, inching closer. Ira feels happy and then faint. He closes his eyes. Jake holds his hand.

A voice breaks the spell. "We'd be free by now if we'd all worked together."

"Austin," Jake murmurs, but it can't be. Ira sits up and opens his eyes. His vision is obscured by pulsating shadows.

"We'd be out by now!" Austin yells. Ira's stomach tightens.

"Why is he here?" Ira mutters to Jake.

"Because his fucking hole was a failure."

"Fuck you," Austin says.

Ira focuses his eyes on Austin, who is standing right in front of them. His bleeding face and deteriorating skin look like a gruesome Halloween costume. His dark goggles look like bug eyes. "It would have worked if we all had worked on it," Austin insists. "But no, you guys had to do your own thing. What exactly were you doing?" His tone is infuriating.

"You look like shit," Ira says.

"You look like roadkill," Austin says.

"You were initially very good-looking, let that be said. But now you look like a pizza the cheese fell off of," Jake says.

"Well, you look like a bird with all its feathers plucked off."

Jake anxiously puts his hands to his face.

"Did you start a restaurant?" Austin asks, holding on to the edge of their island. "Can I get a reservation at your fucking restaurant? Did you build a castle with a moat?"

"Your hole wasn't even a hole," Jake says.

"I got it deeper after you left."

"Then why are you here?" Ira demands. He can't believe Austin crashed his deathbed.

"Where do you want me to go, Ira?" Austin sounds deranged.

"Anywhere else."

"I can die wherever I want to," Austin says. He crawls onto the island and sits across from them. The island bobs and drifts. Goop splashes onto their faces. No one says anything for several minutes. Ira can't take the tension.

"Why do straight people come to Fire Island during Pride?" he blurts out. "Are they just bored? Or do they long to be seduced under the boardwalk? Chosen and then convinced, gay for one night, under the cover of darkness . . ."

"My family owns a house here and has for fifty years."

"Whoop-de-damn-do," Ira says. Jake laughs.

"Go fuck yourselves," Austin says.

"With pleasure," says Ira. He scoots to the edge of the island, wanting to leave with Jake.

"Where's the house?" Jake asks. He seems genuinely curious.

"Fifth Walk."

"That's on my morning stroll," Jake says. "Which house?"

"One. It's right on the beach."

"Is it the one with the wooden pillars?"

"Yeah. The gray one."

"It's got double decks?"

"Yeah. Actually, triple decks, if you count the very top, but it's not up to code." Ira feels trapped. He wants the conversation to end.

"It's right by Stone Trail," says Jake.

"Yeah."

"One summer I stayed on Pepperidge Walk, but as far from the beach as you can get." Jake wipes his face of gunk and sweat. "Your grandparents bought it fifty years ago? They must have gotten it for a song!"

Austin nods. Ira crawls back to Jake's side. Austin and Jake discuss the post office off Dune Walk, some guy named Mike at the Casino Café.

"What do you do, Austin?" Jake asks. Ira feels jealous.

"I'm in advertising."

"Oh, really? Ira is a graphic designer."

"Huh. I'm mostly on the business side."

Ira lies down again and closes his eyes while Jake and Austin talk about vacation days and office dynamics. Their grating human voices chip away at the black sky of his mind. But as the minutes pass and Ira feels more and more out of it, their chatter begins to soothe him. Little phrases slip into his consciousness— "double major," "fourth-floor walk-up," "destination wedding"— and linger for a moment, detaching from and reattaching to their meanings.

"Solar panels."

"Couples therapy."

Warm goop is spilling over them again. Ira dreams he's in a dilapidated movie theater. He dreams he's watching Austin and Jake play tennis. They look incredibly sexy. Austin's muscles glimmer in the sunlight. Jake dances merrily around the court, the ball flying past him.

The dream shifts and they're all living in a loft overlooking Central Park.

Everything is slow and dim.

You're dying, his dad says.

No, Ira thinks.

He wants more minutes.

He wants whole years.

Lifetimes where he lives as a woman.

As an outlaw.

A street musician.

Lifetimes where he really learns Latin.

Where he's a king.

A benevolent king.

The images stop.

He can't leave himself now.

To die will be like tearing the music out of a song.

It's wrong.

His mind is slipping away.

He doesn't even have to live, he just wants to keep thinking forever.

He won't even say anything—he'll just think!

He'll just watch!

A wave of panic

a wash of relief

Naomi Shuyama-Gómez
The Commander's Teeth

THE OLD AMBULANCE is missing its brakes again and Lorenzo, semipro street racer but also our driver, laughs from the front of the vehicle as if to reassure us that, well, at least we still have the steering wheel and we should be damn thankful for that.

"In one piece, please," Omaira quips. I feel even less safe in the back of the ambulance with Omaira, a hygienist, who braces herself against the portable dental chair and gives tiny yelps for every pothole that makes contact with a tire.

We continue inching along, before Lorenzo is able to force the brakes back in their socket and pronounce the ambulance fine. He tests the brakes again on the empty road. It's a small miracle that we haven't driven off the mountain. I'm in my eighth of twelve months to complete the yearlong obligatory social service known as "rural," where students enrolled in medicine, dentistry, nursing, and bacteriology serve rural communities after graduating. Our sites are chosen by lottery and negotiated through bribes. We work Monday through Friday; on the weekends, we go home and drink, or stay in the barracks and drink. On difficult days, like the one where we lost the brakes or when we descended the unpaved dirt roads of Yumbo in first gear, with Omaira vomiting out of the window, Lorenzo and I take the edge off by thrusting mechanically against each other.

Dentistry had interested me since I saw my grandfather without teeth. We'd just moved to the city, into my uncle's house, and my grandfather was playing basketball in the empty lot behind school with much younger men. He was elbowed in such a way that four teeth fell, twinkling on the cement. My grandfather hadn't motioned for a break from the game, hadn't been scared of the blood he spat. Instead, he picked up his four teeth and put them in his pocket. A decade later, after he moved in with us but before the lung cancer took him, I would study my grandfather's dentures when he left them in the bathroom. I ran my forefinger over each beautiful, polished stone, stark against the blue bathroom sink.

Over the months, I've developed a uniform and a routine; my barrack rises at five A.M. and I tuck old jeans into even older boots. I stretch stiffened joints, shrug on the lab coat I've waited six years to wear, now yellowed from overbleaching. We eat our breakfast standing up, waiting for the old ambulances to grind to a stop at the end of a footpath snaking around the barracks.

"Your Ferrari is here," Lorenzo calls out.

We climb in the back, balancing gear, exhaustion, and canisters of pressed juice. Every morning Lorenzo, Omaira, and I follow the winding mountain roads to where we are stationed for the day. I've gotten so used to the bleating city traffic that the quiet rumble of the rural's commute still unnerves me.

Omaira carries the conversation with Lorenzo while I watch the morning light leak through the panels of my fingertips curling around the grab handle dangling above my head. They say last night there were reports of increased FARC activity. My skull makes contact with Omaira's chin when the ambulance brakes just in time for a lone Chiva bus collecting its passengers. It took some time for the three of us to be able to sit in silence comfortably, and longer still to develop camaraderie. Omaira had to first confront me about Lorenzo. She cornered me in the mess hall and asked if he was as bad a driver in bed as he was in the ambulance. I told her she should find out.

During our rural, the land we work is protected, secured by the military we sometimes hear marching along the road in single file. The young men, most of them drafted through mandatory service, patrol the mountains, and stir the vegetation as they wait for orders. Every twenty minutes we pass clusters of flattened rooftops thatched brown and tiled red, small islands of human intervention in contrast to the lush jungle.

Up in these mountains, orchid bees glint like black opals in the sun and when the Cauca River swells to a flood, farmers use zip lines to move across safely. The few villagers out on foot, sensing the ambulance, hardly glance up from their path as Lorenzo weaves around them. He has worked as a driver for years now, and if Omaira and I accompany him, we never have real trouble at the checkpoints. Yet, if I look too hard, I can see the movement of a different kind of uniform, underneath the dense foliage, like fish rippling just below the water.

Though we arrive late because of the stop-and-go ambulance, the community leader welcomes us with a smile. Sometimes it's a tent, sometimes a villager's home. This time a wilted finger offers us a concrete room with working lights and running water. "You'll be setting up here."

Lorenzo has been to this site before and knows the safest place to park the ambulance. He helps carry the equipment we've brought along into the bare room. The villagers think he is the dentist and children, several with hair rust-colored from malnutrition, follow behind him. Lorenzo motions to the locals who have gathered for medical attention. "For dental work only, please follow me." He splits them into groups based on the level of emergency. At first, we had distributed comprehensive cards that asked patients to rate their pain and levels of discomfort. We passed around pamphlets showing the anatomy of a mouth and offered tips for preventative care. But it turned out the paper was better suited for tinder than instruction. Now Lorenzo and the community leader take turns asking each person, "What is your name? How old are you? How much does it hurt and for how long?" They share a clipboard between them to note their findings. Later, I will use the clipboard to match the patients with procedures. While Omaira butters the floor in polish, I set up the instruments and test the faucet. The cleaning chemicals and sun heat up the room. Sweat skids across the fold of her elbow as Omaira works the mop.

When I worked in the trauma unit, I brought along a notebook. I didn't want to forget how the patients described what had happened to them. I wasn't required to summarize or document their injuries according to standard medical terminology. Instead, I recorded. One patient characterized a rubber pellet fired at his eyeball as a red flower forced to bloom open. Another said she could feel the shards of ice grinding in her leg after a motorcycle crash. I noted other details of these encounters: How a patient's mother taught me to use a poultice of milk bread to draw out splinters. An elderly woman tilted her head back and moaned softly as I searched through her scalp, parting her hair with my fingers, to retrieve glass. A wife clutched me by the collar and asked if her husband would love her the same after we restarted his heart. Sometimes I circled close to understanding what they meant, but I still didn't know how to receive these offerings.

Though the volunteer rotations often fell on national holidays when the hospitals were most short-staffed, I liked my shifts at the emergency ward better than the work in the rural. Visiting the city's marketplace, among the street vendors in woven wild cane hats, I could be invisible. The vendors also prepared for surgery, expertly arranged their produce on low tables, and hawked samples of their ripest fruit. No one paid me mind while I sorted through the spill of produce as long as I kept a hat on, too, the one my mother had worn. A crowd afforded a degree of security, my parents had instilled in me.

It was made clear to me during the rural that I only knew what to do if they came to me in pieces; I was used to sliced fingertips, bullet holes, broken bones, smashed limbs, and allergic reactions. With equipment, I could stitch scalps shut. I always knew what was expected of me and wasn't in charge. Here, in the villages, I look into mouths like open graves. I fill cavities, extract teeth, see them once and never again.

The barracks we stay in during the rural program were once a school the government had appropriated and turned into a military post, and now they serve the graduated students working the area. They are still coed because they hadn't expected many women to graduate with degrees in medicine. The supervisors hadn't even installed a second toilet. It doesn't matter what time of the day I use the single-stall bathroom because with twenty of us to a classroom, there is always, always a queue. My government sheets are clean but stained. Mosquito nets are the paper-thin dividers sectioning each cot. I've made a lot of beds in my life, but this is the easiest, only a pillow, a blanket, and two small suitcases under the bed. I sleep in it like I've slept in all the others.

By the third week I'd been watching the cobwebs expand across the ceiling corners but hadn't mustered up the willpower to disturb them. Lorenzo'd been paid to drop off some bottles for the weekend when he invited me out for a drive. I'd always felt inept at the chess game of social interactions that led to fucking. I was never sure if I was interrupting. It had been the same way in dental school but with an international student. Xian. A name like that spilled a glow over everything. We'd been lab partners, assigned at random for the semester. In the study rooms of the college library, Xian and I made out for hours, high on whatever she could get, and low on food and sleep. In the dark of her apartment, we were bodies grinding each other down, a knife and sharpening stone.

Lorenzo leaves with the ambulance to pick up lunch. The first patients brought in are usually the elderly; after examining their smiles, Omaira teaches them how to brush their teeth and floss. She's also the children's favorite. I try to be gentle, but they sit the most still for her, reaching for her pretty hands. Not ten minutes later, the two windows darken with bodies in camouflage. I can hear the butts of guns clicking against the concrete exterior of the room we're occupying. A woman from the detachment, long hair braided down the front of her rifle, opens the door. The FARC commander enters with a security detail. If he has this many bodyguards pacing behind, I figure he must be someone of importance.

The woman I'm working on glances over and gets up out of the chair quickly, almost tripping over her sandals. "I have to go," she says.

"We still haven't finished," Omaira pleads.

The woman presses a warmed candy into my hand and apologizes. "Sorry, but thank you," she calls out, darting out the door before Omaira can hand her one of the little goodie bags of toothpaste, toothbrush, and floss we prepared hastily last night.

Through the open door, I see the queue of patients has disappeared. I study the soldiers crammed in the room. The commander looks about forty and the others can't be old enough to have started shaving. The shortest one smiles at Omaira and then covers his mouth to hide it, as if ashamed of the condition of his teeth. He asks for the door to be closed, the commander does, before calling us forward.

. . .

Early on in the rural program, I went to the home of a farmer Lorenzo knew. We stayed late to finish examining his five children's crowded mouths, shovel-shaped incisors and dental crowns carrying the Carabelli cusp. The farmer invited us for dinner. We had to leave the ambulance behind to hike up to his village. For the hour-long walk, we were prepared to go on foot, but he insisted on bringing us up on the mules he'd taken for his children. He warned us to keep our mouths shut, or they'd house wings, motioning to the insects around our faces.

Along the way, we passed a place where the forest was slightly less dense and the farmer said that there had been an outpost. We didn't ask whose it had been. Only the curfew, discarded gasoline drums, and weathered sacks of sand remained as markers.

We hadn't expected a welcoming. By the open kitchen we met extended family members, neighbors, and friends. They were the sort of people with eggshells rattling in the watering can, the type that saved the fat drippings to flavor bread. Wind pierced the forest's canopy and ruffled the tangle of limbs from palms and ferns. The farmer's wife told us proudly he could kill and field dress any animal. As if to prove himself, the farmer shot a chiguiro, took a knife to its fur, and confirmed my suspicion that everything looks the same skinned. At any moment, I thought, the rain would break, and we'd moved quite a distance from their homes. I searched for a tree to get behind but no one else moved to find shelter.

After hanging the animal by the paws, the farmer broke the pelvis with a pop. The thunder rumbled closer and I couldn't stop from bracing myself, even as I figured he knew which storms we could weather out in the open jungle. The meat would be tender, the farmer assured us. He pulled an intestine through, and left the innards to plop like fish on the forest floor. Though it was getting dark and I had trouble seeing then, I made out tapeworms writhing among the still pulsing organs.

. . .

The commander wears his years on his neck and hands, the brown rubbery skin creasing deeply along his forehead, knuckles, and mouth. Omaira begins to hum into her face mask. Unlike his bodyguards, the commander isn't carrying a noticeable weapon, his rank only evident by his men and posture. The commander is thin, but with a paunch stretched along his midsection. He holds his hands behind his back, like an uncertain child, and looks us both in the face.

"Don't worry," he says, "I'm only here for treatment." Omaira hums louder.

There are times I've thought about being taken, wondering whether my family could afford my face on national television or if the government would care enough to organize a rescue mission. Whose hushed voices would exchange my name after gathering for church? I imagine Lorenzo returning to find us gone, trembling for eight silent miles without us. Or maybe he won't return either.

"Do you have any pain?" I ask stupidly.

The commander motions for his guards to remain posted at the door and sits in the dental chair. "Here," he says, "and here and here."

I change my gloves and face mask before I place my fingers under his stubbled chin. "When was the last time you saw a dentist?" The warmth from his skin transfers to my cold, latexed hand.

He blinks. "Years ago."

I adjust the bib and peer into the mouth of the commander. Omaira clinks the mirror against his teeth to check the molars and I use the sickle-shaped probe.

"Occlusal wear, gingivitis. At least three teeth that I'd recommend extracting. Bicuspid, bi-rooted. Premolar." A mouth is like an autobiography. I read for the vices that can be gleaned from its state. "Sir, how old are you?"

"Thirty-three," the commander replies.

Omaira touches the cross at her neck. "Jesus's age."

During the season of pomegranates, we ate so many that each of my long, thin fingers purpled and browned. I traced the downy sideburns against Xian's face, down the bumps of her sternum and the purple-blue veins of her wrists. "E-mi-li-a." She sounded out each syllable and swayed like a stalk as she spoke. Xian read my notes from the emergency room and showed me pictures of her family. She insisted on sleeping with all of the windows in her apartment open so that she could listen to the frogs coo through the night. When the wind blew in from behind the metal bars permanently installed over the windows, the gauze of her skirt flapped like a butterfly.

Xian asked if I was afraid of beginning the rural. "Someone could hurt you," she said. "Someone could take you."

She knelt behind me and I watched her cup my breasts—her thumbs hooked around my nipples. I could feel the tips of her long hair on my back before Xian burrowed her head into it, tickling me with a flutter of her eyelashes, and I could smell late summer in the river, the way I always could as a child.

When I fit him in the cheek retractor, I see the commander as he is. Labial frenulum between his front teeth stretched taut, the gums exposed in a sick smile. The commander's teeth are ground down and stained the same color that I imagine my uncle's charred bones would be if we were ever to be reunited.

Ideas tumble in my skull; I could hurt him if I wanted to, and to different degrees: a few scrapes across the gums, some heavy-handed excavations, unnecessary extractions, and insufficient anesthesia. What does he know about dentistry?

I find a cavity to press on.

The commander winces. "You are very young. So young."

My supervisors made me wear red lipstick while shadowing them to appear older. "I'm certified," I reply evenly.

"Of course. Do you know what's wrong?"

I nod. "You need long-term procedures."

"Just do what you can today."

When we met up, Lorenzo and I drove to the town and parked in a restaurant lot. We had sex urgently; I kept his hands busy with the slick pulsing between my legs. I gripped him in one hand, pulling back the foreskin to the base, and lowered my palm to his penis, dry-rubbing the head. Stay up, stay up, I pleaded. With men, I had trouble figuring out how hard I could go.

He pressed his knuckles into his eyes, while I continued to apply pressure.

"Dentists are sadists," Lorenzo said, and it sounded a lot like absolution.

The noise the explorer produces as I scrape it across the enamel of the commander's teeth is not unlike the squeaks of chalk across a blackboard. The layers of plaque folding over themselves remind me of the avocado seeds I planted with my mother in the windows of our sunny apartment in the city. We sat in the kitchen and used a cuticle pusher to peel the drying brown coat, unveiling the smooth fleshy second layer of skin. We skewered the pit with three toothpicks and dangled it over the mouth of a glass jar to watch the hairy water roots extend. The years passed and the fruit we'd grown was small, misshapen.

I continue to scrape the calculus bridge from the commander's bottom front teeth while Omaira prepares the injections. I make circular strokes with the scaler. Omaira places the gurgling evacuator in the corner of his mouth, suctioning away the bloodied saliva and calcified flecks. I use the water pick to continue dis-lodging tartar deposits and bits of food. I press the needle into his gum and pump the shot of Novocain slowly, evenly. His full mouth, holding wires and instruments, somehow reminds me of the house I grew up in with the pots of baby tears and wild thyme spilling from the kitchen.

I put my weight on his jaw and crunch the molar with the for-ceps, once, twice, and then once more. I pick out the tiny shards from his gums. Dig around for the fragments in the root. Fish for the nerve. In this inaccessible jungle, my heart is a hammer keeping steady the minutes. The FARC killed my uncle, I mouth under the surgical mask as I work. After his disappearance, my uncle's house in the city became ours.

We'd finished fucking in the back of the ambulance when I told Lorenzo I felt guilty that the families couldn't afford the things they gave us. Cramped beside me on the hospital gurney, he grunted that pride was expensive.

"They trust me, and I make holes in their heads."

"You doctors," Lorenzo sighed, "better than in the chest."

He caught me looking at the stab wound he'd acquired from a run-in with the police and smiled. "I can't help it; they fall in love with me and when I have to reject them, they try to kill me."

On the farm, each of my parents slept with a haversack packed at the foot of the bed. My dark-haired mother kept preserved foods and dried herbs in hers, the things we would need if we had to flee in the middle of the night and didn't know if food would be readily available. Each item was weighed against others—I'd caught her debating aloud, was she packing the engraved hand mirror because she missed her father who'd given it to her, or just because it was Wednesday and he had died on a Wednesday and so she always thought of him on Wednesdays? My father, in his bag, kept a pistol and handfuls of seeds in hollowed-out gourds.

When he shook them, I thought I could hear the rain. During those midnight marches, I was too young to take anything of value, but made a habit of picking up a stone to prove to myself the next morning that it hadn't been a dream.

I look around the room now and cannot locate a single item worth taking. The midday heat droops everything it touches and the meager lights flicker in the sickening way they do when they're barbecuing bugs. The commander continues to surrender his mouth as the folds in my palms prick and my grip wavers. Omaira must notice his knuckles whitening as he presses them against the armrests but doesn't offer her hand to hold. The soldiers step closer to the commander and I wonder if I'll see the lid of another coffin thumping shut.

A month ago, on the Saturday night drive back to the dormitories, I was the first to notice blood splattered on the highway dividers and the only one who saw two socked feet poking out from under a twisted plastic sheet. They were thick for the weather we'd been having, and clean and white, despite their owner lying on the road.

Lorenzo remembers an outstretched hand, but not much else. The one-lane road curved where the police car was parked and we had no choice but to drive very close to the body, to the distressed police officer handling the report. The window was rolled down and if I extended my arm, I could have pinched the sheet and slipped it off.

The body under the white plastic shroud was the most naked anyone could ever be. I reached my hand across Lorenzo's thigh. He tensed.

I have to work quickly if I want to finish treating the commander before Lorenzo returns. If he catches up to us, maybe he'll try something stupid and that won't end well for anyone. I grip the forceps around the second tooth, rocking it back and forth to loosen it from bone, and feel a trickle of cold sweat slip under my white collar. The commander's steady curve of lips frames my view and the words to the Hippocratic oath come back to me before I twist the tooth free.

"Are you missing anyone?" Lorenzo asked.

"No."

"We're not worth kidnapping, are we? They just kill us."

My mother's brother had lived in a neighborhood with night guards who carried small handguns; one walked up and down the streets from six P.M. to midnight. Another man relieved him at midnight and kept watch until six A.M. The high walls of the yards were embedded with colorful broken glass. My uncle threw me a surprise party for my twelfth birthday at his house. He catered the event, rented a band, and hired entertainers. He invited his friends and their children, the whole block except for the house of a known dealer. When the party spilled onto the street, I saw the dealer's two children, dressed well and playing with expensive toys. They lingered at the front of their house, watched the inflatables go up through the rungs of the gate. "Sorry," I mouthed, relieved that it hadn't been my decision to exclude them.

Lorenzo sat up and held me by the shoulders, running his fingertips down the vaccination scars that had left grooves like the pips on a domino down my arms. "Had you ever seen a dead person?"

"Sure," I replied. "We have to go down to the morgue. Twice, at least."

He told me he'd seen a few. In Lorenzo's village by the river that slices Colombia, fishermen pull the disappeared out of the Magdalena with the catch. He explained, "It's customary to adopt them. We've places for them, marked NN in the cemetery. Sometimes people name or pray or cry for them. My mother did."

Later he asked what he'd been wondering since he found out where I was from, the things Xian never could have known to. Lorenzo waited until he got what he wanted from me, that where I was from, the town I'd spent my early years in on the farm, some hadn't said yes and there came the sort of harvest that forced the workers on all fours. The paramilitaries mowed on suspicion, and limp, lopped sponges bloated in the field until the military came to bury them. The newspaper's missing person inquiries and obituaries grew to ten pages long. A young priest called to bless the fields gathered us around the aspergillum, poised high and cracked like a whip. The widows shifted their rings from left hand to right. We kept our haversacks stocked and continued the drills.

After I told him what he wanted to know, Lorenzo went quiet, and from the inside of the ambulance, we listened to the stray dogs growl to each other.

Sweat drips in fine chains down my upper body. I uproot two more teeth and offer the whole ones to the commander in a clear bag. "Thank you," the commander says in a thickened voice, his face swollen and drooling. "Thank you for your work." The commander peels several bills from the modest wad in his breast pocket. Omaira, ashen faced and trembling, takes the money from the commander's hands and returns the change.

"Do I tip you?" he asks.

"No," Omaira says hurriedly.

"We can't accept them," I explain.

The commander explores with his tongue the slab of gauze where posterior five used to be. Three other wads of cotton are wedged between molars. I imagine him trying to understand how these wounds can be good.

.   .   .   .

After the commander leaves, Lorenzo returns with the food. "Do you think they'd believe us, if we told someone?" Omaira asks. Lorenzo places a hand on Omaira's shoulder and she shrugs him off. "We could identify the commander by his teeth. He didn't tell us his name, but he must have been important. He looked it."

Lorenzo backs away from Omaira. "I don't want to be responsible for revenge."

She turns to me next. "You know. He let you take them out."

I hand Omaira the teeth fragments in a clear bag, and her upper lip begins to quiver. "Tell the director, then." A few tears creep down her cheekbones and into her mouth. I offer her a tissue and she seems to relax.

"Well," Omaira says, "I don't think anyone else is coming." Lorenzo begins to pack up our supplies, the surfaces sticky from bug spray and nervous sweat. I pocket the commander's teeth and steer Omaira outside.

Famished now, I check for anthills and clear a place to eat on the ground. Under the sun, we stir rice, potatoes, and chicken drumsticks into the stew, which is thick and threatening to spill from the containers.

When we arrive at the school-turned-barracks-turned-dormitories, Lorenzo drops Omaira off and then takes me to the room where he stays during the week while he works up in the mountains. That night as we sleep naked, swaddled in Lorenzo's arms, I feel certain I can recognize Xian's wingspan. When Xian spooned my warm back, I studied the walls of the dormitory while she kneaded stiffened muscles. I imagined a man parting Xian's legs as if he knew what he was looking for. I was already mourning the life that could have been mine.

A month before I finish my assignment, during a night that pours the kind of rain that makes the worms slip out of the earth, Lorenzo, too, disappears into the jungle. By then, I've managed to glue some of the pieces together, used dental bonding to re-create the commander's molar. As we stand mud-sunk in our usual spot,

Omaira tells me she's drafting an official letter to the director. It feels familiar as church, the waiting, and we train our eyes to the shadows of wings gliding across the dirt road. Omaira leans the weight of her body against the dental chair. I watch the birds tap their feet to mimic the sound of rain, while in the drying road, just a few meters ahead, the worms inch back to their burrows, or fry onto the rocks under a merciless sun.

Rodrigo Blanco Calderón

Translated from the Spanish by Thomas Bunstead

The Mad People of Paris

I ARRIVED IN PARIS on November 23, 2015, ten days after the Bataclan massacre took place.

The Parisians bore their grief swathed in a kind of invisible shawl. The silence of those days was a scarf made of the very air, wrapped close around the necks of the locals and us foreigners alike.

"Yes, *peculiarly* cold this winter, isn't it?" said Mme. Rachou in her elliptical Spanish, when I brought this up.

The feeling solidified when you rode the metro. Nobody talked. The babies didn't cry. And the dogs, which you're allowed to take with you on public transport there, didn't make a sound either.

The apartment I got for myself was on the south side of Paris, in an area called Le Kremlin-Bicêtre. The university was in the north, in Pontoise. And for the entirety of the metro journey, which would take an hour and a half, sometimes two hours, I would hear no conversations, not a single word being spoken.

The only people who said anything on the metro were the mad people and the drunks.

In the case of the drunks, they tended to congregate at the ends of the platforms. Many of them were Russians. They had red, chapped faces. They were like the leftover bricks from a building site.

The mad people, on the other hand, were always alone—each connected up to the throng of voices inside their brains.

It wasn't much different at the university itself. My stint as a guest researcher at the Laboratoire Linguistique, Dictionnaires et Informatique was due to last a year. This laboratory was, from what I could ascertain when looking into options for internships abroad, one of the most advanced institutes in my field, which was the application of computer science to questions of linguistics. But my colleagues didn't seem to be programmed to say anything more than the cold, punctual "*bonjour*" they met me with each morning.

Certainly, my below-par French didn't help.

The only opportunity to vent was on Wednesdays and Fridays, when I went to evening classes—language and French culture—at the Sorbonne.

The classes ended at six P.M. and a number of us sometimes went to one of the cafés on Boulevard du Montparnasse afterward. A Korean couple, a Dutch woman, and two Algerians, along with myself, were the regulars. The common language was English. We'd sit and talk for an hour, then go our separate ways.

And it would be back to the silence.

I would walk down to the Vavin metro stop and, rather than going home, get on line 4 in the direction of Saint-Michel. Almost without my realizing it, my footsteps would once more lead me to 9 Rue Gît-le-Coeur. I'd stand before the commemorative plaque and reread the names of the legendary guests at what was once known as the Beat Hotel: "B. Gysin, H. Norse, G. Corso, A. Ginsberg, P. Orlovsky, I. Sommerville, W. Burroughs."

I'd try to guess which room Ian Sommerville and William Burroughs had stayed in. It was there that the fresh-faced computer scientist, recently in from London, had accompanied the much older writer in the inferno of one of his countless detoxes.

I tended to feel very despondent on the way back from those excursions. In the metro, I thought about what would happen if I started shouting. From the look of me, people could well mistake me for an Islamist. And yet I was sure that the same would happen as I'd seen so many times when the normal run of things was disturbed in any way: in the end, my fit of madness would be buried by the stunning imperturbability of Parisians.

Other times, I had the idea of abandoning my doctoral thesis and putting my energies into developing some kind of software that would process the language of those voluble Paris down-and-outs. I envisaged a miraculous interface that would transmit the messages they were sending. I fantasized about the effect my discovery would have: the inhabitants of Paris getting to discover how alike they all were in their various solitudes. The end result being a global, fraternal embrace. Maybe even an orgy.

Clearly, I was depressed. It wasn't long before the panic attacks began.

Or something very similar, because they never spiraled. Although, as Bogdan would later explain, the worst panic attacks were precisely that: the sense of an infinite anguish growing and growing, but never quite managing to overflow. Nobody bats an eyelid, and that's when you start thinking you're really losing your mind.

One Wednesday, the urge to start shouting became unbearable. I was in a metro car, riding a Saint-Michel–bound train. What stopped me, or saved me, was looking up and finding a phrase somebody had scrawled on one of the doors:

Parlez vos voisin!

The person who wrote it must have been either a sage or someone who'd been driven to despair. Or both.

I looked to my right and saw a man, a handsome blue-eyed Caucasian, somewhere in his fifties and smartly dressed. He was busy on his cell phone. I checked the graffiti again to make sure I'd understood what was undoubtedly fate stepping in to give me an order: "Talk to thy neighbor!"

I got ready to use a phrase in my rudimentary French, one of the *formules de politesse* we'd learned in class.

But when I turned to face the man, I couldn't speak. He was still looking at his cell, only now his free hand was engaged in a very specific, and quite horrifying, activity.

Nobody else in the car seemed to have noticed.

I watched with a mixture of disgust and fascination. The man was picking his nose with his middle finger, which then traveled directly to his mouth. At times he left it resting on his tongue. Or he let the residue get stuck on one of his front teeth. You could see from his expression that he liked the taste. And he went on doing it.

He got off at Saint-Germain-des-Prés. And I, just as the doors were about to slide shut, followed him off the train.

Coming out of the station, I saw the man walking ahead toward the corner where the Deux Magots café was. I followed him at a distance and he soon stepped inside the L'Écume des Pages bookstore. I went in after him and pretended to take a look at the new arrivals table. He went all the way to the back. He returned carrying a squat-looking book; it was thick, but the cover can't have been larger than half a sheet of paper. I couldn't see the title or the name of the author. The man paid and went out. I waited for a few seconds before following him. I saw him cross the boulevard, heading south. The walk sign on the pedestrian crossing came on again, and taking long, loping strides, I gained on him as he started down Rue Bonaparte.

The man was moving very quickly, and I lost sight of him. Moments later, the narrow sidewalks gave way to the wide-open space of Place Saint-Sulpice, with its fountain out in the middle and the majestic church at the far end. These were names and coordinates I would come to learn later on. For now it was only a case of spotting him going up the church steps, and then hurrying after him without asking myself where we were.

When I went through the church door, I was immediately struck by the deep beauty of the interior, like that of a pool of water suspended high above. Though I didn't know why, I experienced a profound sensation of guilt. It was as though the Baroque concavity of the nave had been flipped over and had pierced my sternum.

I caught sight of the man. He was kneeling on a prie-dieu in front of a priest. They were on the other side of a glass screen that separated them from the aisle.

It took me a few moments to understand that what I was seeing—which looked more like a bank manager's office than anything else—was the confessional.

Still keeping my distance, I went along the aisle.

I spent a short time looking at the main altar in the central nave, the lateral staircases, and all the screens and ornamentation. I went around the back of the altar, which brought me to another aisle, and it was then that I found myself at the Lady Chapel.

I sat on one of the small chairs arranged around it.

The statue of Mary is framed by marble columns. She appears with a baby boy in her arms, and she's crushing a serpent underfoot. She stands on an orb representing planet Earth; the serpent is trapped between this and her foot. The orb, in turn, half protrudes from a stream of molten lava that threatens to spill over the edges of the frame. Yet it doesn't. It's as though Mary, via the weight of her immaculate foot, immobilizes the serpent and at the same time turns everything around her to stone, thereby stemming the evil that wants to devour the world.

That image gave me strength, but at the same time it troubled me. The thought I had was this: What happens if Mary lifts her foot?

I forgot about the man. I lowered my head, said a prayer under my breath, and started to cry.

As for the man I had seen, who turned out to be named Bogdan, I saw him again a fortnight later, again inside the Church of Saint-Sulpice. Later on I found out that, while I had been going back there evening after evening hoping to catch sight of him once more, he'd been going to different churches. Churches, as I would also find out, were one of his two great passions. The other one being zombies. Everything to do with zombies.

In the churches, Bogdan confessed. He wasn't a Catholic, and though he felt guilt for certain things in his life, it didn't weigh that heavily on him. He was Romanian but had lived much of his life in West Germany. With the fall of the Berlin Wall and the breakup of the Soviet bloc, he went back to Romania and there became a pioneer in the world of financial services. He made a lot of money, and three children and two grandchildren arrived along the way. He'd put off enjoying his success and made many sacrifices, and just when it was coming time to retire, time for him to enjoy his life alongside his beloved wife, she died.

Now, more than a year after her death, he felt it was his duty to try to be happy, and that he had a license to do whatever he wanted.

As well as Romanian, Bogdan knew English, Russian, and German. But he'd always wanted to learn French, hence his decision to spend a year in Paris. He was taking an online course and, after every lesson, would go out and try to practice. The issue, unforeseen by him—it's something no language institute or embassy will ever tell you—was the reticence of the Parisians.

And that was the challenge he had been facing when, visiting one of the city's many churches one day, he happened upon the solution. Stepping inside the confessional was the perfect opportunity to practice his French, given the fact that the priest had no choice but to listen to him. And, unlike psychotherapy, it was free.

Now that they had gotten to know him, his confessors had even started correcting his vocab and pronunciation.

"And I've improved quite a lot," Bogdan said. "You should try it someday."

We were having our first beer together in the Café de la Mairie, across from Place Saint-Sulpice.

So as not to raise suspicions, Bogdan avoided going to the same church more than once a fortnight. He told each of the priests a different story. Or, rather, variations on or offshoots from one single ongoing story. To avoid confusion, he had a notebook to which he consigned what he said each time, along with the basic coordinates: priest's name, church, time of confession, and penance.

"And where do you get your stories from?" I asked.

"From my novels," he said.

In this new life of his, Bogdan had decided to fulfill another of his ambitions: to become a writer. The novels, or what he understood as such, would be based on his own life. An anodyne existence interrupted, when least expected, by something staggering: a zombie attack.

"Obviously, I never talk about zombies when I'm confessing. But I do manage to get across the sense that my life's in danger. And so I've also come to see that this is precisely what a good novel is: a zombie attack always being imminent, but never actually happening."

At that moment, Bogdan was working on a novel set in present-day Paris, which had its customary joie de vivre on show but was also riddled with the fear of terrorism. More than ever, this was a Paris under the long shadow of the city's first bishop, Saint Denis, whom Bogdan furthermore considered the first zombie of the Christian era.

I don't know whether Bogdan finished his novel. In fact, I don't know for certain that he ever wrote a single page of it. But he did show me the stained-glass window in Saint-Sulpice's with the terrible image of the decapitated saint hugging his own head to his chest. On another occasion, he showed me the inlaid statue at Notre-Dame Cathedral that repeats the same motif, as well as the one in Suzanne Buisson. I went with him to Rue de Mont-Cenis and walked the three miles that, according to legend, Saint Denis walked holding his severed, bleeding head in his hands, before collapsing in the place where they would go on to build the great basilica that now bears his name. And where, additionally, the remains of all the French monarchs are buried, from Clovis I to Louis XVI and Marie Antoinette, the two last true monarchs of France, who—as I ought to know very well, Bogdan said—were also beheaded.

Bogdan's explorations weren't limited to Paris. He went to see churches in all corners of France. I was never asked to join him. He'd sometimes take off with no notice for two days or an entire week at a time.

I would become desperate.

To begin with, as a way to calm myself down or simply to fill the time, I gave his advice a go. I went to Saint-Sulpice's, and to Saint-Séverin's as well, and confessed. I adapted the story of Sommerville and Burroughs: Bogdan was a Moroccan poet and recovering alcoholic; I, on the other hand, remained a Latin American computer scientist working in linguistics. Instead of the infamous Dreamachine, he and I were working together on the "Kremlin-Bicêtre project." When I tried to explain how the software worked, the priests started looking at me like I was from outer space. And at that point I dropped the whole masquerade.

Mme. Rachou unwittingly gave me the name for the project. It was a day when the urges to start shouting were very strong. I remembered the underground mantra, *parlez vos voisin,* and went and knocked on her door. Mme. Rachou, as well as being my landlady, also lived right next door.

"Oh, yes," she said when I brought up the subject. "We have a long history of mad people in France."

I'd told her how struck I was by the number of disturbed people in the city. And particularly on the metro.

Apropos of that, she explained the story of the name, or at least part of the name, of the neighborhood we were in. If you went up Avenue Général Leclerc you came to the Bicêtre Hospital, one of the oldest and most historically significant *asiles des aliénés,* which at other times had been a prison—it was there that Louis XVI said that the vagabonds and mendicants of Paris ought to be locked up.

"And what about the 'Kremlin' part?" I said.

"Oh . . . *je sais pas,*" she said.

The information I've just given is provided on a panel outside the hospital, alongside a map of the building. However, the fact I found most striking was the following: it had been there, in Bicêtre, on April 17, 1792, that the guillotine was first trialed.

I immediately thought about what Bogdan would say when I told him this new fact I'd learned. Then his continual rebuffs came to mind, and I decided I wouldn't tell him anything.

That which I spitefully kept to myself in his absence, later evaporated completely. My interest in Paris's psychiatric hospitals was the only proof of an incipient interior life that, the moment he came calling, I instantly forsook.

That life, nonetheless, gradually came to transform my doctoral mission.

One morning I found a book entitled *Le Kremlin-Bicêtre: Identité d'une ville,* by M. L. Fernández, in the university library. Its author explains the origins of that *ville's* name by first explaining that the Bicêtre Hospital harked back, via some mangled pronunciation, to the Bishop of Winchester Jean de Pontoise, who had been awarded the land in that area in 1286. The "Kremlin" part, on the other hand, was part of a great business strategy. In 1812, on the return of Napoleon's devastated army after the Russia campaign, large numbers of the veterans took refuge in the hospital. As a way of attracting this clientele, a local tavern owner with a nose for business had the idea of opening a bar named Au Sergent du Kremlin, and in time, with the bar's rise in popularity, the name ended up extending to that whole outlying area of the city.

Other pieces of information emerged over the course of those months. Connections that would briefly illuminate a system of signs otherwise enveloped in fog.

The problem was Bogdan.

But what interest could that presentiment of mine hold when Bogdan showed up at my apartment and, without so much as asking if I wanted to, took me salsa dancing in a place overlooking the Seine on the Quai Saint-Bernard? How was I going to solve the algorithm France had become if he, after we'd been dancing, asked me up to the terrace of the Arab World Institute for a drink, thereby, with that view over Paris in the spring, deactivating all my fears?

Then, one day in May, Bogdan announced that he was leaving. He wanted to spend a couple of months looking at churches in the north of France, and from there move on to Belgium.

I didn't want to say goodbye. Nor did he insist. I shut myself in my apartment and cried for a week. Then I came back to earth. I felt completely empty, ready to think.

Mme. Rachou thought I'd been away on a trip.

"You look very pale, young man. Are you feeling okay?"

"Yes, Mme. Rachou. Nothing to worry about."

"Your friend, the Russian, left this," she said, handing me a package. Opening it, I recognized the squat book. It turned out to be a copy of *The Hunchback of Notre-Dame*.

"He isn't Russian," I said.

Mme. Rachou's answer pulled the rug from under me completely:

"Of course he's Russian." She smiled as though to forgive my naïveté.

I took the book with me to the university that day.

He hadn't written any dedication. There were only some underlined phrases in the introduction relating to Gothic architecture in churches and the many restorations undergone by Notre-Dame.

What did it all mean? Maybe he'd known from the beginning about my following him? What had Mme. Rachou meant by her answer?

I started to investigate. I soon established some of the historical context, which at the same time would help my argument should anyone ever decide to put any money behind the project. As I continued to read around, I was able to home in on what I was really trying to find—for example, when I came across talk of the Saint-Rémy-lès-Chevreuse psychiatric hospital, which had wings for mentally ill people set out according to the revolutionary calendar, I knew I was starting to see what was really in play here.

When I read the news about the attack in Nice, during the Bastille Day celebrations, Bogdan immediately came to mind. I don't know why, given he'd said he was heading north, not south. I spent a number of days poring over everything that emerged to do with the attack: articles, reports, videos, the statements of the people who had been present.

Before July was out, there was the attack on the Church of Saint-Étienne-du-Rouvray. I had hardly so much as read the headline and I already knew, this time beyond question, that Bogdan was involved. Not only because that church was in northern France, or because of the two terrorists' horrifying decision to slit the priest's throat, but because of the two nuns and two parishioners who had been inside the church at the time and were taken hostage. One parishioner was French, and the other was Russian.

There were no photos of the sacrifice that took place, nor did the names of the hostages who had witnessed it appear. But such proof was beside the point. Now all I wanted to know was Bogdan's connection to everything that was going on. Did the attacks have anything to do with him? Or was it all confirmation that, in spite of his hoax confessions, he was actually in danger? Or, the strangest possibility of all, had Bogdan worked out some way of anticipating the attacks? His confessions, the supposed zombie attacks—were these not coded references to terrorist activities?

Anxiety began to boil up inside me, and this time it seemed like the lava would overflow. But then I remembered that I had the book.

I went and found it and started going through it again.

Something told me to check that Bogdan hadn't hidden a piece of paper somewhere between its pages. Doing this, I happened upon a number of paragraphs he'd underlined in the lengthy notes section contained in that edition. Specifically, the second and fifth notes to page 68, which, following on from the also-lengthy introduction, corresponded with the second page of chapter 1.

These two notes made reference to the *fête des fous*, or Feast of Fools, a remnant of the Roman Saturnalian festival celebrated by the clergy during the Middle Ages. The activities that made up this carnival, in which a false bishop, archbishop, and even pope (*un pape des fous*) would be elected, were taken on by the wider populace, and in particular young *écoliers*, leading on several occasions to brawls and disturbances, imprisonments, and the whole event's being outlawed.

The notes also mentioned a book called *Histoire et recherches des antiquités de la ville de Paris*, by Henri Sauval, which Victor Hugo himself had made liberal use of in the construction of his cathedral.

The interesting part, at least for Bogdan, who made a note in the margin, wasn't only the evident relationship between these "clerics" (in the medieval sense of the word, as revived by Julien Benda in his famous book) and the makers of the Enlightenment encyclopedias, but also the fact that Hugo's and Sauval's dates didn't match up.

Sauval had the feast happening on the day after Twelfth Night: January 7, that is. Whereas Hugo had the two celebrations on the same date: January 6—the day the novel begins. Was Twelfth Night, associated in continental Europe primarily with the Three Kings, the *same* as the Feast of Fools? Did this constitute backhanded criticism of the Restoration? Veiled support for the Revolution of 1830, which was already beginning to raise its head and in fact exploded into life on July 27, only two days after Hugo started work the novel?

I initially took the comparison to be Hugo's way of casting

aspersions on the monarchy. But, looking at it again, a more profound interpretation was suggested: when the powerful have their feasts, it's just mad people and abject drunks having a high time. What else could Bogdan have meant by the emphasis he'd placed on Louis XVI and Marie Antoinette's having been France's "last true monarchs"? Wasn't this ultimately the same mistrust as Hugo's for any form of "restoration"?

There were too many questions. So many, in fact, that I only managed to work out—through an instinct I'd thought completely extinguished in myself—where the answers were certain not to be. And that was in the outward, surface-level Paris, lovely to a fault, where the calculated staying power of its architecture has combined with the tourism industry to turn the past into a single, undifferentiated weft.

It was in the subterranean city that I would have to go looking for Bogdan.

I've learned a great many surprising things, living in the Paris metro these years. The first being that the Kremlin-Bicêtre project was already a reality a long time ago. Some of my companions, when they're in high spirits, or rather when the booze takes them to the brink of delirium, go so far as to say that it's always existed. Under other names, and taking different routes, but always coming out in this place that is both origin and spillway.

The second is that Parisians, to a one, confess. You only need to look at them from the platform, going around in those glass-sided booths, so reticent, so unforthcoming, while at the same time saying—shouting, at times—so much.

The third is that Russian is a beautiful language, which when mixed together with French, alcohol, and the cold, becomes something prophetic.

What we have done down here is to prefigure that which, sooner or later, will end up happening up above. The victory of the Front National, for example, was predicted by one of the Saint-Lazare station's cells (which is one of the oldest), long before Le Pen Sr. came on the scene.

France's imploding is another recurrent topic of conversation, one that only we—Russians or French, it doesn't matter anymore—link back to its original cause: the nostalgia we felt for our fleeting empires (and even the Revolution), and for the hell we failed to unleash. The older guys always end up telling the stories of the disaster that was the Russia campaign. The incomprehensible loss of life that seemed to punish, rather than to reward, the advance. The promise of entering Moscow, only to find the city absurdly empty, razed to the ground by the Russian army itself.

We are the only ones capable of understanding that a young French person has it within them to point a machine gun at their classmates, or at the people in the café where their parents used to go, and, with a cry of "Allah is great" or "Death to all immigrants," open fire. It's in those moments that we accept the truth of the matter: other people ought to be apprised of these things. Which means that the project, and completing it with somebody from outside, remains as pressing as ever.

I nonetheless feel that I am the only one who understands the true importance of the interface. I am occasionally surprised to find myself sitting alone in the Kremlin Tavern, at the table at the back, arguing. But it doesn't stop me.

This is the reason I still go out.

I go to Saint-Sulpice's to look at Mary's immaculate foot and see how long we have left.

Then I get on one of the metro trains, taking up position between the confessionals. If someone is careless enough to come and sit next to me, I start picking my nose. And if not, I just read the writing on the doors, the seat backs, and the walls, looking for the hidden truths, just as the saints, the mad people, and the lovers of Paris do.

Shelby Kinney-Lang

Snake & Submarine

Not long ago, a friend in California—call her Esmé—
became severely ill with a rare and rapidly progressing
cancer, and has been posting updates about her condition on a
medical blog, which appears on my Facebook feed. In an entry
from last month, she describes all the ways in which she has been
saved: she is saved in Christ, of course, but also, and she doesn't
mean to sound trite to list this second after Christ, saved by Britney Spears's fourth album, *In the Zone,* which she played on repeat
when she was a freshman in high school and estranged from God,
uncertain if her travails, which at the time felt monumental, were
possible to surmount; she was saved by Glenn Gould, and by
Degrassi, and by Richard Fleischer's *Fantastic Voyage,* in which a
submarine crew is shrunk infinitesimally and sent into a scientist's
dying body; I pay particular attention when she says Tolstoy has
saved her, that writing can save, or she hopes that it can, because
this is how I know her, from a class in college in which we read
Tolstoy in translation and often spent long Massachusetts afternoons talking with excitement about *Anna Karenina.* I am not
sure, I tell my wife, while we walk along a dirt road in the Berk-
shires adjacent to our home, what it means to be saved by Glenn

Gould or Britney or Tolstoy, if Esmé means *ars longa, vita brevis,* or if she means that from a distance some spiritual part of her has been redeemed because of these essentially faithless works, or something else entirely, something that may or may not correspond with an immaterial soul—which was always a disagreement between us during our Tolstoy conversations, that she believed such a thing existed and I did not.

So as a kind of test, as an act of, I don't know, saving her, preserving what I know about her on the page—aware that I can't save anyone, that a man setting out to save a woman is a tired trope—I begin to write about a character I name Jolie, a composite, and after a few pages, if I squint, I can see in Jolie a number of people from my past, one of whom is Esmé, this particular friend who wonders about the saving power of writing, hairless from chemo, twenty pounds lighter, or so the pictures she posts to Facebook show, her figure hollowed to a Munchian scream, except, could it be, Esmé is smiling, she's filled with joy, or affects joy, even lying in a hospital bed with a nasogastric tube taped to the front of her pale face and playing Pokémon, reverting to a childhood diversion at what is possibly the end of her twenty-nine years of life. She reflects in her medical blog how she spends some of what might be her last moments on earth choosing to capture and instruct virtual creatures, which as a father-to-be I read as her displaced longing to parent a child she will likely never have. She describes how she visited an OB-GYN specialist to have an ovary laparoscopically removed; it was subsequently sliced into strips that still have viable eggs, each strip of which was preserved indefinitely in liquid nitrogen. The doctors do not know to what extent the chemo and radiation will impact future fertility, Esmé writes, but she and her husband plan to try to conceive when her cancer journey, as she calls it, concludes.

I continue to write about Jolie, thinking about Esmé, when after a few more pages I notice that Jolie resembles someone I once knew, in fact they share the same body, a girl I met in León when we were both nineteen, walking the Camino de Santiago after I renounced my Evangelical faith (and all faith), and this American girl, whose name was M, who wanted to be a wildland firefighter, described with the strange specificity of a mind that had the capacity to write fiction how she'd one day own a submarine she'd navigate through dark waters. M was a devout but liberal Catholic, so that the arguments that engaged us on those belly-long summer days walking across the golden plains of Spain were among the most intellectually difficult of my life. I cannot imagine, in retrospect, anything of what we discussed was particularly well-informed, having read nearly nothing at that point in my life save for a little Camus and Fanon, which was enough to convince me of what I had secretly begun to suspect in the preceding years, that there was no God, that existence indeed preceded essence. I can still see M clearly, the honey-colored nape of her neck when her hair was up in a bun; her defined shoulders moving beneath a Gore-Tex hiking shirt in the moments before she hefted up her heavy backpack; the peculiar, lovely geometries of her face, dark chestnut eyes, oblong dimple in her right cheek. Something about the Camino drained us of all sexual tension; our bodies became merely bodies, and if we should see each other in various states of undress, as we did each morning and evening we walked together, there was nothing about a glimpse of flesh, no matter how evocative in other contexts, that we found very interesting. We parted in Santiago de Compostela—I continued to Finisterre, the end of the earth, and watched the sun set over the Atlantic— having walked nearly three hundred kilometers together, having slept by each other, above or below in bunks, napping off the path side by side in the shade of a chestnut or eucalyptus tree, stinking and bloody-footed, promising to exchange emails, though of course we never did.

We met again by chance, this woman M who happens to have Jolie's body, in a small college town in Western Massachusetts four years later. By then M had married and divorced, had come home to her parents' house on Crescent Street, twenty-three years old, because she did not want to live in a city across the country with an evil ex-husband. She drifted through the streets of her hometown, unable to figure out what it was that she wanted to do with the rest of her life—not return to graduate school, she was at least sure of that—and then she came across me by the brick-stove bakery, seemed overjoyed to see me. We walked together for quite some time, until M said God was no longer with her, by which she meant there was no God. She told me this that first day, as if conceding a point in an argument we had been having those last four years. We were standing by then outside her large Victorian home with its single dark blue tower, which I recalled, speaking to her that fall day a few weeks before she disappeared again, was the wood-floored turret in which she had grown up, where in spring every morning soft sun fell on her face from a slatted skylight, where she stayed up some nights reading Augustine and Saint Thomas Aquinas, and where she had learned to kiss boys. For those three weeks before M drove to Montana, maybe, or Idaho, some place like that, the sugar maples and oaks shaking off red and yellow leaves, she invited me over to her house every day. I met her father, a hirsute man who was active in the local farmers market, and her mother, a professor of religious studies at the college. M was the youngest of five siblings, all the rest of whom were dispersed across the nation. We were changed, the attraction that four years prior did not exist now seized us animally, having multiplied in that time, so that we each experienced a kind of hunger in the presence of the other, a body-flush brought on by proximity, even though I secretly could not fathom what she saw in me, especially because she was newly faithless, still racked with guilt whenever we were together. She told me so right away, as if all that time I had been encouraging her to atheism for this precise reason. We would climb up to her turret every night, spend long hours together, from which vantage I noticed at sunset the windows darken with a clotting-blood color like the background of a Munch painting, then reverse themselves each morning.

So after writing a number of pages, I knew that this is what

Jolie looked like, this and a few other people from my past arising in her.

Jolie woke one day with cramps, a pain she thought at first was menstrual, but as the cramps grew in intensity, as she worked that morning and into the afternoon stocking groceries at Trader Joe's, as the April day lengthened and then contracted again, and she returned to the apartment she shared with her boyfriend, the pain became the horizon of Jolie's mind. She did not understand yet the extent of her illness because she had not yet gone to the hospital. She had a particular type of pride, so that in the last few days, as her abdomen grew tender, as she became more and more nauseous, she decided it was an early period, the stress of too much work. She thought even now that she needn't go in, that she might tough it out, whatever *it* was, even though that day had become a kind of hell. After all, with what money would she pay the ER bill? The pain was a creature, an active, pulsing pain that slithered around in her abdomen, maybe menstrual, maybe not, and left her shivering and disoriented. Pretty soon she found herself curled on the couch hours before her boyfriend was due home, trying not to think.

Her boyfriend was named Finley—they were still unmarried after six years—and he was easily startled by the slightest movement in the Southern Californian brush whenever they went hiking on dirt paths in a nearby canyon. Grass and stalks of flowers had shot up in a superbloom, the dirt path walled in like a hedge maze. His nerves were alert whenever he hiked; he was sure that lurking in the thickets were coyotes, cougars, and above all, worst of all, snakes. A slight rustle in the bush would send him leaping back, or trotting ahead, though it was always only a bird, or the wind, and never, though they'd lived in Irvine for four years, a snake.

When he found Jolie coiled on the couch that evening, returning from his internship at a law firm at which he'd been placed by his law school, he felt the same sense of dread that overcame him in the canyon, of snakes bellying in the underbrush.

He went to her and kneeled and she told him what she was feeling, her face pale and sweaty, shivering from the pain beneath the fleece blanket she'd pulled up to her neck. She'd spent the last few hours on her phone, watching videos of car crashes with the sound off, makeup tutorials, reading articles about celebrities, determined not to check her symptoms online, which is what Finley would have done straightaway.

"We're taking you in," he said, trying but failing to conceal concern he'd hoped to conceal by uttering received language that he realized only after he said it was a phrase most often associated with detectives, and not paramedics.

On the drive, the highway was, as Jolie's boss would say, a parking lot. For the longest time, perhaps because she was from Montana, she thought this was a metaphor her boss used simply because he was a manager at Trader Joe's, an expert as it were in parking lots, but eventually realized, provincial girl she was, that in fact it was a common saying. They braked and drifted forward and braked again, the evening light movie-scenic orange.

Without asking, Finley called Jolie's mother, a nurse, whose voice came in over the speakers in a loud "Hello?" Jolie had been too disoriented by pain, too seized by the taillights on the freeway, to notice what he was doing before her mother's voice sounded suddenly over the car's speaker. Her mother was one of the reasons Jolie habitually avoided doctor's visits, that and because her insurance was no good. Unless there was a broken bone, or a serious fever, her mother insisted (when Jolie was still a child) that Jolie was fine, that the fever or rash would resolve on its own.

"Hi, Mom!" Finley said, a grating appellation Jolie had asked him many times not to use. Finley described Jolie's situation. The traffic picked up a little, so that they could accelerate for a few hundred yards, but then the pace slowed again, the visual din of red brake lights flashing in direct correspondence to the slithering pain, light and pain bleeding together, until the exit for the hospital came into view. They'd only gone a couple miles down the highway, but it had taken twenty-five minutes.

"Does she have a fever?" Jolie's mother asked.

He spoke while Jolie listened. She began to understand that maybe there was something seriously wrong.

As if to hedge against the wrongness of her condition, Jolie interrupted and said, "I'm fine, Mom. It's just pain."

What Jolie's mother said next was the same thing M's mother told me during dinner one evening in those three weeks when I stopped by to visit, when we would eat food prepared by M's father, elaborate salads with farmers market fare, or baked squash, or thick lentil soup, and talk delicately around national politics, never about religion, even though M's mother said grace every evening. They might play a record during dinner, not choral music, though I don't recall what. On this night, they were talking, in an almost indecipherable familial shorthand, about M's ex-husband and the conditions of her leaving. Her mother had been so looking forward to the possibility of M's bearing children—children like many of her siblings already had.

"But then that thing happened," M's mother said.

"Mom, stop."

"I didn't like what you did."

"Not for you to say."

I felt stupid, listening, decoding, and realizing for the first time that there might have been, from what I understood about the content of their shorthand, a pregnancy, a source of pain and conflict between M and her ex-husband (and now M's mother). M's father, with a glint of sauce on his brown beard, looked down at the beef lasagna he'd made, while M's mother stared hard across the table at her.

"The body is an altar," M's mother and now Jolie's mother over the car's speaker said, maybe at the same moment, though for different reasons, in different worlds, an idea I think, but I don't know how, will help preserve the life of Esmé, who is possibly dying in California, the condition worsening. "The body is an altar."

At the end of each blog post, Esmé gives a thanksgiving to God. There is not merely or only despair in her recounting of the many medical procedures she undergoes: that she cannot eat solid foods because of a new tumor in her intestines that grew rapidly in the outpatient days between doses of chemo; that she vomited when they put in the NG tube, clogging it; that her skin is rashing all over her bald head, which once grew thick, dark hair; nor of course is there only joy in her posts, though sometimes she affects joy, or perhaps truly feels it, I can't tell: that she has seen this or that friend, that so-and-so has dropped by with a Game Boy loaded with Pokémon, that the oncologist stayed after her shift to pray with her. What is striking is the way in which hope and despair face each other in equal measure, mediated through the grace of God. She says that she is saved, but practices mindfulness anyway with a cancer group in order to be in the here and now. Like M, Esmé very well might have been a writer, only she's interested in other things. At the bottom of the page, after she has signaled that she is loved by God and loves Him in return, there is a button the reader can press to donate money for her medical expenses, which, though she does not explicitly address them, are suggested to be enormous.

The body is an altar. Jolie did not fully understand what this meant, would turn it around in her mind in the weeks and months that followed: the CT scan, the biopsy of her ovary, the surgeries, the chemotherapy. Finley followed along skittishly, but with increasing resolve. It turned out the pain was a blessing in disguise, gallstones that were easily removed, and without which the cancer would likely not have been discovered until it was too late to effectively treat. They'd caught it early, in other words, the doctor said, standing with his notebook like a detective, as if ovarian cancer were a burglar who'd just broken into her home but hadn't had time to take anything too precious before he was caught.

But of course, Jolie thought, there was something precious taken—one ovary, the other possibly out of commission after chemo. There was a way, however, the doctor told her, to potentially preserve fertility. So the ovary was laparoscopically removed and subsequently sliced into strips of viable eggs, each strip of which would be preserved indefinitely in liquid nitrogen. She found herself, at twenty-nine, without her left ovary and fallopian tube, in and out of the hospital, growing thinner and paler, hairless, looking at herself every now and again in the mirror and seeing looking back that figure in *The Scream*.

The body is an altar, or maybe her mother had said the body is an alter, as in alteration, as in altered, her body is being altered, will be altered, all bodies in motion are altered without end, amen. Upon her body, there will be sacrifice, or the sacrifice is the body itself.

Jolie asked Finley one day months later what he remembered about their initial car ride to the hospital, if he remembered saying, so cheerfully, "Hi, Mom!" But he did not, and also did not recall Jolie's mother saying anything about being altered because he was too busy looking out for giant slithering snakes on the evening highway parking lot, those creatures coming with bared fangs to swallow whole him and his soon-to-be fiancée—he proposed before surgery. Esmé describes a procedure on Maundy Thursday in which a medical sheet was drawn across her naked body, like a cloth pulled over an altar (I realize now), the same position in which Jolie had lain for the initial biopsy, blue sheet over torso—but what sort of altar? What could M's mother possibly have been trying to achieve, if M in fact had had an abortion, saying something like that, "The body is an altar," with me at the dinner table?

M had stopped eating, maybe the record scratched, and she said she was quite done with this conversation, though she would not later disclose what it all had meant, instead describing the incredible pressure of the deep ocean, increasing the lower you journey. I felt hopelessly lost, not unlike how I sometimes felt during our conversations on the Camino, when it seemed better I should concede that not only did God exist, but also that I had an immaterial soul that would persist eternally after my body decomposed.

The Maundy Thursday procedure ended with a consultation with a palliative care specialist, a woman in her thirties who had come to know Esmé fairly well, better, in all likelihood, than I have ever known her. Esmé reports on her medical blog being struck by the fact that the palliative care specialist squeezed one socked, unwashed foot at the end of the visit; she is unable to resist reading the symbolism of this gesture, does not know how this will all end, she writes, but knows she is already saved—which perhaps, though maybe I'm cynical, reveals her fear of the opposite, that there is no saving, no salvation, no persistence—filled by God's love.

There was a risk Jolie's cancer would return, a suggestion that conception would prove difficult, and prohibitively expensive. And it was expensive, when she and Finley decided to try, borrowing against Finley's future (he was already awash in debt) for the technical procedures that would require a mixture of animal passion and medical knowledge. Noncancerous tissue and eggs from the ovary that had been removed were now replanted near her belly button, near skin scarred from the original surgery, so in the months after, there would be two raised pink lines on her left lower abdomen, like a bite from a snake.

But before all that, there was an altar, a wedding at a ranch in the canyon in which Jolie and Finley sometimes hiked, where Esmé was married in California. Finley's father made the altar himself, flew out from Massachusetts, screwed trellises into wooden crates weighed down by bags of sand, and threaded flowers and gauze through the trellis holes. In the background, the sun-bleached hills, gold with cholla. Jolie had grown enough hair for a dollop of shampoo, wore a simple strapless satin wedding gown showcasing the honey nape of her neck, so that all of her friends said she looked good, not only because she was a bride ("the bride" they continued to say), but because she no longer looked sickly, dying, like she had looked for over a year.

M emailed me not long ago, surfacing from the deep blue, to say she hoped I had found peace, whatever that meant, a correspondence that happened to arrive the same week that Esmé died. My wife found me crying at the computer, reading the last blog Esmé wrote. In it she arranges her prayers alongside her daily mindfulnesses, to be in the here and now, one mantra of which is what Jolie repeated to herself the night she was married, mindful of the inhalation of breath, mindful of her recovering body dancing with Finley on the parquet floor in the three-walled barn; she had not died, had tasted death and then whirled away. Say this is the best I can see for Esmé, what I hope, what you might call a saving prayer, that she is whirling through the barn like Jolie, still alive right now.

Jacob M'hango

The Mother

THE WORLD HAS A SOUL, and it speaks in mysterious ways, or so Sepo had learned from Tombi, who, in that village far away, had amassed a large following—of mostly women—who'd attended all of her weekly meetings down by the stream, who'd spread word of her to the neighboring villages, and who'd heeded all of her divinations without question, because they'd *truly* believed her a genuine prophetess.

It was in that village that Tombi had defied all patriarchy and tradition, and there, the tale of Tombi and Sepo will be told, and retold, for generations to come.

But, perhaps we should start at the beginning.

The village elders said that all of nature existed as one, and had only one purpose: to ensure its own survival. They read the signs and found correlations between the seen and the unseen. On the day she was born, they asserted that Tombi's arrival had cast ripples through the spiritual realm, and they said:

Tombi did not cry at all, not like other infants. This is a sign.

Though the ground beneath the village shook, she entered the world on her feet. This is a sign.

And, *That girl looked at our faces as if she'd seen us all someplace before.*

This is a sign.

Sepo was born two years later. When she'd first become conscious of herself and her surroundings, she'd found it hard to believe that the famed Tombi was her *sister*. The way people fawned and flung themselves at her feet like that, it seemed much too overbearing, but Tombi didn't seem to mind. This was all she'd ever known.

In the years that followed, however, her sister would come to yearn for an average childhood; to roam free as other children roamed, and play silly games with her friends, just as Sepo did. But, their parents had strictly forbidden her from mingling with other children—not until the arrival of her first blood—and so, Tombi spent her days sitting quietly in the shade of the mango tree outside their house, watching her sister and her friends play games like Kamgolobi and Gonje.

Sometimes they would play Sipoti-Sipoti—if the boys were around—but Sepo had once told her that most of the boys were bad mannered and lewd, and that she much preferred to avoid them altogether. She said that Danga (the boy with the big teeth resting on his lower lip) and Chipaso (the boy who spoke with a lisp) were the worst of the lot. Danga, she said, would often pull his ujeni out of his shorts and dangle it in a girl's face, and Chipaso didn't know how to keep his filthy hands away from their breasts.

And Tombi privately wondered to herself what she would have done, if she were the one whose breasts had been so unwelcomely fondled.

Sepo knew that her sister wanted nothing more than to be an ordinary child—to be free—and her own enjoyment of such was never without some small guilt.

Sometimes, when she and her friends were out playing their games between the mud houses of the village, she would think of Tombi at home, and picture her with her oblong face and her kind brown eyes, just sitting there on a reed mat in the shade in front of their house, and when the day of Tombi's first blood finally arrived, Sepo was almost as happy about it as she was.

For the very first time, her sister was allowed to leave home, and make friends, and actually join in on their games, and when she did, there never seemed to be anything so *special* about her at all. She had no impressive abilities and, in fact, lost at pretty much every single game, every single time.

She was also prone to injuries, and when she got hurt and bled, she bled just the same as all the other girls.

And she said it made her feel like she finally belonged somewhere.

Their parents, however, along with the village elders, still seemed bent on denying her any semblance of a normal life.

People told her that she was *very* important, or that she was the reincarnation of some powerful ancestor who'd returned to save the world. She was told that she was different, and she had only to patiently wait upon the gods to deliver her true calling.

Above all, they said it had been a *grave* mistake to have allowed her to leave the house in the first place.

And so, to keep the peace, she bid her fleeting freedom a reluctant farewell and resigned herself to staying at home, and alone, for the rest of her life.

When Aunt Malambo—her mother's thickset elder sister—visited from the city and suggested that Tombi spend some time away from the village, their parents would initially hear nothing of it.

She reasoned exhaustively, however, that it could *only* benefit

Tombi to see the world, and learn about the ways of other people, and then continued to reason thusly for a long time, until finally, it was decided that if Tombi should leave, then Sepo should leave with her.

The sisters soon learned that all the stories they'd heard told around the village, about the *grandeur* of Aunt Malambo's big city home, didn't quite equal the reality of what they'd found waiting for them. They'd journeyed right through the city—until they'd left all those tall, shiny buildings and fancy city cars far behind—and even further still, until the very tar road beneath them began to steadily narrow and thin and vanish altogether, and then arrived, at last, in a place where all the houses appeared to be slumped over in disrepair.

Huddled, Sepo thought, the way she and her friends would huddle together whenever something had frightened them.

The difference between this place and the village, however, was that while the houses in the village had thatch over them, and there was far more space to play in, the houses here were cramped, tin roofed, and appeared about as stable as chickens standing in the rain; as if they could fall over at any moment.

But it was to be their home, and despite all appearances, they'd found their stay at Aunt Malambo's house to be most welcoming, if not enlightening.

During their visit, Tombi and Sepo witnessed the type of unimaginable dramas they'd never seen play out in the village. Every now and then they'd see some young man sprinting by with a bloodthirsty crowd of stone-throwing, chain-wielding, plank-bearing men giving chase, shouting, *Kawalala!* And sometimes they'd see a naked woman running by with the mob at her heels, shouting, *Hule!* and incensed women would cry, *Go find your own husband!*

Regardless, the change of pace and scenery turned out to be just what Tombi had needed to truly break out of her cocoon. Cheelo—the soon-to-wed last-born daughter of Aunt Malambo and her equally loving husband, Uncle Lukosha—was their only cousin still living at home. Sepo watched real joy thrum to life in her sister, as Cheelo introduced them to all of her friends in the neighborhood.

And then, of course, she introduced them to that young man, Mbwete.

Now, you may be wondering how it all turned out the way it did.

While Mbwete, himself, would prove entirely unimportant, what followed would never have come to pass, had he only just decided to mind his own business.

Court was in session. The headman cleared his throat loudly and motioned for the crowd to simmer down.

With a drooping head and palms squeezed together between her knees, Tombi cut a miserable, slouching figure on the central reed mat. Her yellow-dotted green chitenge dress came all the way down to the ankles, but still, she felt naked. Though her gaze was lowered, she could still see everybody around her; note their exact positions, their movements, feel their eyes upon her, and all the hatred she felt in their staring cut deep into her heart.

Sepo, dark circles beneath her eyes, was seated with the other women to her right. Her sister looked exhausted, almost dried out, thought Tombi, and imagined she'd rustle like autumn leaves in the hug she so yearned to give her.

Tombi is a witch, they said.

She is trying to destroy our way of life; she's been struck with madness by the gods!

And, *She must not spend another day in this village.*

The men to her left, in particular, had made no effort to hide their desire to see her punished. They wanted her banished. They leveled accusation after accusation at her, stripping her of every bit of dignity. And when she said nothing, when she responded to their direct questioning with only silence, the headman—to vigorous nods of agreement—labeled her as insolent and disrespectful.

The women to her right were no less unforgiving. There was something piercing about the way they looked at her. Even those who'd initially come to her defense—saying that she still deserved respect, no matter what—now wanted her gone, and they called her a *witch* in hushed tones, and championed her doom.

Confined to her little reed mat, trapped between masculine ire to her left and feminine loathing to her right, she could feel the fury and the disgust coming together, swirling all around, united against her.

Tombi kept her head bowed down, eyes upon her lap, and waited.

The headman swatted a large, black fly from his furrowed brow—furrows deeper than those she'd seen plowed into the village maize fields—and then nodded his bearded, meaty head toward a raised hand in the crowd. A Rubenesque young woman with tousled hair, from her seated position, lowered her arm and announced:

She said it herself, that she had stopped the rain. I was there when she said it. She also said that she had driven the fish away from our side of the river. She said it was to teach us a lesson!

The woman turned to look directly at her.

Tombi, did you not say it?

A wave of murmurs swept through the crowd, astonished faces darting from one to the other. The headman swatted the stubborn fly from his too big, stubby nose and glared at her.

Her silence was met with even louder murmuring, demanding to hear her speak, asking each other what had become of this once shy and respectful woman before them.

The headman lifted his face with a grunt of displeasure and nodded toward another raised hand to Tombi's left. An elderly man with thick eyebrows struggled to his feet and said:

Should we even be listening to her? She has grown a following that is splitting loyalties in this village, even in this chiefdom. They think she is a prophetess, but it is nothing but witchcraft! And a witch is no prophetess!

He clapped his hands at Tombi, barely able to contain his magma, and added:

Now this! This is why we encourage young men to marry from our stock. We have many ripe young women in this village, so it is beyond me why Mbwete—in spite of his upbringing—chose to ignore this village and all the other villages in our chiefdom, and bring from the city a woman whose upbringing we know nothing about.

At the mention of his name, Tombi finally lifted her gaze.

She turned her head slowly to the left.

And looked directly at Mbwete.

Who shifted uneasily on his stool.

The soft-spoken, unassuming young man—who'd spent only a year living with his parents in the city—had all of his offers for Tombi's hand obstinately rebuffed by Aunt Malambo and Uncle Lukosha.

And so, she and Mbwete simply eloped to his village.

And Sepo, of course, had followed.

There was little doubt that he'd truly loved her, at least, in the beginning.

But after three years had gone by without any sign of pregnancy, a salvo of emasculating talk had finally worn him down. So, he put thatch on new walls. He'd taken a new wife—Tina—only three months ago, and her belly was already swelling. An otherwise svelte young woman with braided hair, she was seated right now beside her own sister, Sepo, and hadn't removed her glare for an instant. Of all the women present at the trial, the loathing burned deepest in Tina's heart. Tombi could feel it. The way Tina looked at her felt as if she had the ability to see right into a person.

Perhaps she'd seen into Mbwete, too. Perhaps she'd read that empty place in his heart; his desire for a second wife. A *childbearing* wife.

All she had to do was show up.

And on the score of her masquerading as a prophetess, continued the old man. *This village, like all the other villages, has one true prophetess as chosen by the gods, and stationed in the chief's village. Our gods have not chosen this woman. Therefore, the only way to restore order in this village is to banish her!*

He retook his seat, all bristle and brimstone, to a roar of forceful nodding.

The headman looked around pensively. He looked over one shoulder toward his statuesque kapasos, standing at attention behind him, and then over the other. The chief had offered assurance that the prophetess, of whom the man had spoken, would be attending the trial to play her part. But she had not yet arrived.

The headman slapped himself hard against his sweaty cheek in a renewed effort to get at the fly, and then turned back to the court.

Ambuya Nkumbu's hand dropped at his irritable nod. She said:

I am very happy that, so far, we are in agreement over what to do about this young woman. I admit that I was one of those who stood in support of her when Mbwete brought her to this village. I do not speak for her now.

Tombi said nothing. She remained unmoving, and indeed, unmoved.

The gray-haired woman continued:

I was born here. I've grown up here. Not even once have the gods tried to change our way of life. As women, we have always collected and prepared poison for our men to use, for catching fish. But the river that has always sustained us is drying up, and has no fish, and we are now starving because of this young woman.

Ambuya Nkumbu splayed her gnarled hands and stretched her spindly fingers, as if spreading seeds of approval over the other women.

And all because we have refused to change our way of life? Tombi doesn't want us to use the poison, but how many fish would our men catch, to feed this village, if they used only hooks? How much more would we have for our headman, to pay tribute to the chief, if we did not use the poison? Don't bother answering me. I just want you to think about it.

Next, the overconfident Kalasa—the thirtyish-year-old man with large, uneven teeth—stood promptly and said loudly:

What I especially don't agree with is that we should stop our charcoal business. We are only using the resources our gods have given us. How unwise it would be to die of thirst when our legs are in water! Even the gods themselves would laugh at us.

A murmur of agreement ripped through the court.

He continued, *It is not like the village sees no benefit from this enterprise. We burn the trees, package and sell charcoal for the benefit of our families. There are also people at the market whose lives depend on our supply of charcoal. What would become of them if we heeded this woman's rambling?*

The sun beat down upon the thatch roof above their heads. Every now and then, a breeze blew through and cooled the sweat trickling down the back of Tombi's neck, and her heart tom-tommed like a drum in her chest, drying out her throat, making her feel drenched and parched at the same time. This thing should have been over by now.

Tombi has also strongly condemned our chitemene farming system. What she refuses to understand is that when we clear new land, we burn those trees and the ash acts as fertilizer in those new fields. It is not because we cut trees that we don't have rain; we don't have rain because of this witch! She has bewitched the sky, and so has she the forest, that it will not yield food for our sustenance. This witch must not spend another day in this village!

Kalasa lowered himself onto his stool to another energetic murmur of agreement.

The paunchy headman stroked his beard. He made as if to speak, lips parting, pushing his tongue forward, but before he could, Tombi rose suddenly to her feet to the collective gasp of the court.

She could bear it no longer. The time had come for her to speak.

I am the Mother! said Tombi in a resonant voice, both gentle and powerful—like the mellifluous rush of many waters—and swept her gaze from person to person. Their eyes darted away, as if trying to escape from their sockets.

The headman cleared his throat three times, pushed himself up by the armrests, and bellowed, *It is against tradition for a woman to stand in court, or to speak without permission. You are no one's mother, woman! Sit down! You have no authority here!*

I have authority everywhere, replied Tombi, matter-of-factly.

A hush settled over the court. She looked straight into the headman's big bulging red eyes without blinking and, without a word, he retook his seat. The crowd reeled as if a shock wave had moved through them, stunned at what was unfurling before their eyes, but not a single person dared utter a word.

I am the Mother, the Benevolent, she continued, and turned to each person present as she spoke. *I give life and sustenance to all of creation.*

I am the Mother, the Omnipotent. You see my power when I shake the ground, when I raze your houses, and when I flood your fields.

I am the Mother, the Omniscient. I have set laws and timings in place, to mark when the seasons start and when they end; to determine when day replaces night, when youth gives way to old age, when life succumbs to death, when you bleed, and when you don't.

I am the Mother, the All-Loving. I nourish all of creation with my love. I let it fall like rain, choosing not who, or what, to refresh. I am love itself.

I am the Mother, the All-Seeing. I blaze my eye at you and your activities by day, and I twinkle my many eyes at you and your activities by night. I was before you were, and I will be long after your fleeting lives have ended and your skulls have become soil.

I am the Mother. I am you. You are me. I am everything. And everything is me. You are not the only dominant species to be contained inside of me. There were others before you. And if you don't stop hurting me, there will be others after you.

The beleaguered headman, whose back hadn't once touched the high backrest, lumbered to his feet off the edge of his seat.

Enough! I will listen no more to the ravings of this madwoman!

He looked around the court, and then fixed his eyes on Tombi and proclaimed, *In the name of the gods, whom you have gravely disrespected, I hereby banish you from this land! Now, woman, will you leave peacefully?*

Her answer, by way of staring directly at him, and then quietly shaking her head from side to side in the negative, fueled a fresh surge of gobsmacked whispering through the court of onlookers.

The fuming headman, visibly ruffled by her continued defiance, said:

Then we will reconvene here tomorrow with the prophetess, for your incontestable sentencing.

Tombi and Sepo watched the sun complete the final quarter of its daily lap. It became a big red ball, as it began to disappear behind the hill that always cast a shadow upon the drying stream; the same shadow that would then spread across the bushveld and enfold the village, enabling them to see the stars and the moon as if they were on a dark, domelike canvas.

They sat on the mat outside Tombi's hut. Silence filled the space between them. And then Sepo finally spoke.

Tombi, what you did today was strange. How is it that you can appear so weak, yet so strong?

Her sister turned to look at her.

The prophetess wasn't there today, she continued. *Do you think she will come tomorrow, to serve the final banishment on behalf of the chief?*

No.

Will there be rain and food for these people, if they completely refuse to listen to you?

No.

Is there any hope at all?

Tombi smiled, only slightly, and then turned away.

Yes.

You know, it's a pity that I wasn't allowed to speak, as family. It would have been better if some of your followers had come to speak for you.

Silence.

Are we leaving this place tomorrow?

Silence.

Tombi didn't say a word. She kept her eyes up, and watched the stars.

Sepo woke with a start in the dead of night to the sound of many passing feet hitting the ground in front of her hut. She threw away the blanket, came out from under the mosquito net, pulled on a chitenge, and tiptoed to the door.

By the time she'd opened the latch, the *hiss* and *whoosh* of the roaring fire had permeated the air. Once she was outside, none of the village folk—who'd now trooped out of their homes to watch—needed to tell her that it was Tombi's hut that was on fire.

Her screams—*I'm burning! I'm burning! Please help me!*—pierced the quiet of the night.

Sepo had slumped to her knees, paralyzed and wailing, before she'd even realized it. Nobody rushed toward the burning hut; they all just stood and watched on, as the hungry flames brightened the sky in total discount of the stars and the moon, devouring the thatch and the poles.

When, finally, the entire roof fell in with a burst of glowing embers, it marked both the crescendo, and muting, of Tombi's bloodcurdling cries.

Through her tears, Sepo could see many of the villagers who had been in attendance during the trial that day. Among them stood Mbwete, holding Tina's braided head to his chest, arms around each other's waists, and watching. Just like all the others, they watched it happen without trying to help, and said that it was the will of the gods. That the witch had gone too far, and witches got what witches deserved.

As the wattle and daub of her sister's hut began to come apart and burn away, so, too, did the villagers begin to disperse. Sepo, alone on her knees, watched all the doors to the nearby huts begin to close, watched all the lights go out, one by one.

Before long, only a smoking ruin remained.

And silence.

Sepo sat there in the gathering darkness until she could weep no more. Staring at the ground, she had picked apart the varied shapes of harried footprints in the moonlight, leading away from Tombi's smoldering hut.

The footprints of the displeased gods, who had run away, after torching her sister's hut and securing the door shut with a chain.

Alone in her bed, Sepo wondered what she was going to tell her parents. What would she say to Aunt Malambo and Uncle Lukosha? How was she to tell them that the gods had burned Tombi alive in her hut, to cleanse the village of witchcraft? She shuddered at what was to follow at dawn. The men would retrieve Tombi's charred body from the ashes at sunrise, the prophetess would pronounce a curse upon her soul and ask the gods to keep her in darkness. Her body would be spat on, and buried far away at a secret place in the forest, and nobody would be allowed to openly mourn her.

How would she say these things? And would the gods, or the villagers, even permit her to return home?

At that very moment, a steady wind pummeled into the door and the light of the kerosene lamp flickered wildly. She turned and found the latch undone—she must have forgotten to close it properly—and the door slightly opened.

She got up, and was about to shut it when the door suddenly swung all the way in. Sepo fell backward in surprise and looked up.

Stand up, said a voice from the darkness. *Quickly, get dressed.*

Sepo lay there sprawled upon the ground, petrified and blinking stupidly.

Hurry, pack your things.

With trembling hands, she got up, and did as instructed.

And before she left, she took the kerosene lamp and hurled it into the wall.

As Sepo marched down the footpath in the dreamlike semi-dark of the night, balancing the ukwa bag on her head with her hands, she listened to the steady footfalls of the shadowy figure in front of her, and kept pace.

The sputtering and spluttering in the distance behind them merged with the trill of the crickets in the surrounding underbrush. Sepo paused on the footpath to gaze back across her shoulder, and admire the way the roaring blaze licked at the sky above the village.

She imagined Tina's head resting on Mbwete's chest, her skinny arms wrapped tight around his waist, and all the others looking on, and all of them thinking that it must have just been in the family.

She also considered the confusion of the gods, let alone that of the village folk, when, at sunrise, they'd find no bodies to desecrate.

She lingered, staring for a while longer.

Come on, said Tombi, coming back up the path toward her. *Let's keep walking.*

'Pemi Aguda

The Hollow

THE HOUSE IS UGLY, Arit decides when the taxi drops her off in front of her new assignment: too many roofs clambering over each other like crowded teeth, and flaking walls the pink of a tongue. She shrugs her tote bag higher and knocks on a gate so black she checks her knuckles for soot. A young boy, maybe fifteen or sixteen, opens to the sound.

She is from the architecture firm, she explains, here to measure for the renovations, and is Madam Oni available?

He waves her in. Madam Oni isn't home, but Arit can proceed with her tasks. His name is Lucky, and he is happy to help if she needs more hands.

She nods, and he retreats to the backyard, leaving her alone. She scratches at the inside of a wrist.

Arit faces the house, and the house faces her. She loosens another shirt button. Even the breeze is balmy, a warm exhalation. She crosses the compound, surveying, analyzing. An overgrown garden a strange tint of green and a gaping carport with no cars, gravel that scatters under her tennis shoes and fences that loom too high, lean too close to the two-level building. Her brain is already simmering with solutions, although she will not design this remodel. She is new at the firm, one year out of university, which means she will be doing the grunt work—measuring, measuring, measuring—until she earns trust. She slings the office camera around her neck, clips the measuring tape at her waist.

What is a house? What do we want from it? What makes it beautiful? Arit's uncle, the man who wooed her to architecture, told her that only when she could answer these questions for herself and for her client should she take pencil to paper. The front door opens at her touch, and she enters, looking.

A long time ago, there was a woman who lived elsewhere in the city. What is a house—this woman wondered, as her husband dragged her body, like a mop, over faded terrazzo floors—but a pressure cooker, a vent pipe screaming steam?

Arit starts by re-creating the ground-floor plan on paper. Her strokes are precise and sure. Little arcs for doorways, short slashes lancing them. Two lines for a wall, another between for a window. There is power in drawing a line into existence, and Arit is deliberate with it, careful.

The interior is cool, and as she moves from room to room, extending her diagram, the sweat on her skin evaporates, leaving a chill. It is a still, contained coolness, one that smells of air that is trapped, waiting. She can neither hear nor see an air conditioner. She pushes curtains apart. The light seems to hesitate at first, but then it floods in, glancing off the surfaces, filling the spaces, revealing the house to her.

Arit believes that buildings are among the most objective expressions of history. She notes the carpet—gray, vaporous—paws it with a foot to confirm its solidity. The walls: stucco on concrete, a beige that hides dust. She places a palm flat against a wall—the texture tickles. Her hand comes away moist. The curtains: brown, patterned, the kind that were ever present in Nigerian movies of the nineties. The windows live in recesses: narrow, arched, paired up. Furniture is standard family fare: two sofas, two armchairs, one coffee table. There are no paintings, no photographs.

The logic of the layout is lost to her. She turns a bend, expecting to find a room, but no, it is another lonesome nook hosting two cloudy windows. That explains all the roofs. She retraces her steps, and here she is in a guest room, sheets taut on a double bed. Back she goes, and she is in the kitchen now, long and slim with dull-green tiles. The counters are black marble with whorls of white, coiling smoke in a dark night.

Tired, she leans against the sink and looks out to a gnarled backyard—high grass and naked trees. Her drawings make no sense. The walls do not meet on the page, the lines dangle and hang. The house resists containment.

"Well, what do you think of this house of mine?" Madam Oni asks, materializing just inside the back door, a bag of vegetables in hand. Arit reels. The woman has asked her question with urgency or annoyance, as if for the fourth time. Her hair is graying and cut close to her scalp. Her skin is dark, shining, smooth, save for a forehead that furrows and cheeks that sag. Her eyes are narrow, ellipses of bright white punctuating her face. Somewhere in her fifties or sixties, not much taller than five feet.

"I am confused," Arit says, honesty overwhelming professionalism.

Madam Oni snaps, "What were you expecting? Something straightforward?" Arit has no answer. "Can you fix it?" Madam Oni's voice has softened, almost beseeching. "Can you fix it?"

A professor once said that a successful renovation must allow the legacy of the original to shimmer through, to carry forward; and Arit is wary of the hardness of the word "fix," the incisions of the x. She shakes her head. "That's above my pay grade, ma. I'm just here to measure for the as-built drawings. My supervisors will then discuss any solutions with you."

Madam Oni lifts the bag to the counter, turning her back. "Can I have the kitchen for thirty minutes? Lucky, the gate boy, can help." Her tone is cool again. Arit is dismissed.

"From the relics of household stuff," Honoré de Balzac wrote, "we can imagine its owners in their habitat as they lived"; but as Arit glances at her watch, she sees that three hours of her life have evaporated in this house, and all she can imagine is that no one could live here. She senses an absence, an omission—familiar somehow. Madam Oni, too, seems exhausted, shoulders hunched, head hanging. Arit apologizes and brushes past her client to work outside.

What is a house?

During the evenings Arit's parents worked at their struggling supermarket, her uncle would watch her, and his favorite bonding activity was an architecture lesson. A roof? Floors? Walls? Arit would venture, always logical. But every answer she gave was wrong. No, he would say, try again.

The woman who lived in a pressure cooker had married a man who waited to reveal the evil festering in his guts. It oozed forth after a few years of marriage, in the form of mistresses, gifts bought for them with the woman's money, as fists to her cheekbones, a foot in her belly, full pots of soup flung at walls, okra sliding down like tears, doors locking her out after trips to the market, doors splintered in the middle of the night.

This woman had a son, and as she stowed him away in cupboards to save him from his father's cruelty, under beds, behind chairs, she wondered, what is a house but a large handbag with many hidden zippers and pockets?

Arit's classmates hadn't understood why her ambitions didn't transcend houses. As they aspired to design government buildings and malls and banks and museums and memorials and schools and hotels, cantilevered inventions of steel, muted cubes of concrete, sloping façades of timber, otherworldly curves of glass fiber, Arit had drawn houses: floor plans, exterior elevations, mechanical, electrical, plumbing. She didn't care about schools of style, she cared about unity, about a calming cohesion. She sketched on the blank pages of her novels, between chapters, her dreams filled with sectional 1:20 door and roof details.

The house is the square root of all architecture, her uncle told her. But Arit told peers that her obsession was more about growing up in flats with no storage and shoddy workmanship, with damp windowsills that sprouted mushrooms, with wall edges that left scratches. She quoted their oldest lecturer back to them—over time, bad environments can induce bad mental health—and they accepted her explanation as truth, though she wouldn't meet their eyes. They identified with it.

From the outside, Madam Oni's house is comprehensible. With Lucky eagerly holding one end of the measuring tape, Arit's site plan and perimeter measurements come together in little more than an hour. She looks up at the house again. The pointed arches of the windows would be better suited to a church, a sanctuary, a building that evil skirts around, passes over.

On the inside, Madam Oni has disappeared, and Arit's calculations still don't add up. She checks and rechecks lengths and widths and heights and never gets the same reading twice. The tape retracts into itself and bites her fingers, again and again. This uncertainty, this shiftiness, this impossibility, causes a ringing in her head. Unmoored, dizzy, she feels as if the walls are the floor and she is leaning against the ceiling, her torso wedged into a window frame. A fear clunks up her ribs, puncturing her breaths, a fear that nothing is real and everything is upside down and elementally wrong. She turns into another lonely corner, seeking a way out, and the sun is streaming through two slender panes, lighting up the carpet, a holy burning.

What does it mean for a house to be fixed? Arit wonders. *To make firm, stable, or stationary // to repair // to set in order or in*

good condition // to put in a position to make no further trouble //
to get even with or revenge upon // to kill, harden, and preserve for
microscopic study . . .

Madam Oni reappears and guides Arit to a chair, a warm hand
on her elbow. They take a few steps, or they cross through several
rooms. The woman pushes a plate of Cabin biscuits and a cup of
warm Milo to her. Arit, who associates these with her childhood
and rain, looks out to see that, yes, it is indeed raining, and she
blinks repeatedly, reminding herself that she is not fourteen and
she is an adult and she is safe.

The woman who lived in the large handbag with many pockets
made a plan. She sold aso-ebi from a tiny shop in Balogun Market,
saving all the profits, every tip. She sold zobo at church events and
ofada rice at community gatherings, the sun darkening her skin,
firewood smoke staining her lungs. She opened a bank account,
hid the multiplying money from her husband, whose character
grew weaker, and the power in his swings, in his words, stronger.

She bought land in a part of Lagos that wouldn't become popular for another eighteen years, a part she had to access by foot
because the closest bus stop was twenty minutes away. She hired
an eager draftsman who advertised his services in colorful letters
under bridges, in scratches on the battered hoods of danfos. And
when it was time to build, she oversaw the project herself, breathing her fear into the foundation, sweating her resolve into the concrete walls. She rinsed herself at the site so her husband wouldn't
smell new beginnings on her. "Soon, no more," she chanted in her
head every night he added a scar to her skin, every night she added
a terrified scream to her son's memory.

When the last shingle was nailed to the roof, the woman put
her son on her back and left, taking nothing else. That first night,
they slept on the bare floor, burrowing into each other. A house is
freedom, a house is an escape. This one sensed their dread, their

relief, and stood vigilant, ready to protect. How can you know a house if you don't sleep in it? Some say that light is the success of any building, but what new angles might darkness reveal?

That last night, Arit's uncle took the pencil from her hand, shading the windows on the front elevation dark, shuttering the paper house they'd designed together. "It's nighttime for our inhabitants," he intoned in a cartoony voice, and Arit laughed, enjoying this effort of imagination, the breadth of it.

When she wakes in Madam Oni's house, it is still raining and—according to her watch—well past midnight. She is lying on the couch, warm and protected in its embrace. The half-drunk cup of Milo is on the low table before her, biscuit crumbs glittering on the plate. Madam Oni is asleep in an armchair, her head nestled on her shoulder. Even in sleep, her eyebrows are pinched—anxious, guarded. The only light in the room is from the outside lamps, glowing up the thundering rain, turning the water to sparks.

This is unprofessional, Arit thinks, staying so late in a client's house. Why didn't the woman rouse her, ask her to leave? She wonders if she should be afraid of Madam Oni, but decides no. Her skin doesn't prickle; she senses no terror.

She stands to find a bathroom and shuffles around until she is guided to the foot of the stairs. Though she technically has permission to access the entirety of the house, to complete her measurements, she hesitates. Because the sleeping woman is unable to stop her, Arit feels she's crossing a boundary. But then she notices her left wrist, jittering against her thigh. She climbs.

Nothing creaks as she moves through Madam Oni's house, nothing betrays her; and in this silence, her attention returns to her wrist, to the pulse ticktocking under thin skin. No door opens to a bathroom. Instead, she finds two small bedrooms, one with slippers peeking from beneath a wardrobe, the other with no furniture but an old-fashioned stool, its three legs carved of a rough wood. At the end of a hallway, past an empty lounge, is what must be the master bedroom: a king-size bed, a mattress with no sheets.

As she steps in, the stillness intensifies, breaks across her face like cobwebs. Not a serene calmness, but a muzzled nothingness. Like a familiar hand across a mouth. The woman who lived in the house of freedom was found by her husband. On that lot so far away from everything, he climbed the gate, breaching the perimeter, cutting his shin, trailing blood across the compound. He broke a lock, nothing but death swelling in his chest, coating his throat.

The house bristled defensively around the sleeping mother and son, inhaling and exhaling, and the man felt the draft on his neck, on the meat of his hand gripping the knife. He moved from room to room, hunting, but every turn took him back to where he began. The walls shifted, the floors wavered—he was bewildered. Each door led to a hallway that led to a dead end, the sharp arches of glass twinkling at him, promising pain. Exhausted and dizzy, he leaned into a corner, seeking an anchor, protection—though from what, he didn't know. He felt a loss of control. The house balked at his weight, at his entitlement to support. It closed on him, deviating and rearranging itself until a hollow appeared, between walls, between floors, between worlds, and there the intruder was folded in, trapped, never to hurt again.

A house can be a prison, too.

When the woman woke, she sensed what had happened to her hunting husband. She picked up the knife. The house seemed different around her, heavier. She flung open the windows and kissed her son, who stilled within her embrace, transfixed by the bloodstained floor.

She carried him to the kitchen with a new lightness in her heart, which she imbued into fluffy balls of akara, the aroma of frying beans shaking her son loose. They ate together, the deep freezer their table, and spoke of flimsy things, laughing and licking salty oil off their fingers, never once looking over their shoulders.

. . .

Arit's uncle shuttered the windows of the paper building that night, then let the yellow pencil go. He pushed the cup of warm Milo to her side. What happens in a house stays in it, he told her, his fingers circling her left wrist—her drawing hand. What happens in the dark must never see the light. His voice had dropped the jokey register, cloaking her protests. His hairy hands traced further, sketching patterns on her skin she would never forget. Architecture is about negotiating borders, he whispered.

She was fourteen.

The woman and her son lived in peace in that house that was also a prison, in the certainty that they were safe and secure. The boy grew into a man. He married a short dash of a girl with shiny, dark skin and full, sagging cheeks. The new wife added her laughter to the house. Her songs rose like incense to the rafters.

When the woman lay dying, she pulled her son's wife close, and with breath that smelled of wilting vegetables, she whispered the story of the house that had protected her. The wife smiled at her mother-in-law's deathbed gibberish and patted her old, scarred hand and forgot.

She painted the house a baby pink, softening it, hoping for children to fill its spaces. She cultivated a garden. Her husband knelt beside her in the damp soil, and they planted tomatoes and aloe vera and lemongrass. She made him elaborate meals, and he wrote her elaborate letters. They made love in every room.

But the years introduced a sourness to their marriage. Her husband changed. He came home from his bank job frustrated—by customers who screamed and a woman supervisor who always demanded more and colleagues who didn't respect him—and he took these frustrations out on his wife.

The house stirred from slumber, moved in righteous anger—

because hadn't it protected this man when he was only a scared boy?

Waking to behold the rooms shuffled around her, the wife finally remembered her mother-in-law's story and knew her husband was gone. Her knees framed the new bulge in her stomach, and she cried with sadness and relief and indignation and gratitude.

Madam Oni switches on the light in the master bedroom. "What you will find here," she says to the frozen Arit, "is a big, fat nothing."

That night, late, after her uncle had gone, Arit took an eraser in her left hand to the house they'd drawn together. Friction, friction, until the paper wore thin, until the shreds were indistinguishable from the rubber shavings, until her wrist ached where his fingers had circled first.

The wife was pregnant and alone, and she wailed and wept. The house watched, absorbing her tears, moisture beading on its walls, refracting the morning light.

The wife left the house with the taps running and the drains stopped, but she returned to dry floors. She threw rocks at the windows, but the cracks thinned and vanished before she could turn away.

"I didn't ask for your help," she screamed at the ceiling. But when a bowl of blended peppers slipped from her hands and crashed to the floor in bloodlike splatters, she fell to her knees with a towel and wiped and wiped and wiped.

. . .

The following day, Arit's parents sat her in their cluttered living room, her feet almost touching theirs on the threadbare rug. Outside, it rained. She wouldn't look up, afraid of what they might see in her eyes.

"Your uncle is dead," they told her, then broke down weeping. "We know this is hard for you—your favorite uncle." And they reached for her and embraced her, mistaking their own tears for hers.

"How?" Arit asked.

His house, her parents explained, it had just folded, collapsed. Late in the night. He was inside.

The wife lived in the house her mother-in-law had built. Mother and child, healthy and happy. She seemed to forgive the house its action, and the house slipped into hibernation, content with this truce. The wife focused on her son, who grew tall and lithe. She kissed his forehead, broad like his father's, and pinched his cheeks, full to dropping like hers.

Years passed. The boy loved his mother. On his way home from school, he brought her gifts of plantain chips and kuli-kuli. He joined her in the kitchen, slicing yams and whisking eggs. When her lower back ached, he trod lightly on her, to massage the knots from her muscles, both of them sure that he would know when to step off, that he would mind the line between pressure and pain. She smiled at him, adjusting her depth of field so that he was her center, her star, and the house and what it held dissolved into a background blur.

Arit's uncle had taught her that architecture is the material realization of a vision. Why wouldn't it work the other way, too?

. . .

So one afternoon, as the wife walked past the closed door of her son's room and his too-young girlfriend said, "I'm not ready, stop, I'm not ready," she quickened her pace, pretending not to hear. But a house can't make such a choice. The boy was gone in the morning.

The wife took a hammer to a wall, wailing again, "Give him back," making no dent. Because he was just a boy, her boy, and she'd expected he'd have time to learn, to unlearn.

Arit no longer draws houses with her left hand. Instead, she uses her right. And she hopes that if she respects the power in a line, and is deliberate with it, and careful, she can atone.

Always logical, Arit.

The woman remained in the house, seeking hints of her son in the skirting, in the junctions between walls and ceilings, in the dust patterns on windowsills, in the shaped shadows on floors.

The house gave her nothing.

And she responded in kind: she stopped painting; she stopped all maintenance.

Still, the house stood strong, stubborn in its principles, in the duty breathed into its foundations so many years before by the woman who needed it, and refused to crumble around the woman who resented it.

There is no gray zone with a house, it is all definite lines. How else could it stand?

What is a house?

As Madam Oni finishes the story of the house, Arit looks out to see the sun coming up. The rain has stopped. "I woke one morning, and I was tired of searching for my son," Madam Oni says, breaking the silence. "Every angle in every room, every window placement, is a reaction to my son, to my husband, to my father-in-law. I'm living in that reaction, haunted by it. And I need this house to be fixed, so I can forget."

"There is no fixing," Arit says. An itch blooms angrily on her wrist, and she scratches. Friction, friction. "It doesn't work. No fixing, no forgetting."

Madam Oni shakes her head, rejecting Arit's conclusion. She presses her hand over Arit's, stopping it. "I can't believe that. I have to try. *We* have to try. Please."

Downstairs, a sustained sound, like the ringing of a tin cup, a cry in its hollow.

What does justice cost? What are clean hands left to carry?

Arit disentangles herself from Madam Oni and walks to the narrow windows. The new morning colors bleed into being. There is no fixing. A collapsed house cannot un-collapse. Rubble is also an objective expression of history. But Arit won't be its warden. She won't be stuck.

Soon, Arit will walk out of this house and never return. She will pick up a pencil with her left hand and sketch something light, something abstract. She is tired of paying, of carrying.

A house is a pot, a house is a bag, a house is a prison, a house is a supplication, a house is a justification, a house is a child on your back, weighing you down. A house is a house, and you can erase it, wreck it, tear it to the ground. A house is a house, and no, you can never forget, but you can walk away.

Cristina Rivera Garza

Translated from the Spanish by
Francisca González-Arias

Dream Man

Strange things always happened to him with her, but
what surprised him most was the way in which he would stop
loving her for long periods, sometimes for whole years. During
that time his lack of love would become an almost natural discipline: he'd walk unhurried, play with his son in the morning, read
the newspapers, work, or chat with friends in trendy restaurants,
both complain about, and enjoy, life. At those times, Fuensanta,
his wife, would smile more and sleep better. Whenever she came
upon him unawares on the balcony, leaning on the iron railing
with his gaze lost in the treetops, she didn't ask him, "What are
you thinking about, Álvaro?" Instead, she'd run her hand over
his shoulder and move away, sure of herself, without suspecting
anything. But then, without any obvious reason, it would happen once more: he loved her again. At times the emotion was
provoked by the smell that wafted from the bakery on certain July
afternoons. Sometimes everything began to happen again because,
by chance, someone said words that he had heard only on her lips.
Solanum tuberosum. At other times, he'd receive messages, brief
notes written on onionskin paper or monosyllabic telegrams that
fluttered onto his desk weightlessly like the swaying of a dry leaf.
They were the signs of her proximity.

At those moments he studied his own life, and with unpremeditated urgency he'd appeal to grandmothers and aunts in search of information. He wasn't completely sure of what he was looking for, but he couldn't rest until he found it. And so, between mugs of hot chocolate and sweet rolls, or in the middle of big family meals that took place over long wooden tables, he'd listen once again to stories of his childhood with feigned inattentiveness. He had been a happy child. Born in the month of April in the bosom of a stable family, he had never wanted for anything. He had had more than enough light, nourishment, pampering, bedtime stories, and the affectionate pats with which anyone awakened by a nightmare is lulled back to sleep. His needs had not been excessive and for that reason he developed an even and placid temperament, given to good company and easy laughter. Since he was the youngest of three children and the only boy, he soon became his mother's and father's favorite, although for different reasons. His early years transpired without mishap among loving relatives, vacations at the seaside, and books. Right between dessert and coffee, but still under the influence of those stories, he verified once more what he already knew: there was no pathology in his life that could have led him to her. No trauma or complex predisposed him to seek her presence.

But that was not what he felt the first time he loved her. It happened in the winter, during one of the most pleasant periods of his life. He had finished his university degree in engineering and had married a woman with gentle manners and a true gaze. Still childless, the newlyweds spent time enjoying their bodies in different landscapes. They liked to travel. Sometimes they would opt for grand voyages across continents while other times they'd take short weekend getaways to neighboring cities. They'd go to Cholula, Cuernavaca, or Tepoztlán, guided by strong intuitions rather than specific plans. On those occasions they drove carefully, listened to music by dead composers, and admired the mountainsides monosyllabically. One of those trips took them to Toluca, a high-altitude city whose greatest charm was the cold. There they stayed in a small, graceless hotel and a little before nightfall, instead of having a bite to eat and going to bed, they decided to put on their coats and take a walk under the arcades of the city hall. The cold made them quicken their pace and lock arms energetically.

"My bones ache," said Fuensanta, rubbing her hands, "I'd rather go back."

"I'll go with you," Álvaro hastened to reply.

"But this is what you came for, Álvaro, to walk in the cold." Fuensanta reminded him of his wish and pushed him toward the sidewalk, urging him on.

Still undecided whether to let her return to the unfamiliar hotel or continue his walk in the wind, he saw her recede little by little until she disappeared around a corner. The cold, which had the virtue of putting him in a good mood, made him react with unaccustomed energy. He turned, lengthened his stride, and more rapidly than usual he crossed the downtown area without paying too much attention to the few nocturnal passersby or the buildings characteristic of a drab, and perhaps too new, city. Spurred on by the gusts of wind that were coming from the snow-covered Nevado de Toluca volcano, Álvaro left the downtown area and penetrated the steep and asymmetrical streets that came and went without warning. Soon he didn't have the slightest idea where he was, but instead of worrying him, the disorientation and the cold sharpened his senses: he was as awake as he had ever been, and for that reason content. It was while in that state of physical and mental alertness that Álvaro saw her for the first time.

It was already past ten when he began to feel tired. As fatigue overcame more and more of his body, he paid greater attention to his surroundings. There were squat shabby houses with big iron gates, fried-food stands where people milled around the fire, pharmacies, neon signs, stairs. Trying to get his bearings, he came closer to a lamppost but the light disappeared as soon as he reached it. At that moment he became aware of the danger. He was in an unknown neighborhood in a strange city late at night. In addition, it was cold; a sharp, overwhelming, pitiless cold. He turned in every direction trying to find a taxi but the street was deserted. Desperate, he approached a couple of nocturnal pedestrians to ask them the fastest way to reach the city center, but neither of the two looked him in the eyes, and they passed by his side without saying a word. Still excited by the cold, but beginning to feel afraid, Álvaro went up a steep slope until, breathless, he was forced to stop and vomit because of the effort. He was bending down in front of a small window when he heard moans: it was the faint sound of two people who had just made love. Then, forgetting his situation, he peeked in between the slats of the blinds and observed them. A half-dressed man and woman were still intertwined. The weak light of the lamp and the purplish brocade of the sofa lent the scene the patina of an almost unbearably remote past. There were numerous golden statuettes on rectangular tables as well as oil paintings with thick wooden frames hanging on the white walls.

While the man hurriedly zipped up his pants and knotted his tie in front of an oval mirror, the woman lay immobile on the sofa. Perhaps she was waiting for something: a word or a caress. But nothing came. From under a dress of sky-blue silk emerged a long white leg ending in a high-heeled shoe of the same pastel tone. Then, as if she had sensed his presence, the woman let her head fall back over one of the edges of the sofa, and stared directly at the minuscule orifice of the window. Irregular bangs flowed over her temples, crowning a pair of big translucent eyes. Álvaro was sure he had been seen and ran away. Once again with labored breath he reached what seemed to be an expressway, and there he stopped the first taxi he saw.

"I'm going downtown," he said, "to the Guardiola Hotel."

The taxi driver gazed at him in the rearview mirror with a look of complicity but didn't ask any questions. Then he lit a cigarette and turned up the radio. Conchita Velázquez's most famous song filled Álvaro with melancholy. The lyrics reminded him of the scene he had just witnessed, and he imagined that the couple in the old house had made love *as if tonight were the last night*. An air of uselessness, an aura of lost time, an echo of urgency hovered over them. When he finally arrived at the hotel, Álvaro paid and, upon opening the door, was surprised by the cold once again.

"But it's so cold," he said, more to himself than to the taxi driver.

"Well, what do you expect, it's midnight at the end of November," answered the man without taking the cigarette out of his mouth.

At that moment he thought of the absurd garb of the woman on the sofa: a sky-blue silk dress on a winter's night, a dress with narrow straps in a place like Toluca, the city with the highest elevation in the entire country. Then he turned up his coat collar and crossed the street.

Fuensanta was asleep, and she did not wake when he slowly settled himself under the covers. He tried to get closer to glean some heat from her but restrained himself since his hands and feet were like chunks of ice and he didn't want to disturb her.

Immobile, with his eyes open in the darkness, Álvaro waited a long time for a warmth that did not come. Then he heard the staccato of high heels on the floor tiles in the hallway, and without knowing why, he hugged Fuensanta as if she were his salvation.

"It's nothing," he whispered in his wife's ear when she opened her eyes.

"Did you finish what you had to do?" she asked with a sleepy smile on her lips before shutting her eyes again.

Despite the innocence of the question, Fuensanta's words put him on the defensive. What was it that he "had to do"? Trying to find the answer, he fell asleep.

The morning light forced him to change his position on the bed several times, until, fed up with the sun's relentless pursuit, he decided to get up when there was no longer any shade under which to find refuge. Grudgingly, he opened his eyes, and the empty room overwhelmed him. Fuensanta was no longer under the blankets or any other place. He was going to call her when he saw the note on top of the bureau. *I'm going for a walk and then I'll have lunch in the hotel dining room. Meet me there a little before twelve. Kisses, Fuensanta.* The little hands on the clock indicated that it was still possible for him to get there on time. He had a quick bath and put on some faded jeans and a plaid shirt. The image he saw in the mirror was that of a normal man. All around the room were big clean windows through which the clear and sharp light of the highlands penetrated. Álvaro searched for Fuensanta's face among the diners, and when he saw her half-watermelon smile he realized that she wasn't alone.

Fuensanta was sharing a light lunch with another woman. "Look, Álvaro, this is Irena," said Fuensanta as soon as she saw him.

There was an excitement in her voice like that of someone who has found a treasure or the correct name of a street in a city without street signs. The stranger raised her face and Álvaro was unable to pronounce a single word. Mute, immobile, afraid of being exposed, he could barely manage to look at her. She no longer wore the absurd silk dress but a pair of brown corduroy overalls over a white T-shirt that made her seem much younger. Chestnut-colored bangs covered her forehead and framed the same big, sad eyes that he had seen the night before. Her ponytail and a simple amethyst necklace gave her the look of an old child. When Álvaro finally shook her hand, the noon light sparkled on feminine skin.

"Pleased to meet you," said Irena.

Her voice was exactly as he had imagined it: soft but deep, as if it emerged from moist zones below the stomach. In his confusion, Álvaro forgot that he was hungry.

"Álvaro, Irena knows this region very well," announced Fuensanta euphorically. "She's gathering wild plants from the foothills of the volcano, isn't that so, Irena? And she wouldn't mind if we accompany her today."

"Unless, of course, you'd rather just stay in the city and peep around the area."

Irena's words seemed transparent, but Álvaro knew immediately that they weren't. He had no doubt that she had seen him. *Peep*. He had been found out. But she wouldn't tell on him. That seemed to be the deal. Álvaro agreed to go up the mountain almost immediately: he had no other choice.

"It's getting a little late, but we still have a few hours of broad daylight left."

Irena guided them through narrow streets until they reached a cherry-colored pickup truck. When the door was opened a cloud of dust made him cough. There were rusted tools on the floor, maps, compasses on the worn seats, and dirty napkins. Álvaro settled himself into the back as best he could, and Fuensanta became copilot.

"And these bags?" asked Álvaro, pointing to a pair of knapsacks full of cans and other tinned foods.

"It's my sustenance for this month," Irena explained, without letting up driving at what seemed an excessive speed. "I have a cabin near Raíces. I spend almost all my time there, especially during the winter harvesting season. I don't come down to the city very often," she muttered between her teeth, looking at him in the rearview mirror.

"How interesting," said Álvaro, listening to her as one does to a liar.

The landscape distracted him. Light fell tenuous and sharp on the cornfields. In the distance the horizon was almost blue, and like the high sky, unreachable. Farther away, the volcano awaited them, fearless, secure, eternal. There was something threatening in the snow that covered it.

"It must be terribly cold at night," said Fuensanta. "You'd like to live around here, Álvaro, isn't that so?"

Before he answered, Fuensanta added: "Álvaro loves the cold, Irena. I don't know why."

Irena looked at him again in the rearview mirror; an unusual shimmer emerged from a crack in her pupils.

"It must be because no one can stay still in the cold," said the woman.

Álvaro lowered his eyes and considered running away.

Irena turned off the highway onto a dirt road. She drove for another stretch, avoiding the pine tree trunks until she stopped the vehicle in a totally green, solitary spot. Once there, Irena began to walk. Fuensanta and Álvaro followed close behind. The landscape captivated them. The pine trees that covered the mountainsides seemed to transport them someplace else, an enchanted forest where children get lost, the primeval, mythical forest. The pine trees blocked the sun's rays and soon the visitors were cold. Without paying attention to them, Irena stopped to examine closely a small flower with delicate lilac-colored petals.

"*Solanum tuberosum*," she said, raising her face toward them as if she were repeating a magical lesson.

Fuensanta and Álvaro exchanged uncomfortable looks.

"Irena, we're freezing," explained Fuensanta with just a hint of impatience. In response, Irena stood up and walked hurriedly.

"There's only one way to get over that, Fuensanta." She turned around to look at her. "Let's run."

The smile on Álvaro's face was a combination of fright and desire. He was beside himself, running downhill without thinking of his wife, without thinking of anything. His body had taken over and guided him up and down, as if a prize awaited him on the other side of the hill, and on the other side of his respiration. Breathing hard once again and with a fresh urge to vomit because of the altitude, Álvaro was almost dragging himself by the time he arrived at Irena's cabin. She was seated on a rock waiting for him, near a lamb that she treated with unusual familiarity. When he reached her, they smiled at each other, and were going to say something when they heard a scream.

"Álvaro!" Fuensanta's voice indicated that something serious had happened.

Without hesitation Irena went toward her and came back with Fuensanta leaning on her shoulder. She had sprained her ankle.

"Álvaro," Fuensanta mumbled when she came near him.

Her husband observed her as if through a thick fog and didn't move. It wasn't until the third or fourth time he heard his name that he stretched out his arms and carried her.

"Everything's all right," Álvaro stammered.

Irena opened the door of her cabin and invited them in. The fire in the fireplace made them quiet: its gentle heat and the orange light of the flames seemed eternal. While Irena bandaged Fuensanta's ankle with expert hands, Álvaro glided noiselessly through the space. He touched the stone and wood walls, caressed the book covers, the upholstery, and the curtains. Like a modern-day Saint Thomas, he touched everything in his path, trying to convince himself that it existed, that it was real. In some infinitesimal spot in his brain, deep within his dreams, there had existed a place like this. But he had never seen it before. He had never been inside it.

"What exactly do you do?" Álvaro asked with genuine curiosity, as he glanced at books on meteorology, issues of the journal of the Botanical Society of Mexico, theses on genetic improvement, and pencil sketches of very small plants.

"Irena does research for an agronomic institute, isn't that so?" interrupted Fuensanta.

The woman kept quiet until she finished adjusting the bandage around Fuensanta's ankle. Then, with visible signs of satisfaction on her face, she got up.

"Let's have a drink," she said, picking up a bottle of cognac and three glasses without waiting for a reply.

Between sips she explained that she was in charge of a census of wild species that grew on the slopes of the volcano for an agricultural research institute in Arizona. She was interested above all in potatoes. *Solanum tuberosum.* She worked for a team that was trying to find a nonchemical solution to the problem caused by the late-blooming *tizón,* a fungus that, among other things, had destroyed entire harvests in nineteenth-century Ireland, causing the famine that led to massive emigration to the United States. Irena illustrated her narration with leaves afflicted by the disease, bringing them closer for Álvaro and Fuensanta to view, as if they were myopic or genuinely interested in her scientific research. Little by little as her interlocutors' questions decreased, Irena changed the topic. They spoke for a bit about the climate, and some more about Mexico City, and finally, they were quiet. The lamb's bleating made them jump up from their seats.

"We're far away from civilization," murmured Fuensanta, undoubtedly animated by the cognac.

"Yes," mumbled Irena. "Absolutely."

Álvaro didn't open his mouth except to ask for more alcohol. While the amber-colored liquid was poured into his glass, the image of Irena wrapped in a dress of sky-blue silk seemed even more absurd than it had the night before. Surely he had made a mistake. He must have seen something else. There was no connection between the woman in overalls who studied plants and the woman reclining on an antique sofa after having made love with a man who was undoubtedly cruel. His rapidly increasing curiosity kept him alert. Fuensanta, on the contrary, soon fell into a tipsy doze.

"You can stay here tonight," Irena said when she noticed Fuensanta's languor. "Tomorrow I'll take you back to civilization," she joked.

The wrinkles around her mouth aroused him. Her way of keeping still with her gaze fixed on the fire drove him crazy. With one thing and another, Álvaro realized that he wanted to get to know her. What is there beyond civilization? he asked himself in silence. Love, he answered immediately. Outside, all around him the primeval forest acquired the darkness of mystery. Or of terror, he added to himself.

. . .

It seemed that they wouldn't be able to return the next day either. A light snowfall and a problem with Irena's truck prevented them from going back down the mountain to the Guardiola Hotel, back to their car and to their normal life in Mexico City. Civilization. Irena prepared a lentil stew on a wood-burning stove, in between descriptions of conifers and helobial plants, and behaved like a perfect hostess. Everything in her behavior indicated that she was enjoying the extended company of the tourists. Far from feeling at ease, Fuensanta and Álvaro soon found themselves exchanging looks of deep anxiety.

"We have to get back today whichever way possible," Fuensanta said without worrying about good manners, tired of beating about the bush and broaching the subject in roundabout ways.

"Work, you know," Álvaro explained, trying to smooth over any unnecessary gruffness.

"I understand," their hostess answered with a smile on her lips but without doing anything else.

After eating, however, she went out to the pickup carrying a toolbox. Álvaro volunteered to help, but she declined his offer.

"Fuensanta may need you," she said. "I won't be long."

In her absence, both Álvaro and Fuensanta automatically undertook an inspection of the place. Their curiosity made them break with preestablished social codes. The cabin, which had been a welcoming hut the night before, was now a hermetic cave, full of signs of decay and malignant air. However, nothing they found seemed important or stood out. The biology and botany books were arranged one after the other in perfect order; the Mazahua rugs matched the onyx statuettes and other crafts from the surrounding areas. There were work boots next to the bed, thick woolen sweaters, and a pair of binoculars. Everything was in harmony with Irena's personality: her books, her silences, her projects. The cabin was completely hers. It fit her like a glove.

"Look," Fuensanta called to him, showing Álvaro a bundle of letters with stamps from Denmark. "They don't seem to be from Arizona."

Álvaro wasn't listening because in between the pages of a book on zoology he had just found the photograph of a man. He was dressed in a sky-blue suit, and from underneath a thinly trimmed moustache emerged a pair of thick, sensual, almost brutal lips. The felt hat that covered his head seemed to belong to another time.

"It's him," he exclaimed. "So everything is true."

"What's true?" Fuensanta asked from the other side of the house. Álvaro hesitated for a moment, but finally decided to lie.

"That we're shut up in a cabin in the middle of an enchanted forest," he said in a jocular tone, putting the photo in one of his coat pockets.

Fuensanta didn't smile. Outside, a light layer of snow left white islands on the landscape and on memory. They observed the light of the mountains without saying anything; then they saw the sun beginning to set. A dizzying anguish forced them to keep quiet.

"And if we never get out of here?" Fuensanta asked with a mixture of regret and anger. "We should never have accepted this absurd invitation."

The choice of the term caught his attention. *Absurd.* He too had used it the night before. Despite the fact that nothing sinister could be detected and everything seemed in order, the word sprung up naturally. Irena was absurd. Her cabin in the middle of the enchanted forest was absurd. And there they were, hugging in front of the fireplace, sleepy with uneasiness, also absurd. The lamb's insistent bleating was absurd. And absurd too was the cold that had brought them to a city without charm, and to a sleeping mountain watched over by a dead volcano.

Irena returned a little after nightfall. She came hurriedly, in the company of a thin little man dressed in a red poncho.

"If it weren't for Ezequiel you'd have to stay here," she announced.

Hearing her mention him, the man lowered his eyes to hide his satisfaction. Then, without transition, Irena guided them back to the truck. Like the day before, Álvaro got in the back, while Fuensanta was in the copilot's seat, from where she nervously observed the speedometer. As they went down the mountain the tall pines gave way to dry willows and later to the stoplights of the darkened city. Both of them breathed with relief when they reached the streets of the downtown area.

"Thank you for everything," Fuensanta said in a cutting tone as soon as she opened the door of the vehicle.

Irena smiled a crooked smile.

"The pleasure was mine," she said as if she were in reality saying something else, looking at the windshield.

Suddenly, as he placed his foot on the ground, Álvaro grasped with horror that Fuensanta didn't intend to give Irena their address or phone number in Mexico City. Everything seemed to indicate that she meant for the absurdities to end there, under a dark sky at the door of the Guardiola Hotel. At the last minute, just before following his wife, Álvaro turned and took out his wallet from his back pocket and with unpremeditated daring, extracted one of his cards.

"Look me up when you go to Mexico City," he said, in a natural tone that was obviously a sham.

Irena, however, took the card with an outstretched arm and an open hand, as if she had been waiting for it forever. Once again taken by surprise, Álvaro thought that Irena was in reality in a place outside civilization. And for that reason he loved her. One, two, five minutes. Then the cold forced them to say goodbye in monosyllables.

It took a month for Fuensanta's ankle to heal. As they resumed with difficulty the normal rhythm of their lives, both Álvaro and Fuensanta chose to omit the word "Toluca" from their conversations.

Neither of the two pronounced Irena's name. Despite being absolute, the omission was not the result of any agreement, but rather of a fleeting sense of dread that made them close their eyes before actually falling asleep. At those moments, the two entered the enchanted forest through different paths. Fuensanta advanced above the landscape with slow cloudlike steps, while Álvaro ran among the trees at top speed.

In all his visions, Irena held his hand, gliding alongside him with the rhythm of a shadow, like something superimposed. Then, when Álvaro and Fuensanta woke up in the same bed, the two exited the forest in the same way.

Álvaro thought of Irena for a few days, an entire week perhaps. The image of the woman slipped in through the cracks in his schedule, with the onslaught of the cold, or the nostalgia for a green place. Sometimes, especially when he observed the tops of the trees from the terrace of his apartment on the thirteenth floor, he imagined that he loved her. The emotion that immobilized him then was huge. He trembled, experiencing a feeling of hunger in his mouth and stomach, followed immediately by an immense urge to vomit. Little by little, between family meals and television programs, he lost sight of her inside him. Then he forgot her, like one forgets those things that never happened.

Later, when Fuensanta and Álvaro didn't say the word "Toluca," it wasn't due to precaution but rather to having given it up. The two of them had managed to find the exit from the primeval forest. But they were mistaken.

Álvaro caught sight of Irena a second time under the jacarandas of April. He had gotten together with Sonia, his older sister, in an open-air café where they had arranged to meet to catch up and talk about unimportant things as was their custom. Before ordering the requisite cappuccinos and deciding between the raspberry tart and the cheesecake, the two hastily opened a cigarette pack.

"If Fuensanta saw me doing this she'd kill me on the spot," said Álvaro with a cigarette lighter in his left hand.

Sonia shrugged her shoulders and urged him to continue with the bad habit they had begun a long time ago, at the start of adolescence's winding road.

"But she can't see us, Álvaro," commented his sister, while she exhaled smoke in the direction of his face with secret pleasure. Whether it was to avoid the irritation from the smoke or to enjoy alone the taste of tobacco on his lips, Álvaro closed his eyes. One, two, five seconds. When he opened them he didn't see Sonia, but Irena. She was crossing the threshold of the doorway with her sky-blue silk dress, a pearl necklace, and the exhausted attitude of a cow on its way to the slaughterhouse.

"Did you see a ghost? You turned so pale."

When Sonia turned around in her seat to identify the cause of her brother's confusion it was too late. Irena was fleeing in a white limousine whose tinted glass prevented Álvaro from seeing inside. After the incident, brother and sister didn't have coffee or eat anything. Chain-smoking, Sonia tried to make sense of a story that Álvaro narrated in half-finished sentences, halting stammers, and ecstatic smiles.

"It's a woman, Sonia," he said to her. "A woman I met in a forest."

Sonia, who had been privy to her brother's romantic ups and downs for years, just kept quiet. There was something in the story that attracted and bothered her at the same time. It wasn't Irena's double life, or Fuensanta's ignorance, or the infantile tone with which Álvaro described his metaphysical affair.

"I didn't know you liked the cold so much, Álvaro." Finally she had hit upon the answer.

The story bothered her because it was based on information she was unfamiliar with. The person whom she thought she knew by heart was now slipping away from her because of a very small but essential reason: the cold. One always missed something.

"It's not such a big deal, Sonia," replied Álvaro without conviction.

The cold. He liked it, it's true, but he didn't know since when. It had been a sudden thing, he was sure; one of those convictions that are born, grow, reproduce at breakneck speed, and never die. Perhaps everything had begun that wintry morning in which the immobile city had covered itself with white clouds, trying to find a bit of warmth, and he, on the other hand, had taken to the street at a rapid pace, conquering the whole of it. Irena was right: during the cold, everything was permitted but movement was required. That was its charm, its particular fascination.

The chat with Sonia ended on a note of distrust as well as resignation. Despite the fact that all the words they exchanged had been gentle and reasonable, the two avoided looking each other in the eye when they walked together toward the garage.

"Keep me in the loop." Sonia laconically said goodbye.

The following day Álvaro found a bouquet of flowers and a manila envelope on his desk. The joy that invaded him was comparable only to his fear. What was Irena looking for? What could he give her? The image of a mad Irena, tied to his ankles like a steel ball, made him hesitate when he breathed in the aroma of the tuberoses that she had sent him. His office mates' curious gazes pierced the glass like thousand-year-old swords and that made him stop, open the envelope as if it had to do with a family matter, and read with a blend of patience and astonishment: *Meet me at the Café Siracusa at 4:15, Irena.* What bothered him most was the fact that she didn't seem to have the slightest doubt that he would keep the appointment.

The Café Siracusa was an old-fashioned place frequented mostly by midlevel office workers and women with big plastic bags. Álvaro went once in a while because it was only a few blocks from his place of work, and above all because no one knew him there. Whenever he wanted to escape or hide, he'd go to the Siracusa as if it were a secret paradise or a refuge frozen on the shores of time. The big prints of Greek theater, the temples of Apollo, and the Euryalus Fortress that covered the walls lent that effect.

As always upon arriving he went to the bar, ordered a whiskey on the rocks, opened the newspaper, and waited. This time he knew something was going to happen.

Irena arrived half an hour late with damp hair.

"I'm sorry, Álvaro." With her khaki slacks and blue shirt she almost seemed a normal woman. "But it's still difficult for me to gauge distances in this city."

It seemed like a logical excuse to Álvaro. "Let's go over there, is that okay?"

They moved to a table surrounded by some red overstuffed chairs. Irena ordered a sandwich and a bottle of mineral water. When the waitress left, the two realized that they had absolutely nothing to talk about.

"Why are you spying on me, Irena?"

The question was said by another person inside him, some impolite and tactless person, without the slightest sense of mystery and the complexities of seduction; someone who was afraid.

"You're the spy, Álvaro," Irena responded naturally, as if the topic of espionage were common between two people who were getting together for the first time without knowing each other yet. "Give me back Hercules's photograph," she added in a low voice, as if mentioning the topic were more painful for her than for him.

Álvaro opened the manila envelope and extracted the picture. "It was a stupid reaction," he said. "I didn't mean to keep it."

Álvaro had never felt as he did at that moment in the Siracusa, seated next to Irena for the first time: he was naked and he was unable to lie.

"I know," she said, caressing the back of his hand and making him look at her.

Then, like the strangers they were, they talked about the weather, not mentioning the man in the photograph or Fuensanta. Nor did Álvaro dare ask Irena what brought her to Mexico City, and she didn't volunteer any explanation. Without much to talk about, they ended up telling innocuous jokes. Both were in a good mood.

When Irena finished her sandwich, and Álvaro his third whiskey, the two left the Siracusa without anything in particular in mind. Together, holding hands, bumping into people in a hurry, they seemed like children walking aimlessly, or two idle adolescents. It was almost dark when they came upon a park with dry plants and wilted chrysanthemums. They sat on the grass and continued their meaningless conversation. The weather. Both of them loved the cold. Then, without planning to, they stood up together, and kept walking until they found the Sorrento Hotel with its doors wide open. At 10:35 P.M. they made love for the first time.

They spent the next two days together. They'd have breakfast in the Siracusa and then walk without any fixed destination until hunger pangs brought them back to the café. Then they'd play Chinese checkers on plastic boards, buy sunflower seeds, and strike up conversations with homeless people, and at night they'd make love with extraordinary calm. They acted as if they had all the time in the world or as if time had stopped forever at an island port. Álvaro phoned Fuensanta, and after failing to come up with a plausible lie, he simply asked her not to wait for him, said that he would explain later. Neither Irena nor Álvaro acted like a furtive lover: they didn't hide or search for dark places to kiss with passionate hurry, and they didn't change their names. On the contrary, the two walked the city streets as if they were invisible. If someone had stopped to greet Álvaro, he would have said with the utmost naturalness:

"Surely you must be confusing me with somebody else. I'm not Álvaro Diéguez," and the interlocutor would have believed him.

If someone had grabbed Irena by the elbow, she would have excused the other person's error.

"You're mistaken, sir. My name is not Irena Corvián."

And both of them, in the strictest sense, would have been telling the truth.

When the moment to say goodbye came, they shook hands with no rush or dramatic gestures.

"Thank you for everything," said Irena.

"The pleasure was all mine," replied Álvaro.

Then he accompanied her to the parking garage where the cherry-colored pickup was waiting for her. When he saw her leave, he realized that he knew almost nothing about her, and with relief, he was aware that he hadn't offered any unnecessary information either. Then he walked back to his office, eyes cast down and a half-hidden smile on his lips. The aroma of the tuberoses confirmed to him that nothing had been a dream, but the note in the manila envelope made him wonder once again: *Don't kid yourself, Álvaro. I don't exist. Irena.*

Both Fuensanta and Álvaro had forgotten his inexplicable disappearance for two whole days when, by chance, he remembered the event. It was at one of those gatherings of good friends where familiarity and red wine lead inexorably to the discussion of a controversial topic: gender inequality.

"And what would you do if you were men?" the men asked the women in a provocative tone, trying to put them between a rock and a hard place.

One of them, the wife of Álvaro's best friend, said frankly:

"I would be more attentive to the emotional needs of my wife." The subtext made more than one of them blush, and put others in a bad mood.

Immediately there were giggles.

"Well, if I were a woman," said the husband in question, "I would put on sexy nightgowns and make passionate love every night."

"Well, if I were a man," insisted the same woman, "I would make a superhuman effort to learn how to listen."

As the volume of the matrimonial dialogue increased, the hosts moved around the table offering cigarettes and wine.

"And if you were a woman, Álvaro?" asked Fuensanta, more to

silence the couple who were on the verge of an argument than to find out what her husband thought.

Álvaro let out a nervous laugh, reached for his wineglass, and to the surprise and disapproval of his wife, accepted a cigarette. Then he kept quiet.

"So?" asked Sergio, the host, expecting a reply.

"I would wear sky blue, and forgetting would be easy for me." The silence around the table was as profound as his own astonishment.

Álvaro had just remembered Irena.

"And what in God's name does that mean?" asked the interrogated husband, trying to provoke something similar to his own conjugal quarrel.

"I don't know." Álvaro refused to say anything more.

He smiled at him, raised the cigarette to his lips, and, a second later, exhaled the smoke with singular satisfaction. He had decided to go to the Nevado de Toluca one more time. Suddenly, he felt like running in the cold and telling stupid jokes.

"Well, if I were a man, I would be exactly as I am," Fuensanta informed the gathering, considering the matter closed.

Little by little, people left. The angry couple went away with remorseful expressions, and in the end only the hosts, as well as Álvaro and Fuensanta, remained, sitting in chairs on opposite sides of the living room.

"They seem to have problems," said Nélida, the hostess, resuming the thread of the conversation. "But who doesn't?"

"Discreet individuals," replied Álvaro with an ironic note in his voice, while he observed Fuensanta from the corner of his eye.

"Or otherworldly beings," added Sergio.

It was in this way that they eventually came to the subject of sirens. They spoke of Ulysses and the Mediterranean, and ears filled with wax; they made comments about firm-breasted mermaids that appeared on lottery tickets, discussed the one described by Hans Christian Andersen; and then, by chance, they ended up in the Toluca Valley.

"But there isn't enough water there," commented Álvaro, with genuine interest.

"There used to be," said Nélida, an anthropologist who they knew had been researching the history of the Chanclana, a famous mermaid made of *tule,* or bulrushes, who, according to oral tradition, had the ability to destroy men.

Relishing the others' attention, the anthropologist described the ancient lakes of the region as "generous" and "inexplicably beautiful." Then she explained that although it dated from time immemorial, the legend of the mermaid had recently come into vogue among the fishermen when, due to the construction of a dam, the lakes had disappeared.

"A veiled criticism of modernity, no doubt," she determined.

It was in this way that they exited the territory of otherworldly beings and arrived at the more pressing, though more abstract, topic of postmodernism. Álvaro by then was on his third cigarette of the night without paying the least attention to his surroundings. A slight, blissful tipsiness repeated the name of Irena in his right ear.

Sirena.

Álvaro didn't return to Toluca until several months later. First, he had been incapable of finding a sufficiently logical pretext to explain his trip to a frigid valley without mentioning the name of the other woman. Then he waited in vain for Fuensanta to go away for a weekend to Tepoztlán with her girlfriends from college. Finally, as the days and weeks passed, he forgot about it. He forgot that he had wanted to go up the mountain, high above the air, until he reached the season's snow. His tasks distracted him; his daily rituals fascinated him once more. When the possibility of going opened up in front of his distracted eyes, he couldn't believe it. It was the second weekend in November when Fuensanta announced with a smile that her parents had given her a ticket to go to Cancún.

"I suppose the heat will do you good," he said.

It was at that moment that Álvaro became aware of his chance: he would go in the direction of the opposite climate that his wife was traveling to.

Álvaro left Mexico City on a Friday at three in the afternoon. He was taking an extra pair of boots, his leather gloves, and a black coat inside the trunk of the car. He had even taken the precaution of buying a first aid kit. The music of Leonard Cohen accompanied him as he crossed the Desert of the Lions and then La Marquesa, *I'm your man*. The high green band of the pine trees, the blue of the sky, the lightness of the air. Everything that reminded him of a being inside himself that responded to the name of Irena. This was her context: an agglomeration of houses and people at the highest altitude in the country; a junction of Spanish broom where moisture had turned to stone and then absence; a valley where everything became confluence, plant, bird. Álvaro crossed the periphery of the city through an expressway, observing it from afar, from all possible angles, and then he went toward the Guardiola Hotel, where he asked for a room and ordered his usual whiskey as well as a pack of cigarettes.

The decision to go out was unpremeditated. The cold pushed him outside, and just like the first time he had been in the city, it invited him to take a walk in the winter gale. Once again Álvaro let his body guide him, knowing beforehand that at any moment he would arrive at the old house where he had seen Irena wrapped in an absurd silk dress approximately one year ago. When he was in front of the black iron gate, his hands pressed the buzzer and smoothed his hair. He waited. He waited without knowing what he would say, or even imagining what he was looking for.

"But, Rolando, how good of you to come back." The woman had opened the gate a crack with excessive precaution, but as soon as she recognized him, she opened the door wide and embraced him. Álvaro, taken by surprise, let her do as she wished.

"It's wonderful you've come, really," the woman repeated with tears in her eyes, "your sister needs you so much. You can't imagine."

In effect, Álvaro couldn't imagine it. Still hugging him, the woman led Álvaro through a narrow hallway until once again she opened another door, a bigger one made of wood. Inside were the gold statuettes, the oil paintings, the lamps that radiated a wan, tenuous light, the Persian rugs, and the sofa upholstered in purple brocade where Álvaro had seen Irena make love with a man who was in a hurry. Suddenly full of sorrow, he gazed across the space and became quiet.

"Hercules, isn't that so?" Someone inside him asked the question in the form of an affirmation.

And the woman nodded.

"He's getting worse, Rolando, that man's jealousy is suffocating her," she said with her half-shut eyes and pale lips.

At that moment, just before the woman began to speak again, a slow, deep, and terrible noise invaded the room. It was a tremor, a shaking of the earth. Soon, the rumble became more intense, and after what seemed an eternity, silence returned, a silence as loud as the noise itself.

"Antonia!" A cry came from another room.

Summoned, the woman excused herself and immediately ran out. The dust that the shaking left behind transformed the atmosphere. Álvaro barely managed to stand up with his energy depleted by fear, and as he tried to arrange some of the statues and other objects that had moved, he found the photograph that explained the mistaken identity. Irena and a man identical to her were embracing in front of a bay that seemed to him gray and icy. Undoubtedly it was Copenhagen. The image of the twins moved him.

"You look so much like her, don't you?" said Antonia as soon as she returned.

Álvaro turned, and with astonishment and pleasure, never before having felt so puzzled, he confirmed in a mirror that, in effect, his face and Irena's had a slight family resemblance. He hadn't noticed it before, but at this moment, he was grateful for the error. Because of it, not only had Antonia taken him into her confidence, she also shared stories that would have been difficult for him to imagine.

"Is everything okay?" asked Álvaro.

"Yes, young man, don't worry. My daughter gets very nervous when there are tremors, even one as mild as this one," she explained.

Then she offered him coffee and more conversation.

"That man is terrifying, Rolando," she continued her story. "When he's here—fortunately less and less often—he's angry all the time. He's always criticizing your sister and doesn't leave her alone: that she doesn't know how to cook, that she leaves glasses of water all over the house, that she doesn't rejoice in his successes or lick his wounds when he fails, that she doesn't dote on him. It's unbelievable. I sincerely do not know what Irena does to put up with him."

"She must be in love," Álvaro dared to guess. "Still," he added doubtfully.

Antonia looked at him as if through a fog, with a sadness that was difficult for her to hide.

"I don't think she is anymore, Rolando. But you're right; how she loved him!"

Antonia turned her face toward the corner of the room. "Imagine leaving behind her life in Copenhagen to come and shut herself up in a dump this size. Without any family. Without anything. Why did they let your sister do something like this?"

"Irena was already the legal age when everything happened, Antonia. Remember?"

Someone inside Álvaro listed reasons in a firm and logical manner. Someone looked at the photograph of the twins with an odd, bitter, treacherous nostalgia. Someone was in pain.

"She must have been very much alone, I suppose. Perhaps it

was a moment of madness," murmured Antonia with an absent-minded gaze between sips of coffee. "That's what happens to women who study a lot, isn't it?"

Álvaro smiled. Then he nodded in order to keep silent, just because. At any rate, Antonia wasn't paying attention to him anymore. She had shut herself up in an internal world full of stories that as she herself said could not be expressed in words. Suddenly the image of Hercules made Álvaro's blood boil and for the first time he was afraid for Irena and for himself. Abruptly, the memory of a winter afternoon in Copenhagen restored peace to him. Then, disconcerted, he realized that he had never been in Denmark. He needed a cigarette.

"I guess it's because of her daughter, don't you think? If he weren't hiding her, surely Irena would have already left, isn't that so, Rolando?"

Although the information startled him, he tried to maintain his composure. He nodded in silence, as if he accepted the validity of Antonia's opinions, and then, nervously, he asked if he could smoke.

Antonia's weak and sorrowful tone echoed his, as she asked for a cigarette in turn.

"She's going to be four in December," she observed before lighting her cigarette. "He said he's keeping her abroad."

"Yes," muttered Álvaro.

The smoke from his cigarette rose in the air with the slow pace of sorrow. Álvaro felt an immense urge to get up and leave, but his unease prevented him from applying his energy. It was already past two in the morning when he finally decided to cross the wooden threshold and return to his hotel.

"Take care of yourself, Rolando. You never know what that man is capable of." She kissed him on each cheek, and without saying anything more, she closed the door before he had time to thank her.

When he got to his room he fell into a deep sleep. He was

both tired and fed up. The illicit affairs of a normal man were surely more vulgar, but also less confusing. If it were only a matter of harboring hopes, of having his way with her on the nearest bed and letting himself go. It wasn't rocket science. Furthermore it happened all the time. A man had sex with a woman, while she made love with him. That was the thing, the whole point. Disgusted, Álvaro covered his head with the pillow and stopped thinking. Before completely shutting down his awareness, however, he remembered Antonia's error and he smiled wanly. Irena's twin. Her brother. A man with whom she had shared a winter afternoon facing the gray sky on a pier in Denmark. The man she trusted.

A dream he couldn't remember gnawed at the nape of his neck when he got up, took his customary bath, and had breakfast. He was uneasy; even inside the hotel room he turned his face from left to right as if someone were watching him from afar. He heard footsteps that stopped without warning, and voices that persisted inconsiderately. When he shut the door of his room he checked the pockets of his pants and his jacket with the feeling that he had forgotten something. He didn't find anything. He was getting ready to descend three flights of stairs when he saw two men dragging a gigantic black bag.

"Whose body is it?" he asked jokingly, suddenly in a good mood.

"Nobody knows."

The response left him speechless and made him tremble inside. He had never before been near a dead person. Still without reacting, he stood aside to let the men and their enormous bundle through. Contrary to what could be expected, Álvaro was hungry when he got to the restaurant. He wanted to fill his mouth with fruit, hot and spicy foods, and festive colors. When his order came, he sniffed the coffee and food several times before ingesting them.

For his trip to the volcano he chose music by Sibelius. He drove carefully, probing his mood: sometimes he felt he was going to get there too late; at others, he felt like getting lost on purpose. The dilemma was resolved only when he observed the very white, high clouds in the sky: he'd go up the mountain, up the path, into the thin air. He had to see Irena. He had to confirm that she was real, that in some area of the world the forest existed, and within the forest, the cabin, and in the cabin the woman dressed in sky blue who was carrying something in her that belonged only to him. *Sirena.* When he left the highway behind to take the dirt road that would lead him to the cabin of his soul mate, Álvaro was smiling. The smile accompanied him while he walked under the pine trees and saw a flock of lambs. Then, when he opened the door of the cabin, the smile evaporated; he was aghast.

"But, Irena, what happened to you?"

The woman was crouching in a corner of the house. She was hiding her face behind her knees, and from her matted hair emerged a pair of nervous arms in clumsy and syncopated movements. Her moans filled the atmosphere of decayed matter; it was something incomprehensible. Álvaro came close to her and when he did so, Irena tried to become even smaller.

"No," she said.

It seemed as if she had lost her mind.

"It's me, Irena. It's me."

The woman finally turned to look at him. Her face was crisscrossed by scarlet-colored scratches and bruises. Her lips, opened in furrows of fresh blood, pronounced his name while her swollen eyes tried to identify him.

"Rolando," she said, and hugged him.

Then she fainted or lost consciousness. At any rate, she closed her eyes and rested. The insistent bleating of a lamb reminded him that he was far from civilization.

With the help of his first aid kit, Álvaro was able to dress some of the wounds, but since Irena did not come to, he decided to take her to the nearest hospital. He wrapped her in a blanket and walked the stretch of path that separated them from his car. Breathing heavily but with his energy intact, undoubtedly because of the adrenaline, Álvaro managed to make out from afar the withered face of Ezequiel, the little man who, the year before, had helped them get out of that inhospitable place. Stretched out on the backseat, Irena looked like a bundle of bones, a flower shorn of its petals, a broken line.

"But she's a woman," Álvaro said to himself, "remember that she's a woman."

He drove as Irena had done before, at lunatic speed. The emergency guided him all the way to the hospital. When he arrived, a distracted doctor ordered X-rays, and after examining Irena, looked at him suspiciously.

"Are you her husband?"

"No, Doctor. I'm her brother," said Álvaro. "Her husband's name is Hercules."

"I see," said the doctor.

A couple of hours later, Álvaro found out that Irena had three broken ribs and was suffering from the secondary effects of a nervous breakdown. When the doctor suggested filing a complaint with the authorities, Álvaro hesitated. He had never been in a situation like this one. He didn't know exactly how big the enemy was; he didn't have the slightest idea of Irena's preferences; nor did he know if he should trust the police. The thought of notifying Antonia now passed through his mind, but Hercules's proximity made him afraid again. After thinking about it for a little while, he decided to bring Irena to Mexico City. He wouldn't be able to lodge her in the apartment on the thirteenth floor, but he thought of a room with big windows in the Sorrento. That way, far from the volcano and from Hercules, she would heal and he, her brother and lover and confidant, would be able to see her whenever he wanted during her convalescence. That night, while he slept in the bed next to Irena, the smell of disinfectant in the hospital produced another dream. Just like the one that had awakened him in the Guardiola Hotel, this dream had no name. He couldn't remember it.

It wasn't until Sunday that they returned to Mexico City. On the trip Irena was awake but stubbornly silent. She let herself be led around like an invalid or a little girl. At times she gave the impression that in reality nothing interested her very much, especially her life.

"Where are you taking me?" she asked when they crossed La Marquesa.

"To the Sorrento," answered Álvaro, looking at her from the corner of his eye, trying to put her in a good mood.

Irena made a face that didn't quite become a smile and afterward she fell asleep.

Without having agreed to, both gave the names of each other's siblings when they asked for a double room. Rolando and Sonia. Through the windows the city was a gathering of fireflies.

Taking advantage of Fuensanta's absence, Álvaro slept in Irena's room that night. Every so often when he looked at her, he'd wake her up to give her the medication and then he'd tuck her in once more. He didn't exactly know what kept him close to her, remembering and forgetting her with equal ease, but he supposed that it was something powerful.

"Perhaps you're my destiny, Irena," he whispered softly, so that no one would hear such a hackneyed phrase.

Then, with renewed vigor, he substituted it for another he imagined to be more exact:

"Maybe you're my fate."

This time he fell asleep.

The first week Irena spent in the Sorrento was marked by disorientation and confusion. Álvaro arrived everywhere late, and everywhere he seemed distracted and in a bad mood. Fuensanta constantly asked him, "What are you thinking about, Álvaro?" which added to his silent resentment.

"Leave me alone, Fuen. It's nothing," he managed to say with his mouth full of lies.

Then he'd go running to the hotel as if his life depended on it. It was obvious that Irena wasn't expecting him. By her sudden starts, her nervousness, by the way in which she chewed her nails, one knew she was expecting someone else. Hercules. The cruel man.

He asked her about him one Thursday afternoon, just before sundown. Irena sat down on the bed and cracked her knuckles.

"Do you really want to know?" she inquired before deciding to speak.

He could not help but be fascinated by the threat implicit in her question. Álvaro immediately responded that yes, he wanted to know.

"Hercules was so different, Álvaro," began Irena with her gaze fixed on a cold and distant place. "When he knocked on my door the first time, he had the eyes of a lamb and the attitude of a needy person. He didn't know anyone else in Copenhagen who spoke Spanish and when he found out that I lived in the building, he turned up right away. Two or three months later everything changed. He had the ferocity of a wounded animal, and however much I tried, I couldn't get him out of my house. Or my life."

Irena fell silent. She turned to look at him and then, observing the intense colors of the sunset, continued: "I was pregnant."

The silence that followed was a long one, thin as a needle.

"And in love, I suppose," said Álvaro, encouraging her to go on.

"No, not in love. I've always been a woman of fragile loves, Álvaro," she said with a half smile on her face.

It was the first time he'd seen something like that since she arrived in Mexico City.

"He didn't love me anymore either, but Hercules is cruel. His lack of love turned into hate, and hate into this"—she pointed to the bruises on her face. "Do you believe me?" she said, interrupting herself.

"Why shouldn't I believe you?" asked Álvaro, surprised.

"Hercules is like one of those characters in a horror novel," she continued without answering his question. "He's charming in public, but when he's alone he's powerless against his own bile.

He produces it in enormous quantities. He gulps it down but he often chokes on it, and then he spits it out and dirties everything around him. I don't know," she said, changing her tone to one full of compassion. "Perhaps he had an unhappy childhood."

Álvaro kissed her on the nape of her neck and lay down by her side. A cloud of melancholy was raining blue water inside the room.

"Or perhaps everything is due to his addiction," she added with affected carelessness. "Drugs put him very much inside himself, you know, where his worst self is."

Álvaro for the first time felt that his life was out of control. He couldn't endure Irena's confessions, although he himself had induced them with indiscreet questions and opportune comments. He had expected something else. A story of love with strong passions and inexplicable obsessions. A woman prepared to give up everything for a man, or perhaps the contrary. But it was nothing like that. Irena's was a story of "fragile loves." His disappointment was huge. The more he knew, the more uncomfortable he felt, the more out of place. And what if Hercules were to go looking for him to give him a good beating and take his wife back to the enchanted forest? Would it be worth it? He wasn't even sure anymore of his interest in Irena. He was surrounded by confusion, degradation, deterioration, decay. Irena was an ambiguous woman.

"You, on the other hand, have always been the man of my dreams," murmured Irena, as if she could read his mind.

It was as if Álvaro were seeing her through the lens of a very sunny day. He half shut his eyes and with incredulity repeated the phrase *I've always been her dream man*. The grammatical mingling of the sentences produced an emptiness in his stomach. For a moment he didn't know if he was the dream of a woman or the man who dreamed of a woman who was dreaming of a man dreaming of a woman. A linguistic vertigo forced him to close his eyes. When he opened them, he was in his bedroom, underneath the blankets, his right arm barely touching Fuensanta's shoulder. Around him the sun's morning rays were already shining.

That morning he had a phone call from Hercules Corvián. Just as his wife had done, he made an appointment with Álvaro to meet at the Siracusa at four fifteen that afternoon. In his voice there was not the slightest sign of doubt: he was sure that Engineer Diéguez, as he had called Álvaro, would come to the meeting.

"Antonia is right, you look a lot like Rolando," said Hercules by way of introduction.

Then he took off his hat of a bygone time, led him toward one of the tables in the back, and without asking Álvaro, ordered two whiskeys.

"Perhaps I am."

Someone inside him was playing with language, motivated by fear and desolation. Someone inside him observed Hercules with an almost feminine apprehension and unshakable rancor. He would not let himself be defeated. He would not let Hercules defeat them. That man with a withered face and bony hands could do nothing against him, against her, or against reason.

"I'm going to tell you about it because I'm sure she filled your head with lies," he began.

A minute later and almost without transition, Álvaro found himself listening attentively to the story of Irena told through a mouth with thick lips and stained teeth.

"Irena is obsessed with the idea of being the victim of the whole world. Now it happens that I'm her executioner, isn't that so? Don't let her make a fool of you, Engineer Diéguez. About the beating, ask Ezequiel; and with respect to Copenhagen, remind her of the many humiliations she made me go through. She'd put me down all the time. How could someone with a doctorate in sick plants lower herself to be with a guy like me?"

The hate that came out of his mouth had no bounds. As he spoke without tolerating any kind of interruption, a fragility full of pointy edges seemed to break his puny body in two; but then, as his words continued to pierce the atmosphere with sharp arrows, the hardness of his gestures gave him the appearance of a commonplace, vulgar man.

"And surely she never told you about the times she beat me," continued Hercules, extinguishing a cigarette in a round ashtray with brusque movements and without paying attention to Álvaro's confusion and annoyance.

"My God, Hercules, don't be ridiculous. Everyone knows that when men make women mad, they react by trying to hit them, but they just don't know how," said Álvaro with a tone of boredom in his voice, and without really believing what he was hearing.

He felt as he did at that party where he remembered Irena, the party where a couple slung accusatory insinuations at each other until embarrassment forced them to leave. What was Hercules looking for by giving him his own version of the facts? To clear his name? To pass himself off as a good guy? He wouldn't be able to, thought Álvaro, and not because his version wasn't as valid as Irena's, but because the hate he emitted when he talked, and that filtered through each of his sentences, made his words suspect. Hercules was at a crossroads: the motivation that pushed him to fight on was the same that doomed him to failure. Without hate he could win allies, but without hate there was no point in tormenting his wife, the mother of his daughter, his partner. When he was preparing to leave, Álvaro could only look at him with compassion and disgust. He barely mumbled a couple of syllables by way of farewell, and left running in the direction of the Sorrento. He needed to see Irena. He needed to tell her that he was in agreement, that Hercules was in reality a cruel man, and that she was in danger. She had to leave her cabin, her enchanted forest, the cold of the Nevado. She had to go away however she could, return to that institute in Arizona perhaps; she had to save herself. She had to take care of herself, take her medications, stay well for their walks together, for the silly innocence they shared. Álvaro's mouth was full of words for Irena, but when he reached the room at the Sorrento, she had already left. *Don't kid yourself, Álvaro. I don't exist.*

Three days later, while Álvaro was still torturing himself trying to decide between searching for Irena and forgetting her forever, Fuensanta informed him that she was pregnant. At that moment his dilemma was resolved with the immediate initiation of a new life. A life marked by the warmth of another, a life without cold. A life without Irena.

Álvaro was happy. When he looked at himself discreetly in the mirrors of his house, a pride that was real, though cautious, crossed his face. He felt satisfaction. He had a job that he not only enjoyed, but that allowed him to live with decorum and more. A stable and lasting affection joined him to his wife. He had Mariano, a son almost two years old in whose eyes he found inexhaustible quantities of peace and hope. He had friends, books into which he could delve alone, and favorite cinemas. He had a routine that steered him through the chaos of everyday life. He had a future, hundreds of them. At thirty-three, Álvaro had attained everything he had dreamed of at fourteen, perhaps even more. At the age of Christ, he could not find any reason to complain about life, while he did indeed have much to be grateful for. Álvaro knew this. It was enough for him to observe the nearness of Fuensanta and Mariano to verify that he was a whole man.

During Mariano's second birthday party, however, a strange sensation transformed the tranquility of his new life. It was an old, fuzzy, wounded feeling. It had been consuming him for a long time until, weak, pale, and moribund, but still alive, it reached his feet. The feeling that made him stand still and hesitate came to him from within the pages of a book. It was *Sirens of the Highlands,* the most recent book by Nélida Cruz, the anthropologist in whose house he had witnessed the embarrassing fight of an incompatible married couple.

"Thank you, Nélida," said Álvaro upon receiving it.

The book was a precious object. The care taken with the edition was noticeable not only in the quality of the paper and the font, but also, and perhaps in particular, on the front cover: an oil painting by a local artist in which beings that seemed only half human looked at the reader with eyes full of an almost divine sadness. Álvaro observed the painting for a couple of minutes, with a curiosity that seemed to belong to someone else. Then, when he recognized her, he placed the book on the nearest table without saying a word. He was sure that one of the faces was Irena's. Until that moment he hadn't thought about her for three years.

"What are you thinking about, Álvaro?" Fuensanta asked when Mariano was sleeping in his room and the dishes, slices of birthday cake, and deflated balloons filled the apartment with melancholy.

"Nothing, Fuen," he answered with an unaccustomed meekness in his voice.

Then, without saying a word, he put his arm around her waist, drawing her toward him, and as he observed Nélida's book from the corner of his eye, he held her close to him for a long time. As soon as Fuensanta went to sleep, Álvaro retrieved the book and began to read it in one of the armchairs in the living room. He skipped the first chapter, where Nélida showed off her theoretical knowledge by quoting Geertz, Bakhtin, and Taussig with a prolixity that bordered on the irritating. Nor did he read a chapter where the anthropologist described in detail her method of gathering data. He skimmed through a long historical section where sirens of the whole world and from every period appeared and disappeared at will. Álvaro's attention was drawn to a short chapter near the end of the book, in which the author tried to describe, without much success, the story of a tiny siren that hovered around the Lagoons of the Sun and the Moon in the crater of the Nevado of Toluca, the dead volcano. While he read hurriedly, a chill ran up and down his spine. He stopped. He read once more.

As we have seen, the stories of mermaids of the highlands follow a more or less regular pattern. Among all of them, however, there is one that stands out for both the physical characteristics attributed to the said mermaid, as well as the faculties in which she takes pride. This legend has its origin in the ranches near Raíces, especially those nearest the crater. It involves a mermaid with sky-blue skin and very small physical proportions that vary according to the informant. Thus, the siren of the volcano is at times as small as a hand, and at others, as big as a local deer. In neither of the two examples does she manifest human dimensions. In contrast to the traditional Chanclana, whose principal faculty is to attract and destroy men, the sky-blue siren is timid and hides from others while taking on human guises. When men come upon her the dénouement is always fatal, although not immediate. It is said that on seeing her, men find something inside themselves—certain gestures, inclinations, thoughts, perhaps—whose fascination leads them, eventually, to madness. Her malignant work sometimes takes months, and, more frequently, whole years to produce effects, but these effects are inescapable.

Álvaro closed the book and, shaking his head, went to the bedroom where Fuensanta's warm and relaxed body awaited him. He took his clothes off, put on his pajamas, brushed his teeth, and, finally, slipped under the covers. When he closed his eyes, the vision of a gray plain kept him awake. It was the North Sea, immobile and stark. At three in the morning he decided to get up. He went to the kitchen to prepare some tea, and observing the tops of the trees from the thirteenth floor, he pronounced Irena's name for the first time in a long while. He was concerned about her fate. He wondered about the three ribs that in all certainty had been broken by Hercules. Then he cursed himself with a growing sense of guilt. He thought he had behaved like an imbecile, abandoning her at the moment when she needed him most, but then he remembered that it had been she who had disappeared without a trace. The feelings she provoked were confused and contradictory. Besides, he had had good reasons for his forgetfulness—the birth of his son. When Álvaro finally returned to bed, a light and uncomfortable sleep pervaded him. When he awoke his bones ached.

Two days later the perfect excuse to undertake a return to Toluca came: the publishing house that had produced Nélida Cruz's book was organizing a presentation in the city's cultural center, and the author invited them to attend. Fuensanta accepted immediately and Álvaro, without visible eagerness on his face, did the same. Suddenly memories pursued him. He tried to scare them away with his son's smile, but it was all useless. First came a feeling of cold, and then, the wan light of the highlands, the pine trees, the dirt path, the cabin, a lamb and its horrendous bleating. Then Hercules's face, framed by the walls of the Siracusa, appeared in all its crudeness. He tried to stop the memories, but by then he couldn't do anything. He was in another place and it was a lost cause. Álvaro knew that he had a secret that bore the name of a woman, and he also knew that the fact of having it upset him. Furthermore, that irritation was accompanied by fear. And if he found her again? And if Doña Antonia ran into him on the street and called him Rolando? And if he came upon Irena in Hercules's arms? What if he didn't find her? Álvaro was forced to smile and recognize that he lacked answers to any question related to Irena.

They started out early, before the traffic drove the city insane, but after the sun came up. Fuensanta was in a good mood, humming to popular songs on the radio and observing Mariano's face from time to time. Just like Álvaro, she considered herself a whole and happy person. When they were approaching the highest city and were already on the boulevard bordered by willows, Fuensanta's attitude changed.

"We came to this city a few years ago, do you remember, Álvaro?" she said, looking at him from the corner of her eye, as if it had just come to her mind.

"Yes, a few years ago, Fuen," mumbled Álvaro, doubtful that Fuensanta could have ever forgotten the trip they had taken so that he could enjoy the cold for a few hours.

Then they were silent and within that silence they crossed the city and left it behind. Without consulting her, Álvaro had decided to go up the mountain, up into the thin air, toward the foothills of the volcano. They crossed abandoned ranches, cornfields, barren slopes. They observed the gray, unreachable clouds. They counted the pines and the oak trees. Álvaro left the highway behind, took the dirt road, and soon they found themselves surrounded by different shades of green. They were in the enchanted forest. With Mariano in his arms, Álvaro walked up and down the slope with an unaccustomed hurry, a hurry that accelerated his breathing, making it almost impossible. Even then, he didn't stop until he glimpsed the cabin where, just a few years before, they had spent the night in Irena's presence. The disappointment on his face was immediate and obvious. The cabin that he remembered as picturesque and friendly was now an accumulation of discolored and badly arranged wooden boards. Surrounded by other little shacks of the same type, Irena's cabin was pathetic.

"Álvaro!"

He didn't notice Fuensanta's shout. Álvaro continued walking toward the place without listening or seeing, without feeling anything other than a strong expectation. When he reached the door, some children opened it from the inside and, without heeding him, ran around him as if playing an ancient game. They were dark-complexioned children with their cheeks red on account of the cold and the dry air, children with an easy laugh and unfamiliar faces, children wearing huaraches and thick sweaters of coarse wool or ponchos that were too big. The children's voices, mixed with the lambs' bleating, created disorder, a noise that irritated the senses. Álvaro continued on his way. He crossed the threshold of the door and although the darkness prevented him at first, he tried to see what he had seen in the past: a cabin like the lit-up interior of a walnut. Instead, he encountered the wrinkled faces of two men and a woman who were exchanging muffled murmurs while they drank some hot potion in clay mugs. There were no books, no fireplace, no colorful textiles on the wall, no candles.

"What can I do for you?" asked one of the men with some hostility and without getting up from his chair.

Álvaro was about to answer when the woman came closer, took his face between her rough hands, and began to cry with something like sadness.

"But it's you, Rolando, how late you've come, how late this time, young man."

It was an older Antonia, with the same voice of surprise and an almost unrecognizable face. It seemed as if she had aged a hundred years.

"Don't look at me like that. It happens to everyone. Don't be afraid."

Certainly Álvaro was afraid. Suddenly he became aware that he was carrying his son and that he didn't have the slightest idea of where Fuensanta was. Furthermore, he was surrounded by ragged children, monosyllabic elders, and dirty lambs, inside a hut that could perhaps protect them from something but definitely not the cold; a hut that in addition did not open up in welcome but, on the contrary, closed itself, rejecting him.

"Irena," he managed to stammer, "Irena."

Suddenly, the name seemed to him unbearable, his presence there ridiculous. Antonia looked at him calmly, took him by the arm, and made him sit down at the table. Her movements were so slow that they seemed to him eternal. By then accustomed to the dim light, Álvaro recognized Hercules's face in a large photograph that covered one of the windows of the place. It was the face of a smiling man under which a motto in red and green letters was inscribed: "I'm a friend of the *mexiquenses*." It seemed to be part of a political campaign and to belong to a different era.

"You're late, young man," repeated the old woman as she served him hot coffee in another clay mug. "I warned you that your sister needed you; I told you many times, Rolando."

Recrimination filled her voice and made her tremble with something like a mixture of passion and sorrow. Disturbed by the accusation, Álvaro was about to confess that he wasn't Rolando, but at that moment Mariano extracted himself from his arms and ran toward the group of children that were still playing around the cabin. His concern forced him to stand up, but one of the men held him by the arm with the strength of a boy of twenty.

"Nothing's going to happen to him. Let him play with his friends," said the man in a tone of command.

Then he stationed himself in the doorway in a threatening position. Little by little, as Álvaro began to identify Mariano's voice among the other children's voices, he became calm.

"Why did you come?"

The question the second man was asking him was full of the same unfriendliness and the same recrimination he had heard before.

"I don't know," Álvaro said after thinking about it for a while. "Really, I don't know."

Then he collapsed. The sincerity of his response won him the sympathy of the elderly people seated around Irena's table. Their gaze, which had been rude earlier, settled with compassion on his back.

"Losing a sister is the worst thing that can happen to somebody," murmured Antonia in a barely audible tone. "Especially when they were the only children and twins, besides."

While they all nodded in silence, Álvaro was filled with sorrow and terror. Sorrow for the sister he had lost without even knowing it, and terror because the confusion of identities was going so far that it was confusing even him.

"I'm not Rolando," he affirmed suddenly, thinking of Sonia, his real sister.

"Oh, son," answered the woman, placing his hands in between hers, "it's always the same. When the pain is so great, you always wish you're not who you are."

The tone of understanding ingrained in her voice was a sign of her age, her gray hair and long striated wrinkles. Álvaro started up from his seat.

"No, Antonia, I'm really not Rolando," he repeated with more anguish than firmness in his voice.

"And I'm not Antonia," murmured the woman in a joking tone, trying to show him the extent of his foolishness.

Convinced that the conversation was useless, Álvaro continued to stand and looked through the windows. In the distance, the enchanted forest was still immobile, indestructible, crowned by large gray clouds. Nearby, the group of children was running as if the natural shape of the world was round. He recognized Mariano among them, and then, he discovered that holding the boy's hand was a little girl whose face he forgot and remembered with astonishing ease.

"Who is she?" he asked the old people while he pointed to a slim girl with chestnut-colored hair who it seemed was taking care of his son.

"Little Mariana has always liked children, isn't that so?" they remarked among themselves as if in reality nobody had asked them anything.

Álvaro went out of the cabin and toward his son with the intention of rescuing him from an undefined but imminent danger.

"Uncle Rolando," the little girl shouted at the same time that she stretched out her arms to him.

Álvaro couldn't avoid opening his own arms wide to receive her in them. Then, no longer knowing how to act or what to do, he surrendered to the ambiguities.

"Come," said Mariana, taking his left hand.

He followed her with his son in his arms. The girl, who was dressed in brown corduroy overalls and work boots, guided them with confident steps through the pine trees and solitary paths full of sharp-pointed rocks. They went up the mountain, into the thin air, until they left the forest behind. When they did that, they penetrated the amorphous body of a low-lying cloud. Then, to his complete surprise, they found themselves in front of the lagoons formed by the water in the volcano's crater. The landscape surrounding them was desertlike, useless land. Álvaro was tired but the timeless beauty of the place eased his breathing. Mariano, asleep in his arms, was not able to observe the tense stillness of the waters, the delicateness of the air, the meager warmth of the sunlight that filtered through the cluster of gray clouds.

"My mother went away in that direction," Mariana announced to him as she looked toward the lagoons.

There was no sadness in her gaze. In her eyes, the green color associated with hope radiated from her translucent pupils. She kept quiet for a moment while throwing little white stones toward the Lagoon of the Sun, and then, as if the trek hadn't required any effort, she turned to look at him to indicate that they should return. This time Álvaro didn't obey her. He took off his jacket to cover his son's body and sat down in the same spot where he was standing.

"I can't go on anymore," he told the girl with complete honesty.

"That's what my mama always used to say," answered Mariana, who, without any premeditation, turned her back to him and began the walk back.

Observing the growing distance between them, Álvaro suddenly understood everything that had happened and knew what he had to do. He called to her. He shouted her name and asked her to wait for him. Then, he took her hand and guided her down the slope with a firmness and wisdom that he was just discovering. Slowly, stopping here and there to pronounce the names of some plants, Álvaro walked with his two children until he arrived at the cabin. There, surrounded by the old people, the lambs, and the other children, Fuensanta was waiting for them with a look of distress and her muscles tensed. When she glimpsed them in the distance, the joy of seeing them return safe and sound mattered more than her anger. She ran to hug them.

"Let's get out of this place, Álvaro," she whispered in his ear. "Everything is cursed," she added while she looked around her, encompassing it all within a long and watery look.

Álvaro obeyed. He took his son in his arms, and, carefully, with the speed of someone who is trying to elude death, he began the walk back to the car. He didn't say goodbye; he didn't turn around; and while he advanced hurriedly, he didn't hear anything except his agitated breathing. When he saw the car in the distance, it occurred to him that it was a matter of his own personal salvation. Then, with the same nervous speed, he opened the doors and awaited Fuensanta's prompt arrival. The syncopated movement of their bodies drove him crazy: he didn't know what he was seeing, or what exactly to pay attention to. A knee. A forearm. The heel of a shoe. An eye. Two. They had to leave immediately. As soon as he heard the door slam, he turned on the engine and stepped on the accelerator. It wasn't until a couple of miles later that, looking at the rearview mirror out of the corner of his eye, he realized Mariana was in the backseat.

"And what are you doing here?" asked Fuensanta in amazement, noticing her at the same time.

"My mama told me that one day you'd come for me," answered Mariana in a terse and natural voice, looking at Álvaro in the rearview mirror. "She said that you had always been the man of her dreams," she added, looking at the landscape through the windows, no longer paying attention to them.

Fuensanta repeated the last sentence through her teeth and kept quiet. Álvaro did the same. Mariano, sleeping in his car seat, contributed to the gathering silence. Mariana didn't say another word. The volcano covered with snow watched them from afar.

The situation, like all those created directly or indirectly by Irena, was absurd. Álvaro couldn't understand what a girl with a serious expression, who looked out with a weary gaze that did not correspond to her age, was doing in his car. He didn't know what explanation he would give Fuensanta when, no longer surrounded by the children, they sat down at the table to talk. Nor did he know who Irena was or had been. Above all, he didn't know who the dream man was. As they left behind the enchanted forest, the only thing that Álvaro could do was look out of the corner of his eye at the rearview mirror, hoping with all his heart that he would not find Mariana's face. However, that face continued to be there every time that his nervousness or incredulity forced him to spy on the backseat of the car. Mariana, Mariana Corvián. What would he tell Fuensanta? What would he keep quiet? Within that silence, while the city came closer with its curved spinal cord of lights, Álvaro once again spelled out the word "absurd." Everything, without a doubt, was absurd.

Fuensanta didn't break her silence when they got back to the apartment. Without saying a word, she prepared to feed her son while she showed Mariana where the towels and the bathroom were. When, freshly bathed, the little girl was ready for supper, Fuensanta placed a bowl of cereal on the table, which the child ate without appetite. Then after both children were fed, Fuensanta led them to the bedroom, where she tucked them in, turned off the light, and said good night. Afterward, she went to the balcony, where Álvaro was waiting for her with a contrite expression. Fuensanta observed her husband with a questioning look, but not with distrust. She knew him well. She knew that Álvaro was not the kind of man who suffered from romantic passions or single-minded obsessions. She had faith in him.

"So," she said, bringing a chair closer and placing a bottle of tequila and two glasses on the little table, and asking him, to his complete surprise, for a cigarette.

"None of this has a logical explanation, Fuensanta," murmured Álvaro.

"I know," she answered. "Or so I imagine," she corrected herself.

The human silence that formed between them was voluminous and uncomfortable. But the night of the city crept up on them, with a multitude of disorganized noises that were difficult to identify. Without saying a word, they clinked glasses for the first time.

"Mariana is the daughter of a cruel man and a timid siren," began Álvaro with an ironic smile half-outlined on his face. "Mariana is the daughter of Irena, Fuen. Do you remember her?"

Fuensanta remembered. She had barely heard the name when she wrinkled her nose, and with a couple of weary gestures asked Álvaro for the lighter. Then, after lighting her cigarette, she went to the wrought iron railing and rested her arms on it.

"Her father is, or was, a shady sort who it seems had taken her abroad, perhaps to Copenhagen, without Irena's permission." Someone inside him knew stories that he personally was unfamiliar with, and then handed out explanations with unheard-of aplomb. "It seems that Hercules is, or was, a local politician."

"Hercules Corvián? The candidate?" The incredulity on Fuensanta's face was genuine.

"Do you know him?"

"Everyone knows him, Álvaro. He's the worst kind, connected to narcotics trafficking it seems," she said exasperatedly, and then, without transition, she said loudly, "What can a man like that and a doctor of sick plants have in common?"

"Violence," said Álvaro immediately, surprising even himself. Then he told his wife about the hospital incident, omitting Irena's stay in the Sorrento.

"How could a woman like that, with all those words in her mouth, allow herself to be beaten up by a jerk like Corvián? No, Álvaro, it's too hard to comprehend," concluded Fuensanta, who at this juncture was more interested in the story itself than in the way Álvaro had found out about it. "Didn't you ever see him in those TV ads? A guy with no class, with his outmoded hat and the look of a shameless, down-and-out bum. It's horrible." Álvaro was astonished by his own ignorance. Never in his life had he seen the ads that his wife was referring to, but all her descriptions corresponded to the man whom he had once met in the Siracusa. In his confusion, they clinked their glasses a second time.

"I think they met in Copenhagen but I don't know anything else."

"She must have gone crazy. Isn't that what tends to happen to women who study a lot?"

Without meaning to, Fuensanta was repeating Antonia's words. Then, again without any transition, she pressed him to continue:

"And about Mariana, how did you meet the girl?"

"Like you, Fuen. I met her today."

The sincerity of his voice won over his wife's sympathy. She came closer to him.

"She doesn't act like a child, Álvaro, did you notice that?" she said in a murmur. "She looks at you like a grown-up; she behaves like someone much older."

Álvaro nodded in complete agreement.

"I think Mariana has witnessed some terrible things in her life, Fuen," Álvaro said, as he narrated his trek toward the volcano's crater: the Lagoon of the Sun, the Lagoon of the Moon; *My mother went away in that direction,* the black water, the cold wind, the clouds where gray exploded in a thousand tonalities and textures, a still life. "I don't know what we're going to do with her," he concluded with a question mark in one eye and a plea in the other.

Fuensanta kept silent and looked out at the night, indicating she had understood. The decision would be hers and hers alone. The tequila on her tongue awakened her senses.

"At the beginning I thought that Irena was a friendly woman, Álvaro," murmured Fuensanta, "but her way of repeating the names of plants wasn't normal, was it? It couldn't be. Did you also notice that she didn't feel the cold?"

Fuensanta asked and answered her questions simultaneously.

Rather than conversing, she seemed to be elaborating a monologue that had been deferred for a long time.

"I should throw a jealous tantrum, shouldn't I?" she went on. "I should ask you where this happened, how you found out about it, when, and at what time. But Irena wasn't a woman who could provoke jealousy in another, Álvaro. Compassion, pity, perhaps: something like that."

Fuensanta was silent again while she searched for the exact words, the most precise terms, but she couldn't find them.

"Irena wasn't looking for love. You could tell that from a mile away, Álvaro. She wanted something else. Protection perhaps. Maybe protection from herself. A way to leave."

"She found it," he muttered, observing his wife's faraway eyes.

"Her dream man." Fuensanta repeated the words several times, as if hypnotized. "How curious, Álvaro, what a turn of phrase. Did I ever tell you that I also came to think that a woman had dreamed you up for me? Yes, don't laugh"—she gave his shoulder a gentle push and took another sip of tequila—"I always thought that you were the dream of a feverish woman who in her hurry forgot you on the pavement where I later found you by chance, just like you find your blessings. There's no better way to describe what I feel for you."

Álvaro looked at her with amazement, gratitude, and incredulity. Fuensanta had never told him anything like that in her whole life. Not even in the steamiest moments of their relationship, not even at the beginning, when everything had been enchantment and seduction, had she been prey to clumsy sentiments or passionate dramas. Just as she had said at that party where the ill-suited couple had fought in secret, Fuensanta was in reality a man. Sure of herself, fulfilled in her daily activities, contained in the expression of her emotions, at peace with her surroundings. And now this slightly tipsy woman, who smoked cigarettes while she was confessing to him a love greater than he had ever imagined, seemed totally unfamiliar. Still dazed, he raised the glass of tequila to his lips, without losing sight of her: a hitherto unheard-of face, an unrecognizable expression, a hidden woman suddenly revealed that night. He liked what he saw. All of a sudden he wanted to see her like that for the rest of his life. Suddenly he was sure that he was dreaming. Then, as the two struggled to look each other in the eye, a pale light illuminated the scene on the balcony. Both of them turned their faces toward the interior of the apartment, and with surprise they discovered the figure of Mariana, who was watching them from behind the armchair in the living room. The girl was standing, immobile. A wounded statue. They were afraid and felt like running away. Scantily clad in a sky-blue nightgown, Mariana seemed to be a beacon that offered its light to a perfectly calm ocean. A timid siren. Through her big green eyes, another woman illuminated the couple's silhouette.

He was a man who dreamed.

She was too.

Grey Wolfe LaJoie

The Locksmith

THE LOCKSMITH CANNOT speak well. He never liked school.
When he was a child, the others called him Tombstone. They
threw things at him. Bottles and food waste and dirt clumps stud-
ded with gravel. Though he was much larger than they were, he
remained as still and as quiet as he could while enduring these
acts.

The locksmith is not allowed a driver's license. He rides a bicy-
cle from customer to customer, granting them entry. He likes to
think about the number zero. He likes to think about time travel.
He likes to think about shadows. He has watched many videos on
each of these subjects.

When customers engage with him he is polite. The locksmith
nods and goes about his work in silence. As a child he suffered
a traumatic head injury at the hands of his stepfather, and now
he rarely smiles. It is painful to do so. The customers are deeply
troubled by his presence, by his ineffable, clouded expression. But
they must regain access to their homes, to their automobiles.

A woman calls the locksmith. She is screaming. Her son has shut
himself inside her Lexus and refuses to open the door. Her only

spare is with the father, she says, who is out of the country on business. Intermittently she shouts at her son while, it seems, banging on the hood of the car. She asks for an estimate and then gives the locksmith her address. The locksmith hangs up the phone and readies his equipment. Into a heavy black bag he packs his tension wrenches, his small key-cutting machine, his pick sets, a wedge, several blank keys.

It takes him over an hour by bike to get to the large three-story house on the far side of town. When the locksmith arrives, the woman is on her phone, pacing. She lowers the phone and covers the receiver. "Where were you?" she asks. "Liam might have died of dehydration waiting for you!" She wears dark, form-fitting jogging clothes and her gray hair is pulled up in a bun. The locksmith looks past her, toward the deep black car, which glistens like fire. He steps toward the car and removes his bag. Inside the vehicle, a small blond boy watches him, motionless. The woman carries herself back and forth across the driveway speaking gravely into her phone. Sometimes she pauses to shout through the windshield at her son. "You little shit," she shouts. "You're going to have yourself a hell of a week after this, you little shit." The boy does not acknowledge this. He continues to watch the locksmith, carefully. The two of them stare at each other through the glass. Something is being communicated. The locksmith leans down, shuffles through his black bag. The boy watches him in much the way a small animal would—a squirrel or a bird—if it were to find itself frozen in the locksmith's path. With terror the boy watches. From the heavy bag the locksmith removes a long, narrow tool. Abruptly the boy unlocks the car and runs toward his mother.

"Oh, Liam," the woman says, hugging the boy. "Liam, baby, are you okay?" She turns toward the locksmith. "You can leave now," she says.

.   .   .

In particular, what the locksmith likes about shadows is that, although they occupy a three-dimensional area, we can see only a cross section of them. The cross section is a silhouette, a reverse projection of the object which blocks the light. But the shadow itself has volume, dark and imperceptible.

It is still early in the morning, a cold sunny day in December, and the locksmith is riding to his next customer. The shape of his shadow stretches out before him. The customer he is visiting has dealt with the locksmith before. He is a man named Chuck, a Realtor of some kind. Today Chuck is waiting on the steps of a property he has just purchased, a small bungalow with peeling white paint and shattered windows. He is smoking a cigarette and he waits for the locksmith to dismount his bike before speaking.

"They told me this key worked on all the doors but it doesn't. I can't get into the basement." He hands the key to the locksmith and, although it serves no obvious purpose, the locksmith examines it carefully. SCHLAGE, the key reads. The locksmith breathes heavily.

He hands it back to Chuck and follows him into the house. The floor is littered with items of varying familiarity. Things bank up against the corners of each room, soiled beyond restoration. There are wrappers and shards, stray electrical wires, syringes, a phone book ripped to pieces, an old tire. There are baby clothes and animal droppings and a heavily stained mattress. The smell is inscrutable.

Chuck leads the locksmith through the hallway, where every few feet someone has punched a hole into the drywall. Black mold wanders along in snaking bursts, digressing sometimes into these holes. The locksmith is careful not to step on a thing. Chuck points to the basement door, then goes to the kitchen to inspect the gas lines.

The locksmith stands before the door. It is secured with two worn locks, and the work will take him some time to complete. He lowers his bag and begins.

The locksmith does not have friends. He has a pit bull terrier. When he found it, the dog was lying abandoned behind a shopping center. It was peppered with lacerations and unable to walk. He and the dog reside together in his deceased mother's house. Its coat is black but for the white streaks of fur atop its scars and the mist of gray under its eyes.

Each day when the locksmith comes home, the dog will hide under the bed for an hour or two, trembling. In the beginning, the locksmith tried to coax it out with food, but now he simply waits for these episodes to pass. By dark the dog climbs onto the bed and lies at the foot, watching the locksmith cautiously before drifting to sleep. In the mornings it eats, and only then allows itself to be touched by the locksmith. In this sense they coexist.

For two hours the locksmith works with patience and efficiency on the basement door. The first lock is a standard cylinder barrel and takes him very little time, but the second is rather elaborate, a paracentric keyway. He does not label these in words but nevertheless understands them intimately and moves gracefully through the steps required to open them. Chuck has ordered a pepperoni pizza and offers it several times to him, but the locksmith cannot think of this. He must focus on his task. A lock is its own kind of language.

By noon he has fabricated a functioning key for each of the barrels. He duplicates them, puts them on a ring, and brings them in to Chuck, who is crouched behind the oven. Chuck rises and takes the keys. His hands are dark with grease. From his wallet he removes three twenty-dollar bills and holds them out to the locksmith. "Pleasure," Chuck says. The locksmith takes the money and begins to leave.

"Hey," Chuck says, "don't you want to see what's down there?" The locksmith turns back to him, shakes his head, and goes.

. . .

The symbol for zero is meant to encircle an absence, a nothingness. But the unbroken circle comes also to connote, paradoxically, everything. This excites the locksmith greatly. He has learned much about zero. He has learned that mathematicians and physicists are unsure whether zero is real, whether it should be treated as presence or absence. It is an interpretive problem. They are fiercely divided on the issue, he has learned. The answer determines a great deal: the nature of black holes and gravitational singularities and the origins of the Big Bang. The locksmith stays awake late into the night, watching videos on the subject.

He must ride across the river toward a small apartment building where an elevator has locked itself shut. Along the way the locksmith crosses a set of train tracks. On the tracks there is an animal, an opossum. She has been split in half precisely by the train. She is dead, certainly, though her stomach still bulges and writhes. The locksmith sets his bike aside, comes closer to the animal. From within her cleaved stomach there are newborn opossums, nosing their way out. Perhaps two dozen. They are pale pink and blind, moving haltingly into the hard winter light. Their flesh is so thin as to be translucent, the black eyes just visible beneath. The locksmith watches them squirm. He is unsure what to do. They are incredibly small. Each could fit with ease onto a tablespoon. After a time, he lowers his bag and begins to remove his tools. He takes out his tension wrenches and his key-cutting machine and his pick sets. He places them all neatly into a shrub, out of sight. He takes off his undershirt and lines the inside of his large black bag with it. Then, one at a time, he sets the opossums into the bag. In his hands they are crêpey and silken and periodically they seem to sneeze. The locksmith thinks to himself, *Hmm . . .*

. . .

The dog is bewildered by the locksmith's return so early in the day. For a time it stares at him, forgetting to hide. The locksmith finds an old cookie tin in the kitchen. His home is as it was when he inherited it. He takes the tin and lines it with socks. He places the opossums in the tin along with a jar lid filled with warm water. Into another lid he spoons applesauce. The dog watches curiously as he works. It sniffs at the air between them. When the locksmith glances at the dog it turns and leaves abruptly, disappearing into the bedroom for the rest of the night. Nervously, the locksmith looks into the tin. The small animals stumble vaguely into one another and then rest. He sets them on the kitchen counter, beneath a small reading lamp which he hopes will keep them warm. For the remainder of the day he sits and watches them.

In the morning the locksmith goes and retrieves his tools. They are coated in a thin layer of dew and he wipes them down carefully with a rag before placing them back into his bag. The woman who owns the apartment building with the locked elevator is not terribly upset about the delay. The name she gives is Ms. Alice. "People can use the stairs," she says, when he arrives. She speaks with an enigmatic European accent and wears heavy, riotous jewelry. The locksmith follows her up to the fourth floor, where the elevator was last opened. On the way she hums to herself an unrecognizable tune. Her voice leaps about the staircase. The locksmith walks closely behind, blushing at the sound.

It has been a long time since the locksmith has worked an elevator but he has not forgotten. First he must use a universal drop key to open the landing doors. Once inside he can determine the underlying issue.

"You know the great Houdini?" Ms. Alice asks him. The locksmith is kneeling before the elevator control panel, the woman standing behind him. He looks back at her, somewhat distressed. "He started as a locksmith," she says. "At the age of eleven he began as an apprentice for the local locksmith and soon he could pick anything open." The locksmith smiles painfully, nods, and turns back to his work. "Have you seen his gaze?" she asks. "I think he had the most magical gaze. So terribly, terribly morbid his gaze was." The locksmith is trying to focus. He has the key in the chamber but he must turn it just so in order to trigger the doors. Ms. Alice watches with her hand on her chest. "He was Hungarian, you know. A lot of people don't know that. Hungarian and Jewish. They buried him alive but he clawed his way out. That was one of his tricks but he started panicking while he was digging up." Her jewels clatter carelessly as she speaks. "Later he wrote in his diary, 'the weight of the earth is killing.' That's what he wrote. Can you believe that? They had to pull his body up out of the dirt." The mechanism catches and the locksmith steps back. He takes his heavy pry bar and carefully works the doors open. "How lovely!" Ms. Alice says.

The elevator cab is stalled between floors and the locksmith has to crouch and step down into it. It is dim in the cab. The only light comes from the floor above, where Ms. Alice's feet are still visible, rising up from red shoes. The locksmith inspects the service key mechanism. It is a very simple tubular pin tumbler lock. It will take only a little while. Ms. Alice calls down into the shaft. "Are you thirsty?" she asks. "Would you like something to drink?" The locksmith mumbles something quickly. "What?" Ms. Alice says. He repeats himself carefully, his shoulders tense. There is a long silence and then the locksmith returns to his work, impressioning the lock with a blank. "Oh how I wish I could have seen him perform," Ms. Alice says. "Such a handsome, eerie man. Full of miracles. Full of wonder. Keep up your enthusiasm! He always said that! But then of course his final words were something altogether different."

In very little time the locksmith has restarted the elevator's operation. The lights flicker on at once and the doors close and of its own accord the cab begins to lift him. It rises eight stories and then opens up to the roof. Before him, the gray sky unfolds slowly, its cold light flooding the cab. A dark bird drifts down on the wind and lands just ahead of him.

Since he was a very small child the locksmith has thought of time travel. There is one theory which accepts the flow of time as a cognitive construct. This is the locksmith's favorite. According to this theory, were the locksmith to return to his past—such as the last time he saw his mother—he would have no experience of any temporal discontinuity. He would simply look backward in memory, reconstructing his childhood, or forward in expectation, guessing at the future. Were the locksmith to travel back through time, in other words, everything would feel as it does now. The locksmith thinks of this often. He thinks, Who is to say I haven't just time-traveled? Who is to say time ever moves forward? Wordlessly he thinks these things to himself.

The locksmith waits for the elevator doors to close, then presses the button to go back down. When he returns Ms. Alice is there smiling. "That was quite the escape!" she says.

Kirstin Valdez Quade
After Hours at the Acacia Park Pool

Every afternoon since school let out, Laura and her best friend Bernadette had gone to the pool in Acacia Park. There they sunned on towels and dangled their feet in the water and observed the older girls, who draped themselves along the concrete deck close to Joel's lifeguard chair, and the older boys, who dragged each other's heads underwater and blasted the Rolling Stones from competing tape decks across the pool. They ignored the little kids and the young mothers in their skirted suits. The rest of the park was deserted under the clear blue sky, the grass yellowed and spiky, the playground metal scalding. To the north, the Santa Catalinas rose above the bowl of Tucson.

It was hot in the full sun, and Laura wanted to slip into the pool, lie back, let the water rush around the roots of her hair, wanted to feel her muscles push through the water, but she was given to understand that once you were a teenager, you no longer got fully wet; you kept to the edges, and you watched your hair. Laura and Bernadette pressed the warm skin at each other's shoulders, their fingerprints turning white and then red. Occasionally they goaded each other into calling out to Joel.

"Help, Joel!" Laura called across the sparkling expanse of water. "I'm drowning in suntan oil!"

He shook a finger at them. "Don't distract the lifeguard." He winked, then returned to scanning the pool.

Joel was three years older, but Bernadette and Laura had some claim on him because when they were little Joel had lived on Bernadette's street. Now, almost a senior, he'd become clear skinned and square jawed. "His mouth is so sexy," Bernadette murmured, squinting across the pool at him, and she was right. Joel was nearly lipless, masculine, his smile lazy and wry.

Laura lay on her belly, her book propped to block her chest. She kept waiting for her body to even itself out, but she'd just turned fifteen, and still her puny left breast hadn't caught up. Laura had taken to approaching the mirror only in profile. The right was pretty much just right: full and round, spilling ever so slightly out the top of her swimsuit. Normally Laura stuffed a nylon knee stocking in the bottom of her left bra cup, which did the trick, but you couldn't do that when you might get splashed by boys or tossed in the water. Last week, Bernadette had gotten tossed in the water, and somehow even drenched she was beautiful—or not beautiful, maybe, but smooth and laughing. Her thick straight hair, which, dry, was nearly blond, streamed heavy and darkened with water. Everything about her was unblemished and clear. Laura's own black hair was so thin that when it was wet, she was all skull. "You have to fluff it," her mother told her. "Use my hairspray."

It wasn't fair because you most needed great boobs when you were in a swimsuit. Laura had considered just going ahead and stuffing, as she was rarely splashed, but the cruel irony was that the better your boobs, the better your chance of *being* splashed. The thought of a dripping brown nylon streaming out of her swimsuit like entrails was so horrifying that Laura's only option was to tense her left pectoral to push the breast forward.

"You okay?" Bernadette asked. "You look constipated."

· · ·

Laura's breasts notwithstanding, the summer seemed to be shaping up perfectly. But then, toward the end of June, Mr. Swanson from next door ran away with an eighteen-year-old girl who worked at the Breezy Freeze. "Of course I *knew* about her," Laura overheard Mrs. Swanson telling her mother in the aluminum carport. "But I didn't know he'd leave with her. And to Los Angeles!" Mrs. Swanson sobbed into her hands as if she could have borne it if they'd gone to Denver or Wichita.

Laura had a great deal of disdain for this sort of female misfortune. No matter how you sliced it, it was undignified: to be so distraught to have been left, and to have been left in the first place.

"Mrs. Swanson should count herself lucky," Laura told her sighing mother that evening as they scooped leftovers into yellow-stained Tupperwares. "The man is revolting. He still has acne. That new kid takes after him exactly." Which was true. That giant scaly head—Laura had never seen an uglier baby.

Laura's mother pinched her hard on the upper arm. "Where is your compassion?" she hissed. "I hope to God you never have to find out what that woman is going through."

So, because of a single unfortunate comment, Laura found herself committed to a summer of babysitting for a dollar an hour. A dollar! Instead of reading and sunning herself at the city pool with Bernadette, Laura would spend her days with the two irritable, pale little Swanson girls and their sluggish red-faced infant brother.

Inside and out, the Swansons' house was brown: brown carpet, brown cabinetry, brown paneling on the dining room walls. Only the curtains were blue, and these were heavy and long, shimmering pale taffeta, thick with cigarette smoke and kept drawn at all times against the day. Once, three years ago, Laura had waited just inside the door while Mrs. Swanson looked around for her purse to buy a single box of Girl Scout cookies. Now, the whole place smelled of sodden diaper and—a result of the barely effective evaporative cooler—pond water, microbial and rotting.

"The pad for the cooler is old," said Mrs. Swanson the first day, embarrassed. "Mr. Swanson was going to replace it." She bounced the baby hard on her hip. Her makeup was amateurish and haphazard, as though it had been applied without the aid of a mirror. A thumbprint of brown foundation was smeared on her left cheek.

"I can breathe out of my mouth," said Laura.

"I'm going to have to hire someone, and God knows how much that will cost."

If Mrs. Swanson wanted sympathy, she wouldn't get it from Laura. A dollar an hour! Laura's mother acted like it was some huge tragedy that Mrs. Swanson had had to get a job, but filing and answering phones at the bus station didn't seem bad to Laura, not compared to being marooned with three kids in this festering house.

"My mom says you get a thirty percent discount on bus tickets. That's pretty great."

Mrs. Swanson looked at Laura hard through short, sticky-looking lashes, as if to determine whether Laura was being sarcastic, which, Laura supposed, she sort of was.

"Is it great? Where'm I going to go? Los Angeles? Just cram them into my suitcase?" She jerked her thumb at the girls, who were kneeling on the kitchen floor, dully stirring the air in a dented aluminum cooking pot. "Put my pot away, Jean Marie," Mrs. Swanson said. "It's not a toy."

"*Jeannie!*" cried the older girl. "I told you to call me Jeannie!"

Mrs. Swanson handed off the baby. "He needs a change." She heaved her purse onto her shoulder and slammed the screen door behind her. The baby startled, then blinked stupidly into Laura's face.

In the minutes after Mrs. Swanson drove away in her enormous dented Chrysler, everything went to hell. The four-year-old, Melinda, stripped naked and bolted for the door, the baby whacked his head on an open bureau drawer, and Jeannie, the second grader, stuffed the kitten in a shoebox and sent it sailing down the stairs. The stairs were bare plywood, installing the carpet being another task Mr. Swanson hadn't gotten around to.

"Check the baby!" Laura yelled at the older girl, and she ran out the door and down the block, trying to overtake Melinda before she smacked naked into an oncoming car.

Eight thirty in the morning, and it was already in the nineties. At the intersection, Laura grabbed the girl by a sweaty hand, but the child resisted, went limp, and collapsed on the hot sidewalk. Laura dragged her across the concrete for a foot or two, holding tight to the skinny little wrist, while the girl shrieked. "Owie! You're hurting me!"

"Stand up then." Laura gave the wrist another yank, released it. Hot dirt gusted down the street.

Melinda bowed her head and sobbed into the concrete. Laura crossed her arms and regarded the naked child.

A lady Laura recognized from the neighborhood slowed her car and rolled down the window. She looked sternly over the top of her sunglasses. "That child should be wearing clothes."

Stupid cow, Laura said in her head, and turned her back on the woman. "You—" Laura swung Melinda up, digging into her bare skin with her nails. "You're a brat."

"I hate you!" Melinda screamed into her ear.

Laura hoisted the squirming girl. "I hate you more."

Inside, the scene was blessedly quiet. The baby had cried himself to sleep in a shuddering heap next to the china cabinet, and Jeannie was peering into the shoebox. Laura dumped Melinda on the couch. "Get dressed or I'm calling your mother." Melinda curled into a ball and sobbed, small tense buttocks high. Her spine was a knotted cord down her back.

"You can spank her if you want," Jeannie said. "Mom does all the time." Jeannie removed the lid and watched with interest as the kitten staggered out of the box, turning a few drunken circles.

"I think you damaged it," said Laura.

The kitten took an unsteady step, then stopped. Its head drooped to the carpet. Even Melinda had quieted and was watching, fist in mouth.

"I really think it's dying," Laura said, queasy.

"No, it isn't," said Jeannie, but her broad, pale forehead was cinched.

Laura reached for the kitten, but it roused itself and darted under the couch.

The second afternoon, while the baby napped, Bernadette stopped by. She kissed Laura's cheek, then surveyed the Swansons' living room, fanning the sweat off her face. "Nice design concept. It smells like shit in here."

"I know," said Laura, but the truth was she'd already quit smelling it.

Bernadette was wearing a plaid halter dress. She had bad posture, so her shoulder blades stuck out behind her. "Here," she said. "I brought you this." She handed Laura a sweating Breezy Freeze cup. It was a chocolate milkshake, half-melted.

"God, you're a sweetheart," said Laura. Sometimes she wondered what she'd done to deserve Bernadette.

"Poor you. I hate that you're stuck here."

Laura was flooded with affection for her friend. "Yeah, but I'm doing it for us, for New York."

Jeannie scowled at the cup. Only now did Laura notice that the girl's buttons were done wrong on her shirt. She reached out to fix them, but Jeannie shrank from her and crossed her skinny arms across her chest. Laura tipped her head at the girl. "See what I mean?" she said to Bernadette.

Bernadette looked around. "So what, you just sit here all day? I wish we could swim."

"*You* can," said Laura, but she knew Bernadette wouldn't go, not alone. Bernadette had been fat until just before high school, and she was still self-conscious, despite her new height and long hair. Laura sometimes had to remind herself that Bernadette's prospects had changed. With Laura's stick-out ears and skinny legs and asymmetrical chest, the two of them were no longer in the same category, and it was only a matter of time before Bernadette figured that out. "You should go."

"What, and swim in circles by myself? It's not fun without you."

Relieved, Laura shrugged. "I know. It stinks."

"I'd like some milkshake," said Melinda hopelessly.

Laura took a long suck from the straw, eyes on the smaller child, then relented and poured some into two jelly glasses for the girls.

"I don't want any," said Jeannie. She pushed her glass away.

"Rude," said Bernadette, and drank it herself.

Mrs. Swanson told Laura she'd pay her next week, when her paperwork cleared, and then said she'd pay the week after. A dollar was pathetic, but it was still a dollar, and as she endured the shrieks and fights, hauling the swollen baby around the house like a sack of sand, the hours added up, and Laura took pleasure in imagining Bernadette's face when she presented her with the money for the escape they'd been planning since they were eleven. It would be 1980, and they'd leave Tucson behind with the faded old decade, take their places among the slim secretaries and assistants with soft curly hair. Laura would buy the kinds of things those women bought: tartan skirts and brisk heels. Maybe even a high-quality foam falsie, like a chicken cutlet. They'd be roommates, she and Bernadette, and they'd double date, returning home giggling and tipsy together. Some nights, they'd go to movies, the two of them. Other nights they'd just stay in, paint each other's nails like sisters or best friends in magazines.

On those worst days, when the baby squalled and the girls

pinched Laura and each other, Laura could at least think of the money that was coming to her, the fat stack of dirty bills: counting them, smoothing them, tucking them away for the day she and Bernadette would board the bus, never to come back. And if she was a little rough with the kids, if she jerked the baby around and snapped at the girls and pinched them back, well, they were getting what they paid for.

At first, Laura spent the days lying on the couch with back issues of women's magazines dangling over her head, watching soap operas: *Guiding Light* and *The Doctors* and *Search for Tomorrow*. Hour after hour passed filled with nearly indistinguishable actors committing nearly indistinguishable betrayals. She learned the lyrics to all the commercial jingles and the tunes began to gnaw at her like a toothache. Jeannie and Melinda watched, too, vacant.

Sometimes in the afternoons Laura was so overcome with sleepiness, she'd stretch out on the couch and sink under. Sometimes the baby was with her, his head heavy and sweaty on her chest. She awoke from these naps disoriented and sluggish, sitting up with a surge of fear to locate Jeannie and Melinda, who, more often than not, were sprawled a foot from the television screen.

One day when Laura opened her eyes, Jeannie was in the armchair, watching her.

"You used to be nice to us," said Jeannie. Her knees were dirty, and strands of lank hair clung to the grape jelly around her mouth.

"Not likely," said Laura. She wiped the corners of her own mouth and hoisted the damp weight of the baby so she could sit up.

"You were," insisted Jeannie. "You had that garage sale that one time and you gave me all your old Barbies for free."

"Nuh-uh," she said, though of course she remembered Jeannie's excitement at the bounty and the pleasure of knowing that toys she'd once cared about would be cherished.

"Yeah-huh."

She didn't know why she got like this around the girls. The worst of it was that she did actually remember liking them. She remembered holding Jeannie when she was a big-headed two-year-old. And she'd enjoyed being adored. Why couldn't she be that person again?

Occasionally, when the baby was asleep and the girls absorbed in the television, Laura snooped in Mrs. Swanson's drawers and jewelry box. But there was nothing there but thick slimming underwear and stretched brown nylons and some cheap fake pearls, light in the palm. Nothing, absolutely nothing, indicated that any of the normal hopes of a normal woman had been fulfilled.

One morning, Mrs. Swanson opened the door with a dark expression. "Look at this," she said, her voice barely containing its rage. She led Laura to the kitchen. "Look." She jabbed her finger in the air, pointing at the toaster, where a piece of plastic had melted to the chrome. The day before, Laura had set the bag of Bunny Bread too close. She'd noticed but hadn't thought it was a big deal.

"Oh, sorry," said Laura.

"*Sorry?*"

Laura shrugged. "I guess these things happen."

"Do these things happen at your house? Does your toaster have plastic melted all over it?" Mrs. Swanson's voice rose.

"No," conceded Laura coldly. She was thrumming with fury. She didn't have to feed these kids. She didn't have to be here in the first place.

She held Mrs. Swanson's gaze. Laura was on the point of quitting when Mrs. Swanson broke eye contact, flushing. "I'm going to be late," she muttered, and reached for her purse.

Bernadette called every day, and sometimes they talked for two or three hours, Laura stretching the cord as far as it would go to dump fish sticks on plates and retrieve milk from the fridge. Their conversations were long and desultory, and Laura could picture Bernadette lying on her bed doing her ab exercises. "Do you ever get dirt in the corner of your toenail that you just can't dig out?" Bernadette asked. "I tried to get it with a safety pin, but now I'm bleeding."

"Just paint your nails," said Laura with authority.

"What are those hellions up to?"

"Who knows? Swallowing Ajax." The girls were actually playing quietly, and the baby was asleep on the couch beside her, arms flung wide. Laura slowly pulled the pacifier from his mouth. Even in his sleep, he strained his neck to meet it. When it finally came out with a pop, his eyes flew open, but his sleepy eyeballs rolled back in his head and he resumed sucking, his lips working away at nothing. She gave him the pacifier back, then began to tug it again.

Bernadette sighed. "Please just come to the pool today. I'm going."

"Really? Who with?"

"With everyone. Bring the kids. Make them sit in the shallow end. I'll watch one. You don't even have to pay me."

"I told you. They're monsters. You can't put the baby down or it'll scream its head off. My back is breaking. I really think I need a brace or something. Anyway, I'm not allowed to bring them to the pool. Mrs. Swanson said a kid drowned there."

"The pool's only two years old. We'd know if someone had drowned there."

"Mrs. Swanson has personal knowledge of someone who's died in every gruesome way imaginable. She told my mom about some lady who was washing dishes during the monsoon, and lightning struck and she was electrocuted."

Bernadette laughed, and Laura smiled, pleased. "We can tie them to a deck chair. Bring their jump ropes. Joel would love to see you."

"I'm so sure."

"Fine. But it won't be fun without you."

Laura could almost believe that Bernadette meant it. "Stick your tongue down his throat for me."

She hung up, feeling hot and forsaken. It hurt to think of Bernadette and the girls from school trading secrets on the deck, teasing Joel, doing things teenagers were supposed to do. The balance of friendships would tilt. Bernadette and the others were entangling themselves in one another's lives, and Laura wasn't there to assert her presence. Soon when they called each other to meet up at the Breezy Freeze, they wouldn't remember her at all.

When Laura and Bernadette were seven, they spent their afternoons playing Zoo in Joel's backyard. Zoo was Joel's invention. As zookeeper, he locked the girls in the chain-link enclosure that had once housed his dog. They weren't really locked in, could have left at any moment, but he wound a rope around the gate's latch for verisimilitude. Bernadette and Laura were allowed to decide what animals they were as long as they were the same kind and as long as Joel approved their choice. Occasionally, he'd tell them to take off their clothes, and they would. Or Laura would. Bernadette would undress so slowly and unwillingly that Laura would be naked and impatient before Bernadette, giggling, had even undone the buttons on her shirt. Meanwhile the zookeeper would march up and down the length of the cage officiously, his eyes on the animals, who stood motionless while the breeze ruffled their fur. Even now, when Laura thought of Zoo, she felt a kind of illicit thrill: being trapped, being watched.

But then Joel and his family moved into a new house on the edge of town. Laura and Bernadette tried to play Zoo in Bernadette's backyard, but without a zookeeper or a proper cage, the whole thing seemed pointless. There was no one to order them about, no one to push sticks or leaves at them through the fence during feeding time.

They hardly saw Joel again until they started at Tucson High, where, despite being an upperclassman, swaggering and muscular, he'd wink a special hello in the hall.

The last week of July, Mr. Swanson mailed Mrs. Swanson a brand-new Osterizer blender, mustard yellow, with a row of square buttons. Mrs. Swanson lugged it over on Saturday morning to show it off to Laura's mother. In the kitchen she plugged it in and pressed the *Whip* button to demonstrate while Laura's mother looked on, arms crossed.

Mrs. Swanson turned it off but kept her fingers on the glass, flushed. "It's a good one. I don't know how he knew which one to buy."

"Maybe Little Miss Breezy Freeze picked it out," said Laura's mother, and Laura, sitting with her book at the kitchen table, nearly laughed. "She does know her way around a milkshake."

Mrs. Swanson was actually older than Laura's mother, but because she'd married late and was naturally submissive, she was always asking for advice. It was a role Laura's mother was happy to fill, and she readily gave guidance on matters she had no experience with: Raising more than one child, for example. Balancing work and home. Dealing with a philandering husband.

Mrs. Swanson accepted a cup of coffee but didn't add cream or sip it. "He misses the children." She glanced at Laura, then lowered her voice. "He feels bad."

"Run along, Laura," said her mother. Very slowly Laura set her book on the table, placed the marker inside, closed it. "He should feel bad, behaving that way."

"I think he wants to come home." Mrs. Swanson rubbed her temple. "I think he just doesn't know how to say it."

Laura's mother pressed her lips with displeasure. "I'm sure that's the case."

"Well, I won't let him," Mrs. Swanson said defensively.

"I should hope not." Laura's mother averted her eyes.

"I won't. I said I won't." Then after a moment, voice tight, she said, "May I have a glass of water?" She waited tensely while Laura's mother ran the tap, then gulped it down. "My sister says you can't cry if you're drinking water."

That night as Laura helped dry the dishes, her mother snorted, "A blender. That's a pretty poor apology, if you ask me. John," she called to the living room, "if you ever give me a blender, I'm filing for divorce."

"What?" Laura's father called back.

Laura was torn between wanting to fill the hours and wanting to demonstrate to all of them—the girls, Mrs. Swanson, even the baby—that she resented being here. But before long, the monotony began to wear on her, and, just to entertain herself, she began to lug her old childhood books and toys over. Now Melinda rushed at her in the mornings to examine what she'd brought, and Laura felt a flush of pleasure at having been awaited. Melinda would turn each book in her hands. "Will you read it to me now?"

One afternoon, the girls had just finished their tomato soup and were working on Laura's old Snoopy puzzle. Laura was feeding the baby vanilla pudding and hoping that the puzzle had all its pieces—she really couldn't remember. The swamp cooler churned ineffectually. She liked feeding the baby, liked his eagerness, his mouth agape like a baby bird's. He leaned so far forward toward the spoon that he practically fell into his own lap.

"Someone's here," said Melinda.

And indeed, at the back door, there was Bernadette and, beside her, Joel. His long blond hair was crispy from the dry air and chlorine.

Joel opened his mouth wide and pressed it against the window, teeth clacking against glass. Those thin lips were remarkably elastic; they looked like slugs or a science experiment, the network of spongy purple veins flattened wet against the glass.

"Gross!" cried Jeannie, delighted.

After Laura and Bernadette hugged, Laura kept her arm around Bernadette's waist; Bernadette leaned into her. But when Laura hooked her chin over Bernadette's shoulder, Bernadette said, "Get off."

Laura withdrew, stunned. She looked around the kitchen, self-conscious. "You guys want Popsicles?"

"Definitely," said Bernadette. "Sorry it smells bad in here," she apologized to Joel, and Laura felt a rush of irritation.

Laura distributed the Popsicles, snapping an orange one in half for Melinda and Jeannie.

Jeannie frowned. "Why do they get *two* Popsicles?"

"We don't," said Bernadette. "You just get a half."

Melinda's face contorted.

"Shut up," Laura told the girl preemptively. "Why'd you have to say that, Bernadette?"

"My daddy is never coming home," Melinda said sorrowfully.

"That's private," said Jeannie. "Don't tell them that."

Melinda looked near tears. The Popsicle dripped down her wrist. "Hey, wanna see my ugliest face?" Joel asked. He dropped his head into his hands, and when he came up, his eyelids were inside out, the tender red insides exposed to the world. Melinda and Jeannie laughed.

"Your regular one is uglier," Laura said, and he flashed her a mischievous smile.

Afterward, the girls brightened and mobbed Joel, showing off their toys. Jeannie thrust her doll in his face. "She's got underpants painted on," she said, flipping the doll's dress.

"Come with me to the bathroom a sec." Bernadette dragged on Laura's arm, and it occurred to her that Bernadette was behaving the way girls in magazines behaved.

Bernadette shut the door. "I didn't ask him to come. He just kept talking to me. We were practically here before he was like, 'Where are we even going?'"

Laura felt very still. "Are you two . . . together?"

Bernadette giggled.

Laura narrowed her eyes.

"Well, don't ask *me*." Bernadette sniffed her armpits. "Do I stink? I think I might stink."

Obediently, Laura sniffed, her nose nearly touching Bernadette's skin, which was heated and damp from her walk in the sun. "Only a little," Laura said, even though she smelled just the clean, almost non-smell of salt.

Bernadette began pulling open cupboard doors and rifling through drawers. "Four bottles of hydrogen peroxide? God. Doesn't she even have perfume?" She sniffed a can of Pledge, rejected it, and nudged the kitten's litterbox with her foot. "Gah. No wonder it reeks in here."

Laura shrugged.

Bernadette found a worn lipstick and puckered into the mirror. It was too pink and waxy, but she didn't wipe it off. "I wish there were two of him, one for each of us. Exactly the same."

Laura said glumly, "If they were exactly the same, they'd both like you."

Bernadette's giggle was a little hysterical. "Come on. He'll wonder where we are."

Mrs. Swanson didn't pay and didn't pay, and the tedious days passed. "Next week," Mrs. Swanson said, taking the baby from Laura, looking more exhausted as the summer ground on. "At the end of the month."

Laura resolved to quit—walk out the door, leave the Swanson children to shut themselves in the refrigerator—but if she quit she might never get paid, so each morning, she awoke at seven thinking of Bernadette's face when, on graduation day, Laura would flourish the bus tickets, and thinking also of all the things they needed before they could leave: new clothes for their job interviews, new suitcases. So each day she made her way next door in time for Mrs. Swanson to leave for work.

One afternoon, after she'd finished feeding the kids cornflakes,

Laura announced that they were going to make paper. She'd done this project in second grade and remembered the pleasure of spreading the pulp across the screen, of peeling off the stiff sheet once it had dried in the sun.

"Paper," she explained, "was invented by the Chinese even before Jesus was born." She began tearing old grocery circulars and construction paper into squares. On the floor, the baby gummed an ice cube tray.

"That makes no sense," Jeannie said sullenly. "How did the Chinese invent paper if they had to grind up paper to make it?"

"They used leaves and stuff, I guess."

She dropped the squares into the blender, which sat on the counter, shiny and unused. She filled it with water. "We're going to mash it into pulp, then strain it, and it'll dry into paper." Laura popped the screen out of the kitchen window while the girls watched with horror. "Don't look so freaked. We'll put it back."

Laura positioned the screen over the kitchen sink and poured the pulp over it. She spread it evenly with a knife into a rectangle. Brown water dripped down the drain.

"See? It's easy."

Jeannie had crept closer. "Can I try?"

The girls were so young, Laura thought. She'd been Jeannie's age when she played Zoo. She'd felt so free and fierce, but really she'd just been a scrawny kid naked in a cage.

They made a second batch and a third. Laura popped out the other kitchen screen, and the girls brightened and got creative, spreading it into shapes, shaking glitter and small leaves into the pulp.

Jeannie pressed *Frappé* and cried, "We can make a whole stationery set!" which is when the blender began to whine. Laura yanked the plug, but not before the kitchen filled with the horrible smell of burnt electricity. Melinda and Jeannie looked worried. "It just needs to cool," Laura said. But when she plugged it back in, the motor struggled, then died out completely.

"Shit," said Laura. Her stomach twisted. She thought of Mrs.

Swanson's rage, and then she thought of her hopeful expression when she'd showed off the blender, and she actually felt bad.

"Shit," Jeannie echoed. "Mom is going to kill us." Melinda sucked her fist, eyes wide.

The key sounded in the front door, and Laura froze.

"Daddy!" Melinda ran at her father and crashed into his leg.

Mr. Swanson beamed. "Hey there, peanut." He lifted her high with thick forearms, and Melinda squealed.

His brown crew cut looked spiny and fresh, thinning at the top, his big face scoured and painful. A craterous pimple on his temple was bleeding.

Jeannie eyed him from the kitchen doorway, gripping the frame as though her father were a black hole that might suck her in.

Laura's relief turned into fresh dread. "Hi, Mr. Swanson. I'm just babysitting." The best thing, she decided, was to pretend to know nothing about the Breezy Freeze girl or the fact that he hadn't been living here. She wondered if she ought to call Mrs. Swanson or her own mother. She wondered if she should ask him to leave, but you couldn't ask a man to leave his own house. Laura could feel her pulse throbbing in her neck, and her mouth went dry. Could he be dangerous?

Mr. Swanson was watching his older daughter, his hand on Melinda's shoulder. "Jeannie-Bird, aren't you going to hug your old daddy?"

Jeannie didn't reply. Melinda looked from her father to her sister, then slipped out from beneath her father's hand and joined Jeannie in the doorway.

Mr. Swanson's eyes welled.

Laura jostled the baby busily, scratched at some food crusted on his onesie. "Would you like a glass of punch?" She led Mr. Swanson into his own kitchen. She looked uneasily at the mess spread across the counter, the dripping window screens, the sink spattered with brown pulp like vomit. "We were just doing a project. Have a seat."

Mr. Swanson sat at the table obediently. He glanced at the mess but said nothing. He didn't reach for the glass she set before him. He pressed his palms into the Formica, lifted them slowly, then pressed them down again, as though testing its solidity.

Laura's alarm faded. "Want some taco casserole? I made some yesterday."

"I had a burger," Mr. Swanson said. Laura imagined him eating alone at the Woolworth's counter at the end of his long drive. After, he'd have stopped in the bathroom, putting off the moment when he'd present himself at the door of his old home. He would have held his own gaze for courage. He would have picked the pimple. The bus station was just down the street; she wondered if he knew his wife was working there now and wanted to see his daughters alone, or if he'd meant to find her here.

Laura couldn't stop looking at a large blackhead buried deep in his cheek. The skin around it was gray. He had bristles growing out of the tip of his nose, six or seven of them. She couldn't imagine the girl from the Breezy Freeze allowing herself to be undressed by him, to be pressed against his hairy belly.

The girls stood watching from the doorway.

"The blender died, Daddy," Melinda said. "We broke it."

Jeannie elbowed her angrily, and Melinda burst into tears. Mr. Swanson stood, alarmed, and hovered over his daughters without touching them. "Hey, baby."

Jeannie pulled her little sister close. "You need to get us a new one," Jeannie told her father in a loud, clear voice. The child met Laura's eye, and something passed between them, an understanding between equals. Laura was filled with admiration for the girl.

Mr. Swanson brightened. "I will, baby. I will."

"Good," said Jeannie. "We'll need it before five o'clock." She stepped forward and patted her father's arm gently.

When Mrs. Swanson got in that evening, she seemed not to register the new blender on the counter, or the flecked kitchen screens that bagged in their frames, or her daughters' guarded silence. She stood at the kitchen table, her purse still slung on her shoulder, turning the note from Mr. Swanson in her hands.

Not ten minutes later, at her own house next door, Laura had just kicked off her sandals and was serving herself a bowl of tapioca pudding when Mrs. Swanson tapped at the back door, her mouth set in a grim line. Two red spots were high on her cheeks.

"Leave us, please, Laura," her mother said, taking one look at Mrs. Swanson. Laura slipped out, then stood quietly in the dining room, listening.

"He wants to take me to the Western Vista Resort tonight." Mrs. Swanson's voice wavered. "It's new, north of town."

Her mother's reply was low and urgent.

"It's just one night! There's a pool with a swim-up bar!" Mrs. Swanson cried. "I need to hear him out."

More hushed discussion, and then Laura's mother called her in. "Mrs. Swanson has to visit her sister tonight," she said, not meeting Laura's eye. "You'll stay next door."

"All night?" Laura objected, though she was already planning her call to Bernadette.

"I'll pay you twenty dollars," Mrs. Swanson said.

"Fine."

Bernadette and Laura lounged on Mrs. Swanson's bed and smeared oatmeal on their faces. The children had gone down agreeably half an hour after their bedtimes, and the house smelled of the cookies they'd baked and devoured earlier. Laura was unable to take her eye off her reflection in the heavily framed mirror above Mrs. Swanson's bureau. "We look like burn victims."

Bernadette laughed. "Not nice."

Laura wondered if they had some fervent need to tend to their complexions, or if they were doing masks because that's what was supposed to happen at sleepovers. This feeling had been occurring to her more and more recently—earlier in the summer at the pool, for example—a suspicion that she was playing a part. But when Laura tried to decide how her real, most authentic self would act in a given situation, how, for example, she would behave on this sleepover if she'd never heard about other girls at other sleepovers, if she didn't know she was supposed to talk about boys and hair, if it were just Laura and Bernadette in this bedroom with the whole night ahead of them—well, she could not begin to guess.

It was strange, being in Mrs. Swanson's bedroom like this; although Mrs. Swanson had told Laura she'd sleep in here, her presence felt illicit, and not just because she hadn't asked permission to invite Bernadette. The sheets smelled of castor oil and powder and something else thick and adult.

"So," Bernadette said. "I told Joel we'd meet him at the pool at midnight."

Laura felt sick. Was this why Bernadette had come over? So she could more easily sneak out to see Joel? "Go meet him then."

"You need to come!"

"I don't see why you need me."

"Of course I need you! You're my best friend. And I miss you. I've hardly seen you all summer."

"We can't leave the kids," Laura said.

"Sure we can. It'll be an hour. What are the chances one of them wakes up in one hour of the whole night? You don't get paid enough to have your life ruined."

"Yeah," Laura agreed glumly. "Still."

Bernadette lay back, stretching her long brown legs toward the ceiling, and touched her toes. "My first time," she said, moving on as if matters had been decided, "I want it to be on an empty sunny beach."

Laura looked up, startled. "Where do you plan on finding a beach around here?" She could picture it exactly: Bernadette in her blue swimsuit, leaning on her elbows in the sand, lips parted, waiting.

"I'll move to California. Anyway, it doesn't matter. We're talking about our ideal situation."

"We're moving to New York, Bern."

Bernadette sighed hugely. "Right." She flipped onto her stomach and nudged Laura. "Tell me about your ideal."

"Well, I'd need it to be dark," said Laura.

"Why?"

"You know. Because of my boobs. They're lopsided."

"Show me."

"No way," said Laura, but Bernadette's eyes behind the oatmeal were steady, so Laura pulled her T-shirt over her head and unhooked her bra. Bernadette cupped them, one in each hand, tipped her head appraisingly. Laura's nipples tightened, and she felt herself become wet. She closed her eyes, imagined Bernadette leaning close. She smelled oatmeal and the apple of Bernadette's shampoo, and under that, chlorine, and under that Bernadette's own salt smell.

"So?" Laura croaked. "They're hideous. Aren't they hideous?"

"At least you have boobs. I can sort of see what you're talking about, but they're fine." Bernadette dropped Laura's breasts and tossed the T-shirt at her. "No one would ever notice."

She was glad she was hiding behind the stiffening oatmeal. Of course no one would ever notice, because no one would ever look at her. She was as plain and bland and lumpy as the oatmeal shrinking to cement in the bowl. She sipped her water, trying to drown the tightness behind her throat.

They rinsed their faces, lay with slices of cucumber on their eyes, laughed about people at school, but Bernadette became twitchier and more distracted as midnight neared.

"Bernadette." Trembling, Laura touched her friend's clavicle. "Let's not go to the pool. Let's just stay in."

"I thought you'd want to." Hurt passed over Bernadette's face. "Are you jealous?"

Laura dropped her hand. "No," she said, too forceful. "Of course not. I just don't think I should go."

"You can't abandon me." Bernadette was actually pleading, and Laura felt at once powerful and guilty. "Why can't you be happy for me?"

Because Laura's summer was ruined. Because her best friend had drifted away. Because everything light and thrilling would always be denied her. Because she was unlucky, unlovable.

Laura wanted, wanted, wanted. A person couldn't live with this formless longing. She thought of the girl from the Breezy Freeze, leaving school and family to follow Mr. Swanson to Los Angeles; this kind of longing could make you do disastrous things.

"We can stay for thirty minutes," Laura said. "Plus ten minutes there, ten minutes back."

At ten to midnight, Laura and Bernadette crept through the house, towels in hand.

"Are you guys going swimming?" Jeannie stood in the dark living room in her sleep shirt, clutching the kitten. "I want to go with."

"Jesus, you scared me," Laura said. "Go back to bed."

"I can't sleep."

"Lie down and try."

"I want to go with you guys." Jeannie narrowed her eyes shrewdly. "Did my mom say you could have a slumber party?"

Laura remembered the child's skillful manipulation of her father that day and laughed. "You can come if you swear not to tell anyone."

"You've got to be kidding me," Bernadette said angrily as Jeannie dropped the cat and ran off to change.

"Well, what's your solution?" Laura felt suddenly cheerful. "Unless you want to go alone?"

Laura had never crossed the park at night. In the parking lot a single streetlight glowed orange. Underfoot, the ruined grass crackled. It was still hot, though the darkness suggested relief. Somehow Jeannie's presence made the excursion feel safer, but Laura's heart still pumped. Leaning against the fence that surrounded the pool, Joel waited silently.

"I'm nervous," Bernadette whispered.

Joel was shirtless, two shadows at his hips where his trunks hung low. "You brought a kid?" he asked. "Lame."

Jeannie squared her shoulders.

At night the gate to the pool was chained and padlocked, so the only way in was over. Joel scrambled up with that long-limbed weightless grace of boys and monkeys.

"Will we get arrested?" Jeannie asked, voice small.

Bernadette whirled on her. "Feel free to leave."

In response, Jeannie stepped forward, wrapped her hands around the wire, and scaled the fence swiftly.

"Not bad," Joel observed.

Laura tossed her swimming bag over the fence, then shoved the toes of her flip-flops into the chain-link. She hoisted herself up. "Here goes." As she climbed, the fence twanged and vibrated. She thought of Joel's dog enclosure. "Hey," she said. "Remember Zoo?"

Bernadette laughed, climbing clumsily beside her. "Barely. What were we thinking, letting ourselves get locked in? Huh, Joel? What were you thinking?"

"What's Zoo?" asked Jeannie.

Joel stood below them, looking up. "Nice beavs," he said.

Bernadette put one hand to her skirt. "Shut up. You can't see anything."

"Wanna bet?"

"I'm wearing shorts," said Laura.

"Need help?" Joel asked Bernadette.

Laura felt her palms slipping, her inner thighs slick with sweat. She gripped the wires harder. Bernadette clambered over the top, then dropped to the ground.

By the time Laura made it over, Joel and Jeannie were already in the pool, and Bernadette was pushing the skirt past her hips. She was wearing a new two-piece, and in the low light the pink was as pale as lingerie.

"I've got your towel," Laura told Bernadette, and tapped it pointlessly. "So don't worry." Then, when she could put it off no longer, she unzipped her shorts.

The water was warm from the day. Laura pushed off the steps and drifted to the dark middle. She closed her eyes and wondered if she could even feel her body at all.

In the deep end, Jeannie bobbed clumsily, her nose and mouth barely above the surface. "I'm holding my breath. Time me, Laura," she sputtered, and slipped under.

The others treaded water, looking at each other and then away, chuckling quietly.

Jeannie popped to the surface gasping. "That was twenty-eight seconds!"

Joel snorted. "You want a medal or a chest to pin it on?"

"We're not even swimming," said Laura. She felt oddly irritable. "We should at least swim." Stupid. Did she think they came here to swim laps? Was she seven years old? There was a pause in the air, anticipation. "We should go back soon, Bern."

Joel and Bernadette drifted closer to each other.

"I hope there's nothing gross in here," said Laura. "Remember when I found a lizard in the bottom of the pool? Remember that, Bern? Are you two holding hands? God. You are."

Bernadette began to laugh softly, unstoppably. She must have dropped Joel's hand because now she drifted, still laughing, toward the far edge.

"Hey. Come back here." Joel swam toward Bernadette, and Bernadette slipped away from his touch.

"We could play Marco Polo," called Laura.

"Yes!" said Jeannie, gripping the concrete edge of the deep end.

"Sure," said Bernadette, and she swam close to Laura.

"What's so funny?" Laura asked Bernadette. "Why are you laughing?"

Bernadette's laugh was almost soundless. "I'm not."

They put their hands around each other's waists and treaded water like Siamese twins. Under her hand, Bernadette's bare middle was slippery with lotion.

Joel faced them. His slick, skinny shoulders reflected the distant orange light from the parking lot.

"You two are no fun," he said.

"I'll play! Come play, Joel!" Jeannie called. "Marco!" But Joel heaved himself out of the pool.

Strangely happy, Laura lay back so she was floating. She allowed her ears to sink below the waterline and listened to the strange clicks and currents, the sounds of Jeannie, maybe, or Bernadette. The breeze skated over her belly and the mound of her crotch. Above her, the sky was moonless, the stars sharp and hard and infinite. Looking up into that extraordinary depth, she could almost believe she was suspended in space.

"Laura." Bernadette's distorted voice sharpened when Laura righted herself. "I'm bored. Let's get out." She was already sitting waist-deep on the steps, looking at Laura uncertainly.

Along the pool was a narrow tract of grass, and on the grass was a row of concrete picnic tables, where, during morning swimming lessons, mothers read magazines under broad hats. Laura lay along one of the concrete benches, feeling the water trickle down her legs. Her eyes burned pleasantly from the chlorine, and she felt calm and alert. The warm breeze chilled her, and even the sensation of the goose bumps rising on her skin felt sensual and soft. "The stars are amazing." From the deep end, she could hear the gasp and splash of Jeannie's inexpert paddling.

"We both have crushes on you," Bernadette said, and Laura sat up. Bernadette was sitting on the next table, her feet on the bench, clutching a towel around her shoulders. Joel stood before her, his hands on her knees.

"Don't tell him that," said Laura. "He'll get a swelled head."

"Oh?" said Joel. He parted Bernadette's legs, so his hips were between her knees. "Maybe I have crushes on you two."

He leaned into Bernadette, cupped her chin, and kissed her. It was exactly what a kiss should be, sweet, under stars, water lapping, coyotes calling in the distance. It was slow and quiet, as beautiful and easy as a movie kiss. It gutted Laura to see it.

"Gross," she said, her laugh false. "You two are disgusting." Her heart pounded. Bernadette reached up to touch Joel's cheek.

Still half-smiling, gaze never straying from her eyes, Joel pushed Bernadette back against the concrete table, bracing one of his own knees on the bench.

"Wait," said Bernadette. "Ow. My back."

He was over her, and Bernadette tried to twist away. "Joel," she said softly.

As Laura watched, he kissed Bernadette again, deeply. This time it was neither sweet nor gentle. Bernadette tried to turn her head but couldn't. The muscles at her neck were ropy. All at once Laura was unaccountably angry at Bernadette, furious, which made no sense, because why would she be angry at her best friend?

As she watched, Laura was not imagining herself, pinned under Joel. She wasn't thinking about his mouth on her own. She was picturing her mouth on Bernadette's, her own weight over Bernadette's body, Bernadette squirming beneath her. She wanted Bernadette punished. And then that quiet surge. Embarrassed, she pinched her thighs together but then remembered the dark and the fact that her suit was already wet.

Joel's hand was twisted in Bernadette's pink bikini bottoms, and Bernadette's eyes were squeezed shut. Laura couldn't see what his hand was doing, but she could imagine, imagine her own hand, which had touched herself, in Bernadette's suit. Bernadette whimpered.

"No!" said Jeannie from the pool, her voice small and strangled, and this is when Laura finally lurched toward them.

"Get off her, asshole." But before Laura could hit Joel, Bernadette had pushed him off herself.

Joel stepped back and wiped his mouth. "Don't play shy. You've been waiting for me all summer." With a start, Laura saw the protrusion in his bathing suit. She'd known it was like that, of course, but the real thing was startling and terrible, and—this occurred to her despite her sloshing heart—absurd.

Laura glanced to see if Bernadette had noticed, because this was something they'd laugh about together later, but Bernadette was sitting rigid with her arms clamped around her torso, her gaze fixed on the black water of the pool.

Jeannie was standing knee-deep on the step, her mouth agape and eyes wide. Laura had nearly forgotten her. Jeannie was shaking her head silently, mechanically.

"You two," Joel said with such scorn it sounded like an insult.

Laura and Bernadette sat side by side on the concrete bench as Joel pulled on his jeans and hoisted himself over the fence and dropped into the grass. His dark form moved swiftly across the parking lot, and then he was nothing but a smudge against the glow of the streetlights.

Laura's anger at Bernadette had vanished, leaving only soggy self-loathing.

They were caged in here, she thought with sudden terror, looking at the chain-link around the pool. Suddenly she was afraid of Bernadette, afraid of what Bernadette would say, and then her fear expanded to encompass Melinda and the baby home alone.

"Get out," she told Jeannie. "We're going."

They gathered their wet towels in silence, flung them over the fence, climbed. This time, there were no squeals, no shouts of encouragement or giddy fear. The only sound in the night was the musical twang of the chain-link as it rattled under their weight.

They walked rapidly—ran, almost—the four blocks, nearly all the way to the intersection where Bernadette would turn left to go back to the Swansons' or right to go home. Laura's heart sloshed.

"Wait up," Jeannie called, her sandals flapping loose against the asphalt, but neither Bernadette nor Laura slowed.

The houses were dark, and, try as she might, Laura couldn't picture the families safe and sleeping inside. Every house they passed seemed deserted. When she got to the Swansons' the children would be gone, and it would serve Laura right.

"I can't believe I left them there like that," she said breathlessly. "Anything could have happened. They could be dead."

"What?" said Jeannie. "What did you say?"

"That's what you're worried about? Something that *could* have happened?" Bernadette stopped, and Laura did, too. "You just stood there," she said in a low voice. She was shaking.

"But you like him," Laura protested. "You've been wanting to make out with him all summer."

"You were right there. And you just watched."

Jeannie was crying silently.

"I'm sorry, Bernadette." Laura felt certain that if she could make her voice firm enough, or if she could weep with Bernadette, or if she could wrap her friend in her arms, they could share whatever this was. They would be closer for it. But Laura's voice was weak, her arms leaden at her sides. "Nothing happened. Really nothing happened."

"I know that," snapped Bernadette. She turned and began walking briskly toward her house, sandals slapping.

"He just kissed you!"

Bernadette was marching along in the middle of the street, illuminated by the streetlamps.

"I just never thought Joel would do that!"

"Do what?" Bernadette whirled around savagely. "Nothing happened."

Jeannie slipped her hand into Laura's, and an ache cleaved Laura's chest.

Forty dollars a week for three months. Four hundred and eighty dollars.

The Saturday before school started, Laura came home from a movie with two other girls to find that Mrs. Swanson had finally dropped her payment off.

Her mother looked up from chopping an onion and indicated an envelope on the counter.

The flap was unsealed; Laura swiftly ran through the bills. "Sixty dollars?" She flung them on the counter. "That's all she brought? What is she thinking?"

Laura's mother turned from the counter. "Oh, sweetheart. I told Mrs. Swanson that she didn't need to pay you so much."

"You didn't."

Laura's mother resumed chopping, her knife moving assuredly. "She's a mess, poor thing. Working herself to death, behind on her bills, completely responsible for that whole family. And then here she comes across the yard with an enormous sum, far too much for a fifteen-year-old girl."

Laura wanted to slap her mother, to send her reeling into the counter, the knife clattering across the linoleum. Laura wanted her mother shocked and cowering. Instead she took a deep breath. Very evenly, she said, "You need to tell her, Mom. You need to tell Mrs. Swanson you made a mistake and she has to pay me the full amount."

"Sweetheart, I can't do that." Her mother tore into a bunch of celery, turned her knife on the stalks. "You don't need that kind of money." That maddening face: the incredulity, the innocence, the absolute refusal to believe her daughter could be so selfish. "What could you possibly need that kind of money for?"

For so many things. She needed beautiful, transformative clothes. She needed to get out of Tucson. She *needed*. With a pang, she thought of the two bus tickets that she'd never hold in her hands. Even if she did leave Tucson, she'd leave alone, a stranger in the seat next to her.

"Oh, Laura. You're a child. Look how generous your father is to you. You were only really working to keep yourself busy."

"You think I spent my entire summer watching those brats to keep *busy*? Is that what you think? No one works to keep busy."

"Laura, if you can't be generous to a woman left alone to provide for three children, then I pity you, and you're welcome to go right over there and tell her that yourself."

Fury lashed at her. "Do not think I will forget this. I will never forget."

Her mother waved her away, knife in hand. "I suggest you go to your room until you can control yourself."

Again and again, Laura told herself she would march next door and demand her due. She told herself she didn't care if she was rude, if Mrs. Swanson was crazy with desperation and their power shut off and the children starving to death. But school started, and Laura didn't say a thing.

Mrs. Swanson did not, in the end, allow Mr. Swanson to move back home. Laura was as surprised as her mother. "I didn't think she had it in her," her mother marveled. Laura thought of Mr. Swanson, counting out the bills for the replacement blender, thinking he was buying his way back into his daughter's trust. She wondered where he was now and whether he ever spoke to his children.

Laura was no longer called on to babysit the Swanson kids, not that she would have anyway. The baby spent days with an older lady in the neighborhood, and now that Jeannie had turned eight, she stayed alone with Melinda after school. Laura sometimes saw them wandering around the front yard, peering into the gravel as if looking for something lost. When she waved, the girls brightened and waved back, expecting, perhaps, that Laura might cross over into their yard to see them, but she never did.

The few times Laura and Bernadette got together, always with other girls from school, their gazes skittered past each other, and Laura left these outings feeling hollowed out, exhausted from her performance of nonchalance, hurt that Bernadette had seemed to slough her off so completely. Then in October, Bernadette started dating the yearbook editor, a long-haired senior. Now, Laura heard news of Bernadette and her boyfriend from classmates in admiring, hushed tones, about the parties they'd been seen at, the marijuana they'd smoked.

One day after school late that fall, Laura walked downtown to Jacome's to buy athletic socks. She'd joined the basketball team, and among this new group of friends, with their practice drills and in-jokes, she felt a kind of relief.

In Intimates, silk nighties hung from the stiff, posed bodies of mannequins. Detached legs sheathed in beige nylon formed a chorus line atop a lingerie case. Embarrassed, Laura circled, trying to find the socks. Everywhere she looked, hard plastic breasts punched through lace and nylon. Laura turned away from these underthings. In the back corner, on the clearance rack, Laura saw a pale gleam that made her catch her breath. She wound her way to it through the racks, and there in the tangle was Bernadette's pink bikini.

Laura lifted the metal hanger and touched the straps.

"Can I show you a fitting room?" asked a matronly young saleswoman who materialized at her elbow.

Laura nodded and allowed herself to be led down the empty hallway of cubicles. The carpet was soft underfoot, everything cushioned and muffled.

"Now's really the time to snap up swimwear. I'll leave you to it."

Through the slats in the door, Laura could distantly hear the saleswomen talking to each other. She undressed slowly and did not turn to the mirror until she'd tied the straps at her neck. Her hair drooped in its ponytail, messy from the long day. Her white cotton underpants bunched under the bikini bottom, and the pink fabric stretched over her uneven breasts. Above, her face floated, pale and pinched.

She sat on the velveteen upholstered bench and held her own

gaze in the mirror. There was something she should do, perhaps: slide into a sexy pose, or glare with hatred at her body. She touched the tie that dangled at the nape of her neck, rubbed the nylon between her fingers. All at once she missed Bernadette sharply, the pain like her rib cage prized apart.

There was no need for a swimming suit like this in New York City, for any swimming suit, really. "You will have the life you want," she told her reflection in a low voice. She was surprised by her own urgency.

Nails drummed on the door. "How's it going, hon?" the saleswoman called through the slats.

"The suit didn't work," Laura said. Then, turning away from the mirror, she reached up and pulled the string.

Arinze Ifeakandu

Happy Is a Doing Word

I

THEY WERE TEN when the plane crashed. Binyelum saw the blackened remains in his father's *Sunday Times,* they always read the Sunday paper together, passing pages between each other. Just look at this rubbish, his father would say, frowning at yet another headline about Hisbah ("Kano State's Hisbah Cracks Down on Private Schools, Enforcing New Hijab Rule," one headline had said), or, Sharp observation, my boy, which made Binyelum's head swell. The day of the crash, his father did not sift through the pages, deciding which he wanted to read first before sharing with Binyelum; he went straight to the page with the story, shaking his head as he read, muttering under his breath. Binyelum leaned against him, reading at the same time, the way he used to do when, littler, he would sit between his father's legs, asking what this or that word meant, how this or that word was pronounced. This is tragic, his father said, turning to him. Later, Binyelum ran to Somadina's house, waving the paper and saying, Look! It was evening, the sun, huge and yellow, rolling into the belly of the sky. Somadina followed him outside, to the dogon-yaro tree across their yard under which they often sat, watching birds. Binyelum caressed the pictures, his eyes like a dreamer's. One day, he said, he too would fly, and he would not fall.

Binyelum and Somadina and the other neighborhood children used to sit under this tree and sing to the birds—Chekeleke, give me one white finger, they screamed skyward. Every evening, the birds erupted in noise as though, having returned from wherever they had traveled since morning, they could not wait to regale one another with stories about their day. Binyelum believed that he could tell each one apart, and he gave them names even though Somadina told him this was impossible: there were just too many, and they all looked the same, clear white feathers, pale yellow beaks, and long broomstick legs. See, Binyelum said, Sarah had a way of flapping her wings, like a thing about to reveal itself, regal and wild, but Rose was timid and loved the branch hanging close to Baba Ali's fence. That made no sense, Somadina said, and they fought, sometimes with silence, a few times with their bodies, rolling in the sand, over dead leaves, pulling at each other's shirts. By morning, they were friends again, playing catch, watching the birds.

But this was before. Before the plane fell from the sky. Before all Binyelum wanted to talk about was how he would be a pilot when he grew up. Before Hisbah seized the truck full of alcohol and ruined his father's business. Before the evening when, after playing ball, the boys formed a circle around him and he took down his shorts to show them he'd begun growing hair down there. They were all a little shy, until Nnamdi, who was the most senior, said, You be man now o, you fit give woman belle. Binyelum, no longer shy but proud, glanced at Somadina and smiled, as if to say, You see? The next day, they both climbed the short fence into Baba Ali's compound again and went into one of the discarded old cars littering the yard. It seemed ages ago, and not only yesterday, that they used to have their bath together outside, under the eyes of the entire world.

They returned there most days after school, making up excuses to wander off from the company of the other boys. Baba Ali's was the perfect spot, that yard with the dark, quiet house whose windows seemed permanently shut to the world. Baba Ali was never in town, and there was no wife cooking dinner in the corridors, no kids running around outside under the mango tree with branches that stretched to the dogonyaro tree, forming a vast canopy for all those abandoned cars. Who taught them to hide? They never wondered. They were only curious fingers in the mild dark. You like it? Somadina said, not in the voice that he would use with the girls and women years away, he'd not yet learned to treat pleasing someone else as an act that affirmed his power over them. He asked because he wanted to know, and Binyelum said yes, and it was not a performance of surrender at all; this was not a game of owning and being owned, not yet.

Had they been older, and cannier, had their minds been tainted early by the world's caprices, like the mind of a boy like Nnamdi, orphaned at three and passed around from one close relative to another distant one, they would have known how suspect they looked, two boys abandoning the gang almost every evening and wandering off on their own. But they knew nothing about the shrewd, untrusting nature of the world. And so there they were, alone in each other's company, shorts pulled down to their ankles, and suddenly there was sound, and light, and they were no longer alone: they lay there, awkwardly, all around them eyes gawking. I tell you, Nnamdi said, turning to the other boys, smug and knowing. They all stood there in silence, Nnamdi smirking still, and maybe it was that smirk that made Binyelum start begging. Abeg, he said, abeg no report us. Somadina looked from his crumpled face to Nnamdi's smug one, and to the wondering faces of a dozen sweaty, grimy boys, and it dawned on him how much trouble they must be in for Binyelum to plead that way. He, too, began to beg.

For days, Nnamdi hounded them like a potent cloud, taking their break money, sending them on errands, making them race each other so that he could see who the man was and who the woman. One evening, he pulled them aside and made them scale the fence. There were five of them, two other boys whom he'd brought along to look out, and this would become Binyelum's second lesson in growing up, having already learned shame the evening they were found: to always watch his back. Pull your knicker, Nnamdi said, and they both stood there and gaped at him, confused, until he frowned and said, Quick. Good, he said, now do that thing wey una dey do before.

In the same backseat as the first evening, it did not feel the same, did not retain that thrill of discovering something sweet. Binyelum looked down, crying. I no tell you to stop, Nnamdi said from his view in the front seat, and now Binyelum's crying made his body shake, and it made Somadina incredibly sad, he too began to cry. They disengaged, and no matter how many threats Nnamdi barked at them—I go tell your mother, I go report to your class teacher—they did not return to each other, did not look at each other, could not.

That night, Binyelum's mother brought out the belt she hid in the same trunk in which she locked her most expensive lace and Georges and Hollandais. Your body will tell you today, she said, as she whipped him on his back, his buttocks, his legs. She'd never beat him, nor his sisters, like that; in the past, she'd ask them to stretch their hand and spread their palm open, and it had been better because he could close his eyes and anticipate the sting, count the rest before the belt came down, one, two, three. This time, she flogged him all over, chanting that his body would tell him. He could hear his sisters crying in the other room. When his father returned, he woke Binyelum up and they sat together in the living room, the girls asleep on mats spread out on the floor, saying nothing, his father's head bowed for what seemed like eternity, his bald spot round and gleaming like the moon. Finally, he lifted his head. You are a man, he said, calmly, shaking his head—you are a man, Binyelum, my son. Binyelum sat there and cried: it was the strangeness in his father's voice, as though he could no longer recognize the boy with whom he read the papers on Sundays, swapping pages, laughing over the cartoons, solving puzzles, as though Binyelum had intentionally misled him all those years and now that he'd been exposed, there was nothing else to feel but crushing disappointment.

Somadina, on the other hand, went out and came in, not quite like before, but almost. When Nnamdi came to Somadina's house with the news, his aunt, Mma Lota, was there. And why are you only telling us this? she said. She spoke Igbo to Nnamdi, persistently, even though he responded in pidgin, and she stared him down with a fierceness. Somadina stood in a corner, watching. The next morning, smug and bouncy with triumph, he waited by the gate to tell Binyelum what had happened. How he told his mother about Nnamdi, about the backseat of the car in Baba Ali's compound. How, seething, his mother said, Ị sị ginị? You say he made you do what? How Nnamdi stuttered, then fled the room. How after she opened her Bible and showed him the wrong in what they had both done, she'd bought him ice cream. He waited until he almost missed the school bus, until his mother came outside and asked what he was still doing there.

At school, Binyelum stayed far away, as though Somadina had a smell about him, and the next morning Binyelum walked past him on his way to the bus stop, and no matter how fast Somadina walked, he never caught up with him, and no matter how hard he called, Binyelum never turned.

II

The Christmas Baba Ali returned home with a woman, they were teenagers, seniors in secondary school. Somadina's father had gotten a job with AP Oil, and they had moved to a nicer house on a quiet street far away from Sabon Gari, a street where the taps spat clean water and the boys were gentle—that was how Somadina's mother had put it, where the boys were gentle. Somadina liked a girl in his class, Kamara, who was always beating him at physics and math, and Binyelum continued to play on the same field, with mostly the same boys. He'd let Dave, a boy from school, suck his dick a couple of times, always at Dave's house when his parents were at work, the doors bolted shut, the curtains drawn, an awkwardness between them. Outside the walls of that house, they did not speak to each other, did not act like they had ever spoken to each other.

Baba Ali's new woman stayed, night after night, month after month. She set up a light-yellow kiosk under the dogonyaro tree. *MTN, Everywhere You Go,* it said on the body of the light-yellow kiosk from which she sold recharge cards and milk and soap and egg rolls that were soft and sweet, and when the children congregated under the tree to sing to the birds, she shooed them away, the children; in the mornings and afternoons and evenings, women gathered there, talking, laughing, sometimes quarreling loudly, so that people rushed out of their compounds to gawk at them and point fingers. Baba Ali became a face that people saw every day, standing under the electric pole with the fathers and bachelors, a lean, clean-shaven man in the whitest singlet talking politics and football and smiling at the children as they walked to school.

It was Saturday morning, and the husbands had played a football match against the bachelors. Binyelum's father returned home, flopped down on the couch, his red Arsenal jersey around his neck like a towel, his round hairy stomach glistening with sweat. Binyelum got him a cup of water, which he gulped down, Adam's apple rippling.

Binyelum returned to his phone. Dave had texted, Come to the church. He'd recently started attending choir practice with Dave. Last week, in the parish's bathroom, which smelled of Izal, he had been more worried that they were doing this in the house of God than he was about the fact that Dave was kneeling on the bathroom floor, on tiles that looked brownish with accumulated grime futilely scrubbed. It was one thing doing what they did at Dave's house with the windows and doors shut, there, it was secret and safe; in church, he felt the eyes of God on him, blazing with condemnation. Sometimes—especially on those nights when his father, cursing and staggering, had to lean on him to make it home, the entire street staring at them—he wondered if he was the cause of his family's misfortune, if his secret desires were too abominable for God's grace.

Before Hisbah seized the truck full of alcohol, ruining his father's business, his father's bar was the happening place. People went there for his special drink combos, and because whenever a dedicated customer asked for a brand of cognac they'd had on a business trip somewhere far away, he made real efforts to have such a drink in his next consignment. Whatever you call your business, son, his father used to say, be proud of it and aim to be great at it. After his goods were seized and destroyed, he became a silent person, sleeping all day and drinking all night. But something about Baba Ali's return had awakened him, making him join the men again at their football games and their early morning banter about the news.

Ị ma, his father said, looking out the door where the wind was lifting the yellow curtain. I was just there, looking at Baba Ali, e nekete m ya anya, and I hailed him, Odogwu!

Whenever his father got this way, he slipped into an elevated Igbo, untouched by English and garnished with the occasional proverb, the occasional unfamiliar word. Binyelum knew the story about Baba Ali. It had been whispered in the street ever since he was a child: how his wife had woken up one morning, dragged her bags outside, Baba Ali begging and crying behind her, how she'd gotten into a taxi and left. They had even made a song about it at one point, Baba Ali, clean your eyes, no dey cry / Pluck mango from your big tree, chop life, but the adults had scolded and whopped the song out of their mouths. Was he odogwu, Binyelum asked, because he brought home a woman?

His father looked at him, eyes yellow, sprinkles of gray hair on his chin and on his head, lines at the sides of his eyes; it struck

Binyelum like a punch, his father was getting old. Baba Ali and his wife, Aina, had been very close, some people even said they were cousins—a detail he could not confirm, his father said—but love can do that to you. His father paused, eyes trained on the picture above Binyelum's head, a framed photo of his sister, Ngozi, standing behind a birthday cake with one candle in its middle. There was hardly a Sunday, his father continued, that they did not go to church dressed in matching clothes, hardly an evening that Baba Ali did not desert the men to go sit with Aina in the kitchen. Their life, already domed in joy, would have been perfect at the birth of their daughter, but they soon learned, after several illnesses, that she had sickle cell. They watched their child suffer, knowing that the suffering was a direct result of their love. After their daughter died, Aina left. The story went that she loved Baba Ali still but could not risk bringing another child into the world just to suffer, that Baba Ali had tried to convince her to stay, the two of them alone in their marriage, But, I guess, Binyelum's father said, face bright with contemplation, that not even they could survive the blow of such a tragedy.

He fell sick for months after, and we thought he might die. We had to rush him to the hospital one time because he could not move, had not eaten in days. Your mother and some other women had to care for him after he was discharged. And then he closed down his shop in Kano, which was doing very well, moving everything to Kaduna, to a branch that was only just starting out. But he kept the house, he'd lived there since he was a boy.

His father took a deep breath, released it slowly, his stomach rising and falling. You see, my son, he said, many people break after something like that, or they become bitter and hateful. But not Baba Ali, not the man I talked to and played ball with today, so eager for life. That is something.

Binyelum knew the story and all its embellishments, was used to his parents retelling tales with as much vitality as they'd told them the first time, but there was a solemnness to the way his father told it this time, a tenacious optimism, that saddened him.

His father was trying to motivate himself, he realized, by lifting Baba Ali as evidence of the possibility for life's restoration. Binyelum was not sure if he felt the same way, he'd begun recently to think that the forces of life were capricious and fickle; why, he wondered, did some people spend their lives struggling to scrape by while others wallowed in abundance?

At school, Dave had started to sit beside a boy, Somadina's cousin Lotanna, who seemed to have everything, staying back in class to talk to him at break time, holding his hand in the corridors. Dave's husband, their classmates teased him, but he laughed at the name, and soon everybody said it without accusation. Binyelum watched Lotanna talk to Dave, Dave's head thrown back in laughter—it annoyed him, how easy it was to fool people. Lotanna, polished in his school uniform that was always crisply ironed and in the way he spoke, without hurry, as though the whole world were his audience, and good as he was at playing midfield, at tennis and chess, and loved as he was by the teachers, was someone for whom trouble was glamorous and safe, someone for whom the world would bend.

Mma Lota, who was at the house most Sundays, came with the news that Baba Ali had died. When his mother poked her head into his room to tell him, Somadina looked up, grunted, and she said, What, it's my house, and sat at the foot of his bed, glancing at everything as though she wasn't in there every day.

You should come out and sit in the living room, she said.

Moving had been her idea, and though Somadina no longer hated her for it, he could not understand why she continued to be invested in gossip about their old street.

Did Somadina's mother know, Mma Lota said in the living room, that Baba Ali's new girlfriend left him as he fell sick? The poor man, had he not enough heartbreak, his mother lamented. May affliction not rise to us a second time.

I took food to him on Sundays, she continued. Mma Ayo did on Fridays, you know, small gestures here and there—it was the most anyone could do.

What happened to him? Somadina asked.

People say he had AIDS, his mother said. But you know how people like to make up stories. The poor man must have died of loneliness.

Loneliness does not kill people, Mummy, Somadina said, shaking his head.

She rolled her eyes at him. What do you know? You have not seen anything yet.

It had seemed, when they first moved out here, that he would never be able to breathe again. There were no boys his age playing football on the street, and his classmates spoke Hausa, which he did not understand, at break time. He wanted to go back home, he'd told his parents. This is home now, they said. Now, though, he had friends who sat on the living room couch, on the floor, drinking Coke and eating chin-chin, playing PS and arguing in loud voices about Merlin or Greek or whether the guy in that video had actually put it in her ass; friends who thought his mum—the few times she'd dropped in from her shop to get something at home—was cool, the way she did not frown at them like most of their parents would have done.

And he had Kamara. His mother said of her to Mma Lota, She's a wonderful child, so smart and so mature, and the nnwa amaka. I did not know Somadina had big eyes like that.

Mummy! he said, raising a pillow above his head as though to throw it at her.

Kamara had only just started talking to him again. JAMB was around the corner, she'd been studying a lot and so hadn't gone with him to the party where he had a can of Star and large puffs of Faruk's blunt. When his friends dared him to kiss Mary, the only girl at the party, he did it. His friends cheered. When the bottle spun toward Mary, they dared her to take off her blouse, an earring, her skirt. No, she said.

It's the game, Faruk said. Don't ruin the fun. And then he said something else in Hausa, which made the other boys laugh.

The next day, Kamara showed up while he was shooting hoops and stood in the middle of the basketball court, arms crossed. Somadina walked toward her but she lifted her hand, halting him. Her friends appeared at the other end of the court, watching. Come on, he said, is all this necessary?

You tell me, she said.

I'm sorry—you want me to kneel down? 'Cause I will. He began to roll up his trousers to avoid staining them, but she said, Please don't embarrass me.

Binyelum scored 268 on JAMB, and his mother cooked his favorite, coconut rice, to celebrate, and his father was sober that evening, and they sat outside, shirtless in the heat, and talked aimlessly about things that had happened and things that were yet to come. With a score like that, his friends told him, he would surely get in somewhere. At the screening for the Defence Academy, Binyelum did not run into Somadina, and Somadina did not run into him. They took the written parts of the exam in the same hall, Somadina in front, Binyelum behind, the hall full of sixteen- and seventeen-year-olds in an assortment of school colors. Binyelum passed but did not get in. Ibadan released their list, and then Nsukka, and he was not on either.

It rained on the evening he got the *Daily Times* to look up Nsukka's list. He sat outside Mama Ayo's shop with the boys, heads huddled together, as they went through the names. Wait, is this the Somadina we know? someone said, pointing at a spot on the paper. They could not believe Binyelum had not gotten in, the boys said, and talked about how rigged it all was, patting his back, making encouraging speeches. It began to rain, the first rain of the year: it began with a whirlwind, dust rising and swirling, making everyone disperse, and then the sky poured down on everything. A neighbor brought out buckets and lined them up under the roof. Binyelum watched from the window. Did she not know not to fetch the first rain? he wondered.

He got a job washing bottles at a pharmaceutical company a

few blocks away, stopped attending choir practice. You have to understand, he thought of saying to Dave, but instead stopped picking up his calls. Dave showed up on his street for the first time ever, breaking an unspoken agreement. Wetin? he asked, putting on his harsh voice, aware of the guys' eyes on him. Nnamdi stood up. You hear the guy, he said, who you dey find? Binyelum saw Dave's eyes, darting toward him, confused and a little brave, and looked away. Just go, he thought, just go. Binyelum, Dave said, but Binyelum simply glared at him—all those eyes, he thought, all those suspicious eyes.

Nnamdi laughed, putting his arms around Dave's shoulders. I just dey play with you, he said. See as you dey shake. Why you dey find my guy?

Choir practice, Dave said.

A week later, outside Baba Ali's compound, Binyelum and Nnamdi argued over Messi and Ronaldo, and everyone who asked could not believe that a boy like Binyelum, quiet and unproblematic, would throw the first punch. Day after day, his heart ached more, and he often had an urge to cry that could not be tied to anything in particular.

III

Nobody believed it would happen in Kano, Somadina's father said over the phone, and yet here they were, in the middle of a curfew, the entire city still and uneasy, waiting to see if there would be another bomb. Binyelum called his mother and asked her to give the phone to his sisters. Don't go outside Sabon Gari, he said. Be careful. Distance made him helpless. His presence would do nothing real for them, he knew, but he could not shake off the feeling that if he were close, somehow he could keep them safe.

He missed them, that was what it was, a homesickness made urgent by worry. For a whole year he'd been away from home, in Lagos, serving Oga Lawrence. He had balked at the idea at first:

learning a trade was for dull students and village boys with no hope of another way. But after three years of waiting, his JAMB score getting lower with each try, his friends getting into small schools in Katsina and Kogi, he had begun to feel useless. In the company of his friends, he felt unreal, nonexistent, as though life were not happening to him, even though all he could feel was its force: his father always reeking of alcohol, the talk of the neighborhood; his angst about never getting into the Nigerian Defence Academy and becoming a pilot; his worry about his sisters.

In many ways, the apprenticeship was like being in school: after four years, he would be given a shop, goods, and some money to start up his own business. He could always go back to school, he would tell himself at night, lying exhausted on the mattress with the other first-year, Innocent, assailed by his scent, his snore, both of them shirtless, both of them sprawled under the insistent whir of the fan, their shorts rumpled, their thighs golden in the soft light of the appliances. The job was hard, it involved lots of walking under the sun, unloading trucks, sweet-talking often surly customers; it involved, for him and Innocent, starting the generator every evening, going to the main house to help Lady B in the kitchen, sneaking into the living room, spacious and high ceilinged, to peek at episodes of *Grey's Anatomy* or whatever Oga Lawrence's children had decided to watch, Lady B's voice raised in scolding—Useless bush rat!—or little Mary-Ann saying no she would not move her legs so the boys could sweep the floor. Do you know that my smallest sister is older than you? Innocent said to her often. Binyelum liked him, his nightly smell of bitter lemon and fresh bath; his limbs, of a boy who had spent his childhood weeding and tilling; his accent, the *l*'s that rolled into *r*'s, so that "rubber" became "lubba" and "love" became "ruv." There was a softness about him, though, that made Binyelum wary, a gentleness in contrast to his hard face, a way of moving and being that was too familiar for comfort.

Innocent, having served a former oga who in the end did not

settle him, was always ready with advice. Nothing we say or see among ourselves gets back to Oga, he once said, but you never can tell when a Judas might appear, so don't join the other umu-boy in openly bad-mouthing him. The last thing you need is for Oga to get it in his head that you're disloyal, life can get very hard then.

Binyelum wondered how much harder it could get, he felt already like someone walking on broken glass, his life dreary—a necessity, he believed, Growth flourishes in stillness, he'd writ-ten in his notebook where recently he'd begun leaving himself reminders, goals, motivations—sometimes he imagined breaking Oga Lawrence's curfew, imagined getting on one of those hookup apps and finding someone to sneak into the boys' quarters, the way the seniors did with their girlfriends. You don't have to do everything Oga says, Innocent told him. There are ways around these rules. Binyelum listened eagerly but told himself that he would break no rules, he had huge plans and narrow options: he could not afford the cost of recklessness.

The bombs were followed by shootings: a sixteen-year-old boy see-ing his friend off after a visit was shot and killed as they both stood at the junction, chatting. The men were driving an okada, the gunman in the passenger seat behind, the driver speeding away, cries of Allahu akbar lacerating the night as they zoomed off, as the spared boy froze and then fell on his knees beside his friend. They must leave Kano, Somadina's mother said to him every time she called, they simply had to—but his father, his father was stub-born, talking all the time about his job, could Somadina believe it! That boy could easily have been you, she said, and then what would a job mean? What would it mean?

This is the first major fight my parents are having, he told Kamara, holding her. It was dark in the room, there was no power; they had left the windows and door open to let in some breeze, the night crackling with the noises of crickets and toads and with the occasional caw of a nameless bird. He pressed his lips to Kamara's hair, wet and smelling of shea butter. Funny, he thought, how fond he now was of a scent that used to nauseate him.

My parents argued all the time, she said. This one time, my mother threw a plate at my dad and it missed him and hit my little brother on the head.

He placed one hand on her breast and the other on her stomach, twirling his finger around her navel. We will never fight, he said.

She backed into him and he held her tighter. His father had been furious when he chose to go to Nsukka: Who chooses Nsukka over NDA, gbọ? Do you know how many phone calls I had to make to ensure they didn't dash someone else your spot? But Somadina did not care for NDA nor anything else for that matter, did not know what he wanted to do with his life. He was good at many things but perfect at none, liked many things but was passionate about none; he could go wherever the wind blew him but why should he, when he felt, with Kamara, such profound happiness, when he could simply follow her wherever she went?

Was he not tying her down? her friends had argued when they moved in together. Men were already knocking on her door, her parents' door, prosperous men, some of them handsome and nice too. Her mother introduced most of the men to her and she talked to them merely to satisfy her mother. Lying in Somadina's arms, she read their text messages aloud, and they laughed together at these desperate men and their outmoded ways. God, you're an expert at nonchalance, he said to her, this man basically says he cannot live without you and all you say is aww. After a while, they became serious, and he told her he loved her and this was it, the two of them together until death. Here was the plan, he said, here was the plan, she agreed: they would both get a job in Enugu after graduation, find a room at Ninth Mile, and then a flat; they would save up, get married, have two or three children, ideally more girls but boys would also make them happy, wouldn't they?

Sundays were for church and football. Oga Lawrence and Lady B did not approve of girlfriends, because to have a woman was to need money—for dates, and Valentine's Day, and birthdays, and shoes and handbags, and shawarma—and to need money was to steal from Oga Lawrence's business. That was, however, not the speech they gave after morning devotion. Don't get a girl pregnant and derail your life, they said instead.

Don't get a girl pregnant and derail your life, Innocent said as they walked back groggily to the boys' quarters, rolling his eyes. As if they care about us.

Binyelum laughed. In their room, he picked up his phone to find his father's missed calls. He called home every other evening, to speak to the guys, or to his mother and sisters, rarely ever to his father. You never call your old man, gbo, he said when Binyelum called back. He laughed, and maybe if he hadn't the hurt wouldn't have stuck out so much, like a bone jutting out of torn skin, it made Binyelum queasy.

Haba, Daddy, he said, and laughed, too, and then they both waited in silence.

Did you hear about Nnamdi? his father asked.

Yes, Binyelum said. He'd heard, from his friends back home, from his sisters, from his mother: a nine-year-old girl had named Nnamdi as the reason she was injured down there, and her father, a retired army man, had stormed the street in a vanload of soldiers, dragged Nnamdi into the middle of the street, beaten him until his eyes were onion purple, and then thrown him into the back of the van and driven away.

A shameful thing, his father said.

A shameful thing, Binyelum agreed.

They waited, again, in silence.

How is work? his father said finally.

Binyelum gazed out the window, at the milky harmattan haze hovering over the conspiratorial cluster of roofs, at the people, bright in their Sunday jeans and gele and agbada, trudging up and down streets and alleyways, vibrant even in the cold, their noises—of laughter and greetings—rising and merging with the rumble and clatter of drums, with the brash songs and prayers blasting out of the speakers of the Mountain of Fire church down the road. It was so much like home, the riot of everything, the splattering of crumbling, brown-roofed bungalows around that one compound ringed by flowers, the compound in which he now stood, looking out at all these people: Iya Ibeji, whose tomato-crushing machine made so much noise; Baba Bolu the police officer, Bolu who always accosted Binyelum and the boys on their way from the shop, chanting Broda mi until Innocent handed him his PSP for the evening. Binyelum wanted to be the person looking down at everything from the house ringed by flowers. He wanted to be the person who, when his sister texted him saying there was nothing to eat at home, didn't immediately fall into a hole of depression and helplessness. He wanted to be the person who told others when they could date and when they could not. The plush couches in Oga Lawrence and Lady B's living room, the huge TV that started from the floor and rose nearly to the ceiling, the endless rows of Cerelac and Indomie noodles for the kids, the crates of eggs, the cornflakes: he wanted to have all that, a life of ease and plenty. Downstairs, Innocent was washing Oga's car, whistling to Osadebe, his arms, his bare back, shining with sweat. Binyelum wished he could stay home, skip church today, but service was compulsory. If he were in Kano, he'd be seated outside Mama Ayo's shop after football training, staring idly at the churchgoers. How he missed having nothing to do.

For Easter, Oga Lawrence took the family to visit his brother in Ibadan, and Binyelum went with Innocent to his first Lagos club. Walking in, he was frightened by the mass of people—everybody was beautiful, or had mastered ways of making themselves appear so. He felt self-conscious in the ordinariness of his black T-shirt and blue jeans, but a few bottles of Heineken later, he was in the middle of the dance floor, bodies pressed together, people floating from one dance partner to another, it made him think of folks trying on clothes at a boutique. A woman wrapped her arms around his neck, twisting into him. She smelled of sweat and perfume and looked into his eyes as though she'd known him all her life and loved him with a sad, quaking love. He wondered what her story was.

Outside the club later, he stumbled into the street with Innocent, arms around each other's shoulders. It was past midnight. A car sped past them, men sticking their heads out of its windows, spraying the street with champagne and yelling, Na we get Lagos!

Your papa! Binyelum yelled back, then turned to Innocent, laughing.

You're wasted, my man, Innocent said, laughing too.

They got on the same okada, Innocent seated behind, his body warm against Binyelum's back. In their room at the boys' quarters, Binyelum collapsed on his mattress, his shoes still on, he felt sleepy yet wide awake.

Next time we go out, Innocent said, sitting at Binyelum's feet, I'm going to take you somewhere different.

Binyelum looked up at him.

He smiled. It's not as big and flashy, but I'm sure you'll find what you need there. At least you'll dance with someone you actually want to fuck.

Binyelum hesitated. Perhaps it was a ploy: get him drunk, ruin his life in the presence of everybody. But the silence felt heavy with potential. He sat up; slowly, he took off his shirt. They were now seated side by side. He hugged Innocent. How terribly he'd missed it, the warmth and solidness of a man's body. Innocent sat there, letting himself be hugged. What am I doing? Binyelum muttered, chuckling into his shoulder.

You've been alone too long, Innocent said, guiding Binyelum's head onto his lap, where he cradled it like he would a sleeping child.

IV

There were birds in the trees outside the Enugu Premier Secondary School, where Kamara broke up with Somadina over the phone, and in the trees under which Binyelum stood, months after his settlement, scrolling through Facebook as he waited for his bus to arrive. Somadina sat on the bench outside the ash-and-oxblood building, head bent, hands covering it. To a passerby, he would look like a man suffering from a terrible headache. One moment a city is still, he thought, the next there are bombs; one day his father was stamping tickets for independent oil contractors, building a house in Enugu, another at the village—and the next he was struggling to get his tickets signed, could not finish his house in the village, peace giving way to strife.

And one moment, he was telling Kamara he loved her and she was saying she loved him too, and the next they were graduates and she had a dream job in Abuja and he had a shabby one in Enugu, a graduate of physics teaching mathematics to junior students and physics to seniors, and soon she was telling him, over the phone, that she wanted to start a family, could no longer wait, It's complicated, you have to understand, you have to understand. All those years, eight years, had those promises meant nothing to her even as she lay beside him? How could she, he wondered, how could she. The voices of students at play drifted toward him; watching them at break time, the junior boys and girls running after one another, dirtying their school uniforms, the seniors standing in corners, whispering, plotting, being dignified, he remembered his own secondary school days. Suddenly, it was all over, his years of carefreeness, it made him pity them. He felt it in his palms, the wetness, and squeezed his eyes shut to force it back in—what a sight he would be, a twenty-three-year-old man crying publicly, in the glare of the sun.

Finally home, Binyelum collapsed on his bed, exhausted. Today had not been his day: he'd woken up much later than usual, run after several buses before finding a seat and, at the shop, had lost a major sale to his neighbor. The elation he felt after his settlement had long since faded, now when he took the bus to work, he thought of the day ahead with hope and apprehension—would customers flock to his shop, he worried, or would he sit idly all day?—and on his way back, he thought only of his bed.

It was raining, and his room was dark and cold. He'd pulled the drapes; something about the street soaked in water, the rust-colored roofs dripping, people clutching umbrellas as they skirted puddles—something about all this made him terribly homesick. Perhaps it was the ordinariness of rain, the way it subdued people anywhere and everywhere, so that the woman clutching an umbrella down the road would remind him of his mother rushing home in the rain, clutching her old yellow umbrella that said *The Taste of Goodness*.

His phone tinkled with a notification: *Somadina Obi Accepted Your Friend Request*. Scrolling through Facebook earlier as he'd waited for the bus, he'd come across Somadina's profile in his People You May Know. He went back on, looking at pictures. The face, bearded and grown, smiling teeth white against a face so black and smooth, not the boy he had known all those years ago, but boyish still, and familiar. Binyelum scrolled through the page, more pictures: with a girl in front of a water-spitting lion, his arm around her waist, her head on his shoulder. *My World*, the caption said.

He imagined messaging Somadina. He would be effusively familiar, Longest time, my gee, he would say, and Somadina would respond as enthusiastically. He imagined their friendliness evolving into flirtation, that on the loneliest of nights, such as this, Somadina would say to him, I have been thinking of you all my life.

He chuckled to himself, how wild, his imagination. He messaged Innocent about a party they were planning, then went on WhatsApp, where his fuckbuddies were. Wyd, he typed to Yomi and Ferdinand, who lived closest to him. It still surprised him, the leeway they allowed him. He rarely ever texted them back outside of sex, and he lied to them all the time—I am an only child, he once said—lies that he told not to make himself appear in a striking light but to avoid being known, because to be known was to be invested. Sometimes, after they'd fucked, they would cling to him, and the slightest moment would present itself in which he wanted to hold them, too—and then he would feel only encroachment, the air suddenly too soft with feelings. He would hurry into his jeans and say, E go be, like he always did, and leave. In his apartment, he would wash his face in the bathroom sink, looking in the mirror, his hair spiky and tangled, his beard trimmed into a funnel, his eyes, red from smoking, looking back at him, saying, Who is this stranger, who is this man? Twisting the faucet, he would lower his head again, cup his palms under his face, cold water hitting him. Every day he lived, he felt less like himself. Growth, people called it; he thought of it as estrangement.

David Ryan

Elision

THEY WERE PLAYING the cartwheel game out on the lawn. Christopher's toys were scattered nearby—the wooden horse, the bells, the blanket they'd stretched out on for the picnic—and Lily had thought it might be time to bring them in, as the sky was getting weird. Then the dark tips of the forest's pines below the base of the lawn shivered silver, as if a transparent hand had combed itself slowly over them. She felt her stomach grumble, though they'd eaten lunch. Birds shot into the sky above the trees and swam away from the shimmering leaves. Christopher finished his cartwheel—at his age it was more of a controlled tumble—and began pointing at all the birds, the gray specks thickening and twisting, pulling together and breaking apart. Gulls so rarely came this far inland. Now dozens swirled, tangled up in the sky, which had turned from blue just a few minutes ago to a gray-yellow, blurred swelling above them. Robins and crows, a spray of sparrows, falling in with the gulls—erupting from some hidden sleeve of atmosphere. Beyond the deep green lawn and the trees billowing up the foothills, a skim milk sky was pulling in toward Lily and her son, as if following the birds. A deeper gray and yellow atmospheric blur—the outer rim of storm drawing up like the nimbus of a giant angel behind it. Christopher—three and a half now, a little small, a little quiet for his age—reached out and began finger-tracing the birds, inscribing their motion overhead.

Let's get the toys, Christopher, she'd said.

She would someday try to remember these things, try to shape them into a story—to try again to make sense of all that had changed. The recalled moments like small islands in a void—Christopher at three, the forest, the enormous slope of lawn, the comfort within the inscrutable modernist house above, and herself in the midst—islands aching within shouting distance in some giant ocean.

On a radio interview she'd heard a physicist suggest that we live an infinite number of lives all at once. All the outcomes move along side by side. An endless train of mirrors pointed ahead, silent as ghosts. We make a choice and simply step from this mirror, onto another one. Each choice opens another dimension, was the thinking. The past, though, it parts in a single wake behind us. When she heard this, she imagined infinite Christophers inside other parallel universes and saw herself as only a blur there beside him. Perhaps the blur was hope. She wanted to live forever. She wanted to be millions of herself. So that no matter what happened, she'd be there for him.

The breeze shifted and the air turned sharp. The birds collapsed in the sky, then blew apart, as if spat out from an invisible mouth. As if they'd planned this all along.

They were screaming, burst open above. She smelled something burning—not wood or leaves so much as earth, or some friction in the atmosphere itself: air compressed, ready to release, closer now.

Honey, how about we just go inside? Let's see what Daddy's doing.

Christopher pretended not to hear.

Hey. Hey, little guy?

The distant canopy of green at the bottom of the hill flashed once more: a mercurial silver, then the green rose up all flushed.

And then the earthquake began. The ground beneath began to rumble like an approaching truck. Christopher said, Oh.

The sky seemed to shake her, and Lily's legs lost her and she dropped to the grass beside Christopher, handed down to the earth. She covered him with her body. The ground shook as if it might open up and swallow them. The wet grass smelled sharp like burning chocolate and she sat in a kitchen with her mother, a double boiler with burned chocolate in the pan, and then her mind returned to the grass, her little boy.

But that synapse started something. And now she was a mirror that had risen, hovering over them now, this woman blanketed over her small boy. In the mirror she and Paul were in Paris, yet unmarried, an April morning in the Square Gabriel Pierné. The cathedral bell opened the air, its peal burst open the breeze with cherry blossoms, a blizzard of whites and pinks in warm sun. A teenage mouth now brushed against her lips, her own recalled strawberry lip gloss released from the quaking earth. And this memory parted from her now, too, and in its place she was driving too fast in the night as the bore of headlights on the dark road grabbed a bright silhouette of an animal—a small coyote clarified in the seconds' tunnel of light—and her car pulled it beneath itself, and she braked and saw in the rearview a timeless creature staggering away, its raw, red, skinned haunches and ribs red in the taillight as Christopher's tiny hands clutched the chains of a swing, rising toward her and falling away in a blue sky. The sun opening from a cloud over them, blinding his ascent; and then she was in college hiking through a New Hampshire forest, damp raw air, snow and mossy shadow beneath fallen trees, and she could hear the forest clearing in the mountains, the tumbling of trees and the hissing of wet leaves—

Maybe a second had passed: when she was floating above herself and her boy on the shaking ground. Lily lowered down to them, rejoined herself holding Christopher on the shuddering lawn, the earth striking up its seismic distress. And then the rumbling beneath grew quieter and slipped away. A thunder grown distant until it was gone. She was on the grass, pressed over her son. Perfectly still. Across the long lawn, the house appeared unchanged. Everything, unchanged.

From the skirt of trees—a stag, a doe, and two fawns emerged and began to leap, as if dancing, shaking something off inside their bodies. The deer danced a moment longer, then leapt into the forest.

Lily? His voice sounded so small. Her husband, Paul, came out of the house onto the deck. Someday she would remember his voice, too, another island floating in the void. His voice sounded so far away up there. He ran down and then was holding her. Smoke was rising far off west. How much time had passed? Paul had said something about going into town. That he wanted to see if he could learn anything. He'd pulled away in the Range Rover, rumbling off the lane arched with the poplar allée, inspired by the trip to Paris from before Christopher was born. (She would later, and often, recall the town of Saintes, driving through an allée of towering horse chestnuts on their way to Paul's friends' eighteenth-century farmhouse, whose foundation and walls had been pilfered generations before them from the stones of a local, ancient Roman coliseum. She would remember the horses, Poitevins, who his friends had said were endangered.)

Paul had wanted her to keep herself and Christopher out of the house—the risk of tremors, the foundation and walls. Christopher was asleep on the grass, having fallen into an unusually deep sleep. They had been out there an hour and Lily was lying on the buffalo blanket drifting in and out, when the landline in the house rang. She rose and ran up the long lawn. The phone was still ringing as she pressed open the back door. The kitchen smelled like damp earth. She grabbed the phone on the wall beside the refrigerator and said, Hello?

But all that came back was this empty sound. Like a comb pulled through hair, crackling and alive in some negated space.

Paul? Hello? She waited on the static. Several dinner plates had fallen from the cabinets and shattered on the floor. She waited in the silence from the phone, then hung up. Out the long wall of windows overlooking the lawn from the living room a half level below, Christopher was still asleep on the deep green lawn.

She opened the cabinet above the blinking microwave, took out the aspirin bottle, and set it on the counter. She felt around the top shelf with her fingers—behind the vitamins and an old sticky bottle of cough syrup and homeopathic drops. It was an old prescription for Percocet. She'd fallen on ice, Christopher hadn't been born yet. She hadn't needed it back then, she'd forgotten about it. The earthquake seemed to have shaken that memory loose, too. The label said the pills had expired two and a half years ago. But she opened it anyway, and dropped one pill onto her palm. She swallowed it with a sip of water. Then she tapped another pill onto her palm. She felt a giddiness, like she was doing something naughty, and saw the deer dancing just an hour ago outside the woods. Saw herself dancing in front of them, disappearing inside the trees. She swallowed, finished the glass of water, only then realizing how thirsty she was. She poured another and the water began to turn yellow.

White afternoon light came in over the sink window. The power had been out. But she noticed this only now as the electricity kicked back on and the house began humming and beeping, chirping to life. The refrigerator's ice machine shuddered, the microwave, the coffeemaker—their little blue blinking 00:00s marking this moment. She went down into the living room, where the bookcase had thrown a volume of *Encyclopaedia Britannica* and a small crystal tray, unbroken, onto the floor. Two Mexican masks that had tumbled gazed up at Lily, calm, unaffected.

Paul's study door was open.

Lily couldn't recall having ever seen it open. Later, this would seem so odd, even as she remembered the agreement and saw how you just accepted certain things, didn't you? A trusting relationship, you agreed to a certain allowance of gaps. Marriages, their tacit understandings, mutual elisions.

Paul had made it sound simple. A place where he could get away. A simple thing, a room with a door. And the door had grown invisible over time.

But he'd left it open. Paul had been in there working when the earthquake came. Considering his discipline, his attention to habit, it would have taken an extraordinary event to distract him from closing the door.

There in its opening she saw the edge of a mahogany desk, a window beyond, its blinds drawn. She expected someone to step into the space there, to find her staring and to close it. And the giddiness returned. The taboo, as with the pills a moment ago. Something opened in her. As if the distress of the earth had pushed through the perfection of her life, as if she were stepping into this opening it had created and feeling the risk of its never closing.

Down in the living room, she picked up a small windup monkey made of tin and set it on the coffee table. The monkey clapped its cymbals as if from the slightest change in surface pressure. The monkey had been hand-painted in Delhi, from one of Paul's business trips. They were trying to limit their use of plastics. Christopher's toys were mostly painted, made of wood, expensive.

She glanced back outside. He was asleep still on the grass.

Inside the study, there was an accounting ledger on the desk, open. Two picture frames on his desk had fallen facedown. Beside them a little ashtray, and in it, a gum eraser, its dull yellow corners rubbed down smooth.

The accounting ledger there, centered on the desk, thick and bland, old-fashioned. It seemed so strange and quaint in the room, on this desk beside these photos of family. Down the middle a thin red herringbone ribbon snaked between the spine of this open page where she saw handwritten notes. A little square of newspaper taped down at the bottom of an entry. The room was silent. She went behind the desk. She glanced through the study door, into the living room, up through the open kitchen, at the back door of the house, the deck beyond, the driveway, the poplars curved in an arch over the entry. Her pulse was blossoming with the Percocet, a teenage ache was rising in her body. She wasn't doing anything wrong. But that's how it felt in this space.

Paul's handwriting, yes. She would recall later being certain that it was his, reminding herself, because it was important. But even now she felt it was noteworthy, to see his hand in the date and unfamiliar name in the upper right-hand corner of the page. He'd jotted some notes beneath the name, and then a list. She turned the page and found in its upper corner another name and date, and more notes below. The pages were much the same except where the details and notes, or a photograph, spilled onto the next page. She didn't recognize any of the names. How could she know so few of the people he'd thought to write down like this? The little notations, dates of birth, occasionally nine digits resembling a Social Security number, *spouse,* or *sister,* or an acreage, landmarks leading to an address. *Wheelchair* on this page, with the name of a convalescent center, a line with an arrow leading to another name. And the photographs, snapshots—all of strangers. Paul's philanthropic interests, perhaps. She knew that in the past he'd hired a private firm to confirm the reputations of certain charities that approached him. But these photographs, the notes cribbed about them, and these odd news clippings—it wasn't a professional report. This was like a scrapbook of desperation. Flattened and preserved between the pages. A man in this Polaroid arguing with another—shirtless and piggish, an enormous tanned belly pulled taut—outside some sort of sunny bungalow. The photo was taken from a car, an out-of-focus side mirror foregrounded the frame. Palm trees, a little wrought iron grill that laced around the broken brown grass with a yellow cactus garden.

Like a dossier. The next page, another Polaroid, a woman leaving a little pink ranch house. She was unusually thin. She wore gold glitter platform shoes, her short skirt on her sticklike thighs and hips. A couple of bruises on her calf, clear enough in the photograph, and there, on her outer forearm. She looked medicated, and as if by contagion Lily felt the Percocet's effect more clearly inside her. She glanced up at the window, the driveway.

They were people you saw all the time but didn't see. Any page, here was a kid you once knew in school who grew up and passed through life mostly unnoticed, passed through an army of silent grievances, faces that filled sidewalks and train stations and other people's weddings. Faces perpetually slipping away from the glittering prizes. Drifting into a repository of invisibility. But, for instance, this woman here? How would Paul know this woman here? Where was the interest? To name her, to catalog her, to paste down her photograph?

The door was never left open.

She returned the book to the page of the thin red ribbon, pulled the ribbon tight, tucked deep into the spine. Paul's Waterman lay uncapped on the floor. It must have fallen during the quaking and her impulse was to cap it and put it back on the table. But she didn't.

She lifted one of the picture frames, she was holding Christopher at the hospital. He was a day or two old, wrapped in the hospital's striped receiving blanket. The other was an older photograph, a framed photograph whose colors had faded into something gentle. Paul and his sister, Carmen, two teenagers standing beside the aluminum fold-up stairs of a trailer. Behind them a clearing turned to a brown and green woods, and, deeper still, a white-capped mountain rose into a blue sky. She set the portraits facedown again on the desk. Then, quickly, she turned back to the book, turned the pages to the entry of the woman with the gold shoes. She tore a note from a pad on Paul's desk. She wrote down that name, the address. And she left.

She came out onto the deck. The cold air, static and raw. Christopher still hadn't stirred on the lawn. It wasn't like they were nudes. It wasn't like there were sex acts chronicled in the pages.

The woman in the book. The name Lily had taken down. That woman's cheekbones, her eyes, her posture—you could see that she had come apart. But Lily knew, too, that she hadn't always been like that.

People discover things about their spouses all the time.

She'd taken an open bottle of Riesling from the refrigerator on the way outside. She came down the deck steps and crossed the lawn and now she sat next to her sleeping child and sipped from the mouth of the bottle. She was drunk, instantly. This cold wind skating over the heat of her body. Christopher stirred now, extended his little arm as if grabbing at something in the breeze. Lily took a sip of wine and brushed a strand of hair from his face.

The air had a fine, cool spray in it. She heard the Range Rover now, down the lane. It emerged from the copse into the open, and pulled into the driveway. The engine silenced and Lily stood. Christopher woke and they began walking up the hill to the deck. Paul had gotten out of the car. He smiled. His old sanguine self. Already he looked strange to her.

Not much news in town, Paul said. He said some other things— there were emergency vehicles everywhere, the streets downtown blocked off. He described the buckled asphalt and piers ruptured over by the Edgewater, the market. He had talked to a couple of cops. She saw photographs of everything he said, but in every photograph there was nothing of what he said.

And later still she would forget all the things he said.

They went inside the house together. She pretended she didn't see his eyes glance down at his study, at the open door. That millisecond, where she saw a series of alternate futures cascading through the present, the past peeling off behind in the wake of the moment. And she said: Oh, the plates. She meant the plates in the kitchen. It got him to look at her, then down at the broken pieces there on the floor. To break the spell, this gap, to redirect his eye so that she didn't have to see him look at that open door. She felt dizzy from the wine and the medicine.

Christopher opened the refrigerator and now cold steam was rising from inside. He reached up and a carton of milk tipped from the shelf and spilled on the glass and was now pooling over the floor.

Christopher! she shouted. She would recall her rage at her little boy. The milk's puddle, it was nothing. Christopher toddled off crying and she grabbed the milk carton and set it in the sink. She took a dishrag and came back, leaned over the milk and saw a reflection of herself. And in that flash of recognition, she felt an ache like a tiny comet in her chest blink and fade. She heard Paul descend the stairs into the living room.

Later there would come the arguments. Paul's explanations seemed more often to prevaricate than to satisfy. His answers only anesthetized the truth. And there often followed her own self-negotiations over what to do about this: cost-benefit, vulner-abilities, a toddler, a child with medical expenses, a single parent, loneliness. The various protective evasions of her own reasoning. Her own ways of keeping the truth from erasing her.

She was wringing the dishrag's milk into the sink, the milk in which her face had appeared. She held the wrung cloth under the tap and returned to the floor. She glanced down. Paul's study door was closed now. Christopher was there in the living room, rolling a train on the rug.

She would later recall the forest shivering silver over the stark green-black of the pines, as if its rolling shimmer had only then set her life in motion. The pines had been hers back then, as had the lawn and the house. As if that recognition of the trees was the last time her life was one thing, where later it would be another, and another, and another.

But where the ache would return most profoundly was in recalling the pool of milk. Where the reflection of her face stared up at what she was just then. At that time. Before so much was erased. As her hand passed over her reflection with the rag, remov-ing her from the moment forever.

K-Ming Chang

Xifù

I DON'T MEAN I WANT HER TO DIE. I'm just saying, what kind of woman pretends to kill herself six times? I'm saying that she loves to pretend. Some women are like that. They don't know what real means. Like that neighbor I had back on the island who pretended she was pregnant for three whole years. Her belly was a sack of guavas, all lumps, and she really thought no one would be able to tell. One of the neighborhood boys punched her in the belly to prove to his friends she wasn't actually pregnant, and all the guavas came rolling out the bottom of her dress and down the road. Juice sprayed everywhere and greenmeat jellied between her feet. And that woman cried about it too. She cried so hard and so long that the sea came forward and punched her out for spending so much of its salt. Some women will mourn anything, even things that haven't been born. I know a story about another woman on the island who impregnated a goat. In the dream, the woman masturbated—don't believe anyone who says she's never touched herself, she's probably touched herself with all kinds of things, a karaoke microphone, an assortment of vacuum-cleaner attachments, a fake jade statue of Guanyin—and then offered her salted palm to her goat, which licked it clean with its tongue.

Three months later, the goat got big in the belly and the woman cut it open. Inside, there was a baby. She raised it all by herself. The baby walked on all fours for its whole life, even when it was a girl, and you can imagine what the boys thought of her. They probably mounted her like a dog on the street. The goatgirl had a baby every four days, I swear. That's the story I heard. And she ate grass too. Her mouth was always grazing the ground. What I always wanted to know was what happened to the goat after it got cut open? How did they cook it? Kebabs? Goat dumplings? Spit-roasting the whole thing?

That's why I told my daughter not to marry a man whose mother is alive. Best if the mother is a goat or dead. That's the only requirement I have: Don't marry a man with an origin. Set his family on fire. But she tells me it's okay, that she'll marry no one's son because she's a lesbian, and I'm so jealous I could kick her in front of a car, the way I once did to the neighbor's pit bull when it shat maggots on my feet. There aren't even any cars that come down our street anymore—they stopped coming since the police roadblocked the strip mall. They busted that massage place in the plaza, said it was full of Chinese prostitutes. I called the newspaper to clarify: I'm Taiwanese. I used to work there. At night I slept with all the other women, some from the mainland and some from the island and some from other islands too small for even the sea to know them. We slept in that hot back room, folding away all the tables and knotting together like a litter of pigs. The tatami mats were plastic and gave me rashes, but sometimes it was okay too, sometimes I liked hearing those women breathing all around me, all the heat in our bodies enough to burn down the building.

I ask my daughter how you even become a lesbian and she says, first, I have to reject the male gaze. So I tell her the story of my father, who couldn't see except for the shadows of things. She says, *I'm not talking about literal sight.* But I am. I'm talking about literally being seen. Like the time before my daughter was born when my husband caught me dipping my finger into the toilet after I'd peed in it. I licked the finger clean. Thing is, I was told that that's one way to make sure you have a daughter. A neighbor told me that, the same neighbor who got caught shoplifting eggplants. Told her, *Eggplants aren't even good.* Anyway, I got a daughter, didn't I? A daughter who doesn't have to worry about her mother-in-law moving in like mine did. I swear, that woman cut holes in my clothes and pretended moths did it. I've never had moths. I kill those motherfuckers with my own bare hands. I clap them down like wannabe angels and crush with my heels their brittle halos.

I once threw a pencil at a fly and pierced it through the heart, if flies even have hearts. My mother-in-law saw me and said that was my aborigine blood, that habit of skewering things alive. And another time she picked up all my dishes after I'd washed them and said they weren't clean enough. *They're clean enough to see your ugly face with,* I wanted to say. Almost told her, *Go eat out of your own ass, that's all your mouth is good for.* She tried to move into the bedroom with me and my husband. Said some fei hua about how her room down in the garage was too close to the kitchen, which has a microwave, which will kill her with its rays. Wanted to microwave her head until the brain-yolk dribbled hot from her ears. The first time my mother-in-law pretended to die, she staged a fall. She went into the kitchen and wet the floor and threw all my plates to the ground. Those plates were what I brought here from the island all those years ago. Everyone told me not to take fragile things onto a plane, because they break. Something about air pressure or the sky's weight. But all the things I packed were breakable. I brought a glass ashtray that my mother once threw at my father's head. It hit him in the eye and now he can't see the meat of things. He can only see their shadows. So that he could see where my hands were, I had to shine a flashlight on them, cast their shape on a wall. I keep the ashtray to remind myself I have a shadow. Sometimes you can't tell what's a body or what's a shadow. For years I stepped around this big spot on the sidewalk I thought was water or piss or something. Turns out it was the shadow of a tree I hadn't looked up to see. I look at the ground more and more these days. Better to keep your eyes where your feet are.

Anyway, my mother-in-law lay down among all the things (mine!) she broke and pretended she'd fallen on the wet floor. Fallen doing what? The woman doesn't do anything but follow me around all day and tell me to take her to the dentist. Claims she's got teeth cancer, sometimes jaw cancer. Is there even such a thing? For all I know, *I've* got jaw cancer. I ran to my mother-in-law and helped her up, but I could see there was no bruise on her. The only thing she'd done was bite her tongue a little, and it wasn't even bleeding. I'd give her my blood to bleed with, that's how generous I am, but she's never been hurt in her life. After that, she insisted on walking around the house using a broomstick as a cane. I've seen that woman jump three feet into the air to smack a mosquito with her hands. One night I saw her drop the cane and run to the TV so she could catch the opening scene of her soap opera, about an empress dowager controlling her puppet son. You see how fake?

Then the second time she tried, it was with a rope. She tried to hang herself in the pantry, except when I opened the door, her feet were still on the ground. Sure, the rope was around her neck and tied to the rafter and everything, but the pantry's only four and a half feet tall and she was just standing there, leashed to the ceiling. She even tried to pretend she was choking by sticking her tongue out and making these coughing sounds, but when I asked her what the hell she was doing, she paused to say, *I'm killing myself because you are a bad daughter-in-law and what will my son think when he finds out I've killed myself because of you how bad he will feel how much he will regret marrying you choosing you you bitch.* I said, *If you can say all that while hanging yourself, you're going to live.* And the third time was the worst. She stole the neighbor's kiddie pool and filled it up in the yard and pretended to drown in it. Except she didn't fill it up enough and there was only about a knuckle of water in there, and when she thrashed around, most of it splashed out of the pool and then she had to continue pretending to drown in nothing. She flopped facedown and tried to be dead, but the whole pool deflated from the weight of her body—let me tell you, she's got hips like hams—and as the air came out, it made a farting sound. Instead of dying, it sounded like she needed to shit. The fourth time was also a drowning, except this one was in the bathtub. I heard her filling it up and I was ready this time. As soon as she got into the tub with all her clothes on, I burst through the door, said, *Not while I'm alive,* and dragged her out by the hair. Turns out her hair is not very strongly attached to her scalp, so I ended up tearing out a lot of it, and she cried for almost a month about it, told my husband I was abusing her and now she'd have to wear a wig. I know ways to abuse her, and none of them involve her hair. I could heat up a frying pan and press it to her face until the skin sizzles and all her features melt together into an abstract painting. I could push her feet into a pot of hot water and boil them till they rise like dumplings. I could scalp her and then wear her skin like a swim cap.

All my friends say what I'm dealing with is nothing: They have mothers-in-law who have locked them inside the garage on 105-degree days, who have put manure in their food and claimed it was the recipe, as if they have ever used a recipe. The worst thing is when some of them convert our children into loving their nainais better than they love their own mothers. That's when you have to tell your daughters the truth of everything that's been done to you, all the times you were told you were a bad xífù for eating with your head bent over the bowl, for shopping at Nordstrom Rack instead of going to the temple, for overstuffing dumplings into testicle-looking things. So what if I like them big. And then you tell your daughter all the stories in history about mothers-in-law who beat concubines to death with a chamber pot, mothers-in-law who rip themselves open by shoving their sons' full-grown heads back inside themselves, sometimes up the wrong hole, a mother-in-law who wakes you up at three in the morning so that you can drive her to the emergency room because, she claims, she's pregnant at the age of seventy-seven and is having a baby right now, it's inside her, rolling around like a juiced grapefruit, it's sour and screaming, and when you finally get there, an hour later because she tells you there's a shortcut even though the only direction she knows is toward the church, it turns out she has kidney stones and you're going to have to pay for their removal, out of pocket, and the rest is debt you'll have for life, and when the doctor rolls her into surgery, you tell him, *Please just let her die on the operating table,* or *Please pretend to operate on her but leave the stones inside her, make her feel the birth-pain of passing those blessed pebbles through her body.*

But the doctor doesn't listen, he removes them and then stitches her up and she loses basically no blood, and she goes home the next day and tells you it's your fault for using too much soy sauce in all your dishes, even though the reason you add a spoonful more is that she told you in the first place that nothing you make is salty enough. The fifth time she tries to kill herself is when she walks out to the highway—without her cane, of course—and steps in front of an eighteen-wheeler, except by some miracle, the eighteen-wheeler stops right before it hits her and there's an eight-car pileup and we see her on the local evening news. It's a physics-defying miracle, how an elderly woman who is terribly neglected at home—because of course she has to say that on TV—has been saved thanks to a trucker's quick reflexes and the benevolent will of god. She's being called a saint in certain comments sections, and I might have left a comment or two as well, all of them about how people aren't really supposed to live forever, in other eras they would be dead by seventy-seven, and being pulped by an eighteen-wheeler is actually, I imagine, a very merciful end, and it probably leaves a beautiful piece of blood-art on the highway, kind of like a mural you can only see from above.

They even interview her for the *World Journal,* and of course she tells the reporter she doesn't blame her daughter-in-law for not taking better care of her, because how can a woman like her, at her age, be valued in a world like this, where old women are seen as burdens? But god had said otherwise; god had held back an eighteen-wheeler and said, *You are worthy of my love and intervention.* I almost strangle her in her bed after that. I stand over her in the dark and think about it, just think about it. The sixth time, I tell my husband it's all his fault. He should have been immaculately conceived by a goat. Every man loves his mother milk-sour. I tell you, my husband never once took my side. One time my mother-in-law told me I'd overcooked the fish, but that fish was so soft inside it almost dissolved in the light. And my husband said nothing to defend me, even though he'd eaten half the fish himself, and my daughter the lesbian only knows enough Chinese to say, *I don't want, thank you.* Like a damn cricket, she says it again and again. I want her to tell me my fish is done perfect. Look how the bones disrobe. This woman tells me I can't cook a fish? I'll cook her. Later she says she wants the master bedroom because the garage is full of outside-air, and outside-air is full of toxins that are souring her, can't you see how her neck sags, how her breasts are hard as potatoes, how her tongue is purple? I want to say, *Your neck sags because you're an old shit-sack, your breasts are hard because you don't take them out to breathe, your tongue is purple from that time you bit it instead of dying.*

I don't say anything about the fish, and I don't apologize either, so that night she puts her head in the oven but forgets to turn it on. I come downstairs in the morning and she is asleep, drooling, with her head poked into the oven. I ask her where she learned to do this oven thing and she says she's been reading, even though I know that woman is illiterate. She's one of those peasant women who's so short she looks like a pack animal from afar, a body built to carry things. I'm a better mother to her son than she is. That's what marriage is, motherhood, except the man doesn't do you the courtesy of growing up. I tell her, *Next time just swallow the insecticide we keep on the shelf in the garage.* She looks at me angry, because I am supposed to say, *No, don't die, we need you, your son needs you,* etc. I bend down really close to her face and say, *The oven is electric.* Then I tell her, *The way gas works, you could have killed everyone in this house. Is that what you want, to kill your own son in his sleep?*

And that's when she stands up, a foot shorter than me. It's morning and my daughter is waking up. I can hear her in the next room, walking around without socks on even though I tell her you can die that way. I like to be awake before she is. I'm glad she won't have a man. Better not to be a mother. *It leads to many suicides,* I should tell her. My mother-in-law starts telling me this story about how she didn't know she was pregnant. The night her son was born, she thought she was having gas. She was alone. But then my husband slipped out of her like a fish and everyone said, Kill it. That's when she left for the island, the baby dragged behind her in a net. I call her a liar. I won't forget the time she caught my husband washing a dish and called my own mother in Yilan to complain how I wasn't doing my duty as a wife, how I made her son clean in his own home, how I threatened him with a back scratcher into rinsing that dish, and of course my mother believed this and called to tell me I would never grow skin, as if, as if my husband has ever washed a dish, as if he's ever washed anything but his own dick, and even that not very well.

The problem is this, I tell my daughter: Mothers grow up married to their sons, but we're born knowing our daughters will leave us. Not because we want them to, but because we never had them, not really: they belong to the men we give them to. Men, they belong to everything, including themselves. This is what I say: We should separate all mothers and sons at birth and grow them in different dirts. Make the sons grow up alone. And mothers, we'll be fine in our own rooms. Give us a window or two, a view, curtains that open into morning. All those times she almost killed herself, she didn't know death isn't like a man: it won't just take you any time you're on your back. When she finally dies, I won't pretend I'm not happy about it. But I'll buy her a good burial, a full funeral. I'll give her an urn with a name on it, which is more than her family would have done, her family who doesn't even name their daughters. That woman answers to nothing. I can't even pray her dead, because the gods don't have her listed in any directory. When my husband dies, I'll bury him beneath her. And I won't mourn then either. You can have his bones and the moths they'll become. I joke now with my daughter, not that it matters to her, since the only men she'll marry are women, and two women together probably cancel out, become nameless. I point at the sky. The sun, I say, and laugh. When choosing a sun to see by, make sure it's got no mother. The moon, that's the mother. Her eye is always open to watch her sun. *It's not really a light,* my daughter says about the moon, *it's a mirror.* But mirrors, I tell her, are more dangerous than anything. A mirror's only meaning is to multiply. To duplicate. To duty. The mirror doesn't change what is shown to it, not unless someone shatters the glass, and that would be you, my daughter, the fist to my ribs, the one who will never become the moon.

Kathleen Alcott
Temporary Housing

O NLY GREG EVER NOTICED the notch in my tooth, and only
in outline did I tell him about how I got it—how Guin and
I stole that couple's developed film from the "J" cubby at the phar-
macy. Tall and poor, she and I had walked through downtown
Petaluma in each other's clothing, our pupils dilated by one drug
or shrunk by another. People thought we were fucking, or whatever mean verb they'd use to describe what bodies like ours could
do with another, but the closest we came was sleeping naked. The
closest we came was dreaming some vague man on top, and waking up holding a pristine, warm woman. If asked to explain the
end of that friendship, I might still blame the night we ruined that
marriage. It's easier to claim there was one bad day, a cheap little
kindness you can spend against the debt of one bad life.

Guin was originally from Utah, spanked to welts for swear-
ing against Jesus too often, asking about the looks her family had
started to get at church, but I'd been punished more by chance,
and silence. Little-girl dinners I had to fix myself in the pantry,
saltines and brown apples, on evenings my parents wouldn't
emerge after a fight. That Guin and I were poor, or unhappy, for
different reasons—my parents boomer dropouts who came from

middle-class security but destroyed their own chance of it, her mother a missionary never given a thing—didn't register in the aisles of the Grocery Outlet where our families both shopped. During those years when I'd all but dropped out myself, becoming the gossiped-about mystery of the honors class girls who had been my friends, our miseries seemed to correspond exactly. I convinced myself soon after that this was closer to a coincidence, a tacky suitcase you find at a flea market that happens to bear your own monogrammed initials. You register the fact and move on, a little embarrassed that a part of you could be so recognizable, and reproducible.

"You are unwell," a client snaps at me, on what is something like a Tuesday afternoon, something like eight months into the virus. She's angry about my suggestion—an antipsychotic, Latuda, for a pattern of intrusive thoughts about killing her husband—and that I've seemed tired, and elsewhere. "Have you even been listening to the complexity of this, or are you just another pusher? That's what my fucking schizophrenic uncle takes, and I'm not a schizophrenic. I'm a good mother and a *successful* entrepreneur."

"I'm sorry," I say, and roll my chair a little toward the screen to let her know I'm listening. "I hear that you're feeling misunderstood."

The client's thoughts have become the defining feature of all our recent sessions—how they intrude as she watches her husband take the bottles of formula from the fridge, or teach the five-year-old about the lawn mower by giving its different parts funny voices. A screwdriver in the neck! A gas leak while she's out! They flash to her mind like things that have already happened, and can't be helped.

"How could I be running an award-winning *yarn store*," she says, "if I were some dangerous lunatic?" That line I would have repeated to Greg, and it would have fed us for months. *Oh, quite easily,* he would have retorted in apostrophe, his handsome face smiling in a way that tripled my devotion. "Also," she says, "I *hate* that thing you do with your tongue." I start to apologize: it's just a habit of thoughtfulness, how I push it visibly against my teeth, but she closes her laptop and shuts me back into my life. Maybe two hours later, as I take in the pond from our Palladian window—its placement under the side gable is unusual for a Federal house—my phone lights up, a spam call with my hometown area code. *Social Security number soon to be erased,* a voice says, *due to illicit possession.*

It's a good trick, on their part. They must bet on how many Americans might like it, the opportunity to pick up a familiar number, if only for the turn to say *no!,* if only for the chance to say *no longer!*

Guin and I were waiting, that day, on a roll I'd taken of a dreaming, episodic acid trip—mostly of her, a few with the twenty-eight-year-old speed freak she was dating. We took turns slamming our palms flat on the bell until the balding, name-tagged Kenneth appeared from behind the curtain to absorb our complaint and disappear again. We rifled through the paper sleeves from opposite ends of the alphabet, bored with the same old photos of our shiny lip-glossed enemies—posing on Jettas in stretch denim, glittery thongs apparent, or holding each other in mirrors bombed by a disposable's flash—and met in the middle. I found the envelope, but Guin snatched it from my hands.

A childless couple in their early thirties, the Joneses lived near me, five blocks uphill, far from the sounds of the boulevard's traffic that filled my mother's apartment. He taught sixth grade and choir at a grammar school—unhappily, it was known, and pedantically—and she designed websites for people in cities. I'd only ever noticed the dog they followed in and out of their Queen Anne, a saluki whose elegance seemed gaudy in that town of hokey editorials and ripped, bored cops. I loved Petaluma, even as I looked forward to leaving, and felt a pride in where I was from, maybe trained by my father, who had adored it, always honking when crossing back into city limits.

You could see the Joneses' dog outside the café where they stopped in the mornings for espresso, sitting calm and certain. The couple were part of a wave of others like them, leaving San Francisco after the tech bubble burst. They were the same people who would make it so the docks where we drank had gated fences, and the smarter restaurants took down their folksy, loving signs— one day they were pleased to serve you, the next they knew the pleasure had better be yours.

The first photos bragged of their house's restoration— midmorning singing onto lacy white pediments, molded cherubs floating at high corners. I wasn't as compelled by it all as Guin. The subtleties of money, how it could be spent, didn't interest me yet, perhaps because my father had been fixated on a lack of it. He was two years sober when he received his larceny sentence. A winsome barber with sixty college credits in philosophy, he'd run a scam he claimed to believe only hurt the credit card companies, not the customers he charged three times.

By the summer before I left town, my mother was doing her own Sisyphean time, paying off the high-interest debt she'd run up the first year he was gone. There'd been nothing enormous: acrylic turtlenecks, a refurbished off-brand laptop for each of us. She ultimately declared bankruptcy, but in those years she was still trying to make it right, buying drugstore stockings for her job as a legal secretary. Soon they were going to change her position from contractor to employee, she would assure me, though I hadn't asked. I didn't need a doctor, and didn't notice she couldn't go to one. Clothes and books covered the bed she hadn't made since my father left it, asking the same question her face did while she smoked. What was the lesson, could anyone say? For which occasion was she supposed to dress? It must have seemed to her that the moment she stopped picking him off the couch where he'd passed out drunk, he stood up quietly to become a thief.

Guin glanced through the snapshots with her eyes half raised, awaiting the clerk's return. Here was the brass finial, rising above repainted lilacs and blues. Next was a day at Dillon Beach, Mrs. Jones disappearing behind mounds of sand in mauve leggings, the two of them in matching Cal baseball caps. As we came upon the image of her twined to the bed frame with luminous black cords, her face lifted in devotion, the clerk reappeared.

I kept his eye and nodded as he rang us up, knowing as I did that Guin had slipped the envelope down the back of her jeans. As he handed me our pictures, Guin put her hand in mine and thanked him so politely—*Gee, I super appreciate it, Kenny*—that he frowned in suspicion. Guin's manners were a vestige of her Mormon childhood, a way of life killed as suddenly as her father was: his own gun, their garage, eleven in the morning. Guin had been eight, and lied to about the nature of his death, but she'd figured it out by the time she was twelve and they'd moved to California. A dyslexic who never spelled a word the same way twice, she was eighteen that summer, and had earned her GED two years before. After I'd stopped showing up to class, I graduated, barely, through some independent-study loophole granted to those with "trouble at home." If we were free then, it was a peculiar kind of freedom—both the kind of daughters who needed to spy, we treated our own lives like something to be infiltrated, armed and blazing.

The June morning was warm, but not severe, as we left the drugstore and crossed the bridge toward the old mill. Its steel coruscated above the remains of the railroad, which had once carried eggs from the town's farmers to San Francisco. The tracks now stood rotting over the estuary—slow, brown, fetid water the town called "the river." Back at my mother's apartment, a flat sectioned from a Stick Victorian, we took off our shirts and settled on the concrete back patio. It was almost pleasant out there, with a row of plants in terra-cotta plastic, a wobbly glass table sprouting a crooked umbrella from the center, and two wooden chaise longues that could no longer be adjusted, their hardware rusted from winter rain. The only object that worked as it should was the ashtray, a metal contraption that spun and lowered, when pressed, to conceal the butts in its belly. Guin loved that thing, and called it the Forgetter.

Memories, the drugstore packages said, in a bendy font that faded in thickness, toward the word's conclusion, to become confetti. On the table between us Guin placed the image where we'd stopped before. The woman lay on her stomach, her wrists bound together behind her back, her legs held in a V by the cords that secured her ankles to either end of the footboard. Her turned face on the pillow, canted slightly up, didn't look at the camera. As for the gag in her mouth, it seemed like something that had always been there.

Sick, Guin said, as she flipped to the next photo, where the husband appeared alongside the wife in the mirror—one arm crossing her torso like a seat belt to choke her, the other holding up a whip. Guin brought that print closer to look at the leather cord, trying to get a real sense of its harm. *I can't look anymore,* she said, after scouring all of them twice. *We should do something about this.*

When I asked why she was so pissed about some boring softcore, she snapped. *Anyone could have seen these, what he's doing to her.* If she believed her reaction to be on behalf of Mrs. Jones, I felt only a sad jolt of confirmation. Even if I couldn't say it yet, I must have suspected the point of my body was its capture.

Guin sat there fuming, smoke pouring from her mouth toward the sun, but I was as calm as I always managed to be during that spell of my life. Like many children of alcoholics, I could read faces very well—as a psychiatrist, it's been useful—and so those photos didn't alarm me. Anger, fear, love, or hatred: those feelings seemed as absent from the Joneses' bedroom as any other clutter, silenced by the dahlias on the end table, or folded neatly within the lilac throw. I didn't much see the point in looking for them.

But then I've always liked explaining people's lives too neatly, or that's what Greg thought, saying that was why I got into my line of work.

This isn't real violence, I said. Guin looked at me then the way someone does when you brightly call them the incorrect name, long after you ought to have known it—hurt enough, by a mistake so crucial, that a correction hardly feels worth the breath.

I went inside to piss, and as I flushed I heard Guin shout she was leaving, a nasty slam of the gate. These sorts of exits were occurring more often, likely in reaction to my impending escape. In the fall I'd applied to college—drunk, online, receiving no acceptances but one wait list from a mediocre private school I knew little about—and when the letter came, I made the mistake of showing Guin my excitement. The brochure of hideous, brand-new buildings, the palm trees that screamed useless, lifelong debt. *It looks like a bad mall where you can't even shop,* she said, a line I would use as my own to people in my classes. By then Guin and I weren't speaking.

That remark about my job: I think Greg made it the first year in Vermont, when we were thirty and mostly happy, chatting with people in the co-op about novels and politics. He taught rich kids classics at Deerfield, just over the Massachusetts border, and liked chiding them in Greek about ancient questions, being addressed as *Doctor* during coat-and-tie lunches. As for me, as the small-town shrink, I felt I was something like the masonry downtown—designed to protect people, but safe from being changed much by their lives. I loved all the granite in Brattleboro, the quartzite of the Gothic church sourced on Wantastiquet Mountain. That kind of architecture is hard to find in this country, where we were in such a hurry to get started that chopping down a tree made more sense than finding and quarrying the right kind of stone. I felt as devoted to Vermont as I did to Greg, loved its order and drama of time. That the leaves in October were as saffron as the snow would be white, that the mating bullfrogs in spring were as loud as the winter mountains had been silent. In Northern California you get from primeval redwoods to sun-painted ocean in a half hour flat, piney peaks to tawny pasture without stopping for lunch. Sometimes I want to blame what Greg called my lost years on that landscape. Of course it was my father, of course it was my mother, but wasn't it also that a day could feel like a year, that the scope of what you saw could explode one minute and shrink the next? Who knew what you were reacting to, the earth that didn't need you or your life that only might? How could you trust any feeling? To my father, a Southerner who still called the ocean the sea, that climate was thrilling. He had loved small talk about weather as much as the weather itself.

My family was nothing like Guin's, but there *was* one strange coincidence between us, I guess I forgot to say—both of our fathers had killed themselves. He'd *told* my mother he couldn't do prison, she would repeat in the months after the call came from the DOC. And as with many things—how to swim under a nasty wave, how to hike down a steep hill and keep your balance—he had been right.

The Joneses' photos, I thought, couldn't have shocked Guin as much as she paraded: we had learned hooks and jabs from a video we paused and replayed on my boxy laptop, and our party trick— she was more convincing—was to make the teenage Spencers and Brians we knew, sweatshirted creatures with bong-water eyes, bleed from their noses without warning or reason. Local boys were friends, but little else: we had fake IDs used for nights in the city that felt like whole futures and required something like investigative journalism to piece together later. Oblivion or velocity, Guin had her preferences—already loyal to downers, she occasionally needed some all-night chatter—but I could do one or the other as if it were an aimless matter of left or right. For her birthday in the spring, we had gobbled Vicodin and sucked lollipops on the

80 into the city, playing up the irony that we might be girls who loved sugar, waving at sweet old women and calling them ma'am. I loved how an opiate made you aware of your lungs, the shallow breathing that courted those enormous sighs. At the Steinhart Aquarium, yet to be remodeled, redolent still with salt water leaking onto carpet, our breathing felt religious. We worshipped before enormous turtles who had lived forever, the shifting walls of fish whose only job was to be a certain color, and float toward the edges of their life. *Oh, I love that ole dang squid,* Guin said, kissing the glass, swiveling around to kiss me. Those drugs made her devoted to everything and everyone—on our way in, she had gasped at the blue eyes of an elderly security guard and said, *Sir, are you aware you're my husband?*—but I took what I could get.

On nights there was blow or Dexedrine glowing through our pockets, the goal was a room that looked like nowhere with a door closed to everything, paid for often with the tips we both made busing tables. When we had less money there were men in tourist neighborhoods, harmless commuters or Cal State bros, who could be convinced to come along to whichever motel and pitch in. Greg would have been upset if I told him that part, or thought it was something like prostitution. There are so many nice, half-safe places on the way to getting rid of yourself, I wouldn't have been able to persuade him, decent people who only give you what you've promised them you need.

So much I didn't say, and still he was the rare person who knew much about that part of my life—only because I'd had to explain why I'd gone to such a bad college, or could sip some turned wine without flinching, or would know what drug slang meant in an art-house addiction movie. We had met at twenty-six as Americans vacationing in Rome, passing down the stairs from the umbrella pines at the top of the city to the travertine arches over the gold-green Tiber. As a couple we were best when explaining something together, an idea or a poem, and could laugh until tears, holding each other's elbows, about a faux pas or malapropism. The remark

I had made in my failing French: *Hitler and Stalin were one big problem.* The time at a lake in Slovenia when Greg hardly glanced over his shoulder where I pointed, to a fire in an oil drum trash can, and the cavalier way he rebuffed it—*Typical Slavic grill*—right before some of the burning garbage exploded. He'd grown up wealthy, which made me feel his choosing me was a greater compliment, but the way my poverty came up began to be a problem. He wanted to be alone together, to have pulled me cleanly from my life into ours. I still don't know if that was unfair, only that most facts of his background were not things he felt hunted by, and from which he had to cower, or stand up to shoot.

The photos of us I reviewed without her: it was a ritual we typically loved, Guin keeping a hand light on my back. She was comforted by the idea of a record, evidence that her life went on without her memory of it, and I by her *who*-lessness, how in one image she could give off many people—the floppy wave of a toddler, the deep stare of real age. The day of that trip, we'd taken the 6 up from Civic Center to Golden Gate Park, where vanished, gray-complected men my parents might have partied with, still known as Fuzzy Bear and Socrates and Hazy Davy, mumbled as they sold most of everything for next to nothing. Those boomers were like the park's cypress trees to us, everywhere you looked, as unmoving and as pissed upon. There's a photo of Guin, euphoric right after we scored, going down the nearby concrete slides—an oddity in design that requires filthy playground sand in the descent, to create speed, and pieces of cardboard you ride on, gripping either side. The day itself became a segmented spectacle, clearly divided into different situations and the feelings they radiated. I love boundaries like that, clean transitions.

We peaked on the bus ride back to town, filling with anxious laughter we felt bounce down the aisle. By the time we deboarded we weighed nothing, and were no one. Petaluma was still made up of forgotten places, sheds meeting little beaches of scrubs and anise, and we spent a small lifetime in the grass by the abandoned Ghirardelli barn on the water, believing the river was not reflecting pink light but producing it. We needed to be free and outside on those drugs, because of how they could flip your senses—leaves could chirp, light could drip—and work a similar inversion on your life, a punch line you might hear and laugh at but soon forget. *Well, I can't speak for myself,* I panted after a silence, facedown in cool dirt to quiet the colors, fucking up the idiom, and we laughed for a year. Sometimes you make a mistake and it feels like a blessing: lucky and funny: clear and perfect: so much purer than anything you could work for.

When we'd come down enough that buildings no longer felt vicious, we went to visit Tim at the bar where he newly had a job. Depending on the drugs he didn't mention and I never saw him use—was he smoking meth, shooting speed?—he could drink to shouting, captious oblivion or down a twelve-pack with no sign of it. He spent his shifts reading, Tom Robbins novels and histories of ancient civilizations, sagas and victories that played in the caves of his face. The swirls and spikes of his hair seemed like an expression of his intelligence. He'd been accepted to Berkeley but refused to pay for an education he could give himself, a fact most of his conversations eventually included. He had the kind of fine, aquiline face I saw later in sculpture halls, and the Gen X slouch that went with their coffee-shop sofas. Tim could be useful and charming, playing us Psychic TV records and asking what we thought, taking us, when he had a car, out to the ocean, where he made a game of running up the high dunes—surprising us with a kite he'd hidden in his jacket, or reciting the bit of Eliot he had memorized. Maybe it wasn't as much his age that was thrilling but his generation, the art they'd made of the T-shirt, the masterpiece of wasting time.

Guin had been sleeping with him on and off for eight months. Sometimes he seemed to worship her, and sometimes he disappeared, and there'd come a tight coil of days in which Guin was always in my bed, asking anxious, funny questions in the middle of the night. *Darlin', when you finish school could we get a little house out down D Street, and have some chickens and sell the eggs? Do those Ren Faire girls think owning a lute is the same as having a personality? Are you sleeping? How old were you when you spelled your own name?* During those sleepovers we'd roll around cackling, doing impressions of people we hated, pretending to fart into the other's bare ass. Even my teeth wanted to fuck her. I could never decide if she wanted that, too, or if both of us did, whether it was for the wrong reason—that we'd shared everything else. The idea of there being some sound we'd never heard the other make, some face we'd never seen that meant *exactly that,* was as illogical as the fact we'd soon parcel our lives apart.

Hurrying back to my bed on one of these nights in the winter, having gone out in the ten P.M. rain to the store that took our IDs, we found Tim in the empty town plaza. He stood under an awning in a thermal and shower sandals, making the kind of snort he did at a dumb remark, over and over—except there was no remark, just the world around him. I felt Guin's hand clench where I held it. His eyes opened and closed, opened and closed, seeming to rinse almost greener, the simple fact of us offending him. How could we have been there, went the blink of his tic, when he was somewhere fucking else? There was a string of screaming cursing, nasal and elated, and when Guin said *let's go* and took my elbow to walk on, he followed us up some stairs and half a block, shouting and laughing for a terrible minute. Then he saw a left turn that somehow reconfigured him—he made a noise of recognition and disappeared without a word.

Guin wouldn't discuss it when I brought up these episodes later, acting like I'd violated his privacy. I didn't consider how he must have treated Guin's blackouts with the same hushed acceptance. *Respect comes in where love should be,* I once read in Tolstoy, stopping to underline it, thinking that distinction would be easy to see.

. . .

Guin and I saw each other only once in our twenties, at the grocery store where she had taken a job bagging—I saw her, actually,
apron clutched in her fist as she cleared the magazine rack by the
bathrooms, not looking back long as she called goodbye to a co-
worker. Had she seen me where I stood in line? I was twenty-four,
and fooling people in medical school with the silk shirts I hand-
washed in my bathroom sink, a change in the way I pronounced
either and *neither,* and I reasoned it was possible she hadn't recognized me. She'd gotten sober for the first time a few years before,
and I knew she had suddenly married, an ex-con line cook—she'd
worn celery green to the city hall wedding, I saw on Facebook.
Other than that she never posted, and sometimes I tried to google
her, pulled my phone out and typed *Guin di Salvo Petaluma,* as
though she were an unusual domestic problem, and I expected the
internet to tell me what to do, and to hear from people similarly
afflicted. Her life was never online in the way mine was—just
those creepy aggregators of phone numbers and addresses. She
had so many, over the years.

Crossing through the grocery store parking lot a minute later,
I watched her get into her husband's car. Standing on that same
concrete, we'd once run into a former friend of mine, Sophie, who
was star of symphony and debate, and she had sneered with rich
concern. *Um, have you ever considered just coming to school?* Guin's
answer came easily, in the same breath she took me by the waist.
Um, Sophie? Have you ever considered just furiously masturbating?

As Guin and her husband roared by, I was ready to wave, but
her face was pitched down, and it seemed to me he'd hit the gas
before she'd even closed the door.

The photos of us blitzed and senseless I left scattered across the
kitchen table, some dare for my mother to find, and then I read
away the afternoon. Guin showed up drunk two hours later,

announcing her arrival by pitching her bag through my open bedroom window, reorganized under an idea she'd had about what we should do. About what, I said, as she took off her shoes and socks, making a grotesque face at her own smell, then leaning one cheek to the cool promise of the wall. She made a snapping gesture at the bag, gone enough that the pads of her fingers barely made a sound, and I threw it at her harder than was necessary. Moving a hand through loose tobacco and coins and fireworks, ChapStick and condoms and shoe glue, she took out the envelope of photos, and I saw a new little tear at its fold.

Pointing at the neat capitals where Mr. Jones had written his contact information, a Yahoo email address, Guin told me to get out my computer. I bet his AIM is the same, she said, crawling into my bed with the splayed limbs. Take off your jeans, I said, they're filthy. She did, then held them way above her, grinning, poking her head through the two legs. Guin created a new account and added him to the buddy list, and then we waited, watching the videos we often did as we swilled the bottle she'd brought. Again we laughed at Kelsey Grammer walking right offstage during a talk, James Brown calling into a news show hammered, saying *I feel good!* in answer to every serious question, allegations of domestic abuse. These were our favorites: a man falling, a man refusing to fall. Would we have enjoyed these clips if they featured important women? I don't know, just how in that grainy iteration of the internet, they did not exist. This only followed the pattern of the world we knew, triumphs and losses occurring mostly on the male side of things. There were clips of women stumbling and tripping, pert meteorologists accidentally drawing cocks that crossed oceans, but they were almost always anonymous—matronly or preadolescent shapes to be known only for the comical errors they made. When the sound came that meant a buddy had appeared online, Guin grabbed for my computer, roughly pressing the screen way back to squint at it. *Hey,* I said, *that cost money.* The alert was just our weed dealer, and I took the laptop back and primly shut it. *That lady could be in real trouble,* Guin said. *That man could be hurting her. Why aren't you worried about her?*

Because of her face in the fucking photos, I could have said. Because sometimes a small insult pays insurance against a larger, I wouldn't have thought yet, because maybe to be primitive for an hour a day is to be in control for the rest. Instead I asked a vicious question, one I sensed she wouldn't remember fielding anyway. She'd already dropped her bag onto the porch and put one leg out the window, and I propped myself up in my bed. *Are you trying to tell me Tim loves you while he fucks you?*

Guin returned to my bed, briefly, mounting me on my hip bones. Give me your hand, she said, laughing, and then she spit in it, smoker-thick and wet, closing my fingers onto my palm. *You're gonna learn so much at school.* I cried in the half hour after she left, loud enough that my mother came tentatively to my door and I sent her away, barking only *Why is it so fucking hot in this house?* Excepting the rare occasion a high temperature lasted into evening, she had the habit of moving the thermostat up to sixty-five at night, saying the early morning fog came in a cold draft. She was a thin, mysterious person, always putting on another sweater, never going farther than her ankles into the chilly ocean, smiling when I begged as a child for her to come, waving and saying she loved to watch me. By the time it was just the two of us I despised her caution, that aversion to the outside air. I would open all the windows and smoke her cheap cigarettes, shrugging when she cursed about her empty pack, saying maybe she should quit.

I'm sorry, I T9'd Guin that night. *I love you. You're right. Let's make that man afraid of himself.*

When I heard about Guin's marriage—he had hit her a few times, she had left him, my mother saw his mug shot online—I felt a real victory for her, then something too close to jealousy. There was no good reason for what had happened between Greg and me: why he'd started sneering if I asked if he'd like to take a bath, walk and see the full moon, why I'd become some corrupt guard assigned to his life alone, asking what that look meant, that gesture, that pause, waking him in the morning to continue the argument. I would hear him brag about me to other people, and I praised him often, too, but in private he'd do and say things that I still can't unsee or unhear. Their cruelty was almost hidden, almost elegant. *I think you talk about your childhood for the attention, darling,* he'd say calmly, *but you already have mine.* One spring he stopped wanting sex, would shade his eyes if he saw me coming naked from the shower, or wince if I squeezed him in the kitchen. By summer he'd moved to the guest room, asking politely for my help in hanging some new art there. Often, I couldn't help it, I'd appear in his door frame to beg and weep. *Oh, here's the quixotic quack again,* he liked to say, rolling his eyes, and often in the same gesture he reached for his clean, warm handkerchief.

After he was gone, I wanted friends to say about my husband what people must have about Guin's, that he was a bad man, or how it was something bigger than him, the drug he loved, which made him hurt her. But Greg stacked his books so neatly when he left: he looked only like himself in his old maroon sweater, crossing the lawn to his truck until the boxes were loaded. There was his pageboy bob I loved, his high rower's ass I used to hold in the shower. We were married by that pond, we ran through that house, yelling some news that would make the other laugh. And all anyone could say, bored with my wretched mourning, was that he had been a person.

I had tried to get Guin alone, the few days after she'd slammed my window shut, but she was always at Tim's apartment. It was a top-floor one-bedroom he took great pride in, regaling us often with battles he waged against his landlord. *That motherfucker,* he would say, *is dealing with somebody who knows his rights as a renter.* After Guin had turned me down twice for whiskey by the river, I agreed when she invited me to his place, though I had sworn myself against it. The last time I'd gone, I'd refused to join them in the shower, and Tim had mocked my weak explanation. *I'm really already clean,* I had said.

I stood there knocking a long time before they let me in. It was seven P.M., and I had passed by windows where families were just sitting down to dinner, fathers standing over tables with large serving spoons, children unfolding blue napkins. Tim kept his door locked and dead-bolted, and when Guin finally opened it, wearing a black lace bra and grass-stained jeans, she looked damp and peaceful. In his room he kept a bed on a low, imitation-wood frame, and in the kitchen a pool table. He'd been teaching Guin to play, all that spring and summer, and she took to it naturally, sliding the cue behind her back as if it were a part of her body. She was good at everything process-oriented she tried, tools and games and diagrams—that year she'd built a solar panel, taught herself fifty birdcalls.

The moment I was inside, Guin crawled back into bed with him where he lay smoking and holding a beer on his bare chest. They were so far in their drunk they'd turned placid and kind, Tim telling me there were Chinese leftovers in the fridge if I was hungry, Guin asking from her place on his shoulder what the weather had done all day. I gestured to a glass quart of tequila on the floor and began to catch up. When I asked Guin if she'd told Tim about the photos, she made a strange face, as if this were not the time—then, seeing his interest, she laughed and produced them. *If anyone deserves to be fucked,* she slurred as he flipped through, *it's that serious prince of a dog.* It was my thought that we call Mr. Jones, but I used words like *somebody,* playing in the hypothetical realm of juvenile humor. *Somebody should call him,* I said, *and tell him the police have the photos? Like the clerk reported them?* Tim spread them in a careful grid across the peaks and valleys of the unmade bed, chin tucked into his hand like the scientist he might have been. *Oh, so they were maybe in my class at Berkeley,* I remember him saying.

I saw the suggestion as airy and unreal, only something to feel better for joking about—but Tim lived beyond that, in the place of real rent and real anger, and soon was dialing the number on speaker. The moment rippled in a sensation I remembered from childhood, of a secret feeling exposed by adult force. The malt ball I'd stolen from the plastic grocery bin, rich and perfect in my cheek: lost to the trash can as my mother demanded, replaced by mealy shame. Guin leaned back on the bed behind where he sat up, saying maybe we should talk about it first. She called him *honey* then, something I hadn't heard before and that made me look at her another way. In it was a wish for peace that was nowhere in how she held her body, the muscled shoulders that appeared to meet the wind before the rest of her. Guin and I exchanged a look as he started to speak, something like a man as he first enters you, that tentative question of cruelty or kindness—*Will I hurt you or love you,* their faces always seem to say, *or is there something in you that might allow me both.*

Yes, am I speaking with Matthew Jones, we heard Tim say, sensed the pause and the assent. The voice he used was one he hadn't around me, clear and clipped. *This is Lieutenant O'Reilly down here at the Petaluma Police Department. I'm calling about some photos you took, reported by a concerned citizen. That's right.*

Once he was really going, Guin wouldn't look at me, just started to press her feet into the curve of his back. I could tell she was deepening the pressure there the more he refused to acknowledge it with any kind of glance back or touch, hinting at the kick that lived somewhere within her. Guin reached for the bottle between Tim's legs, trying thinly to get in the spirit of things. And then, for a moment, she seemed as if she might smile, looking like someone gamely following a story spoken in another language—only a thought behind at first, but soon dissociated from it entirely.

Well, my first question, sir, and pardon my impertinence, I think is the word, but is that your wife in those photos, or another consenting party? I see. And do you have any way of proving that?

The man's faltering equivocations came in a rush, making

amendments as they went. *We were enjoying ourselves privately,* Mr. Jones said, *and as far as I'm aware that's perfectly legal, but I'm, uh, of course happy to help clear up any misconceptions, officer, truly sorry for any alarm.* Tim went on to clarify that, because of Mr. Jones's status as an educator in town, the department had a policy in place for anything untoward. However Guin or I had imagined Mr. Jones, cold with control, smooth with luck—he was something else on that call, namely uncertain on which part of his life he was meant to insist. The honor of his wife? The law as he knew it? The meaning of his privacy? The goodness of his heart?

Guin made a noise, a horsey exclamation from her fat, pursed lips, and Tim shot his hand back to cover her mouth. I could tell she was tonguing his palm, and in retaliation he tightened his grip and pinched her nipple, moving the phone away from his face to giggle. I hated them and I hated everything around them, the butts wilted in glass, the condom wrappers blooming on the wood crate that was the bedside table. *Is your wife at home, sir? Of course you'll understand I'll need her to tell me she was absolutely complicit. If you'd prefer, I can come down there, have a talk on the porch.*

No, Guin said, into Tim's fingers. *Stop it.*

Fucking prank, we heard Mr. Jones say in the background. *Probably. Small town. I don't know, to be sure . . .* And then there was his wife's voice, calmer than his, saying something like *let me take care of it.* Mrs. Jones spoke her name firmly, sincerely, and I watched the sound of it pass over Tim's face. He hadn't planned that far, or had only expected to move against her resistance—only to mock these people in an underhanded advance against their bigger part of the world. Saying something specious about protocol, spewing bullshit numbers, naming a bullshit code, Tim asked whether the gag in her mouth was definitely what she wanted. *Are we done,* she said.

It was clear then that the woman had never believed his lie. Understanding this, Guin's eyes were filling as she pressed her fingernails into her temples. She curled her toes into Tim's back.

Before she erupted—would she cry, would she hit?—there were always signs like this, her insides protesting their limits. She lived in her body as some people live in temporary housing. Unsure how long the arrangement will last, they ruin the walls with holes and marks, they slam the cheap doors. Tim began to speak in the high shriek I'd heard that misting night we'd run into him, adding an affected babying lisp. *Do you hate your yuppie life so much that having your gerbil of a husband tie you up is the only way to come?*

Guin was on top of Tim then and slapping his ears, trying to wrest the phone away for a long time after the Jones household had gone silent. *Fucking stop it,* Guin kept saying, for too long after he had. As the phone fell from his hand and his giggle accelerated, I grabbed my jacket and pulled it around my sweatshirt, leaving his door unlocked. My hood was up against a thick mist as I walked home, and I felt glad to be obscured. I knew how soon I would pay for misunderstanding what Guin needed: To feel righteous about a crime that didn't involve her, but was hers to define. To fantasize inviolably, and indefinitely, about some justice only she could dispense.

I stopped going back to Sonoma County, in part because it lost its weather—I used to love that drizzle and fog, but now it only floods or catches fire. Guin and I spent a decade angry at each other, but the year we were twenty-eight we returned to our friendship and confessed. She had found me online and sent me a note rich in her singular misspellings, telling me only a little about her ex and the heroin, which always went unnamed. There'd been *hard work and a little bit of luck,* she said, but now! She was clean. She was new. We talked about Suboxone and her first-ever bout as a single person, the audiobooks she loved on politics and psychology, the granny unit she had triumphantly rented, a few towns over from Petaluma, despite bad credit and an eviction and a mug shot on her record. Once a month, for most of six, we'd skype—the internet was another one now, capable of bringing our lives closer together, but still faulty enough that her face might slow down, her language stop. *I don't know what happened,* I notice everyone always rushing to say, just as Guin and I did, after a connection drops. Why? Don't we know exactly what happened, that the kind of intimacy made possible by twitching screen is improbable to begin with? That if you know behind you is the safety or danger of your own home, that if you can't smell someone starting to sweat, or see the way they curl their fingers when they mention a certain person's name, the version of life you get and give can't really be trusted?

That's what happened with Guin and me, ultimately. During a conversation that was creaking anyway—she seemed far away as she was, and was answering most questions about the past few weeks with a limited set of *good, okay,* and *not the best*—her face poured into bits. Two minutes later, she took advantage of the conversation restarting to ask about me. Were my patients behaving themselves? As I began to describe a client's unique delusion, Guin's husband called her name, and then he moved onscreen to kiss her forehead. *Anything from the store, babe?* She blushed deeply, saying something quickly about smokes, and sent him away.

We were silent a long time, the country between us redrawing our faces in pixelated revolutions if she shifted or I did. She apologized first for the state of the connection, saying the internet was bad in what she called *west county.* They'd gotten back together a few months before, she admitted, when they both were sober, and I knew, I knew—I *knew*—by the way her glance fell that they were no longer. He'd been living there and they were doing sobriety together, she said, hoping I'd say something accepting—but I had returned to who I'd become again, and I refused even to ask how long.

The lie had been as beautiful as she still was, but I'd forgotten how she smelled, that she was handy with a pocketknife—the time she had, with loving conspiracy, convinced a waiter to send a crying child a milkshake in an IHOP. Devotion rarely goes on without novel surfaces, isn't that right? Without the grain of new situations it can be confirmed against. Greg, when I told him about the call, nodded in sympathy. He scrounged up some stained little words that we've all, in heedlessness, used. *There is only so much you can do.*

It's funny he could say that when he'd heard the sound I'd made, on that call, when I saw the face of her husband. I cried out in the way I do when I see a cockroach, as though it's the first time and I haven't been living all my life in these fucking American houses, built quickly of pest-friendly wood. If you get from one side of this country to the other, or the bottom to the top, you find out that even the wealthy are living in buildings that were not meant to last, and that the American imagination is selfish and short, and that the shrug we give when someone else needs something is a consequence of how long our memory is, and how far we can see into the future—and the answer to all of it is, well, about a hundred years. That's how long the walls will stand if you do nothing, and that's also the scope of history you're expected to know or care about. It's a friendly, easy figure, because it stretches just about one life, indicating any person's decades as an exception, not a pattern. There are accidents of passion, here, not designs of cruelty. And so we go around chirping *life is short!,* which is a way of saying *my life is mine!,* which is a way of saying *best of luck with yours!*

Greg moved out just before the virus, actually—I don't even have that to blame. In the first six months of it, I seemed to spend my sadness only on my friends' and clients' lives, laughing at the right moments, adjusting their medications, often avoiding the diagnoses that would do little to help them and everything to set them against me. You tell a person they're a recognizable type, you call a symptom specific to a pattern of others, and they're likely to rage or turn mute. Few of us want to believe that our pain is so common it can be treated.

In my personal life anyway, I've tried to select against certain categories, and have never gotten it quite right. Greg had accepted exactly one drink in his life—his father was an alcoholic, too—and I'd *chosen* his sobriety, his pellucid memory. Living with him I learned his religious tidiness, to empty rooms in order to sweep them. *Oh, love,* he had said, laughing, in our first apartment together, looking at my dishes as he washed them, *would you let me teach you?* I was then twenty-six, and the undersides of my pots all looked almost caramelized. *How funny that you never,* Greg said, kissing me, *learned to wash the bottoms of things.*

He was careful and tender with all his senses, coming home with dark chocolate and olive oil soap in his tote bag, straightening the rooms we slept in so that nothing bigger ever sat on anything smaller, and all the angles were right. But once he was unhappy, his tongue seemed to fatten with another decade, and his pupils expanded, as he stayed up all night reading the internet, until his brown eyes seemed only to be black. He had the snap of a drunk, the lurching impulses that hated to be seen. Toward the end I woke once, frightened, around three A.M., to the bed frame vibrating with a deep, frantic bass, Mahler's Fifth booming from his office speakers a floor below. As if I were his neighbor, I knocked timidly, asking if he might turn that down. And he stomped across the room, slamming a hand down to quiet the noise, his eyes flashing that deep black and holding mine. He would say things I imagined had been once said to him (*Do you think you're the first person to suffer?*) or pose a mean, specific question (*You never got over your father dying, did you?*) and behave with no memory of it the next day, when I might find him whistling as he cleaned the kitchen, or arranging narcissi in my office with a lucky wink. Even as they horrified me, I envied him those outbursts. Because the worst things I've said or done, and the worst said and done to me, have worked on my life more quietly, like some embarrassing, insuperable superstition—keeping me from walking where it must be safe to, assuring me I know something other people don't.

I waited an hour on my porch for Guin, knowing she would come, thinking of the Joneses' house nearby—the dog who might be passing from room to room, wondering about the change in the way his people were speaking, the lights maybe not turned on at dusk. Through the walls behind me was the bed where I slept, the narrow corridor of sink and pantry where my mother drank her coffee alone by the small, high window. The unhappiness of my life in that apartment was perfectly tailored, shaped like the two of us, and I knew the unhappiness beyond would be a surprise for which I had no retort prepared.

When Guin showed up, I announced straightaway we would return the photos. She nodded and took the package from her bag, handing it to me with a look she must have learned in her childhood—was her sin so bad? Would she be forgiven? I could see in the streetlight how battered it was, the photo on top of the pile a little bent at an edge. I didn't ask why the stack seemed slimmer, or about the tape she'd run on the envelope where it had torn, in some kind of apology. Even her anger she couldn't really care for, or be loyal to, in the way so many people do for the rest of their lives, using the same language to describe it. *My father's narcissism was one of small differences,* a client will tell me, again and again, seeming proud of their articulation. Whatever Guin's failings, she never gave me the same sentence twice.

In college I didn't mention her, though I understood that I was desirable mostly because of the print she'd left on me. She had taught me how you remove a bottle cap with any edge, how you breathe around a cock in your mouth or run backward from a bottle rocket. *You're not going to be this sad your whole life,* she had said once in bed, holding me from behind, her ribs bigger than my ribs, her voice clearer than my voice, and I knew it was something like an insult. She was standing at the perspective of distance between us she already saw. Even if I could drink to nothing with her, stay up on speed and get sliced to ribbons by hateful daylight, I eventually felt the need to return to myself. Faithful student I was at heart, I wanted the home in my mind that would ratify anything I'd done, convert it into some lesson or anecdote. In the middle of my first semester of college, I heard from my mother that the Joneses' dog had gone missing. Flyers punctuated the neighborhood, using the word "love," entreating the town's sympathy. My mother admitted that she'd seen it—trotting downhill, one early morning she was half asleep and smoking out front—but its beauty was such, its certainty so evident, that she could not stop to worry. From her voice on the phone, I understood that she knew this was wrong, how it's those creatures most easily alone you're supposed to call after as they run toward traffic.

Can you imagine losing your dog the same month you lost your job, she asked, but I wouldn't take the bait, wouldn't ask how or why. That was roughly the position I held on anything having to do with Petaluma, and that might be why we never really talked about the time after Dad died, when she'd kept the apartment too warm and we'd acknowledge each other like roommates. Once, when she came to visit me and Greg, and he had slipped off to fix dessert, the topic did come up. Her thin hand grabbed for mine, and she smiled wetly in the sweet candlelight and mentioned those years and said, *Someday, babe, when we have a sign the time is right.*

I did tell a friend the full story of what we did to the Joneses' marriage, recently, during a series of Zooms about what she was willing to do for her husband's pleasure. With the pandemic on, they needed something new in their life, but it would have to be a compromise, she reiterated, and I agreed: he'd been watching the kind of *down, sex-pig!* porn where women's makeup forms runnels down their alarmed faces, and she was interested in shibari, if she could get the right kind of silk ropes from Japan. The friend had been calling often, and I would allow her to repeat her banal remarks, or call me back when her contractor needed to run through something on her kitchen's renovation. Listening to my details of fifteen years before, she laughed at the mischief of it all, and repeated a line I sensed she had read on internet forums about that kind of sex. *Sometimes the bottom is the top.* Then she changed the subject.

It had been so nice to say Guin's name, but the friend had asked nothing further about her, who she had been to me or what she'd become to herself. The next time she texted I vanished the text, the next time she called I silenced the call, the next time she emailed I archived the email. I told myself I was bored by the conversation. False power, voluntary confinement, doesn't interest me. If you add it up, the leather with the lotion, the cruelty with the kindness, doesn't that only get you somewhere neutral? And that's worse than being alone—which I actually like fine—given the lie of being together.

All I had wanted, on that call, was the chance to say the outrageous, impossible words that had become true a few weeks before. It was the only conversation in which it would have been appropriate, because I had never really mentioned Guin to anyone else. She had existed before I became myself. It would anyway require so many steps down their empathic ladders, those lawyers and doctors, a series of bleak facts going lower and lower, deeper and deeper, and by the time I got to the phrase, they would have been worn out. Because first, I'd want to say how once she was sober again she realized her wisdom teeth were so painful she had no choice but to pull them and that two thousand dollars was impossible . . . and so her landlord had cut off the electricity . . . and when the virus hit she was living in a trailer without water, which was meant to be temporary . . . she had a good job at a restaurant but all but two of the front-of-house staff were cut . . . and the NA meeting that was important to her didn't go remote, for some reason, and it felt wrong to start a new meeting on a screen, with intermittent Wi-Fi . . . and actually . . .

She died.

It was Tim who let me know, calling me on repeat from midnight in California, and I picked up in my sleep, as weak and confused as he must have remembered me. My terror, when I heard his voice, was so pure it touched everything—it made the rug I brought my feet onto rough, the books splayed all around me in my bed jagged and menacing. He said something first about Guin being the love of his life, testing out how it sounded. I could tell he was outside, and I remembered how natural he always looked near a streetlamp, as thin, and as cold, and as punitive.

There was no euphemism: Guin had not "passed on." "Four milligrams of pure fucking fentanyl," he announced. "She never did anything lightly, which I have to admit I fucking admire." That he and Guin had not talked in some seven years, that he and I had not in fifteen, that she saw my life as a put-on and I saw hers as a curse on mine—these things weren't a part of the conversation. Shortly after relating some gruesome details, he switched topics, but I was still thinking about the week she'd been alone with her dead body, and only vaguely registered what he said next. He had heard I'd become a doctor, which didn't surprise him. He wanted to tell me about a combination of *ingredients* he'd been using to treat a recurrent sinus infection—maybe we could talk, have a *meeting of the minds,* get it on the shelves. I could feel myself readying the condescending remark, that I was not that kind of doctor, that he hadn't the right to . . . and then it drifted away, easily as an hour does when you spend it lying down. I couldn't hold on to my offense at his having called me, asking myself in the next instant what I'd kept the same number for, if not this. You must want to be reached, I told myself. You must need some part of you that goes all the way back.

"Do you want to meet up?" Tim said. "A drink for the old days." *Well, where are you,* I asked, rather than answering I was in Vermont. I was convinced, somehow, by the short-circuiting of his mind. Even his ruined thinking was clever, understanding that I had left and couldn't have really, daring me to deny it.

"Downtown," he said, like the answer was obvious. I clarified my location, apologizing, and he got off the call soon after, pulling the phone away from his mouth to shriek, "Oh, is that fucking *right,*" to something or someone I couldn't see. And then I knew it, certain as the draft through the bedroom window—that if he'd been three blocks away, that if I could walk to him I would have, saving the buttons of my coat for the walk through the weather.

The days or weeks after seem to fall down, their natural order like something you only narrowly catch, the save so close you've already imagined the irretrievable break. Some people go and you can't imagine the bridge, how their bodies went from being memories to being silence, but it wasn't difficult to picture Guin dying. She had practiced a long time. What bothers me about her death, the thought that cracks my chest open to a sob in the bulk-food aisle, is that I believe it so easily I keep trying to remember it. That the last place she'd ever gone was one where we'd never been together—it's the force that holds me down in my bed until noon some mornings, and makes me wrench my stove from the wall to sweep behind it another.

The fentanyl I keep in my bedside drawer, for months after I hear about Guin, an insult to her, I know—that I got it easily and legally and paid nothing, that I can keep it hidden in a room where I read and clean, sleep and masturbate. *There is only so much you can do,* to use Greg's phrase, but in another selfish context—as in, only so much you can do of this drug, if you want to come back. The threshold is famous, the bottom. I know I wouldn't have gotten it if he had still been nearby, in his tidy other bedroom, and also how lucky I feel to be alone with her—in my mind, I mean, in my body.

"I just think you're unwell," the client chirps again, how many sessions after the first time I can't truly say. "And I want you to know I respectfully decline the opportunity to work with you anymore." *You are the only one here,* the HIPAA-compliant office software informs me after that, so why do I stay there a moment longer, looking at the frame of my life as it's been presented? The window that's best for western light, the row of plants we all keep to remind ourselves of an outside. Then I float upstairs, thinking I'll get some laundry together, and I take a pill. It happens so easily: the idea of *once* has always seemed friendly. I could forgive anything in myself or in him, Greg liked to say, a compliment one day and an insult the next.

In the depth of August, Guin and I pass up quiet, sloping streets. Outside the Joneses' house, we stop, maybe hoping to learn something about that man and that woman, but in their lit bedroom the curtains are drawn, and all we can understand is that they are together. I push the photos into the mailbox that stands on a post, and we continue up the hill to the park we like, situated high above the rambling town. From a damp bench we take in Petaluma, the enormous grain elevator and the purple hills occurring all around it.

You wanted to hurt them because they're lucky, I say to Guin, and the underside of that sentence is that there is nothing she could do to make her life like theirs, but there's plenty I could, and will. Guin cocks wide and clips short, and when I start to bleed from my top lip, when I feel the notch in my tooth where it will be forever, she laughs brightly as a toddler who has just understood that ice can melt, or green give way to blossom.

She doesn't tell me that Tim has taken some of the photos, and she can't know that a few weeks from now he'll be over at McNear Elementary in the middle of the night, supergluing them image-in to the tilt-and-turn fifties windows of the choir classroom. It's not her fault that the children who trot in on their first day of school will see those adult secrets, those strange expressions, as part of their view of outside, or that their teacher will seem scary as he tries to pick them off, cursing when he finds he can't cleanly detach one part of his life from another.

It's dark early in Vermont, and a sound is more likely to come from within the house than out, a faucet, a radiator. As for my life, I've got thick, hand-knit socks on, a full glass of cool water, and a third pill, now, another half a milligram: it's such a small thing against such a big house. Narcan in the drawer, she might have teased me for that, and fuck her. What did I owe her? A call every day? A check every month? A plane ticket would have been easy, an inpatient spell someplace else where her ex couldn't wait in the parking lot. I could have given an apology for her life, not because it was my fault, but because it should have been somebody's. In my bedroom the objects have been rearranged since Greg left, end tables and necklaces, oils and creams. There's the rug from Athens, the vase from Sausalito, another pill on my tongue, then a dull, happy truth. It makes my ribs bigger, lets each breath go farther.

I laugh when I know it! The absurdity in counting! Six? When was the last time you saw one in real life, a number? I can only speak for myself, but I never see a pretty wall of trees, or a stark impasse of mountains, and know there are twelve. No one ever goes on loving someone because it's been so many years. They might just be a category, numbers, something that helps other people understand what we don't need to.

Somewhere under the covers, somewhere under my mind, we snake our way through town in the middle of the night, up and down the gravel of those little alleys, named *School* and *Telephone* and *Pepper,* seeing into the back sides of magnificent houses. *Half-gabled, cross-timber.* She's learned to describe the homes of other people, faithful and tender as the owners must be, pointing with her chin tucked on my neck. *Frieze, coffer.* I kiss her for knowing, I adore her again, she walks deep into shadow, I go deep in my body, lick my tooth where she's chipped it, she forgives us all distance, we come from the same place, we are parts of the same life.

Maybe we aren't girls, surely we were never children, but we might have the talents of animals, sensing everything that wants to kill us, and that we need to kill. Hills aren't a problem, gates we can perch on, dark we can see in, and now we're quiet by the glow of that couple's back window. What's the ancient idea, we've read it somewhere, we turn in the chilly bed to find it, we turn her face in the light of other lives to tell her. We're born knowing everything, which is why we wail. We begin to forget, which is how we can stop. And here's the thing: here's the thing: here's the strangest, loving thing, which helps until it doesn't, which is kind until it's wicked:

At the end of your life, you've forgotten the most.

Eamon McGuinness

The Blackhills

P AT RATHIGAN LEFT SKERRIES at 23:50. A group of men tried
to hail him at the edge of town but he ignored them, double-
checked the light on his roof sign was off and picked up speed
as he drove the coast road towards Balbriggan. The Irish Sea was
quiet, the moon high and bright.

He pulled into the small lay-by at the Lady's Stairs, the sea hidden by large trees. Reversing and parking next to the bottle bank,
he kept the road in his sights, then took out a yellow microfiber
cloth from the glove compartment and wiped down the dash,
meter and ID. He left the key in the ignition and his door ajar,
and shivered when the cold air hit him before taking a deep breath
through his nose. From the boot he took a cardboard box of emp-
ties, all rinsed: vodka, beer and wine bottles, two jars of sauce
and a small bottle of Calpol. He looked around after each drop,
winced at the sound of the glass echoing in the quiet night, then
put the box back in the boot.

The odd car went by. Pat kept an eye on the road, checked the
time on his phone and opened the back passenger door. It was
five minutes after midnight. He walked to the base of the stairs.
The gate was locked, but easily hoppable, the streetlight beside it

a harsh orange. He blinked hard and looked down the overgrown path leading to Barnageera Beach and whistled twice. He heard rustling, then a return whistle. He rushed back to the car and started the engine. A few seconds later, Mick Rathigan scuttled across the tarmac, head low. He dove into the backseat and pulled the door closed as Pat spun left out of the lay-by, taking the first right under the railway bridge.

—You're a lifesaver, Pat, a fucking lifesaver.

Mick reached through the front seats and grabbed Pat's left arm.

—All right, Mick, all right. Lie down.

—I won't forget this.

—You're shivering.

—It was fucking freezing down there.

—There's a blanket and some food beside you.

—Thanks, Pat. I haven't eaten all day.

Pat beeped at the bends as the road wound up towards the Blackhills, while Mick scoffed the roll and bag of King crisps.

—Which way are we going?

—Through the hills. Stay down.

—Let me know where we are.

—Climbing now. Ardgillan coming up.

—Nice one.

—Did you manage to sleep?

—I drifted off but was too nervous. I got a bit of shelter in the old changing spot.

—Was there anyone about?

—A couple of people walking dogs and one swimmer, but I was well hid.

—I can hear your teeth chattering.

—I'll be grand once I warm up.

—I'm taking the left here at Ardgillan.

Pat turned up the heat and put the foot down on the straight stretch of road as they passed the new cricket club on the right.

—No Elvis, Pat?

—Not tonight, I can't enjoy him in this mood.

—Fair enough.

Passing Saint Mobhi's graveyard, Pat blessed himself, reduced his speed, dropped to third gear and glanced at Mick over his left shoulder, who was lying flat on his back, his legs twisted down behind Pat's seat. They made quick eye contact before Pat refocused on the road.

—Passing Milverton now.

—We're flying.

At the T junction Pat turned right onto the Skerries Road.

—How's everything at home? Mick asked.

Pat looked in the rearview mirror but couldn't see any trace of Mick.

—Grand, given the circumstances.

—Has Lilian been sleeping through the night?

—Don't talk about Lilian, Mick.

—Fair enough. I was just asking.

Pat ran his left hand through his thick white beard and opened his window to let in some air.

—Does Lorcan know about this? Mick asked.

—No one knows and I plan to keep it that way.

—What did Butsy say?

—He has it sorted.

—I knew he was the man to ring.

—The ferry's at four from Belfast. You'll get to Cairnryan at seven and should be in Inverness by lunchtime.

—Amazing, he has a bed and all in the truck.

—I know.

Pat coughed hard a few times and closed the window. They were on the road to Lusk and passed the new estates on the left.

—He's a dodgy fucker, but he's always been a mate. Remember what he was like in his twenties?

—Don't, Mick.

—What?

—I'm not in the mood for remember when. We're coming into Lusk, stay down.

—Anyone about?

—A few stragglers.

—I always thought Lusk was a kip.

The lights at Murray's Lounge took an age. Pat kept looking from left to right, scratching his beard while they waited.

—Here we go, at fucking last.

—Many Gardaí around tonight, Pat?

—A few more than usual.

—Did you pass the house?

—A couple of times, yeah.

—And?

—There's tape still around the gate.

—Was there anyone outside?

—No, the place looked dead.

They were out of Lusk and on the old Dublin Road, passing farms and glasshouses.

—Where are we, Pat?

—Nearing the turn for the estuary.

—I shat myself every time I heard a siren.

—What did you do with your phone?

—I fucked it in the sea after I rang you. If they trace the calls, they'll think I drowned myself.

—Did you call Mam?

—No, she wouldn't understand. If they question you, just tell them I was saying goodbye.

—Grand. We're getting a good run at it now, coming up to Blake's Cross.

—I'll miss it round here.

—I don't wanna hear it, Mick.

—I appreciate what you're doing for me, Pat, I really do.

—I just wanna get you out of this car.

Pat took a left at Blake's Cross. There was a little traffic on the R132, the road dotted with factories, warehouses and garages. He opened his window and changed to fifth gear for the first time.

—Have you heard anything about Sara? Mick asked after a long silence.

—Yeah, I was in with her earlier.

—Where is she?

—Beaumont.

—And?

—She's in a bad way, Mick. A bad fucking way.

—Has she talked yet?

—The Guards are waiting for her to come around.

—I fucked up.

—You fucked up?

—Yeah, I fucked up.

—Fucked up? Fucked up? Pat screamed.

—All right, Pat, calm down.

He slowed the car, dropped to fourth gear and looked back at Mick.

—Fuck off, Mick, it's barbaric what you did to that girl.

—Okay, it's just—

—Don't try to explain yourself.

—Watch the road, Pat.

A car beeped and overtook them. Pat regained his composure and looked forward again.

—You did that to your own daughter. What sort of fucking animal are you? Pat hocked and spat out the window.

After a long silence, Mick spoke.

—Where are we, Pat?

—Turvey, swinging left. Two minutes.

—My heart's beating out of my chest.

—This is it for us, Mick, I'm telling you. Don't contact me again.

—What about Mam?

—Leave Mam to me.

Just off the main road, Pat indicated left into a house. A man with an Alsatian on a leash was at the gate and nodded at Pat as he turned in. He brought the car to a stop and the Alsatian barked and jumped at the door.

—Hush, now, good boy, hush.

—All good? Pat asked.

—Grand. You know where you're going?

—Yeah.

—Go on so, Butsy's waiting for ye.

—Good man.

Pat restarted the car and moved down the long, potholed driveway.

—We're here.

Mick sprang up. There were cars on breeze-blocks and the garden was full of scrap metal and pallets. Butsy's truck was parked beside the bungalow, its cab blue, with "Butler Transport" printed on the side in black lettering. Butsy and another man appeared at the back door of the bungalow and stood under a bare bulb as Pat parked next to a Jeep and trailer. Butsy had a plastic bag in one hand and with the other was holding his Dogo Argentino on a lead. Mick was looking around frantically, his head in between the two front seats. Taking off his belt, Pat switched on the interior light and faced Mick properly for the first time. He could smell Mick's breath and noticed how filthy and unkempt he was.

—Do you have everything?

—I have fuck all but I have it.

—Good, all right, let's go.

—I'm sorry to ask, Pat, but did you bring that money we talked about?

—Of course.

Pat fiddled in the glove compartment and took out a wad of notes and handed it to Mick.

—I'll pay you back, I promise.

—C'mon, Butsy's waiting.

Mick took the notes with his left hand and with his right grabbed Pat's wrist and planted a kiss on his knuckles. Mick's nails ran along the back of Pat's hand; Pat could feel their length and looked down to see the dirt on his brother's fingers. He pulled his hand away, wiped his knuckles with the sleeve of his jacket and scratched his beard with both sets of nails. Mick stuffed the notes into his right-hand pocket and got out.

Dogs were barking nonstop from behind the bungalow. Butsy called the men over and took a step towards the car.

—I'd say you lads could do with a strong drink, am I right?

—Am I glad to see you, Butsy! Mick called.

Pat closed his door. Mick spat on the ground and began walking towards Butsy. Suddenly, a man appeared from the darkness on Pat's left and swung a bat cleanly and swiftly at Mick's head. He fell instantly and the man gave one more solid strike to the back of Mick's skull. Butsy and the other man were running and before Pat had moved, they had Mick bound and gagged and were lifting his body away. The Dogo Argentino growled at Mick before Butsy quietened it with a few strokes to the head. Pat opened the car, took out Mick's blanket and dropped it on the ground. One of the men had a grip under Mick's armpits and the other was holding his ankles, the body floppy and loose. Pat fished into Mick's pocket and retrieved his money.

—Go on, Butsy said to the lads.

Butsy put his hand out and Pat shook it. Together they watched the two men carry Mick towards the sheds at the back of the property. Butsy got on his hunkers and scratched his dog behind the ears, then stood up, interlaced his fingers and cracked his knuckles.

—Scumbag. He won't be missed, Butsy said.

Pat was staring at the ground, shaking his head.

—Fucking savage.

—How's Sara?

—Bad, Butsy, bad. He perforated her bowel. She's having colostomy surgery in the morning.

—He's a fucking animal. Don't worry, he'll be disappeared within the hour.

—I don't wanna know, Butsy.

—It's over, Pat, you've done your bit. Will you come in for a drink?

—Not tonight. I should get going, I've to swing by the ma's.

—Fair enough, we'll sort him out, then I'll hit the road myself.

—Is it an overnight?

—No, I'm back here later. It'll be a long day.

—For sure.

—How are the roads?

—Dead, not a crisp bag blowing out there.

Butsy smiled.

—January, what?

Pat nodded and kicked the blanket.

—Would your dogs sleep on this? He was lying under it in the backseat.

—I'll burn the fucker.

—Thanks, Butsy.

—It's nothing, Pat. Give the car a decent scrub in the morning.

—I'll bring it in for a valet.

—Good idea.

Butsy raised his hand for a high shake and Pat took it, and Butsy then placed his left hand on Pat's shoulder for a couple of seconds.

When he was settled back into the car, Butsy knocked on the window and Pat rolled it down.

—Are Lorcan and his family still living with you, Pat?

—Yeah, the lot of them are in the spare room.

—How old is the granddaughter now?

—She'll be six months in March.

—If you ever want a pup for her just let me know. No charge, chipped and all.

—Nice one, Butsy.

—I've always got a couple of pregnant bitches about to drop.

—Thanks, I'll say it to Lorcan and Elaine.

Butsy nodded.

—A bit late to be going to your ma's, no?

—Blocked sink. I told her I'd sort it. She hardly sleeps, that woman.

—Sinks are a pain in the hole. Tell her I was asking for her.

—Will do.

—Go on, Pat, I'll be in touch.

—Thanks, Butsy.

The man and the Alsatian were still at the gate when Pat swung right out of Butsy's and drove towards Blake's Cross. Mick's smell was in the car so he kept the windows open. The roads were almost empty. He gripped the steering wheel with both hands and kept his eyes forward. Before he hit the Five Roads, he turned for the Man O'War. He passed the GAA club, Oberstown detention center and the pub, took a right at Kennedy's Corner, the left turn at Killary Grove, right again onto Darcystown Road, then onto Baltrasna and the second left into his mother's cottage in the Blackhills.

Using the torchlight on his phone, he checked the inside of the car. On the backseat was the cling film from Mick's roll and the bag of crisps. He shook the crumbs and few remaining crisps onto the grass and stuffed the rubbish into his back pocket. He found a bit of bread on the floor. There was no ham or cheese left, just a crust with a thick spread of butter. He walked to the ditch at the side of the cottage and threw in the bread. He looked around, unzipped, and pissed into the brambles and bushes, then wiped his hands on his pants. From the boot he took out a mini hoover. It made a low whining sound as he went over the seats and floor thoroughly. He sucked up gravel, sand and crumbs from Mick's food. *Filthy prick*, he muttered to himself. He emptied the hoover into the ditch and returned it to the car. He sprayed some air freshener, left the windows open and locked the doors.

The sensor light came on outside the back door. He knocked twice before unlocking and entering the cottage. His mother was lying the full length of the couch in the kitchen–cum–living area, the radio blasting near her head, the fire fading. She looked to be sleeping but her head shot up when Pat entered. Without saying anything, he filled and turned on the kettle. He grabbed two eggs from the fridge and put them in a saucepan. She was taking her time to sit up, yawning and stretching, as Pat leaned over her to turn off the radio.

—Any news, Pat?

—No, nothing.

—What about on the phone?

—I haven't heard anything, Mam.

—What time is it?

—Nearly one.

—Many out there?

—Very quiet. An airport run delayed me.

—Grand.

—Are you hungry?

—No, I had a sandwich a while ago.

He put some kindling and a briquette on the fire, took her plate and cup from the coffee table and left them on the counter.

—I'd say he's long gone at this stage.

—Who knows, Mam?

—I just have a feeling.

—We'll see.

—Did you dump the bottles?

—I did.

Pat checked the sink. It had been spat in; gray, green and speckled with blood. He put on a pair of rubber gloves, lifted the bucket of bleach, stepped into the garden and poured it down the drain at the side of the cottage. There was a frost in the air. He picked out the S trap and ran cold water through it from the outside tap. Under the sensor light, he poked around the pipe with his fingers, removing grease, eggshell, potato peel and rasher fat. When he came back in, he put the empty bucket underneath the glug hole and ran the tap. The water ran through the spit and he had to rub with his baby finger until it dislodged. He looked over to his mother. She was watching him work. Outside again, he emptied the bucket on the grass, then went and filled the saucepan with the boiled water and set a ten-minute alarm. He fiddled around with the pipes under the sink and got the S trap back on, tightening and securing it.

—Is it fixed, Pat?

—We'll know tomorrow. I got a fair bit of gunk out of it.

He poured water from the kettle slowly down the sink. There was a gurgling sound and some spurted back up before disappearing.

—I'll be back tomorrow to check it.

—Okay. Will you bring Lilian with you?

—Of course.

—Your sister rang.

—What did she say?

—Sara is in a bad way.

—I know, she has surgery in the morning.

—Nine o'clock, Deirdre says.

—That's right.

She started to weep and blew her nose into a hankie. The eggs were tapping off the side of the saucepan. He checked the time on his phone. From the press he took out vinegar and baking soda and added them to the glug hole before pouring in a bit more water.

—Mam, don't put anything down here and please spit in the toilet or on the grass.

—It's the dentures, Pat.

—I know, but I'm the one has to fix it. Just throw the food into the garden.

—I don't like encouraging those birds.

—Well, in the bin then, but not down the sink, please.

He checked the time again and reduced the heat.

—Has Mick been in touch?

—He rang and tried to talk but I hung up.

—The Guards will be onto you.

—Why?

—Ye are brothers.

—They'll be onto all of us so.

—Did you not notice anything?

—I knew it was an unhappy house. We all knew that.

—He's lost his way since Margaret died.

—He never had a way, Mam. There are no excuses.

—I'm not excusing him, Pat. I'm just trying to understand.

—I'm finished with him.

—It's different for me. They'll destroy him inside.

—They'd put him with his own, they always keep the pervs together.

—Don't call him that, she wailed.

—Okay, Mam, okay, calm down.

His phone beeped. He turned off the eggs and poured the boiling water slowly into the sink. It flowed smoothly down the glug hole. He refilled the saucepan with cold water, then placed his two hands on the counter, dropped his head and stared at his shoes.

—Go home, son, you're dead on your feet.

—We should have protected that girl more.

—You can't save people, son.

—She's your granddaughter, my niece.

—We're on our own out there, you should know that by now.

—Maybe. Maybe not.

—He'll be out in a few years. If they catch him.

—I don't know, Mam. I'll peel these and head off.

—Thanks, son.

—You go to bed. Do you want anything on?

—Mendelssohn.

She had her own route around the cottage and he didn't offer any help. She gripped the arm of the couch and from there grabbed her walking stick and clung to the radiator and then the door handle. He stayed behind her in the hall and guided her to the edge of the bed until she flopped inside. He put on the CD.

—My purse, Pat.

He found her purse under the cushion on the couch and handed it to her in bed.

—There, Mam, all sorted.

—When are you going to shave?

—Soon. I haven't had time to bless myself this week.

—It makes you look old.

—I am old.

—You know what I mean.

—Good night, Mam.

He did a quick cleanup of the living room, peeled the eggs and put them on a plate in the fridge. He set the coffee table for the morning and refilled the kettle, dropping a tea bag into her cup. He emptied his back pockets and held Mick's cling film and crisp packet in his hand. He opened the hall door and listened. He couldn't hear his mother but Mendelssohn was clear. Throwing Mick's rubbish on the fire, he watched as it crinkled and burned. He put on the fire guard, tapped his jacket for his keys and looked around. He called goodbye but she didn't answer, then turned off the lights and locked the door behind him.

Instead of taking the direct route to Rush, Pat went right towards Balrothery and into Balbriggan. He didn't switch on the radio or any music. The streets were empty as he turned right at the hotel, crossed over the train tracks and picked up speed once the town was behind him and the coast road opened up. The Lady's Stairs and lay-by were empty. There was little wind and the Irish Sea was dark and still, the lights of Skerries Harbour visible in the distance. A blue flashing light hit him as he took the last bend into the town. He bit his bottom lip, slowed down and scratched his beard. A fluorescent yellow and blue Garda

Jeep was parked in the middle of the road and two guards in full uniform were chatting outside their vehicle. He didn't recognize either man. The guard on Pat's side put his palm out and the car was brought to a stop. Pat's knees shook as he wound down the window. The guard nodded at Pat, took out his torch and scanned the car's tax, insurance and NCT. The guard's breath was visible in the air as he leaned down to speak.

—How's it going?

—Grand, guard, just heading home.

—Where's home?

—Rush.

—Are you local?

—All my life.

—What's the name?

—Patrick Rathigan.

—Many out?

—No. A few airport pickups but very quiet.

A car pulled up behind Pat and the guard gestured for it to stop.

—Okay, can I see your taxi license?

—No bother.

Pat removed his driver ID from the dash and handed it over. The guard checked the details and registration plate. He took another look at the license before handing it back. There were two cars backed up behind Pat now.

—Okay, safe home.

—Thanks, guard, have a good night.

Pat left the window down and drove off. Stopped at traffic lights in Skerries, he exhaled deeply and took a second to compose himself. He put the foot down when the lights changed and met only one car on the road to Rush. A group of lads tried to hail him outside the Yacht Bar but he increased his speed and arrived home in ten minutes. He checked the time—01:42—then put his phone on airplane mode.

He sat in the car for a few minutes until his heart rate settled. The houses in the estate, lit by the orange streetlights, looked small and shabby. The green in the center of the estate was patchy and wouldn't be cut now till February at the earliest.

He went in through the side door, his hand shaking as he fiddled with the keys. As he walked, the sensor light came on and he stood on the patio, watching the end of the garden. The light went off then on again then off and he unbuckled his belt and loosened the top buttons of his shirt. He looked at the spot the fox had been digging every night and pissed on it.

In the extension, Pat kicked off his shoes and left them by the door, slid out of his belt, then took off his socks and threw them in the direction of the washing machine. His phone torch navigated him through the debris of toys and baby paraphernalia. He switched on a lamp and the cabinet lights, then lit a single candle and placed it in the center of the island. He turned on the heat for an hour and put on the kettle. At the bottom of the stairs, he stopped to listen to the house. In the front room, he turned on the lamp in the corner, then looked at the street and his car. Nobody passed. He removed his jeans and shirt and put on his house pants, T-shirt and jumper, which he'd left on the couch. He turned on the TV and muted the sound straightaway. He pressed play on the DVD and while it was loading went back to the kitchen and made a pot of tea, leaving two bags in the water. He collected all his clothes and put them in the washing machine, added a few more from the basket and left it ready for the morning. The time on the cooker was 01:56.

Pat cleaned his hands and face in the jacks, filled his nostrils with water, then blew hard into the sink. He hocked out some phlegm and spat a few times into the toilet. Back in the kitchen, he added milk to a cup, grabbed the pot and brought them to the windowsill in the front room. He stacked two cushions at the end of the couch and laid out a blanket. The curtains were open and through the mirror above the fireplace the reflection of the streetlight could be seen. He skipped some scenes till he was where he'd left off the previous night. He unmuted the sound and set the volume to three. In black, with a high collar and open-necked shirt and surrounded by four musicians wearing red, Elvis sang "Lawdy Miss Clawdy" in the round. Scotty Moore was to his immediate left. The faces of the people in the crowd could be seen clearly. Pat smiled and nodded along. He poured his tea and stretched out on the couch, but halfway through the song he heard his granddaughter crying upstairs and the eventual shuffling of feet. The cries got steadily louder and the movements more frantic.

Pat climbed the stairs, knocked on the bedroom door and waited on the landing. Lorcan came out.

—Howaya, Da?

—Here, I'll take her, son.

—I think it's the teeth.

—C'mon, I'm off tomorrow, get a few more hours.

—Are you sure?

—C'mon.

Pat followed Lorcan into the bedroom. A lamp was on in the corner and Elaine was propped up on pillows trying to calm Lilian.

—Elaine, love, I'll take her.

—It's not fair on you, Pat.

—It's fine, I won't sleep for a while yet. G'wan, get a couple of hours.

Elaine held out Lilian and he took her in his arms.

—Are you just in, Da? Lorcan asked.

—Yeah.

—How was it?

—Dead, a few stragglers but nothing going.

—Any news about Mick?

Pat glanced at both of them but fixed his eyes on Lilian.

—No, nothing. Yous go back to sleep, I'll sort this one out.

—Thanks, Da.

—Yeah, thanks, Pat, you're a lifesaver.

—I'll chat to yis in the morning.

Lilian whimpered and jiggled in his arms until he got his grip right and she settled, but he felt something off with her. In the kitchen he switched on the warmer and popped in a bottle from the fridge. He tried not to talk or make eye contact with her, but she was fully awake and pawing at his face. While the bottle was warming up, he changed her on the floor. The nappy was dry, but she had a bad rash. He wiped her carefully, removing some lint from her belly button, and applied cream. With another wipe he cleaned in between her fingers and toes, behind her ears, her mouth and nose. Her nails were long and jaggedy and she had a few light scratches on her face. She didn't like her nose being touched but he held her head as she squirmed and got rid of the dry snots. She cried a little, a sort of heavy wail, but he gave her a plastic toy and she brought it to her teeth. Leaving her on the mat then, he filled a syringe with Calpol and took the bottle off the heat. He checked the time again: 02:17. She hadn't moved from the changing mat but was attempting to flip over. He took the dodo out of her mouth and with two shots gave her the full 5 mg.

In the front room, he propped her up on the cushion with her head raised and fed her the bottle. She drank half in frantic gulps and he put the dodo back in. He sat her forward and rubbed her back until she let out a strong burp. He skipped back on the DVD, pressed play and kept the volume low. Her eyes fixed on the screen. Pat gently sang "Are You Lonesome Tonight?" to her. She squirmed a little so he returned the bottle to her mouth. She took another 20 ml, then drifted off to sleep without being burped. He placed his baby finger in her palm and she instinctively made a fist around it. He stayed like this for a few minutes watching Elvis. His tea was lukewarm, and he drank two cups in a row. He leaned close to her and kissed her on the forehead. Her head was tilted slightly to the left. He picked up his phone and was about to check his messages but instead turned it off completely.

Lilian began snoring, a gentle purr. Pat wrapped her in the blanket and laid her on the floor, surrounded by cushions. He went quickly into the kitchen and grabbed the packet of baby wipes. In the drawer he found the nail clippers, scissors and mirror and returned to the front room. He cut his own nails first. He took his time, stopping to watch Elvis and look at Lilian. When he finished, he cleaned his hands with a wipe, then knelt on a cushion, took Lilian's right hand in his and cut each nail with one strong clip, ensuring not to nick the skin. When the hands were finished, he fished her feet out the bottom of her babygrow and did the toenails, then rubbed both hands and feet with a wipe. She squirmed a few times but didn't wake up. He refastened the babygrow and secured her tightly between the cushions. He collected all the nails in his empty cup.

Standing at the door, he watched Elvis. He skipped forward to "If I Can Dream" and turned it up a little. Elvis was now dressed in a white suit and red tie and sang in front of a giant screen, his name in lights. He was holding the mic in his left hand while his right arm gestured and swayed wildly. Pat noticed the rings on Elvis's fingers. He moved along to the music and when the song finished he shook his head a few times. He repeated the song and while it was playing put the mirror on the couch, knelt down and began trimming his beard. When the song ended again, he restarted the DVD and kept cutting until the black leather of the couch was full of his white hair. He added the trimmings to the cup and poured in the dregs of the teapot. He went into the kitchen, put on the kettle and washed out the pot. He took the cup and rushed out to the garden.

He poured the clippings and trimmings onto the foxhole, running his finger around the inside of the cup to make sure he removed everything. He listened to the house. He could see a lit attic skylight next door. He breathed in through his nose, arched his neck back and looked at the sky, then yawned deeply. The kettle was coming to the boil and blocked out every sound. Suddenly, he dropped the cup on the grass and hurried back to Lilian, leaving the back door open. He found her as secure as he had left her, but she had moved her arms, and they were splayed above her, outstretched. He was panting and took a second to compose himself. Kneeling down, he ran his knuckles along her cheek and listened to her soft breathing. After a few seconds, he went back outside to pick up his cup and lock the back door. He made fresh tea, blew out the candle and switched off all the lights. He left the cup in the front room and crept upstairs. All was still on the landing. He took the duvet and pillow from his bed, brought them downstairs and placed them on the couch. He tucked Lilian in, switched off the lamp, closed the door and drew the curtains fully. The TV screen now illuminated her face, and with a heavy sigh Pat stretched the full length of the couch and let his head drop onto the cool soft pillow.

The O. Henry
Prize Winners 2023

The Writers on Their Work

'Pemi Aguda, "The Hollow"
Did you know how your story would end at its inception?

No, I did not. Some stories come out almost fully formed, but this one changed drastically in the three years I worked on it. Earlier versions had the story narrated in the voice of the house, and then cycled through a number of close-third points of view before I landed here. Even after arriving at this threaded structure, the central question, Arit's question—"What is a house?"—proved more elusive than I hoped. I was trying to reimagine the idea of home inside a story about trauma. After many passes, I saw that if I piled all the answers already embedded in the story on top of each other, it created a particular effect: a culmination of answers that gives Arit the insights, and freedom, to leave this story.

'Pemi Aguda is from Lagos, Nigeria. W. W. Norton will publish her debut short story collection, *Ghostroots*, in early 2024 and her debut novel, *The Suicide Mothers*, in 2025. She was a 2022 MacDowell fellow and is a graduate of the Helen Zell Writers' Program. Her work has appeared in *Ploughshares*, *Zoetrope*, *Granta*, *ZYZZYVA*, Tor.com, *American Short Fiction*, and *One Story*.

Kathleen Alcott, "Temporary Housing"
What details or characters did you cut and leave on the editing floor?

There were a number of scenes that got cut—the original story was quite a bit longer than its already novella-glancing length—including an alternate scene in which the characters harass Mr. Jones online, and a moment on the porch where the protagonist finally comes on to Guin, and a detail about Guin being arrested for hitting her husband. I ultimately felt both to be an unnecessarily explosive, or slightly ill-timed, enunciation of conflict and tension: I wanted the story to feel like some frightening small-town walk where the silence itself is a warning, and every minor sound and shadow feels like a threat. An andante, in other words: slow and steady, because we know something will later come at us fast.

More interesting to me than what I cut might be what I added, after the story had been in a drawer for more than a year and I had not been sure it was meant to come out. I had lost a friend to an overdose and I was deep in grief when I retrieved it. Somehow the pieces about architecture were the vise the story needed to clinch wealth and suffering, appearances and secrets, bodies and minds, in the same motion. Once I had that in my mind, rewriting it was all I could do. I canceled all my plans for weeks.

Kathleen Alcott's short fiction has been anthologized in *The Best American Short Stories* and twice listed for the Sunday Times Audible Short Story Award. She is the author of three novels and a short story collection, *Emergency,* which W. W. Norton published in July 2023. Her fiction and essays have appeared in *Harper's Magazine, The Guardian, The New York Times, Tin House,* and *Zoetrope;* she has taught at Columbia University and Bennington College. Alcott lives in California.

Rodrigo Blanco Calderón, "The Mad People of Paris"
What inspired your story?

The story occurred to me one afternoon when my wife and I were walking through the Church of Saint-Sulpice in Paris. Suddenly, on one side, we saw a transparent office with glass walls. Inside there was a priest sitting at a desk and in the chair in front of him was a man. They were talking. I was very surprised to see that it was a confessional. That was how the new confessionals were. So my wife said that this was a good way to practice French: make up some sin and go to confession.

Rodrigo Blanco Calderón was born in Caracas, Venezuela, in 1981. He has received various awards for his stories both inside and outside Venezuela. With his first novel, *The Night,* he won the 2016 Paris Rive Gauche Prize, the Critics Award in Venezuela, and the 2019 Mario Vargas Llosa Biennial Prize.

Thomas Bunstead has translated some of the leading Spanish-language writers working today, including Agustín Fernández Mallo, María Gainza, and Enrique Vila-Matas, and is twice a winner of PEN Translates awards. His own writing has appeared in publications such as *Brixton Review of Books, Literary Hub,* and *The Paris Review.* He is a 2020–2022 Royal Literary Fund fellow, teaching at Swansea University.

K-Ming Chang, "Xífù"
What inspired your story?

This story was inspired by real advice I had received when I was a child: Don't marry a man with a mother. I was constantly being taught that men and their mothers formed a dangerous alliance that sought to undermine the authority of wives, and this hierarchy was ingrained within family dynamics. It was both darkly humorous and deeply tragic to watch the women in my community keep other women "in line," and the anecdote about a mother-in-law who sees her son wash a dish after dinner and becomes so outraged that she calls her daughter-in-law's family to complain about her son doing housework was another true story I'd been told. I wanted to explore the inherited lessons about daughterhood and wifehood that are enforced among the women in a family, and the way in which patriarchal violence demands endless creativity, destruction, and reinvention.

I wanted to examine the agency and the choices that women make when their choices have been limited for generations, and I was also interested in how queerness interacts with these inheritances. The story's monologue format was deeply important to me, as I was envisioning a character who is only allowed to express their uninhibited opinions to themselves and who cannot outwardly resist their position. At the same time, the act of authoring this monologue and delivering it as advice becomes a way of breaking the cycle. The narrator's interiority is the only way to express their frustration and their violent desire for another future. The driving questions of this story still remain with me: How do we choose which roles to pass down and which to rebirth? How do anger and injustice alchemize into love?

K-Ming Chang is a Kundiman fellow, a Lambda Literary Award finalist, and a National Book Foundation 5 Under 35 honoree. She is the author of the *New York Times Book Review* Editors' Choice books *Bestiary: A Novel* (One World/Random House, 2020) and *Gods of Want: Stories* (One World, 2022). Her next books are a novel titled *Organ Meats* (One World) and a novella titled *Cecilia* (Coffee House Press). She lives in California.

Jonas Eika, "Me, Rory and Aurora"
Is there anything you would like readers to know about your story?

It continues after it has ended. It couldn't have been written if I hadn't read Lars Norén, Eileen Myles, Franz Kafka, and Simone Weil. The moment of exclusion is also the moment of gendering. Finding the right tempo and temper was key; it's all about the narrative *voice*. And adjectives. Adjectives can be pieces of jewelry, I hope: ornamental and precise.

Jonas Eika is the author of *After the Sun* (Riverhead, 2021, trans. Sherilyn Nicolette Hellberg) and *Lageret, huset, Marie* (Warehouse, house, Marie). Besides writing, Jonas teaches writing and does translation from English to Danish, most recently of Jackie Wang's *Carceral Capitalism* (in collaboration with Nanna Dahler).

Sherilyn Nicolette Hellberg is a writer and translator based in Copenhagen. She holds a PhD in comparative literature from the University of California, Berkeley.

Rachel B. Glaser, "Ira & the Whale"
What inspired your story?

Rewatching *Jaws* at a friend's house, I was struck by the wild scene where Quint is eaten alive by the shark. As I walked back to my car, I imagined a man getting swallowed by a whale and living his final days inside. I saw him discovering another person in there but not hitting it off with them romantically. It seemed like a fun challenge to set a story in a whale. I decided I wouldn't let science get in my way. I wrote the idea in my notebook but put off writing it. A month later, there was a news story about a lobster diver who, for a minute, was inside the mouth of a whale before being spit out, mostly unharmed. I was annoyed and thought, *Great, now everyone's gonna write a whale story.* I wanted to finish first, so began writing mine.

Rachel B. Glaser is the author of *Paulina & Fran, Pee on Water, Moods,* and *Hairdo.* She teaches fiction at Southern New Hampshire University's low-residency Mountainview MFA program and writes in a turret in Western Massachusetts.

Arinze Ifeakandu, "Happy Is a Doing Word"
What made you want to re-create this particular world/reality in fiction?

I'd written the first version of the story many years ago, a story about two childhood friends—one gay, the other heterosexual—whose dreams of flying would separate them geographically, one leaving Kano for university, the other stuck at home, his dreams and love life stunted by the country's dysfunction and repressive system. The birds came first, the initial opening sentence beginning, "There were birds . . ." Then that compound in which everything happens, an adaptation of the yard across from the one in which I'd grown up. It was nostalgia speaking, I guess: away from home, in my first or second year at university in Nsukka, I'd returned to that yard, Baba Ali's, that was our playground, and to that wonderful sense of community that was so palpable on our street, a truly beautiful thing to behold. I guess you could call it an ode of sorts. Everything else, of course, is imagined, especially the stories the street tells of its occupants.

An O. Henry Prize winner and a Kirkus Prize finalist, Arinze Ifeakandu is the author of the debut short story collection *God's Children Are Little Broken Things.* He is a graduate of the Iowa Writers' Workshop. He currently lives in Nigeria.

Shelby Kinney-Lang, "Snake & Submarine"
Did you know how your story would end at its inception?

Sometimes I have a destination when I write, especially for longer pieces, like the novel I've worked on for the last couple of years. But for "Snake & Submarine," I felt the tailwind of a force larger than me. This experience of knowing with a kind of lucidity exactly the right word the moment I write it is among the greatest delights of my life. It is also an exceedingly rare experience: like for everyone, most of the work of writing for me is returning to a very imperfect draft, then trying to make what I've written less imperfect. "Snake & Submarine" was different. I finished it quickly, in the state more or less as it appears on the page. Without feeling that inspiration—even only rarely—I don't think I'd continue to do this. I'm grateful that I've touched *it*, whatever it is, this greater-than-me force, even just a handful of times in my life.

Shelby Kinney-Lang is a writer and educator whose stories have appeared or are forthcoming in *ZYZZYVA, Bellevue Literary Review, Witness, Joyland, Santa Monica Review,* and elsewhere. In 2018, he graduated with an MFA from the University of California, Irvine. Born and raised in Laramie, Wyoming, he currently lives with his wife and daughter in New England.

Jamil Jan Kochai, "The Haunting of Hajji Hotak"
What inspired your story?

Like many of my stories, "The Haunting of Hajji Hotak" was inspired by a joke. I had read an *Onion* article titled "FBI Counterterrorism Agent Wistfully Recalls Watching 20-Year-Old Muslim-American Grow Up," which I found hilarious but also oddly plausible. I could imagine an FBI agent growing to feel a disturbing sense of affection for some Muslim family he was surveilling. This figure sort of fascinated me. I wondered how they might come to bond with the family they're surveilling, and I wanted to see how I could complicate that sense of affection over the course of a story. Oddly enough, as I began to write the story from the perspective of the federal agent, I wondered about my own relationship to the voyeur as a writer. That is, I began to question my own desire to know and uncover this family. To love them. I asked myself: "In what way is my desire different than the spy's?" And that's where the second person came from.

Jamil Jan Kochai is the author of *The Haunting of Hajji Hotak and Other Stories,* a finalist for the 2022 National Book Award, and *99 Nights in Logar,* a finalist for the PEN/Hemingway Award for Debut Novel. His short stories have appeared in *The New Yorker, Ploughshares, The O. Henry Prize Stories,* and *The Best American Short Stories.* Kochai was a Stegner fellow at Stanford University and a Truman Capote fellow at the Iowa Writers' Workshop. Currently, he is a Hodder fellow at Princeton University.

Catherine Lacey, "Man Mountain"
What made you want to re-create this particular world/reality in fiction?

It seems to me that a man mountain already exists in this world— that is, we live with the presence of a bizarre, inert heap of masculinity; I wrote "Man Mountain," the story, in order to better see man mountain, this abstract thing. Feminism will always be an inherently radical concept as long as we still live in a world structured by patriarchy; yet the way that feminist thought has been digested and distorted by twenty-first-century memes and marketing has created a kind of fun-house mirror effect. Many live with the illusion of a ubiquitous feminist triumph, while the world remains under the control of the still marionette-ed half-dead carcass of patriarchy. I think in a hundred years many aspects of our current era will be seen as extremely weird, stunted, and grotesque; a story can be a smoke signal to the future, a way to tell them, *Yeah, I know, I know, I know!*

Catherine Lacey is the author of five works of fiction—*Biography of X, Pew, Certain American States, The Answers,* and *Nobody Is Ever Missing.* Her honors include a Guggenheim fellowship, a Whiting Award, and the New York Public Library Young Lions Fiction Award. Her work has been translated into numerous languages.

Grey Wolfe LaJoie, "The Locksmith"
Do you consider your story to be personal or political?

I'm very interested in what it is, or who it is, that we assign to the shadows. It is people, of course, societies, who do this assigning—and the unthinking impulses and attitudes born out of our cultural inertia can obstruct, sometimes, even our most careful seeking. Because of a person's identity, because of their ability or their station, assumptions are made about their value—their moral worth—and the result is not simply that they are seen as inferior; in the mind of another, this person sits in the negative space, society's negative space—unseen, and without meaning—an absence, a zero. But the person that sleeps out on the street, or in the prison, or the slum—the one who is believed to have nothing to say, nothing to contribute, merely because his articulation is disregarded and deterred—this person in fact contains universes, libraries, infinite worlds of truth and beauty, which nowhere else exist. Often the most occluded insight is, by virtue of its distance from us, the thing we need most desperately. Anyone cast to the margins by a society knows things about the society that the society could never know of itself, possesses capabilities that it could never—like a locksmith, this person accesses spaces that the others, long ago, forgot the means of entering.

The most bitter thing is not the way that others fail to notice this in some. The most bitter thing is how so many will dishonor this inside themselves—discouraged from speaking, discouraged from acting, and convinced by the world that their agency is poisonous, they sit and they negate their very being. But let me tell you just one secret: a seed sits inside each of us, and it is infinite. Listen very carefully and see what else you hear.

Born in Asheville, Grey Wolfe LaJoie holds an MFA from the University of Alabama, where they also worked as an instructor for the Alabama Prison Arts & Education Project. Their work is featured in *The Threepenny Review, Crazyhorse, Shenandoah, Copper Nickel*, and *Bat City Review*, among other journals. Read more at www.greywolfelajoie.com.

Ling Ma, "Office Hours"
What inspired your story?

What seems like a long time ago, I had jotted down a brief passage about an unnamed character at a university faculty party. Something about the tone made me take notice. It's the paragraph beginning with, "Her default position was that of a dog fighting its way out of a corner. For much of her adult life, she had assumed this defensive crouch, tensed to prove herself against all odds at all times." It recapped the character's career efforts, which had paid off because she had secured a tenure-track position.

Initially, I thought the passage was kind of funny—the severity of tone in describing this striving in academia. But it hinted at a sense of frustration—something about arriving at a place you've directed yourself toward and absolutely disliking where you've ended up—that seemed like a rich place to mine. Even though I didn't know much more about the story or the characters, that sentiment stayed with me. Some years later, I revisited this scrap of writing and developed it into "Office Hours."

Ling Ma is a writer hailing from Fujian, Utah, and Kansas. She is the author of the novel *Severance* and the story collection *Bliss Montage,* in which "Office Hours" appears. Her fiction has received the Kirkus Prize and the Whiting Award, and has been published in *The New Yorker, The Atlantic,* and *Granta.* She lives in Chicago with her family.

Eamon McGuinness, "The Blackhills"
Did you know how your story would end at its inception?

The first scene I wrote for what became "The Blackhills" was the final one in Pat Rathigan's house. At the time, I had no distinct character or story, just an image of a man returning home late at night. Straightaway I knew he'd go in through the back door. My feeling was that he was in his fifties or sixties, that the house was a busy one and the room he entered would be full of baby paraphernalia. I didn't know anything else and followed him as he stepped inside. I wrote this scene with as much detail and precision as I could and put it away.

The second scene I wrote became the opening: a man stopping in a lay-by late at night on the coast road between Balbriggan and Skerries in North County Dublin to put bottles into a bottle bank. I'd written this scene many times over the years but could never fit it into a story. Once I realized the two men were the same character, I knew I had a beginning and an ending and set out to discover what happened between the bottle bank and his return home.

Eamon McGuinness is from Dublin, Ireland. His fiction has appeared in *The Stinging Fly* and *The Lonely Crowd.* He has won the Michael McLaverty, Wild Atlantic Words, and Maria Edgeworth short story competitions. His debut poetry collection, *The Wrong Heroes,* was published by Salmon Poetry in 2021.

Jacob M'hango, "The Mother"
What inspired your story?

The story was inspired by the urgent need to do more in our efforts to protect the planet, and by how—sadly—it seems lost on some people that failure to do so is failure to protect ourselves. Also by the realization that whenever we hurt the planet, we hurt our present and future.

Jacob M'hango is a writer of literary fiction that seeks to explore the human condition. He is the author of a story collection, *Curse of the Fig*, published by Gadsden Publishers in 2018. He holds an MA in history from the University of Zambia and is currently working on a novel.

Cristina Rivera Garza, "Dream Man"
What inspired your story?

Back then, I would have said: mostly the territory—a high-altitude city and region of central Mexico that I knew well but had not written about—and its peoples: indigenous communities brimming with legends of extraordinary beings, such as, against all odds for such a high place with no access to the ocean, sirens. I would have added that I was obsessed with the idea of twins—how some relationships manage to replicate the eerie similarity of twin sisters and to generate, too, the complicity often associated with physical resemblance. Now I can see quite clearly that I was trying to come to terms with the femicide that took my sister's life back in 1990, precisely in that region. There is, I believe, a link between the quiet yet fierce violence emerging from both land and its peoples, especially men, and *Liliana's Invincible Summer*, the book in which I was finally able to explore my sister's life and to join so many others in a search for justice.

Cristina Rivera Garza is an author, translator, and critic. Recent publications include *El invencible verano de Liliana* (Random House, 2021)/*Liliana's Invincible Summer* (Hogarth, 2023); *Autobiografía del algodón* (Random House, 2020); and *Grieving: Dispatches from a Wounded Country,* trans. Sarah Booker (The Feminist Press, 2020), a finalist for the 2021 National Book Critics Circle Awards. She is M. A. Anderson Distinguished Professor and founder of the PhD program in creative writing in Spanish at the University of Houston. She is also a MacArthur fellow (2020–2025).

Francisca González-Arias is a professor of Spanish and translates from Spanish to English and from English to Spanish. Her English translation of the novel *Bordeaux* by the contemporary Spanish author Soledad Puértolas was published by the University of Nebraska Press. She has also published Spanish translations of the poets Emily Dickinson and Donald Wellman. She lives in Cambridge, Massachusetts.

David Ryan, "Elision"
What made you want to re-create this particular world/reality in fiction?

This story seems, looking back on it now, to be an allegory for a particular time of my life. I wrote it after coming out of a period of great uncertainty—questions lingered even after much of that uncertainty was resolved. Our daughter was the age of Christopher, the little boy in this story. And in writing Lily, I was essentially writing myself. Or, perhaps, a combination of myself and my wife. So often, the defining moments of our lives have a kind of seismic arrival—swift and thorough and utterly disruptive of the world we thought we knew. We grasp for answers that don't exist. And this leaves us with a peculiar intimacy with ourselves. The best we can do is hope and try to change, adapt. I leave a lot open in the story, an apt-enough statement for what I learned from that time. John Keats's term "negative capability" suggests that genuine art is created from the ability to step into the unknown and operate with an imaginative capacity that can accept and shape disquiet. The same idea might operate well in life. I'm looking back at that prior time from a much-improved space. There's so much beauty and art in my life now. And so, with this story, "Elision," maybe I had somehow, deep inside, wanted to create this world as a kind of time capsule I might look back on someday in just this way.

David Ryan is the author of *Animals in Motion: Stories* (Roundabout Press). His work has appeared in *New England Review, Harvard Review, The Common, Conjunctions, The Threepenny Review, Fiction, BOMB, The Kenyon Review, Tin House, Esquire, Fence, Copper Nickel, The Best Short Stories 2022: The O. Henry Prize Winners,* and elsewhere. He teaches in the writing programs of Sarah Lawrence College and New England College.

Naomi Shuyama-Gómez, "The Commander's Teeth"
Why was the short story format the best vehicle for your ideas?

What I appreciate most about the constraints of a short story is that compression requires each sentence and paragraph arrangement to be intentional. The short form's brevity lends immediacy to the images selected. For "The Commander's Teeth" I wanted to have enough space to develop the particulars of the setting (late nineties, Colombia) just enough to familiarize readers before using an ordinary act to subvert or shift, even if momentarily, the power dynamics. I had to maintain a level of authority in Emilia's voice, and to accomplish this, I delved into quite a bit of technical, terrifying research on dentistry.

Naomi Shuyama-Gómez is a writer based in the greater New York City area, on ancestral and unceded Munsee Lenape land. Her fiction and poetry have appeared in *Michigan Quarterly Review, The Florida Review, The Minnesota Review, Mount Hope, Reflex Fiction,* and *Rigorous.* She's received scholarships/fellowships from Kundiman, Immigrant Writers' Workshop, CRIT Works, Fine Arts Work Center, New York State Summer Writers Institute, and Asian American Writers' Workshop. Recently, she was awarded *Michigan Quarterly Review*'s 2021 Lawrence Foundation Prize, judged by Julie Buntin.

Gabriel Smith, "The Complete"
What inspired your story?

I'm inspired by anger. *The Complete* is a very angry story. I was angry about politics, and I was angry that the majority of people who seem angry about politics are vapid, self-serving clowns. The endless, entropic repetition of truly horrific governance in the United Kingdom and United States—and the lack of a viable alternative—is partly responsible for the recursive principles I write from. I'm angry because I believe change is possible. This inspired the violent jump cuts. The narrator does remain trapped in recursion, but there are glimmers of breaks.

I was also angry at literature, and I was angry at the short story format. As a reader, I feel let down by modern fiction. I don't think writers are innovative enough or entertaining enough. I believe the reader can tell whether or not the writer was having fun, so I had as much fun as possible writing "The Complete." I believe innovations have been made in other art forms—particularly music—that have not yet been explored in fiction. I wanted to see how many realities I could put into one story while maintaining a semblance of coherence. I wanted vaporwave plagiarism, hyperpop chronology, UK drill recursion—a silent funk maximalism. "The Complete" is an angry manifesto for possibility, and a cautionary tragedy about where we're doomed to stay—a kind of looping, dread carousel purgatory—if we don't try harder.

Gabriel Smith is twenty-seven and from London. His fiction has appeared in *The Drift, New York Tyrant,* and *The Moth.* He was mentored by the late Giancarlo DiTrapano of Tyrant Books, who edited and was to publish Smith's debut novel under his own imprint. That novel will be published by Scribner UK in spring 2024.

Lisa Taddeo, "Wisconsin"
Did you know how your story would end at its inception?

I didn't know how the story would end, I almost never do. I like to surprise myself while I write, to tell myself stories; it might be the only act of self-care I perform with consistency. But I did feel it turning quickly into a tale of revenge. I wanted to examine the generational trauma caused by how we metabolize romantic love, the way we pass down our attachment styles to our children, and how they might help us kick the horrid habits we unwittingly vomited upon them. I am interested in how to stop the cycle of self-immolation at the hands of romance. And more generally how a child can and should be an improvement on their parents.

Lisa Taddeo is an author, journalist, and two-time recipient of the Pushcart Prize. Her first nonfiction book, *Three Women,* was an instant number one *New York Times* bestseller. Production for the series adaptation at Showtime recently wrapped, with Shailene Woodley starring and Taddeo adapting and serving as executive producer. Her debut novel, *Animal,* was a national and international bestseller, with the rights quickly being acquired by MGM with Plan B producing. Taddeo will adapt it for the screen, marking her feature writing debut. She completed her literary trifecta this summer with her short story collection *Ghost Lover*.

Kirstin Valdez Quade, "After Hours at the Acacia Park Pool"
What inspired your story?

I babysat endlessly throughout middle and high school, squirreling away every penny for the glorious escape of college. I prided myself on the quality of care I offered. I brought art projects and picture books, costumes and games. I did not allow television. And I snooped shamelessly. Most of the children were lovely; some were not. One tantruming little boy, who whipped me over and over again with his lasso, fire-hosed urine all over the bathroom. I do not know how he achieved such force and volume; urine was everywhere, dripping from the ceiling, streaming down the shower curtain, pooling across the tile. His sister calmly advised me to spank him. Another child's mother was my own mother's friend. After I'd spent a week of ten-hour days with her toddler, she handed me an envelope of cash that was far less than we'd agreed upon. I felt helpless and humiliated, too shy to point out her error and insist she pay me my due.

As I wrote, I was thinking also about the anxious, itchy loneliness of adolescence, the confusing way some friendships grew apart as we matured at different paces, and the bewildering ambiguity between friendship and desire and resentment. Cooped up for those long days with children, I was so afraid of missing out on my friendships, even as I waited with unbearable impatience for my future to begin.

Kirstin Valdez Quade is the author of *The Five Wounds,* which won the Center for Fiction First Novel Prize and the Rosenthal Family Foundation Award from the American Academy of Arts and Letters and was a finalist for the PEN/Hemingway Award and the Lambda Literary Award. Her story collection, *Night at the Fiestas,* won the John Leonard Prize from the National Book Critics Circle, the Sue Kaufman Prize for First Fiction from the American Academy of Arts and Letters, and a 5 Under 35 award from the National Book Foundation. She teaches at Stanford.

Publisher's Note

A Brief History of the O. Henry Prize

Many readers have come to love the short story through the simple characters, the humor and easy narrative voice, and the compelling plotting in the work of William Sydney Porter (1862–1910), best known as O. Henry. His surprise endings entertain readers, including those back for a second, third, or fourth look. Even now one can say "Gift of the Magi" in conversation about a friendship or marriage, and many people around the world will know they are referring to the generosity and selflessness of love.

O. Henry was a newspaperman, skilled at hiding from his editors at deadline. He spent his childhood in Greensboro, North Carolina, his adolescence in Texas, and his later years in New York City. In between Texas and New York, he was caught embezzling and hid from the law in Honduras, where he coined the phrase "banana republic." On learning his wife was dying, he returned home to her and to their daughter, and subsequently served a three-year prison sentence for bank fraud in Columbus, Ohio. Accounts of the origin of his pen name vary: one story dates from his days in Austin, where he was said to call to the wandering family cat, "Oh! Henry!"; another states that the name was inspired by the captain of the guard at the Ohio State Penitentiary, Orrin

Henry. In 1909, Porter told *The New York Times,* "[A friend] suggested that we get a newspaper and pick a name from the first list of notables that we found in it. In the society columns we found the account of a fashionable ball. . . . We looked down the list and my eye lighted on the name Henry, 'That'll do for a last name,' said I. 'Now for a first name. I want something short.' 'Why don't you use a plain initial letter, then?' asked my friend. 'Good,' said I, 'O is about the easiest letter written, and O it is.'"

Porter had devoted friends, and it's not hard to see why. He was charming and had an attractively gallant attitude. He drank too much and neglected his health, which caused his friends concern. He was often short of money; in a letter to a friend asking for a loan of $15 (his banker was out of town, he wrote), Porter added a postscript: "If it isn't convenient, I'll love you just the same." His banker was unavailable most of Porter's life. His sense of humor was always with him.

Reportedly, Porter's last words were from a popular song: "Turn up the light, for I don't want to go home in the dark."

After his death, O. Henry's stories continued to penetrate twentieth-century popular culture. Marilyn Monroe starred in a film adaptation of "The Cop and the Anthem." The popular western TV series *The Cisco Kid* grew out of "The Caballero's Way." Postage stamps were issued by the Soviets to commemorate O. Henry's one hundredth birthday in 1962 and by the United States in 2012 for his one hundred fiftieth. The most lasting legacy began just eight years after O. Henry's death, in April 1918, when the Twilight Club (founded in 1883 and later known as the Society of Arts and Sciences) held a dinner in his honor at the Hotel McAlpin in New York City. His friends remembered him so enthusiastically that a group of them met at the Biltmore Hotel in December of that year to establish some kind of memorial to him. They decided to award annual prizes in his name for short story writers, and they formed a committee to read the short stories published in a year and a smaller group to pick the winners.

In the words of the first series editor, Blanche Colton Williams (1879–1944), the memorial was intended to "strengthen the art of the short story and to stimulate younger authors."

Doubleday, Page & Company was chosen to publish the first volume, *O. Henry Memorial Award Prize Stories 1919*. In 1927, the society sold all rights to the annual collection to Doubleday, Doran & Company. Doubleday published *The O. Henry Prize Stories*, as it came to be known, in hardcover, and from 1984 to 1996 its subsidiary, Anchor Books, published it simultaneously in paperback. Since 1997, *The O. Henry Prize Stories* has been published as an original Anchor Books paperback. It is now published as *The Best Short Stories: The O. Henry Prize Winners*.

How the Stories Are Chosen

The guest editor chooses the twenty O. Henry Prize winners from a large pool of stories passed to her by the series editor. Stories published in magazines and online are eligible for inclusion in *The Best Short Stories: The O. Henry Prize Winners*. Stories may be written in English or translated into English. Editors are asked to send all fiction they publish and not to nominate individual stories. Stories should not be submitted by agents or writers.

The goal of *The Best Short Stories: The O. Henry Prize Winners* remains to strengthen and add visibility to the art of the short story.

The stories selected were originally published between September 2022 and September 2023.

Acknowledgments

We are so appreciative of our brilliant and hardworking 2023 O. Henry Prize interns: Georgia Brainard and Luke Gardiner. How exciting that from O. Henry, Georgia has launched into a great publicity job in book publishing! Thank you to our insightful and passionate O. Henry Prize readers: Adachioma Ezeano (an O. Henry Prize–winning writer herself), Marion Minton, Sam Quigley, and Cat Gillespie. Thank you, as always, for everything, Dan Quigley, Gus Quigley, Leo Quigley, Heather Clay, Caroline Hall, Lisa Stevenson, and Jen Marshall. In addition to Eddie Allen, Linda Huang, and PRH Audio, we are grateful that Vintage Anchor has added four enormous talents to the O. Henry Prize team: Jordan Rodman, Lauren Weber, Cammi Kaneko, and Sophie Normil. Editor Diana Secker Tesdell's continuous enthusiasm for and belief in the importance of this project through our endless (endless and never-ending) rounds of permission forms makes all the difference. There would be no best-of collections were it not for so many inspired and beautiful writers dedicated to the mysterious, alluring craft of short stories, the winners included here as well as those appearing in all the awesome literary journals continuing to publish despite difficult financial pathways forward. The editors of the journals featured in our contents and in our directory bring fresh art into the world every season. Having the passion and genius of an extremely gifted contemporary writer laser focused on O. Henry was like having the stunningly warm sun shining on us every day, and we are, above all, grateful to Lauren Groff, who has made the best literary playlist, aka the greatest mixtape, of the year.

—JMQ

Publications Submitted

Stories published in magazines and online are eligible for inclusion.

For fiction published online, the publication's contact information and the date of the story's publication should accompany the submission.

Stories will be considered from September 1 to August 31 the following year. Publications received after August 31 will automatically be considered for the next volume of *The Best Short Stories: The O. Henry Prize Winners*.

Please submit PDF files of submissions to jenny@ohenryprizewinners.com or send hard copies to Jenny Minton Quigley, c/o The O. Henry Prize Winners, 70 Mohawk Drive, West Hartford, CT 06117.

Able Muse
www.ablemuse.com
submission@ablemuse.com
Editor: Alexander Pepple
Two or three times a year

AGNI
www.agnionline.bu.edu
agni@bu.edu
Editors: Sven Birkerts and William
Pierce
Biannual (print)

Alaska Quarterly Review
www.aqreview.org
uaa_aqr@uaa.alaska.edu
Editor: Ronald Spatz
Biannual

Amazon Original Stories
www.amazon.com
Submission by invitation only
Editor: Julia Sommerfeld
Twelve annually

American Short Fiction
www.americanshortfiction.org
editors@americanshortfiction.org
Editors: Rebecca Markovits and
    Adeena Reitberger
Triannual

Antipodes
www.wsupress.wayne.edu/journals/
    detail/antipodes-0
antipodesfiction@gmail.com
Editor: Annie Martin
Biannual

Apalachee Review
www.apalacheereview.org
christopherpaulhayes@gmail.com
Editor: Christopher Hayes
Biannual

Apogee Journal
www.apogeejournal.org
editors@apogeejournal.org
Executive Editor: Alexandra
    Watson
Biannual

The Arkansas International
www.arkint.org
info@arkint.org
Editor in Chief: Geoffrey Block
Biannual

Arkansas Review
www.arkreview.org
mtribbet@astate.edu
Editor: Marcus Tribbett
Triannual

ArLiJo
www.arlijo.com
givalpress@yahoo.com
Editor in Chief: Robert L. Giron
Ten issues a year

Ascent
www.readthebestwriting.com
ascent@cord.edu
Editor: Vincent Reusch

**The Asian American Literary
    Review**
www.aalrmag.org
editors@aalrmag.org
Editors in Chief: Lawrence-Minh
    Bùi Davis and Gerald Maa
Biannual

Aster(ix)
www.asterixjournal.com
info@asterixjournal.com
Editor in Chief: Angie Cruz
Triannual

Astra
www.astra-mag.com
AMsubmissions@astra-mag.com
Editor in Chief: Nadja Spiegelman
Biannual

The Atlantic
www.theatlantic.com
fiction@theatlantic.com
Editor in Chief: Jeffrey Goldberg;
    Magazine Editor: Don Peck
Monthly

Baltimore Review
www.baltimorereview.org
editor@baltimorereview.org
Senior Editor: Barbara Westwood
    Diehl
Quarterly

The Bare Life Review
www.barelifereview.org
barelifereview.submittable.com
Editor: Nyuol Lueth Tong

Bat City Review
www.batcityreview.org
fiction@batcityreview.org
Editor: Sarah Matthes
Annual

Bellevue Literary Review
www.blreview.org
info@BLReview.org
Editor in Chief: Danielle Ofri
Biannual

Bennington Review
www.benningtonreview.org
BenningtonReview@Bennington
    .edu
Editor: Michael Dumanis
Biannual

Black Warrior Review
www.bwr.ua.edu
blackwarriorreview@gmail.com
Editor: Jackson Saul
Biannual

BOMB
www.bombmagazine.org
betsy@bombsite.com
Editor in Chief: Betsy Sussler
Quarterly

Booth
booth.butler.edu
booth@butler.edu
Editor: Robert Stapleton
Biennual

Boulevard
www.boulevardmagazine.org
editors@boulevardmagazine.org
Editor: Jessica Rogen
Triannual

The Briar Cliff Review
www.bcreview.org
3303 Rebecca Street, Sioux City,
    IA 51104
Editor: Tricia Currans-Sheehan
Annual

Cagibi
www.cagibilit.com
info@cagibilit@gmail.com
Editors: Sylvie Bertrand and
	Christopher X. Shade
Quarterly

CALYX
www.calyxpress.org
editor@calyxpress.org
Editors: C. Lill Ahrens, Rachel
	Barton, Marjorie Coffey, Judith
	Edelstein, Emily Elbom, Carole
	Kalk, and Christine Rhea
Biannual

The Carolina Quarterly
www.thecarolinaquarterly.com
carolina.quarterly@gmail.com
Editor in Chief: Kylan Rice
Biannual

Carve
www.carvezine.com
azumbahlen@carvezine.com
Editor in Chief: Anna Zumbahlen
Quarterly

Catamaran
www.catamaranliteraryreader.com
editor@catamaranliteraryreader
	.com
Editor in Chief: Catherine
	Sergurson
Quarterly

Catapult
www.catapult.co
Editor in Chief: Nicole Chung
Annual

Cherry Tree
www.washcoll.edu/learn-by-doing/
	lit-house/cherry-tree/
lit_house@washcoll.edu
Editor in Chief: James Allen Hall
Annual

Chestnut Review
www.chestnutreview.com/
editor@chestnutreview.com
Editor in Chief: James Rawlings
Quarterly

Chicago Quarterly Review
www.chicagoquarterlyreview.com
cqr@icogitate.com
Senior Editors: S. Afzal Haider and
	Elizabeth McKenzie
Quarterly

Chicago Review
www.chicagoreview.org
editors@chicagoreview.org
Editor: Gerónimo Sarmiento Cruz
Triannual

Cimarron Review
www.cimarronreview.com
cimarronreview@okstate.edu
Editor: Lisa Lewis
Quarterly

The Cincinnati Review
www.cincinnatireview.com
editors@cincinnatireview.com
Managing Editor: Lisa Ampleman
Biannual

Colorado Review
coloradoreview.colostate.edu/
    colorado-review
creview@colostate.edu
Editor: Stephanie G'Schwind
Triannual

The Common
www.thecommononline.org
info@thecommononline.org
Editor in Chief: Jennifer Acker
Biannual

Confrontation
www.confrontationmagazine.org
confrontationmag@gmail.com
Editor in Chief: Jonna G. Semeiks
Biannual

Conjunctions
www.conjunctions.com
conjunctions@bard.edu
Editor: Bradford Morrow
Biannual

Copper Nickel
www.copper-nickel.org
wayne.miller@ucdenver.edu
Editor: Wayne Miller
Biannual

Crab Orchard Review
craborchardreview.siu.edu
jtriblle@siu.edu
Editor: Allison Joseph
Biannual

Cream City Review
uwm.edu/creamcityreview
info@creamcityreview.org
Editor in Chief: Su Cho
Semiannual

CutBank
www.cutbankonline.org
editor.cutbank@gmail.com
Editor in Chief: Jake Bienvenue
Biannual

The Dalhousie Review
ojs.library.dal.ca/dalhousiereview
Dalhousie.Review@Dal.ca
Editor: Anthony Enns
Triannual

Dappled Things
www.dappledthings.org
dappledthings.ann@gmail.com
Editor in Chief: Katy Carl
Quarterly

december
decembermag.org
editor@decembermag.org
Editor: Gianna Jacobson
Biannual

Delmarva Review
www.delmarvareview.org
editor@delmarvareview.org
Editor: Wilson Wyatt Jr.
Annual

Denver Quarterly
www.du.edu/denverquarterly
denverquarterly@gmail.com
Editor: W. Scott Howard
Quarterly

Descant
descant.tcu.edu
descant@tcu.edu
Editor in Chief: Matt Pitt
Annual

Dracula Beyond Stoker Magazine
www.draculabeyondstoker.com/
tucker@draculabeyondstoker.com
Editor: Tucker Christine
Biannual

The Drift
www.thedriftmag.com
editors@thedriftmag.com
Editors: Kiara Barrow and Rebecca
    Panovka
Quarterly

Driftwood Press
www.driftwoodpress.net
driftwoodlit@gmail.com
Editors: James McNulty and Jerrod
    Schwarz
Quarterly

Ecotone
ecotonemagazine.org
info@ecotonejournal.com
Editor in Chief: David Gessner
Biannual

Electric Literature
electricliterature.com
editors@electricliterature.com
Executive Director: Halimah
    Marcus; Editor in Chief: Jess
    Zimmerman
Weekly

Emrys Journal
www.emrys.org
info@emrys.org
Editor: Katie Burgess
Annual

Epiphany
epiphanyzine.com
epiphanymagazine.submittable
    .com
Editor in Chief: Rachel Lyon
Biannual

Epoch
english.cornell.edu/epoch
mk64@cornell.edu
Editor: Michael Koch
Triannual

Event
www.eventmagazine.ca
event@douglascollege.ca
Editor: Sashi Bhat
Triannual

Exile Quarterly
www.exilequarterly.com
competitions@exilequarterly.com
Editor in Chief: Barry Callaghan
Quarterly

Fairy Tale Review
www.fairytalereview.com
ftreditorial@gmail.com
Editor: Kate Bernheimer
Annual

Fantasy & Science Fiction
www.sfsite.com/fsf/
fsfmag@fandsf.com
Editor: Gordon Van Gelder
Bimonthly

Fence
fenceportal.org
rebeccafence@gmail.com
Editor: Rebecca Wolff
Biannual

Fiction
fictioninc.com
fictionmageditors@gmail.com
Editor: Mark Jay Mirsky
Annual

Fiction River
fictionriver.com
wmgpublishingmail@mail.com
Editors: Kristine Kathryn Rusch
   and Dean Wesley Smith
Six times a year

The Fiddlehead
thefiddlehead.ca
fiddlehead@unb.ca
Editor: Sue Sinclaire
Quarterly

Five Points
fivepoints.gsu.edu
fivepoints.submittable.com/submit
Editor: Megan Sexton
Biannual

The Florida Review
floridareview.cah.ucf.edu
flreview@ucf.edu
Editor: Lisa Roney
Biannual

Foglifter
foglifterjournal.com
foglifter.journal@gmail.com
Editor: Chad Koch
Biannual

Fourteen Hills: The SFSU Review
www.14hills.net
hills@sfsu.edu
Editor in Chief: Rachel Huefner
Biannual

Freeman's
www.freemansbiannual.com
eburns@groveatlantic.com
Editor: John Freeman

f(r)iction
frictionlit.org
leahscott@tetheredbyletters.com
Editor in Chief: Dani Hedlund
Triannual

The Ganga Review
www.lalitamba.com
lalitamba_magazine@yahoo.com
Editor: Shyam Mukanda
Annual

Gemini Magazine
gemini-magazine.com
editor@gemini-magazine.com
Editor: David Bright
Four to six issues per year

The Georgia Review
thegeorgiareview.com
garev@uga.edu
Editor: Stephen Corey
Quarterly

The Gettysburg Review
www.gettysburgreview.com
mdrew@gettysburg.edu
Editor: Mark Drew
Quarterly

Gold Man Review
www.goldmanreview.org
heather.cuthbertson@
    goldmanpublishing.com
Editor in Chief: Heather
    Cuthbertson
Annual

Grain
grainmagazine.ca
grainmag@skwriter.com
Editor: Nicole Haldoupis
Quarterly

Granta
granta.com
editorial@granta.com
Editor: Sigrid Rausing
Quarterly (print)

The Greensboro Review
greensbororeview.org
greensbororeview.submittable.com
    /submit
Editor: Terry L. Kennedy
Biannual

Guernica
www.guernicamag.com
editors@guernicamag.com
Editor in Chief: Ed Winstead

**Gulf Coast: A Journal of
    Literature and Fine Arts**
www.gulfcoastmag.org
gulfcoastea@gmail.com
Editor: Nick Rattner
Biannual

Harper's Magazine
harpers.org
letters@harpers.org
Editor: Christopher Beha
Monthly

Harpur Palate
harpurpalate.binghamton.edu
harpur.palate@gmail.com
Editor in Chief: Sarah Sassone

Harvard Review
harvardreview.org
info@harvardreview.org
Editor: Christina Thompson
Biannual

Hayden's Ferry Review
haydensferryreview.com
hfr@asu.edu
Editor: Erin Noehre
Semiannual

Hobart
www.hobartpulp.com
ee@hobartpulp.com
Founding Editor: Aaron Burch;
    Publisher: Elizabeth Ellen

The Hopkins Review
hopkinsreview.com
wmb@jhu.edu
Editor: David Yezzi
Quarterly

Hotel Amerika
www.hotelamerika.net
editors.hotelamerika@gmail.com
Editor: David Lazar
Annual

The Hudson Review
hudsonreview.com
info@hudsonreview.com
Editor: Paula Deitz
Quarterly

Hunger Mountain
hungermtn.org
hungermtn@vcfa.edu
Editor: Erin Stalcup
Annual (print)

The Idaho Review
www.idahoreview.org
mwieland@boisestate.edu
Editors: Mitch Wieland and Brady
    Udall
Annual

Image
imagejournal.org
image@imagejournal.org
Editor in Chief: James K. A. Smith
Quarterly

Indiana Review
indianareview.org
inreview@indiana.edu
Editor in Chief: Alberto Sveum
Biannual

Into the Void
intothevoidmagazine.com
info@intothevoidmagazine.com
Editor: Philip Elliot
Quarterly

The Iowa Review
www.iowareview.org
iowa-review@uiowa.edu
Acting Editor: Lynne Nugent
Triannual

Iron Horse Literary Review
www.ironhorsereview.com
ihlr.mail@gmail.com
Editor: Leslie Jill Patterson
Triannual

Jabberwock Review
www.jabberwock.org.msstate.edu
jabberwockreview@english
    .msstate.edu
Editor: Michael Kardos
Semiannual

The Journal
thejournalmag.org
managingeditor@thejournalmag
    .org
Managing Editor: Daniel Barnum
Biannual

Joyland
joylandmagazine.com
contact@joylandmagazine.com
Editor in Chief: Michelle Lyn
    King
Annual

The Kenyon Review
kenyonreview.org
kenyonreview@kenyon.edu
Editor: Nicole Terez Dutton;
    Managing Editor: Abigail
    Wadsworth Serfass
Six times a year

**Lady Churchill's Rosebud
    Wristlet**
www.smallbeerpress.com/lcrw
info@smallbeerpress.com
Editors: Gavin J. Grant and Kelly
    Link
Biannual

Lake Effect
behrend.psu.edu/school-of
    -humanities-social-sciences
    /lake-effect
gol1@psu.edu
Editors: George Looney and Aimee
    Pogson
Annual

Literary Hub
www.lithub.com
info@lithub.com
Editor: Jonny Diamond

The Literary Review
www.theliteraryreview.org
info@theliteraryreview.org
Editor: Minna Zallman Proctor
Quarterly

LitMag
litmag.com
info@litmag.com
Editor: Marc Berley
Annual

Little Patuxent Review
littlepatuxentreview.org
editor@littlepatuxentreview.org
Editor: Chelsea Lemon Fetzer
Biannual

The Louisville Review
www.louisvillereview.org
managingeditor@louisvillereview
    .org
Managing Editor: Amy Foos
    Kapoor
Biannual

MAKE: A Literary Magazine
www.makemag.com
info@makemag.com
Editor: Chamandeep Bains
Annual

The Malahat Review
www.malahatreview.ca
malahat@uvic.ca
Editor: Iain Higgins
Quarterly

Manoa
www.manoa.hawaii.edu
    /manoajournal
mjournal-l@lists.hawaii.edu
Editor: Frank Stewart
Biannual

The Massachusetts Review
www.massreview.org
massrev@external.umass.edu
Editor: Jim Hicks
Quarterly

The Masters Review
mastersreview.com
contact@mastersreview.com
Editor in Chief: Cole Meyer
Annual

McSweeney's Quarterly Concern
www.mcsweeneys.net
letters@mcsweeneys.net
Founding Editor: Dave Eggers
Editor: Claire Boyle
Quarterly

Meridian
readmeridian.org
meridianuva@gmail.com
Editor: Suzie Eckl
Semiannual

Michigan Quarterly Review
www.michiganquarterlyreview
    .com
mqr@umich.edu
Editor: Khaled Mattawa
Quarterly

Mid-American Review
casit.bgsu.edu/midamericanreview/
mar@bgsu.edu
Editor in Chief: Abigail Cloud
Semiannual

Midwestern Gothic
www.midwestgothic.com
info@midwesterngothic.com
Fiction Editors: Jeff Pfaller and
    Robert James Russell

Mississippi Review
sites.usm.edu/mississippi-review/
msreview@usm.edu
Editor in Chief: Adam Clay
Biannual

The Missouri Review
missourireview.com
question@moreview.com
Editor: Speer Morgan
Quarterly

Mizna
www.mizna.org/articles/journal
mizna@mizna.org
Editor: Lana Barkawi
Biannual

Montana Quarterly
www.themontanaquarterly.com
editor@themontanaquarterly.com
Editor in Chief: Scott McMillion
Quarterly

Mount Hope
www.mounthopemagazine.com
mount.hope.magazine@gmail.com
Editor: Edward J. Delaney
Biannual

n+1
www.nplusonemag.com
editors@nplusonemag.com
Senior Editors: Chad Harbach and
    Charles Petersen
Triannual

Narrative
www.narrativemagazine.com
info@narrativemagazine.com
Editors: Carol Edgarian and Tom
    Jenks
Triannual

NELLE
www.uab.edu/cas
    /englishpublications/nelle
editors.nelle@gmail.com
Editor: Lauren Goodwin Slaughter
Annual

New England Review
www.nereview.com
nereview@middlebury.edu
Editor: Carolyn Kuebler
Quarterly

Newfound
newfound.org
info@newfound.org
Editor: Laura Eppinger
Annual

New Letters
www.newletters.org
newletters@umkc.edu
Editor in Chief: Christie Hodgen
Quarterly

New Madrid
newmadridjournal.submittable
    .com/submit
msu.newmadrid@murraystate.edu
Editor: Ann Neelon
Biannual

New Ohio Review
www.ohio.edu/nor
noreditors@ohio.edu
Editor: David Wanczyk
Biannual

New Orleans Review
www.neworleansreview.org
noreview@loyno.edu
Editor: Lindsay Sproul
Annual

New Pop Lit
newpoplit.com
newpoplit@gmail.com
Editor in Chief: Karl Wenclas

New South
newsouthjournal.com
newsoutheditors@gmail.com
Editor: A. Prevett
Biannual

The New Yorker
www.newyorker.com
themail@newyorker.com
Editor: David Remnick
Weekly

Nimrod International Journal
nimrod.utulsa.edu
nimrod@utulsa.edu
Editor: Eilis O'Neal
Biannual

Ninth Letter
www.ninthletter.com
fiction@ninthletter.com
Editor: Jodee Stanley
Biannual

Noon
noonannual.com
1324 Lexington Ave, PMB 298,
    New York, NY 10128
Editor: Diane Williams
Annual

The Normal School
www.thenormalschool.com
normalschooleditors@gmail.com
Editor in Chief: Stephen Church

North American Review
northamericanreview.org
nar@uni.edu
Fiction Editor: Grant Tracey

North Carolina Literary Review
nclr.ecu.edu
BauerM@ecu.edu
Editor: Margaret D. Bauer
Annual

North Dakota Quarterly
ndquarterly.org
ndq@und.edu
Editor: William Caraher
Quarterly

Northern New England Review
franklinpierce.edu/nner
douaihym@franklinpierce.edu
Editor: Margot Douaihy
Annual

No Tokens Journal
notokensjournal.com
NoTokensJournal@gmail.com
Editor: T Kira Mahealani Madden
Biannual

Notre Dame Review
ndreview.nd.edu
notredamereview@gmail.com
Fiction Editor: Steve Tomasula
Biannual

The Ocean State Review
oceanstatereview.org
oceanstatereview@gmail.com
Senior Editors: Elizabeth Foulke
    and Charles Kell
Annual

The Offing
theoffingmag.com
info@theoffingmag.com
Editor in Chief: Mimi Wong

One Story
one-story.com
one-story.submittable.com
Executive Editor: Hannah Tinti;
    Editor: Patrick Ryan
Monthly

Orca
orcalit.com
Senior Editors: Joe Ponepinto and
    Zachary Kellian
Quarterly

Orion
www.orionmagazine.org
questions@orionmagazine.org
Editor: Sumanth Prabhaker
Quarterly

Outlook Springs
outlooksprings.com
outlookspringsnh@gmail.com
Editor: Andrew R. Mitchell
Triannual

Overtime
www.workerswritejournal.com
    /overtime.htm
info@workerswritejournal.com
Editor: David LaBounty
Quarterly

Oxford American
www.oxfordamerican.org
info@oxfordamerican.org
Editor: Eliza Borné
Quarterly

Pakn Treger
www.yiddishbookcenter.org/
    language-literature-culture/
    pakn-treger
pt@yiddishbookcenter.org
Editor: Aaron Lansky
Quarterly

The Paris Review
www.theparisreview.org
queries@theparisreview.org
Editor: Emily Stokes
Quarterly

Passages North
www.passagesnorth.com
passages@nmu.edu
Editor in Chief: Jennifer Howard
Annual

Pembroke Magazine
pembrokemagazine.com
pembrokemagazine@gmail.com
Editor: Jessica Pitchford
Annual

The Pinch
www.pinchjournal.com
editor@pinchjournal.com
Editor in Chief: Courtney Miller
    Santo
Biannual

Pleiades
pleiadesmag.com
pleiadescnf@gmail.com
Editors: Erin Adair-Hodges and
    Jenny Molberg
Biannual

Ploughshares
www.pshares.org
pshares@pshares.org
Editor in Chief: Ladette Randolph
Triannual

Post Road
www.postroadmag.com
info@postroadmag.com
Managing Editor: Chris Boucher
Biannual

Potomac Review
mcblogs.montgomerycollege.edu
    /potomacreview/
potomacrevieweditor@
    montgomerycollege.edu
Editor: John Wei Han Wang
Quarterly

Prairie Fire
www.prairiefire.ca
prfire@prairiefire.ca
Editor: Andris Taskans
Quarterly

Prairie Schooner
prairieschooner.unl.edu
prairieschooner@unl.edu
Editor in Chief: Kwame Dawes
Quarterly

PRISM international
www.prismmagazine.ca
prose@prismmagazine.ca
Prose Editor: Kyla Jamieson
Quarterly

A Public Space
apublicspace.org
general@apublicspace.org
Editor: Brigid Hughes
Quarterly

PULP Literature
pulpliterature.com
info@pulpliterature.com
Managing Editor: Jennifer Landels
Quarterly

Raritan
raritanquarterly.rutgers.edu
rqr@sas.rutgers.edu
Editor in Chief: Jackson Lears
Quarterly

Redivider
redivider.emerson.edu
editor@redividerjournal.org
Editor in Chief: Bradley Babendir
Biannual

River Styx
www.riverstyx.org
BigRiver@riverstyx.org
Managing Editor: Christina Chady
Biannual

Room
roommagazine.com
contactus@roommagazine.com
Managing Editor: Chelene Knight
Quarterly

Ruminate
www.ruminatemagazine.com
info@ruminatemagazine.org
Editor in Chief: Brianna Van Dyke
Quarterly

The Rumpus
therumpus.net
alysia@therumpus.net
Editor in Chief: Alysia Li Ying
    Sawchyn

Salamander
salamandermag.org
editors@salamandermag.org
Editor in Chief: Jennifer Barber
Biannual

Salmagundi
salmagundi.skidmore.edu
salmagun@skidmore.edu
Editor in Chief: Robert Boyers
Quarterly

Saranac Review
saranacreview.org
info@saranacreview.com
Editor: Aimée Baker
Annual

The Saturday Evening Post
www.saturdayeveningpost.com
editors@saturdayeveningpost.com
Editor: Steven Slon
Six times a year

Short Story Day Africa
shortstorydayafrica.org
info@shortstorydayafrica.org
Editor: Rachel Zadok

Slice
www.slicemagazine.org
editors@slicemagazine.org
Editor in Chief: Beth Blachman
Biannual

Smith's Monthly
smithsmonthly.com
dean@deanwesleysmith.com
Editor: Dean Wesley Smith
Monthly

The Southampton Review
www.thesouthamptonreview.com
editors@thesouthamptonreview
  .com
Editor: Emily Smith Gilbert
Biannual

The South Carolina Review
www.clemson.edu/caah/sites
  /south-carolina-review/index
  .html
screv@clemson.edu
Editor: Keith Lee Morris
Annual

South Dakota Review
southdakotareview.com
sdreview@usd.edu
Editor: Lee Ann Roripaugh
Quarterly

The Southeast Review
www.southeastreview.org
southeastreview@gmail.com
Editor: Zach Linge
Semiannual

Southern Humanities Review
www.southernhumanitiesreview
  .com
shr@auburn.edu
Editors: Anton DiSclafani and
  Rose McLarney
Quarterly

Southern Indiana Review
www.usi.edu/sir
sir@usi.edu
Editor: Ron Mitchell
Biannual

The Southern Review
thesouthernreview.org
southernreview@lsu.edu
Editors: Jessica Faust and Sacha
  Idell
Quarterly

Southwest Review
southwestreview.com
swr@smu.edu
Editor in Chief: Greg
   Brownderville
Quarterly

St. Anthony Messenger
www.info.franciscanmedia.org
   /st-anthony-messenger
samadmin@franciscanmedia.org
Editor: Christopher Heffron
Monthly

The Stinging Fly
stingingfly.org
info@stingingfly.org
Publisher: Declan Meade
Biannual

Story
www.storymagazine.org
contact@storymagazine.org
Editor: Michael Nye
Triannual

StoryQuarterly
storyquarterly.camden.rutgers.edu
storyquarterlyeditors@gmail.com
Editor: Paul Lisicky

subterrain
www.subterrain.ca
subter@portal.ca
Editor: Brian Kaufman
Triannual

Subtropics
subtropics.english.ufl.edu
subtropics@english.ufl.edu
Editor: David Leavitt
Biannual

The Sun
thesunmagazine.org
thesunmagazine.submittable.com
Editor: Sy Safransky
Monthly

Swamp Pink
swamp-pink.cofc.edu
swamp-pink@cofc.edu
Editor: Anthony Varallo
Biannual

Sycamore Review
cla.purdue.edu/academic/english
   /publications/sycamore-review/
sycamore@purdue.edu
Editor in Chief: Anthony Sutton
Biannual

Taco Bell Quarterly
tacobellquarterly.org
TacoBellQuarterly@gmail.com
Editor in Chief: M. M. Carrigan
Quarterly

Tahoma Literary Review
tahomaliteraryreview.com
fiction@tahomaliteraryreview.com
Fiction Editor: Leanne Dunic
Triannual

Third Coast
thirdcoastmagazine.com
editors@thirdcoastmagazine.com
Editor in Chief: Kai Harris
Biannual

The Threepenny Review
www.threepennyreview.com
wlesser@threepennyreview.com
Editor: Wendy Lesser
Quarterly

upstreet
upstreet-mag.org
editor@upstreet-mag.org
Fiction Editor: Joyce A. Griffin
Annual

Virginia Quarterly Review
www.vqronline.org
editors@vqronline.org
Editor: Paul Reyes
Quarterly

Washington Square Review
www.washingtonsquarereview.com
washingtonsquarereview@gmail
.com
Editor in Chief: Joanna Yas
Biannual

Water-Stone Review
waterstonereview.com
water-stone@hamline.edu
Editor: Meghan Maloney-Vinz
Annual

Weber
www.weber.edu/weberjournal
weberjournal@weber.edu
Editor: Michael Wutz
Biannual

West Branch
westbranch.blogs.bucknell.edu
westbranch@bucknell.edu
Editor: G. C. Waldrep
Triannual

Western Humanities Review
www.westernhumanitiesreview
.com
WHR@gmail.com
Editor: Michael Mejia
Triannual

The White Review
www.thewhitereview.org
editors@thewhitereview.org
Editors: Rosanna McLaughlin,
Isabella Scott, Skye Arundhati
Thomas
Triannual

Willow Springs
www.willowspringsmagazine.org
willowspringsewu@gmail.com
Editor: Polly Buckingham
Biannual

Witness
witness.blackmountaininstitute.org
witness@unlv.edu
Editor in Chief: Maile Chapman
Triannual

The Worcester Review
www.theworcesterreview.org
editor.worcreview@gmail.com
Managing Editor: Kate McIntyre
Annual

Workers Write!
www.workerswritejournal.com
info@workerswritejournal.com
Editor: David LaBounty
Annual

World Literature Today
www.worldliteraturetoday.org
dsimon@ou.edu
Editor in Chief: Daniel Simon
Bimonthly

X-R-A-Y
xraylitmag.com
xraylitmag@gmail.com
Editor: Jennifer Greidus
Quarterly

The Yale Review
yalereview.org
theyalereview@yale.edu
Editor: Megan O'Rourke
Quarterly

Yellow Medicine Review
www.yellowmedicinereview.com
editor@yellowmedicinereview.com
Guest Editor: Terese Mailhot
Semiannual

Yemasee
www.yemasseejournal.com
editor@yemasseejournal.com
Senior Editors: Laura Irei, Charlie
    Martin, and Joy Priest
Biannual

Zoetrope All-Story
www.all-story.com
info@all-story.com
Editor: Michael Ray
Quarterly

Zone 3
www.zone3press.com
zone3@apsu.edu
Fiction Editor: Barry Kitterman
Biannual

ZYZZYVA
www.zyzzyva.org
editor@zyzzyva.org
Editor: Laura Cogan
Triannual

Permissions